THE DAREDEVIL

WATERFYRE RISING 2

NADIA HAN

PROSE & CONCEPTS

For those who have the "fyre" to dare.

.

.

.

"What you seek is seeking you."
— Rumi

COPYRIGHT

First edition Paperback ISBN: 978-1-952820-38-0

Special edition Paperback ISBN: 978-1-952820-39-7

PROLOGUE
ROYCE

MY HEART POUNDED as I walked toward that damn church. I didn't want to come back here, but I had no choice. I almost shit my pants yesterday when I witnessed the murder with my friends. It had taken all my courage to return to this place today.

Dumb idea. Yeah, I know. What the hell was I thinking?

My pulse pounded in my ears as I glanced around, making sure those guys dressed in dark suits and the man with the slash across his face weren't around. His words from yesterday rang loud and clear in my ears. My friends and I had never been this frightened before.

Tell no one, nothing. If you do, they will find you, and they will kill you and your families. Understand?

The thumping in my chest drowned out his words so I could focus on my sole task for today.

Saturday afternoon, downtown Providence wasn't packed because the nearby office buildings were closed. Sweat trickled down my back, and it wasn't from the June weather or the bright sun. Terror was a beast wreaking havoc in my body, and I tried my best not to succumb to it. I imagined myself as a warrior in my video game, trying to defeat the beast.

I can do this. Go in, find my phone, and be out in a few minutes.

Fighting the tremble, I approached the abandoned property, wearing a T-shirt, old jeans, a baseball cap, and a backpack. I glanced at the city map and pretended to be a tourist in case someone spotted me. With several colleges around this area, they probably thought I was a college kid with my height and lanky appearance, which would hopefully help me blend in.

With each step closer to the church, my fingers quivered, shaking the map. Nerves and a wave of nausea stirred in me. I stepped onto the concrete stairs, the sound of my breathing loud in my ears. Returning to this dangerous place either made me really stupid or really brave. I hadn't slept all night because I feared someone would find my cell phone, which I'd dropped during the chaos. Maybe it had been broken. Maybe some homeless guy had taken it. Or maybe one of those dangerous men found the phone and hacked into it, getting my private info and pictures of my home and friends . . .

Shit.

My stomach twisted at the thought, and I forced myself to stop thinking about horrible scenarios. I needed to grab my phone and get the hell out of here and never think about this place again.

If Aunt Klara knew about any of this, she'd be devastated. She'd worked hard to take care of me. My mom died when I was eight years old, and Aunt Klara took me in and cared for me like I was her son. I'd been living with her ever since and feared that one day she might not want me anymore.

Stop the moping already.

Fear numbed me as I made my way to the side of the church, looking on the ground for my cell phone.

"Where are you?" I whispered as though it could hear me. If I couldn't find it, I'd have to pay for a new phone, which wasn't cheap.

The black case with a purple lightning bolt representing my favorite superhero, Thor—the God of Thunder—shouldn't be hard to find. I looked under the bushes and in the scrubby grass and found nothing.

Shit. Where was it?

I just wanted to find it and leave. I walked up to the wall where I'd jumped from the balcony the day before. Was it still up there? No, it couldn't be. I'd had it in my hand because I'd been monitoring my drone, making sure it landed safely, which it did.

I was about to wander to the other side of the church when I noticed a small box on its side, overflowing with junk. I kicked the empty cans, bottles, and scattered papers aside, and my phone gleamed in the afternoon sunlight. Relief burst through me as I picked it up, wiped the nasty goo from the screen, and examined it for any damage. No damage, but also no battery left either. I tucked it into my pocket and would have cheered, but I was afraid that would attract unwanted attention.

As I made my way toward the stairs that led back to the street, a strange feeling settled in me.

"I don't see anything that belongs to him. No need to worry." A man's voice sounded somewhere close, inside the church perhaps.

What if he were here to kill another person?

I knew I should run but froze at the sound of his voice—his accent. Something about it nipped at me. Goosebumps rose all over my arms in such a way that I could almost feel each bump rising from my skin.

Footsteps broke my trance. I hurried down the stairs and raced toward the bus stop two blocks away. As I waited for the bus, I replayed the man's voice in my head. I'd heard that Icelandic accent before. But where and when?

CHAPTER ONE

NERVES STIRRED in me as I glanced out the plane's window, admiring Iceland's breathtaking landscape. Coming back a second time brought an odd feeling I couldn't describe. Excitement? Dread? Something in between?

It was a strange sensation I couldn't pinpoint. It could be nerves stemming from the unknown since this was my first contract job for an innovative beauty product company in a foreign land. Or it was just me trying to find balance in my life.

I had thought the two years with my ex-boyfriend, Julian, had stabilized me. But when things ended, I fell on my ass, bruised, shocked, and ashamed.

Breast implants would make you look hotter. I'll pay for them.

That dress will look great on you if you lose five pounds.

Why don't you add another workout day to your schedule?

The numerous comments from Julian replayed in my mind. How did I put up with that jerk?

He knew about my body insecurity and yet he stabbed me right in the open wound—one that had been healing since I was a teen. Not only did he pour salt all over it, but he also ripped it open even wider.

I wished it was all his fault, but I blamed myself too. Why did I allow him to hurt me like that? Why hadn't I seen the ugly character beneath the handsome face?

No more. No man would ever do that to me again.

I was grateful when I caught him on a date with another girl while I was out at the same restaurant with my friends. Sometimes it takes a shock to wake someone up. No one should depend on another person for their self-worth. I understood that now. Most of all, no one had permission to make me feel worthless.

Stop thinking about that jerk. Focus on the future.

My body relaxed as I switched my thoughts to why I was heading to Iceland. A thrill rushed through me at all the new possibilities. The adventure would remove my mind from the monster living in my psyche—the monster few knew about. I'd be spending two months in this beautiful country documenting NewYou Beauty products. They'd hired me to blog about their unique products made from volcanic mud. With my worldwide following, I could help launch their business globally.

Besides the regular salary, they'd also paid for my flight, hotel, and housing during my stay. Though the pay itself wasn't great, it wasn't important. This was an opportunity to explore the land while I worked. The last time I was here, I'd been rushing and didn't have time to fully discover this country.

I glanced back at my laptop screen, which displayed my latest post on my blog, *Finding Life's Treasures*.

April 5th

On my way to a new adventure in Iceland!

This is my second time in this beautiful country. Have you ever been to a new place and felt a connection you couldn't explain? That would be me with Iceland. The first time, I only stayed for a week. I'm staying longer this time, hoping to find out what that connection is. Perhaps there's a treasure waiting for me.

Have you been to Iceland? Any suggestions on things I should do? Let me know in the comments!

May you find a new treasure today,

M

I closed my laptop, put it away inside my roomy purse, and made a mental note to post again as soon as I was settled in my apartment.

Leaning back in my seat, I thought about my first visit to Iceland—a college graduation gift from my mom. She had asked where I wanted to go, and I chose Iceland. Why? Iceland was a country I didn't know much about, and I had picked it on a whim. Spontaneity could be a good friend. Sometimes it was best to let the universe guide the way because some choices I'd made in the past had been wrong for me. Julian's face wanted to pop into my vision, but I stopped him.

Go away.

I loved to travel and spent a lot of time on the internet browsing all the wonders of the world. I'd started *Finding Life's Treasures* in college, documenting my life. It was like my diary, though I didn't put personal stuff on there. Just my thoughts on places I'd been to. The blog took off, and I expanded to other interests besides traveling. I talked about life and everything that was important to me. It humbled me that people liked what I had to say.

I couldn't help but think about this second visit as a symbol of my renewal. The first time, I found the courage to reclaim my life from my mom. Parents had a grip on their children in unimaginable ways. They shaped their children's beliefs—their lives. Mom was no different. I had grown up under her wing. What she didn't know was that I also developed a monster that changed my life forever—an illness that could only be numbed by seeing new places, meeting new people, and experiencing new things.

That was why I traveled, but no one knew this, and I wasn't ready to share it. Even my close friends Audri and Kiera didn't know this about me. Certain things were better left in the dark.

Now I was ready to reclaim my life from the "monster." No, it wasn't my ex-boyfriend, although he made the monster bigger. Julian didn't have that much power.

Was there such a thing as rebirth? I supposed people deserved as many chances to remake themselves as life required, right? In my book, they did.

A woman with blonde hair walked down the aisle with a pretty girl about eight years old. She carried a book about volcanoes.

"I can't wait to see the geysers, Mom!"

The mom whispered, "Honey, keep your shoulders and back straight while walking. I don't want you to forget your good posture. We have that pageant coming up. The judges will look at everything."

"Okay." The cheerfulness on the girl's face dimmed as

she stood straighter. Her mom missed the frown that came after.

I saw it, and my stomach twisted uncomfortably.

The sight brought on a sour memory. I knew exactly what that little girl was going through and how her life would change—how a monster would grow inside her psyche too.

I tried to look on the bright side. Maybe she'd grow up loving the beauty pageant world and the glitz and glamor it offered. Or maybe she'd be like me—hating it.

I desperately wanted to intervene and talk to the mother, asking her to pay attention to her daughter's needs, but it wasn't my place. So I said a prayer for the little girl, hoping she'd find her way faster than I did.

A few minutes later, the girl walked up and down the aisle, humming a tune. She glanced my way and noticed my Hello Kitty mouse pad.

"I have one like that too. Mine has more hearts on it." Her blue eyes sparkled, lighting up her face.

"Hello Kitty is awesome, right?"

She beamed, and for some reason, I felt the need to say something. "Are you taking part in beauty pageants?"

She nodded. "Yup."

"Does it make you happy?"

"Sometimes." She lifted a shoulder.

I smiled and placed a hand on my heart. "Do what makes your heart happy. Hello Kitty would say that too."

"She's a smart cat." She smiled, waved at me, and walked away.

I didn't know if my words meant anything to her. She'd probably forget about them by tomorrow, but I felt the need to remind her how important inner happiness was.

The pilot spoke into the speaker in English and then in Icelandic, announcing that the plane would land soon.

The plane landed twenty minutes early, and I retrieved my luggage. A car service was supposed to pick me up, so I stood by the door looking for someone holding a sign with my name. A bald man of average height wearing a brown jacket and khakis glanced at his cell phone and then looked at me with a friendly expression.

He strode over with a smile. "You must be Ms. Michelle Yates?" He showed me a picture of my blog profile.

"I am."

"Nice to meet you. I'm Oskar Karlsson. I'll be your driver in the city. Let me get that for you," he said with a slight accent. Reaching for my luggage, he led me to a black Land Rover.

"Nice to meet you too, Oskar."

He opened the back door for me, took care of my luggage, and then we were off. Dark clouds loomed in the sky. "Is there a storm coming?"

"Yes, ma'am. Your flight just made it in time."

I'd never experienced a storm in Iceland, and I didn't know why I wanted to. Normal people preferred nice weather during their vacation to explore and sightsee. Something must be wrong with me if I wanted the thrill of danger. Well, I wouldn't mind the inclement weather if I was safe and dry inside this car or in my apartment. NewYou Beauty had rented the apartment in the middle of the city, so I didn't have to walk far to get to the office.

Metal clanked loudly, followed by another sound, which caused the engine to slow down. More noises erupted, forcing Oskar to pull over on the side of the road.

Nerves rattled my stomach as I glanced at the dark

clouds. Unlike the Providence or Boston airports, the road out of Keflavik airport reminded me of driving through the flatlands of Arkansas, with no buildings in sight. Flat land greeted me on both sides. The idea of weathering a storm while stranded on a road with a stranger didn't appeal to me anymore.

"Oh no." Oskar's worried voice didn't bring me comfort. "Stay here. I'm going to check out the engine." He exited the car, opened the hood, and then quickly closed it when the rain came.

Rain poured, and lightning flashed in the distance. I couldn't help but admire the beauty of the lightning as it cut through the dark sky. I'd always loved watching a thunderstorm in the safety of my home. All that electricity—all that power illuminating the sky—drew me to it.

Thunder roared, and I heard Oskar curse before dropping out of view. I rushed out of the car and hurried over to help him as rain and wind slammed into me, almost knocking me sideways.

CHAPTER TWO

ROYCE

IN MY SKYDIVING JUMPSUIT, I inhaled a deep breath as the wind slapped against my face. Fear of heights had been a weakness I'd overcome years ago by daring myself to jump out of a plane. I almost shit my pants that day when I was eighteen and jumped with a college friend. After that first second of free-falling, the fear disappeared, replaced by an addictive thrill I craved.

Now skydiving was a regular pastime whenever I returned to Iceland.

Skydiving was one of the many adventures offered at Excursions for You. As the owner, I always experienced the adventure firsthand before adding it to the official repertoire. There was no better way to describe that experience to a customer than to have lived it.

Nerves jittered in my stomach, even though I'd done this many times. Looking out of the plane with the door open and the wind snapping did something to my body. Tingles rushed up and down my spine as anticipation churned in my gut.

I looked at the beautiful Icelandic landscape—even on this gloomy day with dark clouds in the distance—with its characteristic green moss covering lava rocks and the unique mountain formations. The view took my breath away as I saluted the majestic volcano in the distance, where it sat like a watchful God.

I turned to Steven, the pilot, and gave him a thumbs up, signaling that I was ready for the jump from 14,000 feet in the sky. I'd be free-falling at 120 mph. Steven—who also enjoyed skydiving—had been my trusted pilot for many years. I'd hired the best men to work for me. Without them, Paradigm Excursions Group—an umbrella for all the excursions around the globe—wouldn't have grown as fast as it did. Excursions for You had been voted one of the top five excursion companies in Iceland for the past seven years.

Adjusting my helmet and goggles, I gripped my harness, inhaled a deep breath, jumped, and dove head down. The wind slapped my face and body, and a thrill enveloped me, giving me this indescribable liberation. My stomach flipped with excitement as I appreciated the atmosphere. I was fully present, feeling all the goosebumps and chills while the wind rushed past me.

On the other side of fear, life offered this blissful freedom—salvation—that could only be grasped when experiencing something exhilarating. It was only up here and during this quiet five-minute moment when I felt alive. Even during the fifty-second freefall, my head was clear of everything except the presence of my body and soul in the sky.

After deploying my parachute and landing on my feet in the drop zone, I noticed the dark clouds creeping closer. I knew there was a chance of a rainstorm, but the ominous clouds signified something worse. It had been a risk to go skydiving today. Usually, when there was potential rain, the company wouldn't recommend skydiving.

But I'd taken the day off from work after the horrendous week I'd just had and couldn't dismiss the opportunity. It was a risk, but I was a man accustomed to risks. Risks had made me a billionaire.

I preferred calculated risks where I looked at the facts and weighed them against liability. Over the years, I'd learned to be more careful with business risks and left the personal thrills aside for when I had time like today.

Out of habit, I fished my phone out of my interior jacket pocket. Oskar, one of my long-time employees, had sent a text about the breakdown of one of my newly purchased SUVs.

"What the fuck?"

I listened to Oskar's voicemail and made my way to his location since I was closer than the emergency crew. Lightning flashed in the distance, and a fat raindrop splattered onto my face.

Cursing, I ran to my white Land Rover, parked along the drop zone. As I shoved my parachute and harness into the trunk, another flash of lightning lit up the sky, followed by a boom of thunder that shook the ground. I hadn't expected this crazy weather today and was grateful I landed when I did.

I had planned to visit the waterfall near my excursion site, but that would have to wait for another day. I had business to take care of now and sent Oskar a text message.

Be there soon.

CHAPTER THREE

MICHELLE

"ARE YOU ALL RIGHT?" I helped Oskar into the driver's seat, settled him in, and rounded the hood to the passenger side.

"Fucking shit! It hurts!" Oskar winced and realized he had company. "Sorry, Ms. Yates. The day isn't going as planned. Probably sprained my ankle."

"Michelle is fine. Is there an emergency number we can call?"

He nodded. "I called my boss. He'll send someone soon. The emergency crew will take a little longer to arrive because we're far from the city. I'm sorry about this."

"Don't be silly. It's not your fault the car broke down and the storm wanted to make its presence known. Hey, I came here for an adventure, and I'm getting one."

He laughed, pulled out a roll of paper towels from the glove compartment, tore off a few sheets for himself, and offered me the roll.

The wind howled, and rain smacked the side of the car. My stomach growled, but the thunder drowned out the sound. Frustration clawed at me, and I placed a hand on my tummy, rubbing it.

I'm not hungry, so stop growling.

The muscles on my stomach twisted, disobeying my order as though the monster from within was testing my patience. I sucked in my gut and showed that I had control over when I should eat.

As I wiped my face with a paper towel, a set of head-lights flashed in front of us.

Hope sparked in me. "Someone's coming."

Oskar hissed and tried to move.

"Don't aggravate your ankle. I can go out and greet whoever it is. Stay." I pointed to him, earned a smile, and exited the car.

It was hard to see with the rain and wind. The white SUV pulled over a few feet away, facing us, and the driver got out, rushing my way.

He came toward me with his massive black raincoat billowing in the wind and the flash of lightning illuminating him from behind. His silhouette cut him like a superhero coming to my rescue, and my heart skipped a beat.

One beat for the beautiful face with piercing green eyes.

Another beat for the surprise of who they belonged to.

Something strange happened to my body at that moment. My body jerked as though a bolt of lightning zapped my head, sending electricity straight down to my toes. Tingles rushed up and down my body. I had no idea what was happening to me. Could hunger be the reason? People hallucinated when they were hungry or thirsty, right? Travelers saw mirages in the desert when, in reality, there was nothing there. But I just had a snack and a drink earlier, so my body should feel fine. Perhaps fatigue had confused my body and mind.

Like New England, Iceland had unpredictable weather, so I was prepared for the sudden rainstorm. But I wasn't prepared for the onslaught of strange physical sensations that made this entire scenario seem out of place.

The rain speckled my face, blurring my vision. Wiping the rain away with my hand, I blinked, and his gorgeous face was right above me. He was so big, towering over me like a Viking warrior.

I wasn't sure if I was imagining things, but time stood still for a moment. My eyes focused on a rivulet that zigzagged down his face and neck. The lightning flashed again, and his green eyes flickered with the flash. I didn't know what was wrong with me, but I couldn't stop staring.

Was that amusement in his eyes? Maybe rain got into his eyes, giving him that odd expression. Or maybe it was just my addled and hungry brain going all weird. That was more likely.

I'd traveled to many places, and each time I stepped foot onto foreign land, I felt like a different person. I could be *anybody* on foreign soil. Nobody knew me. No one knew my past. No one knew my *monster*.

Maybe this odd sensation was the Icelandic version of Michelle.

Thunder shook the ground and yanked me out of my reverie.

"Michelle?"

"Royce?" I knew it was him, but I couldn't let him know I'd been staring at him. That would be too embarrassing.

He took one look at my body. "You're drenched. Get in my car."

My hair, face, and clothes were all soaked. I'd never experienced a "shower" of this magnitude on any of my travels.

"Oskar's injured. I've got some luggage in the back."

"I'll get it. Sit in the front passenger seat."

An hour later, Royce brought my luggage to my apartment on the fourth floor of the five-story brick building. "I need to take Oskar to the hospital."

"Hold on a second." Removing my drenched jacket, I walked into the bathroom and draped it over the tub. Returning to the hallway, I said, "Thanks for the ride. I hope Oskar feels better."

Royce's gaze wasn't on my face but on my chest. I glanced down to see my hard nipples poking through the thin white bra and white shirt, which were both soaked. He had a full view of my breasts. His stare only made things worse.

I gasped and flew a hand over my chest as my body tingled all over again.

He lifted his eyes to my face. "I'll see you later."

Too embarrassed to reply, I stood there as the door shut. Heat flushed my cheeks as I rushed into the bathroom for a quick shower.

I could already tell the next two months would be interesting.

CHAPTER FOUR

ROYCE

FIVE PEOPLE SAT on the other side of the waiting room. I prayed Oskar's ankle would heal quickly. The doctor said he'd sprained it and tore a ligament, which required at least six weeks of recovery. I was down to one man at work now. Oskar was a trusted employee who had been with me from the beginning, so he knew the business well. With all the issues at Excursions for You and my other adventure sites worldwide, Oskar's injury was a bump in my busy schedule.

Out of habit, I checked my phone for updates from my directors at the other excursion sites. Relieved that nothing urgent had emerged, I checked the news for the New England area. I liked being informed about where I lived, even when I was in a different country. As I browsed the feed, a news station for Providence, Rhode Island, popped onto the screen, showing several of my excursion sites as some of the best places to visit. After that segment, the news cut to Dominic Bryson speaking about the low crime levels in the city since he took over as Chief of Police.

My lips curved, remembering him from high school.

He'd pulled his shit together. I never imagined he would join law enforcement, but I supposed people grew up and found their place in the world.

Steering my mind back to my current situation, I drafted an email on my phone, alerting my team at Excursions for You to have someone tow the Land Rover near Keflavik International Airport back to the warehouse. This was a brand-new car, so there shouldn't have been any issues. I needed to chat with my dealership. The maintenance crew needed to triple-check all the vehicles used on the tours and livery service.

This company had been a failing business when I bought it. I transformed it into a successful business where tourists scheduled tours years in advance. Excursions for You fell under Paradigm Excursion Group, which was the umbrella for all my business ventures. I wasn't going to let some fucker ruin my empire. I'd worked too damn hard to build it.

Who the fuck was screwing with me? Property damage cost money and time. I had plenty of money, but time? I'd rather be doing something other than putting out unnecessary fires. Whoever this was had no clue who he was dealing with.

Making this trip to Iceland wasn't on my agenda until costly accidents started. I could dismiss an exploding package left at the front of my office building as some idiot's prank. I could brush off failed brakes on two excursion tour buses even though the mechanic said they had been fine when he inspected them. But six strange accidents in the last few months begged for an investigation. I feared these "accidents" could escalate into something worse.

Anger rippled through me, wondering who was taunting me.

Who had rigged the new Land Rover that was used today? The car had just been delivered to the warehouse yesterday. Did something happen to the vehicle during delivery? What exactly was this criminal trying to achieve? If his goal was to infuriate me, he'd achieved it.

What would have happened to Michelle and Oskar if I hadn't been nearby? The road to and from the airport was desolate compared to other cities. Getting help required a longer wait time.

Why was Michelle in Iceland, anyway? Why did I care? Why did I like the way she stared at me? A shiver had run down my body from her intense gaze, but I'd dismissed the sensation as a chill from the cold rain and wild wind.

But I couldn't forget the way her brown eyes had fixed on me. I felt a familiarity I couldn't understand. Yes, I *knew* her. She was my friend. We hung out with the same group of people, but this sensation was different—a recognition that stemmed from a place I couldn't explain. That intrigued me more than it should have. Why? Because for the first time in a long time, I had no clue why I was suddenly in uncharted territory. Usually, I was a keen observer who loved a tidy explanation, but I couldn't come up with anything regarding this strange feeling.

It had to be all the work issues sending my exhausted body and mind into disarray. I'd worked for seven days with very little sleep and too much caffeine. It was a miracle I could still function.

My mind wandered back to Michelle. She had looked at me as though she'd found something.

Your wet face.

My annoying inner voice had a knack for interjecting dry humor at the most inopportune moments. Michelle probably didn't recognize me with the rain and wind whipping into her face.

The sudden storm was another strange occurrence. The forecast had said a chance of rain, not a thunderstorm with hurricane winds. From a glance, the dark clouds appeared to be hovering mostly near the airport. I understood meteorologists didn't always get everything right.

After sending off my emails, I leaned back in my chair and released a sigh. Michelle's face intruded on my thoughts again. I'd seen her several times at Remi and Audri's home. She was attractive, but I usually stayed away from attractive female friends linked to my boys. Audri was Remington's woman and Grayson's sister, and Michelle was one of her best friends. I didn't have a long dating track record—my choice—and dating anyone within that circle posed a threat to the overall friendship and dynamic of the group.

To some people, it shouldn't matter. But to me, those guys were my family. My friends had helped me survive moments when life seemed dark and unstable. There had been many of them in my childhood.

I stand in the airport with nerves rattling my stomach as the airport officials hand over papers to my new guardian and say their well wishes to me.

I'm terrified as I watch them leave. I don't know this lady standing in front of me or why I'm here. Is Mom okay?

"Where's my mom?" I ask the lady who looks like Mom, but taller and not as skinny. My English is good, but I still have an Icelandic accent. I learn English in school and from speaking with my friend, Magnus, who lives next door. He has family who lives in America, and they visit him often.

The lady smiles at me warmly as she crouches and cups my chin with her soft hand. "You'll be staying here in

America with me. I'm Aunt Klara, your mom's older sister. Your mom isn't doing too well. She's at the hospital."

Aunt Klara is my mom's sister? How come Mom never told me about her sister? Aunt Klara speaks English with no accent.

I'm staying in America? My heart pounds so hard my chest hurts. Tears well in my eyes as fear, anger, and shock twist my stomach. I need to puke.

How can Mom leave me like that? I'm only eight years old. I hear about kids being abandoned by their parents on TV. I never thought it would be me.

At least it's just me and not my sister, who I don't remember much. I don't even have pictures of her. Emma was three years younger than me and disappeared when she was two years old. The police couldn't find her. There are a lot of missing kids in the city. I heard Mom talking about it with the neighbors.

I miss Emma and Mom. More tears flow down my face.

"Aunt Klara will take great care of you." She offers me a tissue, and her kind eyes make me feel a little better, but she's still a stranger to me.

At first, I wonder if she's a kidnapper, but I remember the court documents with pictures of our faces. I don't understand the papers, but the airport officials assured me I'm well cared for, so I guess she's not my kidnapper. I've seen movies about these things.

Still crouching, she takes my hand. "I know you're scared, Royce. Me too. This will be an adventure for both of us. You're my nephew, and I'll take good care of you because that's what family does."

Mom is family. Where is she? I don't say those thoughts

out loud, though. Confusion and fear twist my stomach, and tears burst from me.

"No! I want my mom!" I shouted. Why can't I stop crying? Eight-year-old boys don't cry like toddlers.

"Alda is sick. She's in the hospital for treatment."

Mom has been visiting the doctors a lot lately, but she never tells me why, probably not wanting me to worry.

"Will she be okay?" I ask in a shaky voice.

Aunt Klara sighs. "I hope so."

I don't understand what's happening in my life. I'm scared about not knowing. Shoving my hand into my pants pocket, I tighten my grip over the small action figure of Thor. I pretend I'm absorbing his power and his bravery. In that moment, I play a game with myself. I dare myself to survive— to play pretend that everything is all right. That my mom will be fine, and I'll see her soon.

Aunt Klara presses her lips tightly together. "Your mom loves you. She needs time to heal, and she won't be able to take care of you while she's in the hospital. She'll come over and join you when she's well, okay?"

"Promise?" Hope squeaked in my voice.

Aunt Klara rises to her feet, pats me on the head, and smiles. Taking my little hand in hers, she takes me out of the airport and drives me to her home—my new home.

My mom never came for me. She died a few months later. I opened my eyes, shaking the memory from my brain. The past always came back when I least expected it.

I switched my thoughts over to my friends. Remi, Grayson, Forrest, Arrow, and I met while playing video games. The roleplaying game brought us together to create an innovative game that would change the market—Water-Fyre Rising. Like all things worth having, this video game took time, dedication, effort, and passion. Aside from my excursion companies—in several countries—I devoted my time to creating Level Two of WaterFyre Rising. Back in the day, when I played The Seven Realms with my friends, I had been the "explorer." I was the character who went out to explore places that could be safe havens or hideaways.

I carried that adventurousness into adulthood, applying it to my businesses. While I browsed interesting places around the world for enjoyment, I evaluated whether they'd benefit my business.

My excursion companies had made me a billionaire. People loved visiting places and trying new things. With expert guides, people felt safe and often returned, including sharing their experiences with their friends. I'd learned a lot from my boy, Remington Starke. He'd invested in my first venture, and I appreciated his support and belief in me.

"You're still here?" Oskar's voice snapped me back to reality. He had a cast on his right foot and a crutch assisting him.

"You feeling okay?" I got up from the chair. "You're staying home for six weeks. Got that?"

Oskar grunted. "It's going to drive me crazy. I'm going to drive Sara and the kids crazy."

I laughed, knowing Oskar couldn't sit still.

"Take the time to rest. You've been working a lot. Maybe this was a sign for you to take care of yourself. You can return to desk work after the doctor examines you. Someone from the office will fill your livery service. Don't worry about it."

Aside from excursions, my company offered car services to several businesses in the area.

"You're working a lot too. Take your own advice." Oskar

situated himself in my car, and I placed his crutch in the backseat.

It should be easy for me to drop everything and take a week off, but there was an urgent matter needing my attention. I couldn't go on vacation when someone was trying to sabotage my business.

"I'll make time soon."

"Can you believe I fucking tripped over a goddamn rock and slipped on another? Luck wasn't on my side today. Maybe God wanted me to stay home." Oskar glanced at the evening sky, looking sullener than I'd ever seen him.

Feeling confined wasn't something I appreciated either. "Catch up on your TV shows. That'll make you feel better. Michelle sends you her best."

"Thanks. She was very helpful. Gotta be her worst car service ever." Oskar smiled. "I'll call HR and let them know my situation tomorrow."

After I took Oskar home and made sure his wife forced him to rest, I drove home, passing Michelle's apartment building across the street from mine.

What was she doing right now? Did she settle in okay? I would have texted her, but I didn't have her number. An image of her perfect breasts flashed across my mind, and my cock hardened.

I didn't know why I had never looked at her in that way. She had been seeing someone, and I had too. Mine didn't last long though. Women were like adventures in the wild—there was always a new one to be discovered.

Asshole.

A name I'd been called by former girlfriends when I told them I didn't want to commit. I wanted to explore. Why was I the asshole for telling the truth? I guess I could have delivered it with more finesse. If people wanted finesse, they should attend one of my volcano seminars, where I structured my speech to gain capital for the private firm I freelanced for. Being a part-time volcanologist wasn't about money—my interest in volcanoes made it worthwhile. I was born in a country where most of the landmass was lava rock. To study volcanoes was to study me.

Once settled inside my apartment—a unit in a three-story building I owned—I prepared my speech for next week's conference at the Volcano Museum, where wealthy companies were invited to donate to a charity that funded innovative studies on using lava as a new energy resource.

When I finished, something urged me to type in Michelle Yates on the internet. She wrote for several magazines and had a successful blog called *Finding Life's Treasures*. She was a fantastic writer and photographer, and I needed new images for several excursion sites. Would she be interested in writing some promotional pieces for my business? Did she have time?

Browsing through her entries, I noticed an interesting picture of her looking at the camera. Who had taken it? It was a simple picture, but when I looked into her eyes, my heart did something strange. There was so much emotion wrapped in that simple gesture that captivated me. She appeared to be searching for something.

Weren't we all?

But I *felt* a pull from her. I'd never looked at an image of a woman and felt a connection like this. Again, perhaps all of this was because I needed sleep, but I'd evaluate that later.

That image was for a blog post titled "Searching for Yourself."

We're all searching for our place in the world. Traveling

allows us the opportunity to discover ourselves. Have you been to a place where you felt an undeniable connection? Or met a person who made you feel something? Or found a piece of art that you had to buy? Or ate something delicious that made you recall a happy memory? These are life's little treasures. Small, but meaningful. Drop me a comment, I'd love to know.

I felt like she was talking to me. Perhaps that was the power of her blog. Her words and the images made her post personable, allowing people to relate easily.

By the time I finished reading several posts, I knew more about her.

What are you seeking, Michelle?

I glanced at the time on my computer and yawned. It was past midnight, and I should have been in bed already, but here I was, reading a travel blog and finding Michelle more fascinating than ever.

I went to bed, wondering how her long, curly brown hair would feel between my fingers. Would she look wild and untamed in bed like an undiscovered adventure? Would she let me discover her body? What treasures did she have?

Go to sleep. You have issues to deal with at work.

For once, my inner voice made sense.

CHAPTER FIVE

MICHELLE

ON MONDAY, I sat across from Becca in the café on the first floor of NewYou Beauty Headquarters and sipped my delicious cappuccino, letting the steamy life force energize me. Caffeine was king today, and I needed the power.

The café had a modern appeal, like most of the interior décor I'd seen in Iceland. Geometric-inspired furniture with simple lighting and clean walls decorated with abstract art.

"It's so good to have you join our team, even if it's just for this one project." Becca nibbled on a crepe.

She had blue eyes on an adorable face framed with chin-length dark hair. She stumbled on my blog last year and referred me to the CEO, who offered me a job to promote their new beauty product line on my blog.

"Thank you for this opportunity to work with NewYou Beauty. I haven't done beauty products on my blog before, so this is fantastic. My followers would love this. I love this country. Most of all, I love your unique products. Thanks for the awesome samples, by the way."

"You're welcome. I love using our products too. I'm not

just saying that because I work for the company. The products are truly effective." Becca wiped her hand with a napkin before opening the portfolio. "This is the entire product line. We're a boutique company with a focus on skincare. Can you help showcase our products so we can gain new investors? We have some now, but we'd love to expand."

Flipping through the portfolio, I glanced at the white jars of lotion with moss-green designs and gold accents. "Can I visit the hot springs where you're producing your products? I think people would love to see where everything comes from. A good visual always helps."

"I agree. We have a day trip planned for you next week. Spend a day there, get pampered, and immerse yourself in the lagoon. You have full access to our spas, the gift shop, and the employee-only labs. Our spas are still new, but word of mouth has been helping us tremendously."

I'd tried a sample of their lava mask, and my skin hadn't felt this wonderful in a long time. I couldn't wait to spend a day at their spa.

My phone buzzed, and I picked it up to see the reminder I'd set up to go off every two days.

Food: *Fruits and salads are good for your hair and skin. Eat healthy.*

Daily Exercise: *1 hour of cardio. 30 minutes of weights. 30 minutes of yoga.*

Motivation: *You're amazing! Go buy yourself something.*

Don't forget this: *What are you grateful for today?*

I was grateful for this opportunity to work for NewYou Beauty.

"Hey, Becca!" someone shouted.

I turned, and saw a smiling Fiona Clark sashay toward

us. She wore a black leather jacket with jeans and knee-high boots. Her makeup wasn't overdone, and her wavy blonde hair draped past her shoulders, making her appear like a fashion model. She was a popular blogger specializing in beauty and fashion and had a larger following than me. We weren't friends, more like acquaintances.

I wore a baggy sweater over dark jeans and ankle boots. Seeing her fit figure made me want to rush to the gym and work out for another two hours. I already got in my two-hour exercise at the gym next door to my apartment earlier this morning. Staying fit was important to me.

Fiona looked at me. "It's so nice to meet you in person. I've visited *Finding Life's Treasures* a few times. You've got great content."

"Thank you," I said, tucking my phone into my purse and trying to remain professional as I gauged how truthful her words were. Probably zero on a scale of one to ten. How could I forget she had tried to ruin my reputation a few years ago by starting rumors about me?

I was a forgiving person, but I didn't forget easily.

People like Fiona didn't mesh well with me. I couldn't deal with the fake smiles and dishonest words. She reminded me too much of the beauty pageant circuit.

Becca clapped her hands together. "I'm so glad you both know each other. That saves me an introduction."

Fiona sat down and turned to me. "I'm also covering NewYou Beauty skincare. My followers would absolutely love it. Aren't you a travel blogger, Michelle? Sorry, I haven't read many of your posts. Been too busy trying to keep up with my growing business. We just signed with Chanel to promote their new handbags."

I shrugged, not caring if she did or didn't read my blog or

what fashion designer she signed with. This temporary job for NewYou Beauty had just taken a turn for the worse for me. I'd been excited about the job, but Fiona brought in a distinct energy that rubbed me the wrong way.

Don't let her ruin your joy.

"We have different followers, Fiona. So it makes sense for NewYou to place their products in front of various audiences."

Fiona tossed her hair back as though dismissing my comment.

I wished my girls were here with me. My Super Spy Girls, aka SSG 003, would enjoy an evening gossiping about Fiona and men, not that those topics had anything to do with each other. That reminded me I had to send them a text message later to let them know I'd landed safely in Iceland.

Maybe I could sneak in a few questions about Royce. His face hadn't left my mind since that day he saved me from the storm. My friends were smart, so they'd probably ask questions. I passed on the idea for now because I didn't have answers prepared for my friends. They'd want to know why I was inquiring about Royce's relationships. Not that they'd know, anyway.

"Yes, I agree," Becca said, breaking my trance. She probably sensed some awkwardness stirring in the air. "NewYou Beauty wants every opportunity to promote its products."

Fiona glanced at the portfolio and closed it as though she was done with it. Ignoring her, I pulled the portfolio closer to me and flipped it open again, reviewing the products once more.

"Becca, do you have extra tickets for next week's banquet? I have a friend who would love to attend. She works for a fashion magazine."

"Sorry, we don't have any more."

Fiona pouted. "I thought you had one left over from our chat last week."

"Oh, that was reserved for Michelle."

Fiona twisted her lips, thinking. "If you have another, let me know." She rose from her chair, the Chanel logo on her handbag glinting in the light. "I've got to get to my next meeting. Catch you ladies next week."

When she left, Becca sighed. "Sorry about that. She's a character. Her parents are friends with the CEO, so the company is letting her promote our products. I preferred you because you're more authentic. Fiona doesn't know about that. I want to keep my job, you know?"

I smiled. "No worries, I understand. I'm not a fan of drama. There are people like her everywhere. You just have to know how to deal with them." I leaned in. "Be like me. Shrug them off like a mud scrub." I mimicked the scrubbing motion on my face.

Becca laughed. "Your ticket to next week's banquet will be in tomorrow's email with the link to all the information about NewYou, including a digital portfolio you can browse. The banquet is a charity event at the Volcano Museum. NewYou Beauty is donating to the research team looking for innovative ways to use lava as an energy source. Their discoveries will help our products too. A lot of wealthy people will be there. Four of us from NewYou will attend: the CEO, me, you, and Fiona. A good-looking scientist is giving a speech that most of the office girls are dying to see."

"It sounds like a fancy gala. I only have a black evening dress."

Becca waved a hand. "A black dress on you is perfect. You have an elegant figure. No need for anything flashy."

This time, she leaned in. "I think Fiona is jealous of you. She didn't react like that to anyone else in the office."

"We were never friends, and I don't consider it a loss. I'm only a contractor and not a full-time employee. She has to be respectful to those paying her, right?"

"True. Let me give you a tour of our office. Then you can go home and let everything sink in before brainstorming your marketing strategy. Today is a good day to browse the city. Weather isn't too cold yet for mid-September."

The office building was small, with a lot of glass walls and doors. I met Margaret Evans, the CEO. She was an older woman with short brown hair, giving her a classy look. We'd chatted when she hired me, but it was always good to meet someone in person versus seeing their faces on the computer screen. The company employed about fifty people, including the spa staff. Though it was small, everyone appeared excited about their products.

When the tour and greetings ended, I opted to browse the city. I loved staying in the city, which gave me easy access to everything. I could have waited for a taxi, but what better way to explore than on foot?

Maybe I could see if that gift shop was still around. I'd bought a pair of customized earrings back then, but lost one of them. They had been a gift to myself, and the designer—a young man—created them for me while I waited in the shop. That had been seven years ago.

I went to the shopping area and glanced around. That location was now a hair salon. My heart sank, and I muttered, "Maybe it wasn't meant to be."

Disappointed, I walked back toward my apartment three blocks away. Footsteps sounded behind me. I turned just as a man yanked at my purse and held out a knife in my direction. Instincts had me blocking, screaming like a madwoman, and kicking him. My reaction probably startled him, and he shoved me as he ran off. The force sent me to the ground, scraping my hands.

The asshole! My belongings!

Everything happened so fast. I got up and ran after the thief. He wore a blue cap with a brown jacket and dark pants.

"Stop! Someone help me! He stole my purse!"

Fear of losing my personal items in a foreign country—which would be a disaster trying to get everything replaced—forced me to run faster. Accustomed to running, I didn't lag too far behind him in heeled boots. But his long legs enabled him to stay ahead of me.

The thief ran across the street, but a car blocked him. He rounded the hood and continued. The driver got out of the car and rushed after him. Was that Royce? People stopped in the streets, watching Royce punch the thief and then grab my purse with one hand. With his free hand, Royce gripped the thief by the throat, pushing his back against the wall of a building.

"You fucker!"

"Royce!" I approached him, but the deadly look on his face made me stay a few feet away.

Royce looked at me, and the green eyes that had intrigued me earlier sent a sharp chill running down my spine. At that moment, they looked glacial, like they could freeze the blood in my body. His gaze slid to my hand, which was absently rubbing the scrapes.

"You okay?" he asked, his elbow pressed into the thief's neck.

"Yeah." I lifted my palms. "Just minor scrapes."

The thief paled as he tried to yank Royce's elbow away.

Fearing that Royce would kill the man, I placed a gentle hand on his back. "Thank you for getting my purse back."

"Royce, what's going on here?" asked a police officer with dirty blond hair. He wore a dark uniform and held a baton in hand.

Police officers in Iceland didn't carry guns, which struck me as a little strange. Maybe this country had a better handle on gun control.

The other police officer with red hair stepped up to Royce. "We'll take over."

Royce removed his elbow from the man. "He stole her purse and injured her hands."

The police officer with dirty blond hair looked at me. "Are you okay, miss? Do you need to go to the hospital?"

"Oh, no. I'm fine. I just want my purse back."

Royce spoke to the police officers in Icelandic. Based on the casual conversation, he knew them. The police officers handcuffed the thief and shoved him into their car.

Royce turned to me, gripped my wrists, and examined my hands. "Do they hurt?"

The contact warmed me down to my toes, and the chill from his green eyes disappeared, leaving me mesmerized by how much emotion he revealed in them.

"I'm fine. I was more nervous about losing my wallet."

He handed me my purse and watched as I checked for missing items. I felt his stare on me, and my body yearned for him, which didn't make sense at all.

"Everything is here." Thank God. I'd once visited Milan, Italy, and had my credit card stolen. It took forever for everything to clear. I didn't want to go through that stress again.

"Let me give you a ride home."

"It's just a block away. I can walk."

"No, you're not walking." The commanding tone surprised me.

I didn't like it and glared at him.

"I don't want you getting hurt." He huffed out a breath. "Look what just happened. The thief probably knew you were a tourist, so he targeted you. Let's get you home and take care of the scrapes. You don't want it marking up your pretty hands."

He thinks I have pretty hands?

My annoyance at his commanding tone melted. What did that say about me? I didn't have an answer.

I slid into the Land Rover and buckled my seatbelt. "It's going to take you a minute or less to get me home." The top of the building peaked in the distance.

"That's okay. I'm heading that way. I live across the street from you. See that gray geometric building? That's mine."

"Your building or your apartment?" I asked.

"Building."

"Oh."

I often forgot that Audri's man, Remington Starke, and his friends were all wealthy. Remi, Royce, Grayson, Forrest, and Arrow never talked about their wealth or businesses whenever we hung out. They mostly discussed their Water-Fyre Rising video game—something I didn't know much about. Audri grew up with them, so she knew them better. I only met them through her.

Royce had caught my eye a few times. *Look at him.* With his long legs, the big blond god of sexy fury filled up the spacious car seat beautifully. Remembering the strength that emanated from him just now, my body shivered. He had always appeared casual, as though nothing could bother him. But just now? I saw a spark of power—daring, untamed, and dangerous—that attracted me.

I *liked* it. What was wrong with me?

He was being a protective friend trying to help me, I told myself. He probably did this all the time.

Why did the car ride seem so much longer? The air in the car thrummed with sexual tension. Or was that my sexual energy stirring in my body and mind?

I had to steer my mind away from inappropriate thoughts. He probably had a girlfriend waiting for him at home. I came to Iceland for work. To find myself. Not for sex. Not for a man who looked like a Viking god who could probably make all my sexual fantasies come true.

"Do you have a special deal with Land Rover?" I asked, recalling Oskar had used one to pick me up. These weren't cheap cars.

He flicked a look at me as though I had disrupted him from some secret thought, but there was no irritation on his face. If I had to find an adjective, it would be inquisitive.

He swallowed, and my gaze darted to the motion of his throat. Even that was sexy.

"I own some shares and use them for all of my excursion sites. But I'm looking at a startup brand. They're producing sustainable cars that preserve the natural world. Most vehicles are heading that way, and they're one of the few pioneers who care about the Earth."

My heart palpitated at the surprise. I never pegged him to be an environmental guy at all. I'd met some environmentally conscious people, most of whom were vegetarians or vegans and dressed simply. Royce had a certain rugged style. Whenever I saw him at Remi and Audri's place, he'd worn beat-up jeans and T-shirts that had seen better days, but were expensive brands. Environmental people didn't have the money for designer labels. Or maybe I hadn't met any.

I supposed it was true you couldn't judge a book by its cover, and Royce Viktorsson had me extremely curious.

Who are you, Royce?

The longer I sat in his car, the more intrigued I became. Why was the ride taking so long? Had time frozen?

"I have a Toyota Hybrid at home. It works well." It was dependable, and that mattered most to me.

I didn't have money to splurge. Audri had money, but she never used it the way wealthy kids did, and I adored her for that. She never made me or Kiera feel less than her. I spent all my money on traveling. I collected memories the way some people collected handbags and shoes—though I had a wide selection of those too. My heart was happy seeing the world.

"They're a great car. If you ever need a ride anywhere while you're in Iceland, let me know. I'm across the street." The car stopped in front of my apartment, and a sudden sadness gripped me.

I didn't want to leave his car. What was happening to me? Royce had completely thrown me. I had images to review and blog posts to create. I didn't need a distraction to add to the pile.

"Thanks, but I don't want to bother you. I can call a taxi."

"It's not a bother. I insist. Audri and Remi would be mad at me, knowing I didn't take care of you here."

I laughed. "I'm a grown woman, Royce. Audri and Remi aren't my parents. I appreciate the offer, though."

"I own a tour company, which includes livery service."

Amusement sparked in his eyes. "If I make you nervous, you can call this number whenever you need a ride. There are people on call twenty hours a day. Just call. It's on the house."

I didn't hear anything except *"if I make you nervous."*

"Why would I be nervous?" I asked too quickly.

"Just a hunch. I could be wrong." He leaned over to my side, and the musky scent of his cologne slithered up my nose, moving ever so slowly down my spine like some wicked seduction, making me shiver. "I'm teasing, Michelle." He held out a card with the number to the car service and moved back to his side. I didn't miss the small smile that curled onto his lips.

What was he thinking?

"Thanks," I said, even though I had no plan on using it.

"We should exchange numbers while we're here in case of an emergency."

Now that made sense to me. I gave him my phone to enter his contact information and added mine to his.

After that, I exited the car, waved at him, and rushed up to my apartment, trying my best not to fall flat on my face. Once I got inside, I leaned back into the closed door and released a breath. Nerves twisted in my stomach, but these were a fresh set of nerves. These didn't come from my dark closet.

These came from a man who could influence my body without even trying.

After inhaling and exhaling a few more breaths, I kicked off my shoes, dropped my purse onto the kitchen table, and plopped down onto the soft couch.

Today had been interesting, starting with meeting Fiona, who viewed me as her competitor, to having my purse stolen and realizing my attraction to Royce. A rush of air left my lungs as the last thought solidified in my head. I didn't expect to be attracted to him, but it seemed stronger every time I was near him.

I should start on the NewYou Beauty blog posts, but I decided it could wait. My mind wasn't prepared to work right now. Some girl talk with my besties would be perfect.

I got off the couch, fished my phone out of my purse, and noticed a text from Royce.

Don't be nervous around me. I don't bite.

My heart thudded as a smile formed on my lips. The word "bite" sent my brain into wild territory. Was he thinking of biting me? Where did he want to bite me with his sexy lips? The muscles in my inner thighs tightened as though wanting his mouth there.

This was insane. My attraction to Royce seemed to come out of nowhere. Would the attraction have been as powerful if we had been in Providence? He was devastatingly handsome anywhere he went. The strong-boned face, the magnetic green eyes, and the towering body made me feel safe even when I wasn't in danger. He was well over six feet compared to my 5'7" height. I'd never considered him a potential partner because we were friends. He'd brought a girl to an outing at Grayson's house the last time I saw him, but I'd just broken up with Julian. Kindling a new romance had been the last thing on my mind.

But, God, this attraction to Royce crippled me to some extent. The way he stared at my breasts that day still aroused me. I had to get him off my chest—pun intended—so I could focus on my work. I replied to his text message.

But I do bite.

Why did I taunt? It was as though my brain wanted to

text something appropriate, but my fingers detoured. What the hell?

Oh . . .

A few seconds went by. Did I offend him? Did I cross the line? What was going through his mind right now?

Then maybe I can take you out for a bite to eat.

I bit my bottom lip as joy sparked in my stomach. He'd just twisted my words and asked me out to dinner. I should be extra cautious with a man who could twist things to suit his needs.

What should I say? Did he mean tonight? I wasn't ready.

M: *Not tonight. Maybe next week.*

R: *How about next Saturday?*

M: *Okay.*

R: *Pick you up at 7.*

M: *(smile emoji)*

R: *(smile emoji)*

I smiled, then tossed the phone on the couch cushion like it was something from another world. What did I just do? How did that happen? I was here for work, not for a relationship. Or did he just want to take me out to dinner as friends?

My stomach twisted uncomfortably. Did he flirt with his female friends? Because what I'd just experienced was a *flirtatious* conversation.

Reaching for my phone, I sent a message to my SSG 003 girls.

CHAPTER SIX

ROYCE

WHY WAS I staring at Michelle's response like some high school kid who had just scored his first date? I was a grown thirty-one-year-old man, yet I couldn't help the goofy smile on my face as I entered my apartment.

Something stung my fingers, and I glanced down at the scratch and redness on my knuckles. I didn't remember getting the scratch, but fury had blinded me then.

That fucking thief. He didn't look like a homeless man or in need of money. What would have happened if I hadn't been driving home and saw her rushing after him? She ran pretty fast in her boots, but if she had caught up with him, she would've gotten hurt. Actually, she did. Her palms were scratched up. I hated those marks on her hands. Did they sting like mine? I should have asked her about that instead of dinner.

This sudden need to protect her surprised me. Where did it come from?

Had I done the right thing by asking her to dinner? Maybe she thought it was a simple meal between friends.

We'd had "dinner" as a group at Remi's or Grayson's, but never just the two of us.

Did I want it to be a simple meal?

What the fuck was I doing? Besides her beautiful face, there was something about her that tugged at me. I couldn't explain it. A part of me sought to understand this mystery—to understand her.

I compared the curiosity to my volcanic research for the private team I freelanced for. How many types of lava were there? How could lava be used to serve the natural world? Could part of the volcano be sustainable? I loved finding answers that weren't obvious, and being a volcanologist satisfied that curiosity. Research paid little and mainly relied on grants and donations, but the work was important.

I had plenty of money from my excursion business, so I had time to dedicate to volcanic research, which I incorporated into my Level Two in WaterFyre Rising.

Thinking back to my teen years, I was grateful to have connected with Remi, Grayson, Forrest, and Arrow. Remi started the video game idea as an escape from his home life. He'd invited all of us to join him, knowing that each of us had something to contribute. Little did I know that the video game would save my life too.

Sitting in my office chair, I swiveled back and forth, mimicking the thoughts flowing in and out of my mind. What people said about a person's teen years was true—if I had hung out with a different crowd, my life could have easily gone the other way. My boys gave me a safe haven to explore my dreams, and Aunt Klara offered me a loving home to live in. Even so, I felt an emptiness inside me.

Could a child ever get over his father abandoning him and his mom and leaving them to fend for themselves? I couldn't remember his face. He left us when I was five years old, and in doing so, I'd pushed him out of my mind too. He wasn't important anymore.

Though my mom had a good reason for sending me off to Aunt Klara, that sense of abandonment stirred in me like simmering lava. Every time I thought about my life, my blood heated with resentment toward God or whoever was up there. If God were real, he wouldn't have taken my mom away. The disappointment forced me to pack all my Thor comic books into a box. I couldn't look at him or any other superhero the same way after Mom died.

I always questioned if I was good enough. I knew it wasn't healthy, but that thought was there. Only when I worked on my video game, where I could create my world—construct my own rules—did my mentality change. Like my friends, I wanted to change my present environment. I wanted to become something worthy—to prove I didn't need another's approval to feel complete.

Now I ran a touring empire scattered around the globe. Though success sat beside me, something else was missing. Would it always feel like this? Achieving a goal and still searching for the next thrill?

Probably. Which was why I enjoyed going on new adventures.

Was Michelle my new adventure? She'd probably stab me with her knife if I told her that over dinner.

I had plenty of work to complete before next week's banquet and dinner with Michelle, which was what I looked forward to the most. With friendships at stake, I'd consider it a simple dinner between friends to see where things went. The last thing I wanted was to ruin our friendship and make it awkward between us and all of our friends. I'd let her lead the way.

Shoving all my distractions aside, I checked my email for updates on the Land Rover that had died the day Oskar picked up Michelle.

According to the mechanic, someone had tampered with the electrical wire in the engine. Who? Why? When? I needed those answers.

I fired off an email to my directors from every touring site to inspect the wiring. The last thing I needed was a lawsuit from customers injured during the tours or livery services.

A competitor popped into my head. Could Einar Hallsson from Hallsson's Excursions be that vindictive? In business, anything was possible. Last year, I won the opportunity to promote outdoor gear from a new startup company. Though Einar promised the company a better incentive, the CEO decided to work with me after researching Paradigm Excursion Group and discovering how large my company was. Could that be a reason for sabotage?

It was time I did some digging. I sent Remi a text message.

Royce: *Yo. Is your PI available for a contract job?*

Remi: *He can be. I'm his only employer, but I can lend him to you.*

Royce: *I've got an issue. Need his help.*

Remi: *Okay. I'll give him your info. He'll be in touch.*

Royce: *Cool, thanks. We'll catch up when I get back.*

Remi: *Things okay over there?*

Royce: *I've got it handled.*

Ten minutes later, my cell phone pinged with a short message and a phone number to call. I called the PI and gave him Einar's info.

"I need everything about him and his company," I said.

The PI listened and asked brief questions. I'd heard about Remi's PI and his efficiency, which I valued. I could've hired someone else, but I needed someone dependable.

As soon as my conversation with the PI ended, my phone rang with David Butler's name flashing on my screen. A tight knot formed in my stomach as I picked up the call from the director of my Whitewater Family Resort in Oregon.

"David, is everything okay?"

"Sorry to bother you, Royce, but there's an issue you need to know about."

"What kind of issue?"

David had been with the company from the beginning and taught me everything about whitewater rafting.

"We found a dead body on the trail."

"What?" We hadn't had any issues at Whitewater Family Resort in a long time. A few rafts had flipped now and then, but that was Mother Nature's forceful currents. Nothing we could control. But death? What the fuck.

"I'll be there tomorrow."

"Are you sure? I can keep you posted about the investigation."

"There's been too many unexplained accidents. I want to be there. The police may have questions for the owner."

"Okay, I'll have your lodge prepared for your arrival."

"Thanks." At all my adventure sites, I had a lodge, a suite, or a cabin reserved for me to conduct business during my visits.

I was tempted to call the encrypted number to inform the PI I had another job for him, but I decided against it. It was probably best to let him focus on one thing at a time. I had to sort this out before whoever was behind this destroyed my company's reputation.

Whitewater Family Resort had been the first business I'd purchased and expanded. It held a special significance to me. Not that I didn't love my other sites. I wouldn't have bought them if I didn't love them or see their potential. But Whitewater Family Resort in Oregon represented the beginning of my dream—it started my billionaire empire. Excursions for You was my history, the soul of who I was. My heritage was there.

My blood heated, wondering who was fucking with me. I'd bring down the wrath of God before I let anyone ruin what I'd built with sweat, hard work, and dedication.

"Can you send me the name and any info you have on the person who died? Did he stay at our lodge? If not, let me know where."

"On it."

"I'll see you soon." My jaw tightened as I shuffled my schedule around to make tomorrow's urgent flight.

CHAPTER SEVEN

MICHELLE

IT WAS four in the afternoon in Iceland, which meant it was noon in Providence, Rhode Island. The four-hour difference wasn't that bad compared to other places I'd visited.

How should I tell my friends about Royce? Maybe I imagined this attraction. Maybe Royce just wanted to treat me to dinner because we were friends. I decided talking about Fiona was safer.

Michelle: You guys up for a quick chat?

Audri: Of course! Lunch break for me. What's happening in Iceland?

Kiera: Always have time for my girls. What's up?

Michelle: Fiona Clark is part of my team. Ugh.

Audri: The one who badmouthed your blog to social media influencers?

Michelle: That one.

Kiera: Want me to send her fake designer lipsticks that will swell her lips & prevent her from talking forever?

Audri: You're terrible, K. Love the idea, though. (lipstick emoji)

Michelle: *Wish you both were here.*

Kiera: *Watch your back with that one. She got my friend at Dolce & Gabbana fired.*

Michelle: *Yeah, I don't need the drama.*

Audri: *It's so hard working with shitty people.*

Audri had been harassed by her boss until Remi bought out the company. That poor girl had been through so much. She'd found her happiness now, and I was thrilled for her. She deserved it.

Kiera: *AND she's been with Sebastian since we ended our little whatever.*

Michelle: *What? You didn't tell us.*

Kiera: *Not important. He wasn't my bf. Have something to share when you're back.*

Audri: *You can't dangle 'something' and not expect us to inquire! Who is he?*

Michelle: *Right? Spill it.*

Kiera: *Ha! Nothing important. Lol. Any cute guys in Iceland? I met a Nordic model once. He was insanely hot.*

Audri: *Have you seen Royce yet?*

What should I say? Several thoughts swirled in my head, but they all vanished as if I'd experienced a memory lapse.

Kiera: *What happened?*

Michelle: *What do you mean? I didn't even say anything.*

Audri: *EXACTLY. You took too long to reply. (smile emoji)*

Kiera: *You hooked up with Royce?*

Michelle: *OMG! No! You guys are awful.*

Audri: *AWFULLY curious about our bestie's love life.*

Kiera: *Royce IS a hot guy.*

Audri: He's not dating right now. At least I haven't heard anything or seen anyone. Want me to ask Remi?

Michelle: No!

Kiera: He's probably a workaholic like Remi.

Audri: Remi isn't a workaholic anymore.

Kiera: That's cuz he has you to keep him busy. LOL! (heart emoji, cucumber emoji, eggplant emoji)

Audri: We're talking about Michelle's love life, not mine.

Kiera: It's been a year since you've dated, M. Time to start again. Need me to intro you to a hot model?

Audri: Make sure he has brains too!

Michelle: Let's get on a three-way call.

Kiera: I'll call you in a minute. Need to run to the restroom.

I took a second to breathe after the chat with my friends. I knew it would be difficult to hide something from them. If they saw my face, they'd know something was up right away. I wasn't good at hiding my feelings from my friends. They were like family to me.

I met Audri in my last year at Boston University, studying journalism. Audri had been studying business. She introduced me to Kiera, and the three of us bonded immediately.

Kiera called me and added Audri to our call. I was thankful I'd signed up for international phone services from my provider, for which NewYou Beauty would compensate me at the end of my contract.

"Spill it, Michelle," Kiera said.

"First off, I don't want to meet any of your hot models. Nothing against them. I'm just not in the mood for pretty boys."

"Royce isn't a pretty boy," Audri said. "He's handsome with an edge."

He was *exceptionally* handsome. His rugged looks churned my stomach in delectable swirls, as though my body made its own dessert just thinking about him. I kept the private thought to myself.

"He gave me a ride to my apartment when the livery service car broke down. I didn't know he owned an excursion company."

"Yeah, he owns a lot of them," Audri said. "So, did something happen between you two?"

"No," I sighed. Why should I hide the truth? There was no shame in finding a gorgeous man attractive. "Well, I *am* attracted to him—it could just be a phase, though."

"Hmm . . . I'm not sure about that. Since when have you been nervous sharing your thoughts on a man with us?" Audri asked.

I paused at her comment. *Oh, shit.*

"Audri's right. I don't remember you holding back on your attraction to Julian." I could almost see Kiera's wheels turning. "He's your longest relationship too. Michelle, darling, I think it's time for—"

"SSG 003!" Audri laughed. "You guys did this to me last year, so it's only fair you get to experience it too."

"Might as well take advantage of the fact that we're still young Super Spy Girls," Kiera said. "I can't imagine us doing this in our eighties."

"Speak for yourself. Remi will still call me Agent Sexy Dot when I'm eighty."

"Weirdos." Kiera snorted. "Is Royce attracted to you, Michelle?"

"I don't know." My attraction to him could have

distorted my perception of everything. Could I be seeing what I *wanted* to be true?

"Then we must find out," Audri said. "Kiera, babe, we need to come up with a plan for our girl."

"I didn't call you because I needed a plan. I just wanted to . . . I don't know."

"You wanted us to make a tough decision you couldn't make yourself. We got you!" Kiera said with a laugh.

My friends were obviously enjoying this.

"I don't want to ruin our friendship. What if he's not attracted and finds out that I am? It'll be super awkward."

"Who cares?" Kiera said.

"If it makes you feel better, Royce asked me about you a while ago. I think it was that time you had a big fight with Julian and looked sad. We met up at Grayson's old house. I didn't think much about it then, but now. . ."

I didn't know what to say to that. "Maybe he was just concerned about a sad friend. That's normal."

"Could be," Audri said. "He has looked at you when we all hung out. Maybe he stayed away because he thought you had a boyfriend."

"He has eyes, so *looking* at me or anyone else is *normal*." I laughed at the ridiculousness of this conversation. Though a small part of me wondered if it could be true.

"Stop it with the maybe this, maybe that. Color me determined. We're going to find out the truth," Kiera said. "We'll come up with something for you, babe. If you think of a plan before us, let us know. Sorry, but I've got to run now. Conference meeting with a new modeling agency that needs a photoshoot. We'll chat later."

"Don't apologize. Go! I'll come up with a fabulous plan."

I'd better because their scheme could put me in an embarrassing situation I would prefer not to be in.

"Oh, I can't wait to hear it. See you tomorrow for dinner, Audri." Kiera left the conversation.

"Remi is going to California tomorrow, so I invited Kiera over. We need another girls' night out when you return."

"Agreed," I said.

After a moment of pause, Audri said, "I kind of know what you're going through."

"What do you mean?"

"You're attracted to Royce but afraid that if things don't work out, it could ruin the dynamic between all of us, right? We're all friends. Close friends."

I knew she'd understand more than Kiera because she had experienced something similar.

"Somewhat. My situation isn't like yours, though. Remi is your brother's best friend. He grew up with you. I only met Royce through you. I'm not as close to him as you are. But I do value your friendship and Remi's too. Royce is his buddy." I dropped onto the couch, letting the cushion swallow me. "I don't want things to be uncomfortable, you know?"

The situation looked like it was going to turn sideways. If Royce and I got together and hated each other, we'd be shooting darts with our eyes during group gatherings. Or avoid parties altogether.

"My advice is this—don't overthink it. I did, and it drove me crazy. It delayed everything for us. Remi felt the same way too. Go with the flow, and everything will take care of itself. I know it's easier said than done, but there's no use worrying about something that hasn't happened. If you like him, see if he likes you. You have all these feelings and concerns confusing you. Why not sort them out?"

Audri was right. My brain spun, trying to figure out what I should do.

"Maybe the SSG 003 mission will come to me." I let out a chuckle. "I never thought I'd be in this situation."

"What? You plan on being a nun for the rest of your life because of Julian?"

"No. I just didn't think it would happen so soon. I wasn't looking to meet anyone here."

"The Universe whips you a surprise when you least expect it sometimes. Catch it, examine it, see what it wants from you. Your time for love has come. All the guys before were just *preparation* for the real deal."

Audri and I chatted for a few more minutes until I heard Remi in the background. I released her to hang out with her lover before his trip and replayed the conversation with my friends.

They always made me feel better. Admitting my attraction to Royce made everything more *real*, unavoidable. Even though I didn't have a solution to my predicament, I knew what I had to do.

I was going to find out if Royce liked me.

CHAPTER EIGHT

ROYCE

I DROPPED my belongings off at the lodge of Whitewater Family Resort and hopped into the Jeep, heading to the main office where the director, David, should arrive soon.

Thoughts swirled in my mind as I drove down the dirt path, memories from my time at Oregon State University studying geology and volcanology for my undergraduate and master's. Volcanoes were my link to my past—my heritage. Studying them was understanding where I came from.

More than that, I was fascinated with things buried beneath the surface—magma and other natural resources of the world. People used oil and gas for energy, and I wondered if magma and lava could be used in a similar way. It had been a silly thought from a kid who wondered too much—a kid who wanted more out of life. Even back then, I wanted the thrill, the excitement that made my blood roar. Only those undiscovered things beyond the surface offered me that thrill.

Exploring nature and seeing its danger and beauty was the closest thing to making me feel alive. My first time whitewater rafting was unbelievable. I got to see the various aspects of water, its gentleness, and its fierceness. Nature had both serenity and chaos. I appreciated the constant change that came with the wilderness.

During the summer months or whenever I had breaks between studies, I worked at this resort, a family fun campground that offered hiking and whitewater rafting. It was here that I felt connected to nature in a way I hadn't experienced before. The abundant forest and the sounds of the wild became my companions during those lonely moments.

This place anchored me because the wilderness reflected my emotions. When my mom passed away from liver failure, my life crumbled like the dried dirt in the ground. Nothing could hold it together. When I moved to another country to live with my aunt, I experienced another seasonal change—the gloom of fall followed by the depression of winter. I was uprooted, tossed into turbulent waves of trying to adapt to a new environment. Being in nature allowed me to see how everything could survive despite their differences and whatever weather was forecasted. Things tend to bloom of their own accord, and I let myself become a rock, a hawk, a tree—an aspect of nature that could withstand anything that came my way.

Mom had always loved the ocean, so Aunt Klara and I released her to the Atlantic Ocean, letting the wind and water take her wherever she wanted. Though Aunt Klara gave me love and support—she was wonderful, don't get me wrong—it took me a while to adjust to this new life, new culture, and new language. I was like a fish out of water. But I eventually found my place and understanding when I experienced my first whitewater rafting. The rhythm and flow of the water and its sudden change in course symbolized my life. Some things weren't in my control, and all I could do was go with the flow. I learned to appreciate the various aspects of the river—both the calm and the turbulence.

Despite how I felt anchored in nature, anger and resentment still warred inside me when it came to my family. I guess the forest gave me a safe place to go when I needed to calm my heart. Where was my dad? The memory of a five-year-old wasn't great, and eventually, he faded from my mind. He left Mom and me, so he didn't deserve my thoughts.

Mom never told me why he left, probably because she didn't know. My hatred for him grew every time I saw her exhausted, napping on the couch or drinking too much. But I'd never forget how she'd read bedtime stories or took me to the park. Those precious memories enabled me to work towards my dream. Mom had worked hard to provide for me, allowing me to live comfortably with an excellent education. I missed her, and I blamed him for her death.

It was human nature to blame someone, right? That was how people thought—a rational way of finding solutions that made sense. Being outdoors was my temporary escape from the issues I had to deal with. My mind wandered back to why I was here in Oregon.

Who was to blame for the tourist's death on my turf? Was it an accident? I didn't rule that out, as there had been several minor accidents within Whitewater Family Resort. Accidents occurred, and that was normal, but not death.

I pulled the Jeep into the parking spot, got out, and surveyed the area. Business was closed for a few days for the police investigation and for my team to double-check their procedures, ensuring safety for everyone. Fall brought out hikers and campers because whitewater rafting ended a couple of weeks ago.

From my conversation with David, the deceased man probably slipped from one of the dangerous cliffs that weren't listed on the usual trail route. There were various hiking trails around this campground. Some were safe, while others required more skill. These were marked with an enormous sign stating "Do Not Enter." But to some people, the warning became an invitation.

I had been one of those people who found the risk enticing until I broke an arm in a fall and learned my lesson. Sometimes you had to feel the pain to know it wasn't worth it. It had taken me years to master this self-control—to resist that which posed a threat to me. I had moved on from that kind of recklessness and was now searching for something I didn't even know. But I felt its tug, its silent whisper that nudged me to keep searching.

A leaf fell from a tree and floated in front of me. I grabbed the yellow maple leaf and twirled the stem around, reminding me of the impending fall season. Another year was coming to a close, and yet I still hadn't found what I was looking for.

A teeny tiny part of me whispered, *you already know, but you're too scared to face it.* I had no idea what it was talking about.

Settling in my office, David arrived and knocked on the open door.

"Come in. Sit." I gestured.

"Good morning! For you." He offered me a cup of coffee from the attached local café where his wife worked. "How was your flight?"

"Flight was smooth. Thanks for the coffee. You didn't have to do that."

"Susan insisted." He sipped his coffee and sat on the chair in front of the desk. "She prepared a bag of muffins and bagels, but I told her you're not a breakfast guy."

In his fifties, David had brown hair mixed with gray and a kind face. He wore a puffy brown vest over a long-sleeve knit shirt and khaki pants—the same look he'd worn since I met him when I'd started working here in college.

"Things haven't changed. I prefer lunch and dinner. Please thank Susan for me."

David nodded. "James McNabb checked in to stay in one of our cabins. He came alone. He's a seasoned hiker who's been here before, so I'm not sure what happened. Maybe he slipped or saw an animal that startled him, causing him to trip and fall. It could be anything. Are you stopping by the police department?"

"After our meeting. Any new information I should know since we last talked?"

David shook his head. "No. His family is coming in a few days to have his body shipped back to Providence, Rhode Island."

"He's from Providence?" That couldn't be a coincidence. "Did the police say anything else?"

"No, but the police chief will know more. You're the one making donations to his department, so he should talk."

Thirty minutes later, I sat inside Chief Warren Sutton's office. I'd donated enough money to the city and the police department, so the officials knew me well. Money talked, making things easier whenever I needed an approval for a business expansion.

"I'm sorry about what happened at the resort." Dressed

in his navy uniform, Warren leaned into the desk. He had a head full of white hair and sharp brown eyes. "It appears that James McNabb's death was an accident. There were no signs of foul play. We interviewed all the guests staying at your lodge. No one saw anything out of the ordinary."

I looked at Warren. "Do you know anything else about him?"

"He's a former cop for the Providence Police Department. He was working as a security guard for a bank."

My eyebrows furrowed. Something told me I had to look into James McNabb. "Thank you, Warren. When you get the autopsy results, can you let me know?" I passed him my business card. "It'll make me feel better knowing it was an accident and not a crime on my property."

"No problem."

After thanking Warren, I returned to the campground, informed David to open for business tomorrow, and booked a flight back to Reykjavik tomorrow. Then I wandered over to where James McNabb's body was found, which was on a slab of rock. My crew had cleaned the blood from the surface, making it appear like nothing had happened. I made a mental note to research James McNabb when I got back to Iceland.

I yawned even though it was just two in the afternoon. Functioning on only a few hours of sleep was taking its toll on my body. A walk in the woods with fresh air would rejuvenate me.

Not wanting to think about misfortune or death, I shrugged off all the dark thoughts and walked over to the bridge that gave me an unobscured view of the river where the whitewater rafting took place. As I glanced at the water foaming and breaking over the boulders, I couldn't help but remember taking two different risks before becoming the owner of the excursion site. Buying it hadn't been difficult because I'd been working there and knew how to run the business well. Still, my enthusiasm for becoming a business owner had overwhelmed me, which impaired my judgment. I'd taken a risk with a girl I'd met at a bar. She'd been on vacation and offered me a fun time. My younger self hadn't been able to resist that.

The night before I officially took over the resort, I ended things with her. I'd been seeing her for a week, but according to her, we were dating. I only considered her as a sex partner. That made me sound like a jerk, but that was the truth. I told her it was just sex. It wasn't my fault she misunderstood. Shaking her loose took more work than it should have.

That mistake forced me to reorganize my thoughts for temporary enjoyment. Hooking up with strangers wasn't a good idea even if they had enticing bodies. That stranger could turn into an annoying stalker. Risking my mental or physical wellbeing for sex wasn't worth it. I had been young and didn't know any better.

The following day was etched in my brain because I owned something that was completely mine. I'd worked hard to learn the ins and outs of the excursion business, including being an experienced guide. Everything had gone smoothly until one terrifying incident: I saved a girl from drowning during a whitewater rafting adventure. That pivotal moment was a contrast from what I'd experienced days before when I'd been searching for a thrill.

I took two different risks that week. One brought me temporary pleasure but a headache afterward. The other offered me fear but also gave me the meaning of life. Life was unpredictable, and even though I preferred challenges, the dare, without careful thought, would eventually kill me or prevent me from achieving my dreams—which would have been the same as killing me.

From that day on, I vowed to never sleep with unstable women I met in a bar. These days, I was more careful.

After browsing the area for a few more minutes, I returned to my cabin. A smile formed on my lips as Michelle's face popped into my mind. Where should I take her out to dinner? Did she want the authentic Icelandic food or something in between?

Dinner wouldn't be until Saturday, so why was I thinking about it now? Since when had I thought ahead like this? I'd never cared before. Why did I care what Michelle thought of me?

Maybe she already had a preconceived notion from all the times we hung out as a group. What did she think of me?

You sound like a horny teenager.

God, I needed a good sleep tonight because I was losing my mind.

CHAPTER NINE

AFTER MY CONVERSATION WITH AUDRI, ideas popped into my head. I wasn't going for the License to Kiss mission like she had done when she wanted to know if Remi would kiss her. Kiera and I could see Remi had the hots for her from miles away, but Audri had her hesitations.

I understood her situation now. These feelings were like standing amid a hurricane. With all the uncertainties floating around, I couldn't see beyond what was in front of me.

How should I approach this matter? I came to Iceland excited to work and explore this country. I didn't get to discover it the last time I was here. But now, my attraction to Royce had taken center stage.

I didn't like how a man had become more important than my career. I had put Julian first when we were dating, and he dismissed and disrespected me like a pair of old socks.

Asshole.

Why should I put someone first when I wasn't a priority in their life? I had to be careful where I stepped because the last thing I needed was to crush my heart again.

I wasn't sure if Royce *liked* me in that way. Maybe he was a flirt and had charisma that made women melt, and I was just one of those women who couldn't resist him. What if this attraction was one-sided? Then the entire mission would fail. I shoved that thought aside for now.

I didn't even tell my friends about our dinner date this Saturday. Why didn't I tell them?

Because I'm afraid.

Were these feelings just a phase? I'd experienced them before when I thought a guy was cute and then, a week later, the feelings disappeared. Maybe after having dinner with Royce, my feelings would be gone, and I'd have no issues.

Feeling relieved, I concentrated on my work and logged into the shared drive of the NewYou Beauty employee website. Browsing the images, I created a portfolio for my blog posts, organizing them according to theme and color scheme. This method helped me concentrate on each story segment, allowing the reader to experience NewYou Beauty products on a personal level.

People responded to images, and a picture could say a thousand things words couldn't. But the right words could also add power to those images. I believed that was why people were drawn to my blog. I chose the images carefully, making sure each one mattered.

As I typed my post, a notification popped onto my screen about an incoming email from Fiona. Irritation niggled at me like a bug landing on my skin. Why was she emailing me? We weren't collaborating on any projects, and we weren't friends. She had her own thing to do, and I had mine.

Curiosity got the best of me, and I clicked on the email.

. . .

Hello, NewYou Beauty Team,

I was brainstorming and thought of this wonderful idea that could benefit NYB skincare products. Hear me out. What if I cover the overall social media for NewYou Beauty—including blog posts and other social media platforms since I'm an already established expert in beauty products—and Michelle could cover the retail aspect of the store openings around the world?

This could be a great learning experience for Michelle to expand her blog.

What are your thoughts?

Xoxo,
Fiona

Who did she think she was? *What a bitch.* She had no right to assume what I *should* or *shouldn't* do with my blog. First off, who signed off on a professional email with "xoxo"? And second, who made her the executive decision-maker to push my contractual duties aside to suit her needs? That damn bug was biting my skin, and I wanted to crush it like a mosquito.

I inhaled a deep breath, trying to calm the blood boiling within me. Kiera's words about the special lipstick echoed in my mind. The more I thought about it, the more I wanted Kiera to send Fiona a whole box. Since Fiona considered herself an "established expert in beauty products," she could experience the novelty lipstick that would send her to the hospital or a plastic surgeon.

Stay in your lane, or I'll drag you by your blonde hair to where you belong—right into a pile of shit. Or I'll strangle you with the strap of your Chanel bag so you can go out in style.

Oh. My. God.

I sounded like a horrible person. All of us—every single person, even a priest or a nun—had a side that would retaliate when pushed into a corner. My hands trembled with anger. I got up from my chair, released a heavy breath, and retrieved a bottle of cold water to chill the fire burning inside me.

As I gulped the water down, I envisioned it dousing the fire. I shouldn't let her get under my skin like this.

Let it go. Chill.

Royce's intense eyes appeared in my mind. I recalled the way those green pools had turned dangerously glacial. The frosty green color reminded me of a winter meadow sleeping beneath the snow, and that image chilled my internal heat immediately. My body shivered, but not from anger. Instead, it was from wondering what it would feel like if he stared at me with those captivating eyes under different circumstances. Some might shiver from fear, but I'd tremble with desire.

Jeez. That was a one-eighty turnaround.

Feeling better, I sat back down and read the email in a calmer mental state. Fiona had sent it to the CEO Margaret Evans, Becca, and me.

Margaret didn't need to know about this little nuisance, which was why they appointed Becca to be the liaison between contractors and the company. I knew what Fiona was doing. Her parents were friends with Margaret, so she assumed she could step on everyone else's toes, and no one would react.

Think again.

Fiona didn't know I had very special toes. I imagined my big toe turning into a cute otherworldly creature that turned terrifying—when someone stepped on it—and bit her feet with its sharp teeth until she screamed like a baby. Then I would stare at her, admiring her pain.

Goodness. That was disturbing.

It was a good thing no one could see into my brain because I'd be imprisoned or sent to a psychiatric institution. I should stop watching fantasy movies, which I often did when I visited places filled with magic and lore. Instead, my mind conjured some high-tech fancy shoes with an embedded weapon that would appear at my command. That weapon would stab at Fiona's feet, ruining her designer shoes and reminding her never to mess with Michelle Yates again.

Yes, that was more in line with the Super Spy Girl in me. No one messed with the SSG 003.

Straightening my spine, I drafted my reply.

Dear Fiona,

That was very thoughtful of you. Your concern for me and the growth of my blog is appreciated, but I prefer to keep things the way they are.

I believe my travel blog is successful because I've tailored it to my readers' expectations. My fans love its authenticity. That's important to me and all my clients, including NewYou Beauty. I'm not interested in the retail aspect of NYB, though I know it's very important. There are experts who can better assist in that area, but if you're interested, go for it.

I'll stay in my lane and concentrate on what I came here to do. If NYB believes otherwise, then perhaps my contribution won't be a good fit.

I take my job seriously, and I care about my clients and readers. For that reason, I have to stay true to what I'm good at —portraying products in the most authentic and beautiful way that will attract loyal customers.

Best Regards,
  Michelle

Leaning back in my chair, I read the email over once more and hit send. No matter how angry I was with Fiona, I was a professional and dealt with my issues like an adult. I prayed she would too. My email served two purposes. One was to let Fiona know she shouldn't assume to know what I wanted. The other reason showed the CEO and Becca where I stood. No one pushed me around. I'd dealt with that attitude early in my career when I worked as a newsroom journalist and when I was a beauty pageant contestant. People assumed they knew what was best for me.

But no one could know because I was still trying to figure that out myself. Fiona was used to pushing people around and having things her way, but I wasn't going to tolerate that.

People like her had made my life hell, especially during my pageant years. Those girls and their moms had been ruthless. I didn't have friends. They all considered me the enemy because I had won so many titles ranging from Little Miss Lovely, Young Miss Adorable, Junior Miss Lovely, to Miss Teen Glam many times. I had left that drama behind me.

Drama created unnecessary stress. Who needed that in their life?

Fiona and I had distinct personalities and different

styles. Therefore, what we brought to the table were reflections of us that were unique. At least that was my perspective, anyway.

I refused to give into Fiona's tantrums. A few years ago, she started rumors about my blog being written by someone else, then claimed the travel images were bought from a photographer—whom she claimed to know. I only used images I'd taken personally, or those given to me by clients with permission to publish. It all started when one of my readers commented on Fiona's blog post, suggesting that others check out my blog for travel ideas. It was an innocent comment that pissed her off enough to make me a target. It took a month for things to settle down after I threatened her with a letter from my lawyer—which had cost me money and time.

She didn't have my permission to come into my life and rearrange it as though I reported to her. The nerve.

A headache throbbed in my temple. So much for not letting her bother me. Too late for that. Stress opened the door to many things, and I could almost feel the claws of the monster reaching for me. They felt like a cold chill forming at the base of my spine, travelling up and around to my stomach like frigid fingers that made my body tense. This monster fed on anxiety, and I'd been experiencing a lot of it.

Right now, that monster wanted me to eat a big fat meal that would make me feel wonderful one second and disgusting and unworthy the next. It would force me to purge and then spend hours and hours working out, only to binge again. That had been my dark past, and it had taken me a long time with the doctors to push that monster into the closet.

I could see the old me trying to fight the new me who

knew better. I stood on the edge of a dark past and an unsteady future. All it took was one step over, and I'd return to that place where food was a disease that crippled my body and mind.

How could food be bad for you? There were hungry people all over the world. Bulimia was a dangerous monster that played with my psyche. Though I had locked it up, an unhealthy relationship and a difficult breakup had weakened the lock. And now, with the stress from Fiona, I could hear the doorknob turning, opening . . .

Go eat that sandwich. Get the slice of pizza and the bag of chips. They'll make you feel better. They'll fill the void in you. Then you can go work out and burn off all the calories. Don't let yourself feel empty and lonely.

My body trembled with anger and disappointment in myself for letting it rear its miserable head.

Shut up! Go away!

Clenching my fists, I squeezed my eyes shut and imagined slamming that closet door tight. I stepped toward the future, even if it was uncertain. I was still trying to heal, and that was okay. Healing took time, energy, and patience. I wasn't going back to the doctor. That would mean I had failed.

You're a failure. You need me, I heard the monster say.

In my mind, I placed another lock on the closet door.

My phone rang and snapped me back to the present moment. The name flashing on my lock screen should have comforted me, but it only added another layer of anxiety.

I picked up the call. "Hi, Mom."

"Sweetie! How are you? I assume you got to Iceland safely? How's the food over there?"

I didn't want to hear the word "food" right now. I knew

my mom loved me and meant well, but she never really understood me, which had left a wedge between us.

I resented her for not being there for me when I needed her. She had never listened to my needs and didn't even know I had an eating disorder until I was eighteen. Even then, she didn't know the extent of it. I stopped telling her because she had selective hearing. No one wanted to hear that their daughter was flawed. A flawed daughter didn't win beauty contests. So I pretended to be the perfect daughter when I was really dying on the inside.

"Everything is fine, Mom. I'm just settling in. Everything good with you and Charles?"

Charles Gellar had been Mom's boyfriend for the past few years. He worked for a bank and treated her nicely, and I approved of him.

"We're good, sweetie. I'm happy you're settling fine. I'm calling to let you know we got invited to a big pageant gala this spring. All the winners and their families are invited to attend. We'll need to get a gown—"

"I'm not going."

God must have been testing me today because he kept throwing darts my way to see how I would dodge them. I didn't do too well because a sharp pain stabbed my body. First, it was Fiona, and now my mom.

Mom had no idea what I had gone through. I tried telling her I hated doing the beauty pageants, but she didn't understand. It was the reason I had developed a poor image of myself. In my eyes, the beauty pageant industry exploited children and sexualized them. I remembered wearing these tight outfits, making me look like a Las Vegas showgirl. Children shouldn't look like adults with all that makeup. I never understood why that exploitation was considered beautiful.

I hated myself back then and did something that changed my life . . .

"Aren't you excited, sweetheart?" Mom and I are in line for our first whitewater rafting experience.

I should be excited, but the dark clouds of self-pity and pain grip me. Mom knows I enjoy the outdoors, and this trip is to celebrate my acceptance to Boston University. Needing a change, I'd dyed my hair red, which Mom didn't like.

"I am." A tiny part of me is happy to spend time with her, but the rest of me can't find the energy to smile. The depression has dimmed everything in my life, and I don't want to ruin this trip for my mom.

"After this, we can get our spa treatments, so your skin is perfect for next week's banquet. There are modeling and talent agencies in attendance. You're beautiful, and you'll get signed with someone in no time. We should dye your hair back to its natural brown, maybe add some highlights."

My mom wants me to be someone I don't want to be. She forgets that my education is important, and modeling and pageants take time away from my studies. Sometimes I feel like she's having a conversation with herself because she obviously doesn't hear me, so I've trained myself to only half-listen to her words.

I create a filter to protect myself.

I stare at the powerful water flowing down the river. Water is gentle but dangerously powerful, like the rapids formed from turbulent currents. Can they drown my pain and the expectations of people around me? I'm tired of doing things to make other people happy.

I'm not happy.

What is happiness? I've forgotten. Does anyone care about my needs?

At the moment, all I hear is the rushing of water. The chatter from the surrounding people blends into the sounds of nature. Mom talks to a couple who are our raft companions. There are six of us, including the guide. I block out their conversation. The guide reminds us about something, but I don't listen.

I feel detached from the world—a world that has become dark and miserable. As I look at the woods and river, I want to join them. A sense of defiance stirs in me. I'm sick of feeling trapped. I must break free.

I don't want to be a model or an actress. I don't want people piling layers of makeup on me until I don't even recognize myself. The spotlight burns my face. The way men look at me makes me feel cheap and dirty.

I hate my life. There's no purpose for me.

I have no recollection of getting into the raft, sitting with my paddle in hand. Mom is next to me, adjusting her life-jacket. The guide is at the back, giving directions. Two rafts already went down the river, the people waving back at us. Behind us, paddlers situate themselves into two more rafts.

We move down the river and paddle as instructed. Laughter booms from the raft in front of us, and water splashes everywhere, but I don't pay attention.

Our raft hits something, and we ride with the current. The trees blur around me. The water is so powerful, pushing us side to side, and the raft hits a rock, shaking me from my seat. I drop my paddle and grip the handle to stabilize myself. My mom and the other rafters cheer as the raft slams into a rock.

Another bump tosses me overboard. The currents push me away from the raft, and I hear my mom crying for me. I could swim, but it would be hard against the powerful rapids. Do I want to swim to safety? Do I want to go back to that life?

No. I want my life to end. I want the water to take me with it, so I let everything go.

A sense of freedom overcomes me.

"Shit!"

"Someone help her!"

The voices are drowned by the water splashing into my face, getting into my mouth, ears, and nose.

I'm underwater. It's so cold . . . and peaceful . . . and free. A sense of relief overwhelms me as water fills my lungs. My body goes lax, my brain turns foggy . . .

Something yanks me out of the water, and I'm too cold to move. Am I dead? Hands push at my chest and touch my face, my mouth. I choke and cough out water, and I blink. A silhouette hovers above me. The bright sun behind the person makes it hard for me to see who it is.

Is it God? I must be in heaven.

I pass out.

You see, I tried to end my life that day. Mom never knew. She thought I fell over, which I did, but I didn't attempt to survive. I let the current take me.

When I woke in the hospital room, I lay in bed beside a young boy named Dylan, who had been in a car accident and lost his mom and dad. He was twelve years old and lost everything, but he still had the will to live. He wanted to become a doctor to save people. Everyone in those hospital rooms fought to live in one way or another. Each of them had monsters that wanted their surrender, but they kept on fighting.

From that day on, I vowed to live my life how I wanted and continued to fight my monster. I certainly had to try if a boy much younger than me could do it.

"Michelle? You still there?" My mom's voice called me back to the moment.

"Yeah, I'm here."

"I think you should go to the banquet. We don't have to stay long. It'll show our appreciation."

"Mom, I'm not going. If you haven't heard me before, hear me now—I didn't enjoy those pageants. In fact, I hated them."

"Sweetie, you don't mean that—"

"I do. I'm not attending any more banquets associated with them."

Mom sighed. "There's still time to change your mind. By the way, did you know Brittany has a kid now? That girl was truly something. Such a bully."

"Well, if that's the life she wants, it shouldn't matter. We don't live her life. Maybe she's happy."

"Are you okay, sweetheart? You don't sound like yourself today."

I pinched the space between my eyebrows, trying to release the throbbing tension. "I'm busy and tired. I need to get back to work, Mom."

"Okay, I'll let you go. I'll call back another time. I love you."

"I love you too."

The guilt gnawed at me as I stared at the phone. I loved my mom, but I was also angry at her for not understanding me. There were things I could say that would make her stop nagging me. But that would end our relationship. Was it worth it? She was the only family I had. She loved me in her way, and I was still trying to figure out how to resolve my issue with her.

Get that deep-dish pizza. It'll make you feel good.

The monster was trying to control me again. It knew my favorite comfort food—my weakness.

"Leave me alone," I seethed out loud.

I couldn't concentrate on work anymore and got dressed for a good workout at the gym next door.

CHAPTER TEN

MICHELLE

THE BOUTIQUE GYM was exactly what I needed. It was a lot smaller than the one at home with only fifteen machines.

A girl with red hair at the reception desk beamed and checked me in. I grabbed the treadmill by the wall with a large TV screen. A blonde woman riding a bike on the other side of the room reminded me of Fiona.

Stop thinking about her.

I wasn't trying to, but she seemed to invade my space. My protective armor had weakened after my breakup with Julian. He made me feel like I wasn't good enough for him or anyone. That sense of unworthiness poked holes into my confidence. Even the most confident and courageous person had moments of vulnerability, and I wasn't invincible. Though that moment of self-pity was short-lived, the damage had been done, and I was trying my best to patch up those "holes."

I promised myself I wouldn't give into the monster like I had my first year of college. The stress of being away from home, my mom—all the things I was used to—and studying for my finals had heightened my anxiety. I'd binged on pizza then puked until the day I noticed a bald spot on my head. I'd been losing a lot of hair, and it freaked me out. So I starved myself, thinking that would starve the monster too. I had mistreated my body severely, which forced me to pass out and hit my head on a desk during class. I'd never forget the huge bruise on my face when I woke at the hospital. Luckily, I didn't lose an eye or break an arm.

That incident was a turning point for me. I was pissed at the monster for embarrassing and almost killing me. That was when I shoved it into the closet and locked it up. I had Dylan to thank for reminding me of how precious life was and that my life had a purpose.

Dylan and I share the hospital room. I sit on the chair next to his bed. "How are you feeling?"

"Okay." Dylan forces a smile on his bruised face. He has a cast on his arm and leg.

"How about you?"

"I'm okay," I say as a college commercial comes on his TV screen. "I'll be attending Boston University very soon. What do you want to be when you grow up?"

"A doctor." His lips tremble, but in his eyes, I see determination.

"Why? Why not give up?" I don't know why I'm asking a twelve-year-old boy this question. Maybe when I look at his injuries I expect him to feel grief instead of hope. "Why not give up on everything?"

"I have to live. I have to believe that my parents didn't die for nothing. They have a college fund saved for me. My grandparents will help me with that." He looks at me and I see an inner strength I lack. "These doctors saved me, and I want to

make sure I can save others like me in the future." Tears slide down his face.

I can learn from this young boy. Though he's grieving, he knows what he should do. He knows not to surrender to the darkness. He knows there's meaning to life, and he's fighting to hold onto that belief.

Dylan inspires me to fight the monster inside me. I have to find my place in the world.

I thought of Dylan often. Was he in med school going after his dream?

As my heart rate increased on the treadmill, I imagined myself running away from my problems. Logically, I understood I should face my problems, not run away from them. But this was my method of separating myself from that which had hurt me. I needed the space to think without interruption.

After spending two years with someone, I thought I knew him well. Boy, was I wrong. Some people had a special way of hiding their true selves. Maybe love had blinded me. Had I been in love with him? I thought I was, but when things ended, I was relieved that I didn't need to hear him say those awful things about me or comment on how I should get a boob job like his friend's wife. He compared me to his friends' significant others, who were mostly models or daughters from wealthy families.

It took me a while to realize Julian was just like my mom —he wanted to control me. I was a means to an end. With my mom, she lived the pageant life through me. With Julian, I was an accessory to show off to his friends. He didn't care about me. In the beginning, things were fine, but he revealed his true colors during the last year we were together. Especially when I shared about my eating disorder.

The truth always revealed itself. Sometimes it took longer, but there was nothing more powerful than the truth—it doesn't lie. What I felt for Julian wasn't love. It was a complicated relationship between a selfish individual and a woman still trying to find her way. That was the truth.

I wished I'd met Audri and Kiera in my teens. They could have given me a place to be myself or talk about my issues. But the stress of being a beauty queen did me in. I had paid for the shiny trophies, sparkly tiaras, and cash prizes with my wellbeing.

A memory surfaced, wanting to come forth, and I let it. Why not? It was my way of "decluttering."

Behind the curtains, I hear the audience clapping for the previous girls who have just walked out. Heat swarms my body, and my palms are clammy. I've been doing this since I was six, but I still get nervous before the show. Wiping my sweaty hands on my baby blue gown, I inhale a deep breath.

At eighteen, I should be accustomed to people surrounding me, doing makeup and hair, making sure I'm perfect before the spotlight is on me, but I'm not. I don't like the constant hands pulling at my hair, the strong smell of hair-styling products, and the makeup brushes scraping my face. Thank God this is the last contest before I start college.

I'm so happy I don't have to do this anymore except for the occasional banquets that Mom says I should attend to thank all the judges who voted for me. Mom always wanted to be a pageant contestant when she was younger, but my grandmother didn't have the money or time to take her. I know Mom loves me, and she wants me to have what she never had.

When I was six, I enjoyed pageants because I didn't know better. Over time, I've learned to tolerate it because Mom loves seeing me win. The joy and pride in her eyes makes me temporarily forget the stress. Since this is the last competition, I square my shoulders, inhale a deep breath, and prepare myself for the finale.

The girl in front of me walks out to the stage as another one returns. I know most of these girls because they've been competing for as long as I have. Do they like it? I'm not sure. We aren't close. They seem to love it with their smiles. But then again, I present myself like that too.

I inhale another deep breath as I step behind the curtains, waiting for my name to be announced. The winner of this pageant will get another tiara, a trophy, and twenty thousand dollars. That will help my college tuition for sure. My mom is a single parent and has worked hard to raise me, so any extra money helps a lot.

Nerves jitter in my stomach as I glance at myself in the mirror hanging on the wall. The person looking back at me is different. Much older. I don't recognize her with the blue eyeshadow, heavy blush, pink lipstick, and long lashes. The one thing my mom doesn't allow is Botox. I've seen parents inject their daughters to prevent lines on their foreheads and crow's feet at the corners of their eyes. I witnessed a mother doing it to her eight-year-old once. It's so messed up.

I don't like the person staring back at me in the mirror. She seems soulless, directionless. I don't want to be that person anymore. I'm not six years old anymore. The tiaras I have look the same; they're just accessories. They can't save me or make me happy. They can't stop this pain inside me, nor can they chase away the monster that grips me every day.

Despite that, I can understand how a tiara can give a little girl tangible hope. It gave me that kind of hope when I was six and won my first one. I'd felt love from Mom and everyone around me, but the glitter fades over time.

"Where'd you get that dress?" Brittany Parker slides her gaze down my baby blue dress with iridescent sequins. She's my age and the most popular girl among us. However, she has never won first place, always relegated to second. That explains why she hates me.

"At the store," I reply in a sarcastic tone. "Just like where you got your shoes."

She purses her red lips and makes a distasteful face at my shoes. "My agent got them for me at a boutique in Los Angeles on Rodeo Drive."

I roll my eyes, and I don't care that she sees it. "Well, good for you. Hope you don't trip on those pretty shoes."

From behind me, I hear Brittany whisper, "What a bitch."

Anger boils inside me. Normally, I ignore Brittany. But I don't have that kind of patience today. All the frustration from the past attacks me like a swarm of hornets, stabbing me everywhere. I whirl around and glare at her.

"Don't be a coward and whisper behind my back. If you're going to call someone a name, then say it loud and clear, BITCH."

Brittany and her friends gasp and take a step back from me as though I might attack them.

A coordinator walks over. "You girls behaving? We don't have time for this. We're all part of the same team. We need to get along."

"I'm usually a team player, but when someone steps on my toes, I retaliate." I shrug my shoulders. "Just saying."

"Well, I don't want to hear any more curses from any of you. One more word, you'll be disqualified."

I don't care if I'm disqualified, but I know it matters to Brittany and the other girls. For a moment, I want to walk away from them and this competition, but I want to win so I can shove it in their faces. Those always in second place desire what they can't have.

A Dickinson poem from English class pops into my head. "Success is counted sweetest by those who ne'er succeed." Everyone wants to feel accomplished, including me, but I don't bully people to get it. I've been a runner-up before, so I know the emotions connected to that.

The emcee calls my name, and I step out onto the stage. My heart pounds as lights from the cameras flash. My mom sits in the front row, beaming with joy. Tears well in her eyes, and I know she's proud of me. Smiling widely, she snaps photos, wipes away tears, and snaps more photos to add to the many albums I already have at home.

Seven judges sit at a table at the end of the runway. The man with the beard smirks when he sees me. I don't like the way he looks at me. It makes me feel icky.

In order to make the event go by faster, I pretend to be someone else and smile as though I don't see anyone. My heart pounds as I answer their questions. Before I know it, I'm backstage again wearing the tiara for winning Miss Teen National. Everyone congratulates me except Brittany and her friends.

I go to retrieve my belongings and find orange juice all over my clothes and duffel bag. Furious, my mom calls over the coordinator to complain. I know who did it, but I don't have any proof. With all the energy I've exerted today, I'm too tired to battle with bullies. I'm done pretending to smile for this fake world. Brittany and her friends can be sore losers if they want to. Removing my tiara, I shove it into a fresh bag my mom gives me and we head home.

The treadmill beeped and welcomed me back to reality. I'd been on the treadmill for over an hour and was sweating like a pig. Most people only ran for an hour and hopped onto other machines, but the past pulled me down memory lane, reminding me how far I'd come.

Feeling invigorated, I got off the treadmill and checked my watch. I could make a trip to the grocery store to stock my refrigerator. After a quick shower in my apartment, I headed out to the quaint grocery store down the street.

Grabbing a shopping cart, I browsed through the fruits and vegetables. Keeping the refrigerator stocked with healthy foods prevented the monster from enticing me. Stress often pushed me to crave unhealthy food.

A chill scraped down my back. *Go to the bakery. A chocolate cake is what you need, not these boring fruits and vegetables.*

Ignoring the monster, I continued browsing the fruits. After picking out some apples, I placed the bag into my cart and saw the little girl I'd met on the plane. She wore a cheerful sweater dress and brown boots, looking adorable. That was how kids should look—innocent and without makeup.

She waved at me, and I returned the gesture. Her mom whispered something to her daughter before moving out of sight. I prayed that this little girl would find her way faster than I did. Maybe her situation wasn't as bad as mine.

I got into the checkout line and noticed the couple in front of me. The man had blond hair like Royce, but wasn't as striking. What was Royce doing right now?

Returning to my apartment, I put away my groceries, trying not to think about him, but his face kept appearing in my head. Would it be odd if I texted him out of the blue? Maybe I should just focus on writing my blog posts for NewYou Beauty. I had a good outline planned, so it wouldn't take long to draft a few more posts. Royce was probably busy anyway.

Yeah, working on my blog was the logical solution. But the conversation I had with my friends intruded on my thoughts. How could I find out if he felt anything for me other than friendship? How could I do it without being obvious?

CHAPTER ELEVEN

ROYCE

I REREAD my speech for tomorrow's banquet and revised a few lines. I'd written the speech a month ago to prepare for this important gathering, hoping to gain new supporters for the Volcanic Sustainability Research Program. As a spokesperson for the program, I'd garnered millions of dollars to help the research team find innovative ways to use resources from volcanoes. Being a volunteer researcher, I'd taken part in some of the most profound discoveries.

Volcanoes were natural wonders of the Earth that produced powerful lava, which, if used correctly, could be the next energy source. It would take a while to prove the benefits of lava to the world. Though I'd attended several conferences worldwide, I never missed the one in my homeland, a large section of which was composed of lava rocks.

When I first enrolled in school in the United States, I remembered telling my friends I used to live on lava rocks. At first, they didn't believe me, but after a few Google searches, they were amazed and asked a lot of questions.

Needing a stretch, I stood up from my office chair,

walked over to the tall windows, and stretched out my arms. I stared out the window and looked toward Michelle's building. What was she doing right now?

Why couldn't I get her out of my mind? The attraction started that day when I picked her up during the rainstorm.

My phone rang, and I returned to my desk to pick up the call with a smile.

"How's it going, Aunt Klara?"

"Everything's going well at home. How are you doing over there?"

"Fine. Just making sure the business is running smoothly." There was no need to worry her about the accidents. Aunt Klara had visited many of the excursion sites and knew most of my employees.

"That's wonderful to hear. Don't forget to eat and rest. You work too hard, and I'm not there to remind you."

My chest warmed at her motherly words. She became my second mother when she took me in, and I was fortunate that she loved me just like a real mom.

"Don't worry, I remember."

"Good. I'm calling to let you know I'm going on vacation with some friends to Australia for two weeks. We got a great deal, so I can't pass that up."

"You can go wherever you want and whenever you want. I'll pay for it. You should also retire."

I had all the money in the world to take care of her for the rest of her life. Aunt Klara was a hardworking woman and deserved to live comfortably. I wanted to buy her a new condo by a lake, but she preferred the small house where she raised me.

"I'd be bored out of my mind if I retired. The library

keeps me active. It's a wonderful place for knowledge, and knowledge is power, right?"

I laughed, remembering how she had drilled that into me during school. "Yes. With expansive 'knowledge,' I suggest you stay home. Or volunteer one day at the library. I'd rather you take it easy."

"Are you calling me old?"

"No. Just *wise*. A wise woman knows her nephew cares about her."

"I suppose you learned a thing or two about charisma in school. I pray all those girls aren't victims of your charm."

"There are no victims. I save all my charms for you—the only woman in my life."

"Hold that thought. I need a moment to pick up my eyeballs. They just rolled out of my eye sockets."

Aunt Klara's sense of humor made growing up fun. I had a home because of her. What would my life have been like if she hadn't been around? I thought about that often and was grateful I didn't have to know.

"You wait until you meet the right woman, and you'll forget this aunt of yours. But that's how I prefer it."

I didn't want to continue this conversation, especially the route it was going on.

Changing the topic, I said, "You used to bring home a bunch of books from the library, and the only books that interested me were about geology and volcanoes. The rest were romance novels for you."

"There's nothing wrong with romance novels. You can learn a lot from love stories. Life revolves around love. That's what everyone's looking for. Since we're on this topic, are you seeing someone? Why haven't I met any of your girl-friends?"

Christ. I didn't do an efficient job steering her thoughts elsewhere.

I'd never brought a girlfriend home to meet my aunt. Why complicate things when I didn't have to? If I brought a girl home, she would *assume* the relationship was going to last. It couldn't. There could be nothing more beyond casual dating. I couldn't love her because I didn't believe in love. Love caused too much trouble. The last woman I admitted this to left without hesitation, which was the best solution for both of us.

Love created a lot of pain. I'd witnessed it in my family when my dad left my mom, me, and my sister. If he had been around, would he have been able to find Emma? Mom had gone grocery shopping with Emma and only turned to unlock the trunk of the car when someone pushed her, grabbed my sister, and ran off. Mom wasn't the same afterward. Her heart broke when the investigators said they couldn't find her.

"Aunt Klara, you should know I don't believe in love. Why put a girl through all the trouble when things aren't going to last? I'm *saving* her."

Aunt Klara sighed. "That's sad to hear, Royce. I thought I gave you enough love that you could believe in it."

"Love for family is different. I love you and my friends."

But to love a woman with all my heart was something I couldn't imagine. That would mean I needed to open myself, allow her to enter my heart and know my soul, which was too private. It was best to keep things simple. No one got hurt.

"I *know* you," Aunt Klara said with conviction. "You're capable of so much more. Being able to love your family and friends is an important step."

"Don't you remember what happened to your sister? My

dad claimed to love us, but he left us." Bitterness stung my tongue. "His abandonment broke my mother's heart. I'd be in foster care if it weren't for you."

I hadn't realized my voice held so much anger. Aunt Klara was innocent—she didn't deserve to be on the receiving end of any of this.

A moment of silence pulsed in the air.

"What if I turned out to be just like him?" I asked, revealing a truth I never meant to share.

That had been one fear whenever I started a relationship. What if things got serious and I left my girlfriend or wife? Were there hereditary tendencies I inherited? If I thought like a scientist, logic would lead me to conclude that yes, my father's genes could influence me.

He left right around the time my sister disappeared. No one knew where he went. I didn't care. Though he didn't deserve to be my father, his blood ran in me. I had to be careful about how I handled relationships.

"It saddens me to know you feel this way about love. Your mom wouldn't want that, Royce. As for your dad, perhaps he had a reason to leave. We can never know why someone does what they do. I'm not making excuses for him at all. Don't let his actions influence yours. *You* make your own choices."

What plausible reason could there be to leave your family? I didn't ask that out loud because I didn't want to fuel this conversation further.

"I know you're concerned about me, but I don't have the heart for love. I'm content with my life, Aunt Klara. I have my excursion empire, my volcanologist job, and a video game development that takes up a lot of my time. I'm good. Be happy for me."

"I pray you'll find someone who'll inspire you to love, Royce. Love is very complicated. It's not easy to define either. There's no right or wrong way. Sometimes true love is doing something abnormal. No one can define the 'norm' for us. We're all different."

"Like how you were tasked with raising your nephew? That's not normal either."

"Family takes care of each other. I would've done anything for my sister, just as she would've done anything for me."

I didn't want to talk about this anymore. "Did you already book your hotel? I can book it for you."

"Everything's all set. I appreciate you taking care of me, but you don't have to."

"Of course I do. You took care of me, and I'll take care of you. It's logic."

"I'm not a science experiment, Royce."

"You're more important than that. You're the only family member I have left. Like you said, 'Family takes care of each other.' Right?"

I heard sniffles and knew she was wiping tears from her eyes. She often did this when we spoke about my parents.

"Alda would have been so proud of you right now."

"Parents say that to their kids even if their children are murderers."

She laughed. "Are you trying to tell me something?"

"No."

Though I broke this kid's nose and arm when he and his friend jumped me after school.

I get off the school bus, trying to rush home and retrieve my drone so I can meet up with my boys. We're testing out our drones and seeing what we can capture. As I make my way down the street, I hear footsteps behind me. Before I can turn around, someone shoves me to the ground.

"Fucker!" Dominic Bryson, the popular athlete who supposedly got a sports scholarship to some college, stands before me. His friend, Robbie, crosses his arms and grins.

I jump to my feet and shrug off my backpack. "What the fuck do you want?"

This isn't the first time Dominic has started trouble with me. He doesn't like that his ex-girlfriend has been talking to me. She's only a classmate, but he sees me as the reason for their breakup.

"To teach you a lesson you won't forget." Dominic charges at me. "My girl. My property. Stay away from her."

I'm fucking sick of his privileged ass thinking he can bully me and get away with it. With all the drug deals he does at school, he should be expelled. But money speaks louder than anything else.

I'm not interested in his girl. "She's smart for leaving you, asshole."

"You're going to die, fucker!" He throws a punch at me.

I block his attack and don't hold back as my fist lands on his face. He falls back a few steps and curses.

"Hold him!" he shouts to Robbie.

Robbie complies like a dog and grips my arm, but I'm a lot taller and bigger than them. I punch Robbie in the face, kicking him in the gut. He rolls to the ground, whimpering.

Dominic jumps at me, and a battle erupts between us. We pound each other, and I twist his arm, hear a crack, smile, and throw more punches to his shoulders, neck, and face.

This is the last time he lays his hands on me, and I don't give a shit if I go to prison.

Someone probably called the cops because I hear sirens

approaching. Robbie winces and waves as the police car and ambulance arrive. I'm sure he'll probably tell the cops that I started everything.

Dominic and I are both bloodied and bruised. The cops arrest me because Dominic's family knows them.

Fucking asshole.

I can see that life isn't fair, but I'm not standing still when some shithead thinks he can jump me and get away with it. I mind my business, but obviously, that doesn't matter. I've ignored his taunts in school, mostly because I don't want Aunt Klara getting calls from the school officials.

I try to stay out of trouble, but trouble finds me. That ends today.

From the way Dominic's body lies limp on the stretcher, I hope he will remember the day when I beat the shit out of him and stay away from me.

I sat in jail for a night, and the police let me go the following day. I told the cops I had no parents and lived in a shelter, so they didn't contact Aunt Klara. Lazy asses. If they had investigated, they would've known the truth. Regardless, I was glad they didn't. Aunt Klara didn't look for me that night because I was supposed to be at Grayson's house.

"If you need to reach me, you know how," Aunt Klara said. "I'll send over my itinerary and where I'll be staying."

"Thanks."

"Royce?"

"Yeah."

"Don't give up on love. It is the only thing worth fighting for. Love is priceless."

My lips compressed. I didn't want to make her sad. She was going on vacation, for heaven's sake.

"I'll keep that in mind."

After the call ended, I sat in my office, letting her words sink in. My mind wandered back to Michelle, and I walked back to the window, staring toward her building again.

I didn't believe in love, but I believed in desire and attraction. They were aspects of love, weren't they? If I couldn't have the real thing, I would ensure I got variations of it.

There was one woman who could offer me that.

On a whim, I sent her a text.

CHAPTER TWELVE

MICHELLE

MY HEART TWIRLED as a message appeared on my phone a second after I had sent him a text.

Royce: *Hey. What are you up to?*

He was thinking of me. I couldn't help the smile on my face nor the tiny seed of joy sprouting in my belly.

Pulling out the chair at my kitchen table, I sat down and replied to him.

Michelle: *Being a good girl. Staying out of trouble.*

Royce: *Oh yeah? Define 'good girl.' I think my definition is different from yours.*

I had no idea why I typed that message. There was no intention of sexual innuendo, but I could see how the conversation could do a one-eighty. My world seemed to shift whenever I had contact with him, whether it was physically or via text. This man stirred my body with all kinds of sensations.

I was game for whatever was going on.

Michelle: *What's your definition of a 'good girl'?*

Royce: *I asked you first.*

Michelle: *Ladies first. Or are you not a gentleman?*

Royce: *That depends. My definition is flexible, depending on your definition of a 'good girl.' So what is it?*

Oh my God. The insides of my thighs tightened.

Could it be me, or was this conversation flirtatious and nerdy at the same time? Perhaps the wires in my brain were twisted right now.

Heat pooled in my core, and my body misbehaved from the wild images floating in my head.

Shit, shit, shit. For the first time, my underwear was soaked from a text conversation. I hadn't reacted to a man like this ever. Royce made my body lose control.

I could practically feel my internal fluids trickling out of me, making me gasp. It was a good thing he wasn't sitting beside me because he'd know something was up. I placed a hand over my stomach to calm the jitters.

Nerves weren't new to me. I'd learned to distinguish the variations of them. The ones that plagued me came from the monster that wanted me to spend hours and hours at the gym while whispering degrading things about me. Those nerves had sharp fangs. But these luscious nerves didn't have fangs. These were the kind that reminded me of the thrill from a roller coaster, full of excitement and wonder.

Royce brought on this new thrill I hadn't experienced in a long time, and I welcomed it even though I knew it would pose a threat later. Like most unknown things, the conclusion was unpredictable, but I wouldn't know the answer until I tried it.

What kind of thrill are you, Royce?

I didn't know what I was doing with him, but I couldn't resist the temptation to find out. Just chatting with him elicited a joy I hadn't felt in a long time, and I'd take any opportunity that offered me pleasure.

A hot rich guy like him could get any woman he wanted. He probably had a list of supermodels, celebrities, or rich heiresses from wealthy families at his beck and call. Maybe he was a big flirt and chatting with me or any girl was his normal ritual. The thought soured my mood, so I pushed it away.

Royce: *Excuse me. Have you seen the Good Girl? Did I scare her off?*

I laughed, realizing I'd escaped into my thoughts and hadn't replied to him. Damn wet underwear throwing me off.

Michelle: *Not scared. Just contemplating. My definition of a good girl depends on YOUR definition of a gentleman.*

Royce: *I like how you're playing this game. I know what kind of girl you are—a bad girl in a good girl disguise. Right? (smile emoji)*

I wasn't sure how to answer that. He was probably right. I was a professional and pleasant when working or out in public. But in private, I had a provocative imagination. Didn't everyone?

For someone who loved spontaneity and adventure, I had my collection of secret desires. But I wasn't going to share that with him. Based on his comment, he probably knew. I liked that he knew.

I didn't belong to a particular category. I liked change because it made things exciting, so I could be "good" or "bad" depending on my mood.

Michelle: *A 'bad girl' has various definitions too. I'm a flexible girl.*

Shit. As soon as I sent that message, I could see the image that would pop into his mind. It was vivid in mine, sending more liquid heat to my underwear.

Royce: Do you think your flexibility can sway my hard stance?

Holy shit. I cupped a hand over my mouth, laughing as though someone was in my apartment with me. This conversation was making me sweat.

Michelle: *Maybe.*

Royce: *I know you prefer the wild side.*

Michelle: *How do you know?*

Royce: *I see it in your eyes, the spark for adventure. Someone who loves adventure is a . . .*

A what? My core tightened as I waited for his reply.

Royce: *A wild woman dressed in sophistication. You give off the proper image, but in private, you're improper.*

I dropped my phone onto my lap at his accuracy. How could he read me like that? I never considered myself an open book. Julian didn't even know this about me. Sex with him was . . . just sex, nothing wild or unexpected. I never dared to explore with him because he was too . . . "proper."

A part of me wanted to know how "improper" Royce could be, but the logical part of my brain told me to stay put. *Don't go into unknown territory. There could be traps.*

Michelle: *I neither confirm nor deny, Viking.*

Royce: *Oh, so you like Vikings.*

Michelle: *Not sure if a Viking is a gentleman, though.*

Royce: *You're an angel with horns when they suit you.*

I laughed again. If only he knew I'd dressed up as an angel with horns on Halloween.

I didn't know how much longer I could continue chatting with him and not have to run to the bedroom for a change of panties. I should have done it earlier, but I didn't want to leave the conversation for one second. What did that say about me?

Hooked and crazy.

I enjoyed flirting with Royce. He possessed an adventurous side whereas Julian was all business.

At one point, I was attracted to business executives, thinking they had something I lacked—knowledge. Someone who ran a successful business had to have vision, and a person with a vision knew where he was going. That had been my assumption. Since I hadn't known where I wanted to go, I had hoped my significant other could help me.

I was wrong. No one could help me but me. A man dressed in an expensive suit didn't mean his character was as spotless as his wardrobe.

Did anyone know what they wanted in life? Some people seemed to know, or they made it appear like they did. Talking to Royce reminded me of moments when I felt limitless, where nothing could trap me, where I could do anything I wanted. Even back during my pageant years, there had been a few days when I felt that hopeful. Those precious moments didn't appear often, though. Maybe that was why I enjoyed Royce's company, even though it was just over text messages. With him, I didn't feel the need to be perfect.

Glancing at the nickname he'd given me, I smiled. What would my friends think if I told them about this conversation?

Michelle: *An angel and a Viking have the most interesting conversation.*

Royce: *They do. I think we should do this more often. What do you think, angel?*

Michelle: *I concur, Viking. (smile emoji) (shield emoji) (sword emoji)*

Royce: *Need to take a call. I'll call you after.*

Michelle: *It's okay. You don't have to. Go do what you have to do. We can chat another time.*

Royce: *No, I want to chat again. I'll call you back.*

A sunburst of joy warmed my tummy. Did he mean "call," as in a phone call, or did he mean text? I wouldn't mind hearing his voice, but that could send my body to uncharted territory. I should probably take this opportunity to get a new pair of underwear.

What would he think if he knew his effect on me? He would *never* know. That would give him too much power. Besides, that wasn't something you shared with your . . . umm . . . friend? No. I didn't flirt with my friends like this. Royce was in between a friend and something else—a friend and a sexy Viking.

A smile touched my lips as I entered my bedroom and changed into clean lacey black underwear and tossed the wet ones into the hamper.

Sitting on the couch, I turned on my laptop and concentrated on my blog posts. Reviewing my notes and images, I applauded myself for taking this job. Their mission to help women and men stay beautiful with cutting-edge methods fascinated me. The world was changing at an alarming rate, and beauty products could help people adjust to the fast pace. There were so many products that promised all kinds of things out there, and I'd tried a lot of them, only to be disappointed. Not to mention they cost a fortune. But NewYou Beauty was affordable, and that philosophy sold me because it reached the masses rather than the few.

The writing flowed effortlessly. I'd wait to visit the

NewYou Beauty Resort before I finalized the images. Feeling accomplished after finishing the first blog post and saving it to my folder, I stretched out my arms. A yoga session would be wonderful tonight. My body needed a break from the excruciating exercise from the last few days.

Something smashed into the front window, and a rock landed in the middle of my living room floor, inches from the coffee table where I worked. My body jerked, and my heart hammered. I rushed to the window but stood close to the wall in case something else flew in. When nothing did, I peered out the broken window and saw no one.

It was seven in the evening, and the streets had a few cars passing by. Who would throw a rock into my window? Was it an accident? I lived on the fourth floor, not the first floor. Was it intended for me? It couldn't be. I didn't know anyone here. Maybe it was meant for the previous tenant?

Maneuvering around the glass shards, I picked up the rock and removed the folded note taped to it. Unfolding the note, I read the message, and my heart lurched in fear.

Beauty can't be bought, bitch.

The energy of those awful words pierced me like a twisting knife until I doubled over with a stomachache. I stumbled to the couch, rubbing the side of my stomach to ease the anxiety.

Who would do this? My first thought shot to Fiona. Could it be her? It wouldn't be hard for her to find out where I lived. She probably lived around the area, too, since it was close to NewYou Beauty Headquarters.

Fiona could be vindictive. Was this her way of scaring me away from the project?

Anger bubbled in me. This childish act motivated me to

finish the project, making it shine so brightly that it dulled hers.

My phone rang and startled me.

Royce's name flashed on my screen, and I picked it up.

"Hello?" I said with a shaky breath.

"Are you okay?"

"Someone just threw a rock through my window."

"What? I'll be right over. Don't touch anything." He ended the call.

Too late for that. I stared at the rock and the crumpled note. Placing the phone down on the coffee table, I tried to calm my breathing so I could notify the landlord about the damage. The chilly night breeze entered the window, and I shivered.

A few minutes later, a knock sounded on my door. With caution, I walked over and peeked through the peephole. Relief bloomed when Royce's face stared back at me.

I opened the door, and he filled the space with warmth and safety.

In his black sweatshirt and gray pants, he stepped inside and placed a gentle hand on my arm, soothing my nerves.

"Are you okay?" His gaze searched my face, then down my body.

"I think so. It just surprised me."

He stepped inside. "Show me where."

I led him to the living room window, and he looked out into the street like I had done.

Grabbing the broom from the kitchen closet, I prepared to sweep up the shattered glass, but Royce stopped me. "Don't touch it. I'm calling the police, and they'll need to review the crime scene as is. I'll help you clean up after."

Royce pulled out his phone and called the police, speaking in Icelandic and then English. I watched as he moved around my living room, glancing at the other windows and giving details to the police. As I studied how he took care of things, I realized no man had ever done that for me. Not with this much efficiency.

I didn't even need to ask him. He heard my fear through the phone and rushed over.

He glanced at the rock on the coffee table and reviewed the note beside it.

Reading the note, Royce turned to me with furrowed eyebrows while still in conversation with the police. "See you soon. Thanks."

Then he called someone else. "Oskar, how you feeling?"

His adaptability, readiness, and focus told me he was a man in charge. He was used to multitasking and delegating. I shouldn't be surprised since he owned a successful excursion company. It still baffled me that I didn't know this about him in all the years I'd known him.

Oskar said something that made Royce smile, and something warm blossomed in my chest.

"Since you can't leave the house and want to work, I have a job for you. Can you get the maintenance team to repair the window in Michelle's apartment as soon as possible? Some asshole just smashed it."

While listening to Oskar's response, Royce pursed his lips and peered outside again.

"She's okay. I've got her." He whirled back to face me, and our eyes met. I swore the insides of my stomach shifted at the power of his gaze. "Thanks. Keep me posted."

I was probably too vulnerable from the unexpected event that I didn't have any barriers up, which allowed all these strange sensations to occur. How could he make me feel so much when there was nothing between us?

With his striking face, mouthwatering body, remarkable success, and massive fortune, any woman in her right mind would respond the same way. I wasn't impervious to gorgeous men.

Royce walked over and embraced me. "You look like you need a hug."

His powerful arms tightened around me, making me feel safe. I needed that warmth more than I realized. Today had been horrendous with so many triggers.

I tried hard not to fall apart in front of him. It would be too embarrassing.

With this towering height, he rested his chin on the top of my head easily.

Loving his body against mine, my arms wound around him, clinging to the comfort he offered me. I feared that if I didn't, that monster would get me. Its icy claws pricked the skin around my stomach, and the scent of pizza and fried chicken tried to seduce me. I steered my thoughts away from that weakness. With the anxiety piling up, the monster would break free, so I had to hold on to as much of my strength as possible.

Royce smelled so good—and so familiar for some reason. Yeah, I wasn't myself. This was my first time hugging him, the first time being this close to him. I pressed my face to his sweatshirt and inhaled the masculine scent.

Leaning back, he tipped up my chin. "Feeling better?"

His green eyes bore into me. For a moment, I forgot the fear and anxiety and dove into the gorgeous green, which gave off a different feeling from when he'd rescued me during the thunderstorm. Today, his eyes seemed like a peaceful pasture where nothing could disturb its serenity. I reveled in feeling anchored, as though his eyes were the doors to some fantasy land filled with exciting but safe adventures.

I blinked, forcing myself back to the moment, wondering why he had this unusual effect on me.

Royce could turn off my anxiety like a switch. No one had been able to do that, not even me. In that moment, I knew that whatever was between Royce and me was more than simple attraction.

"Yes, thank you."

"Good."

Did he just sniff my hair? It was so subtle I wouldn't have noticed if I hadn't been keenly aware of his every move.

I broke free from his embrace because I needed the space to think. "Thanks for coming and taking care of everything for me."

Royce ambled over to the broken window. "My men will fix this as soon as possible. The weather is clear tonight, so you shouldn't need a tarp to prevent any rain from coming in."

I should have been the one to think about that stuff, but my brain was currently wandering a terrain called Royce Land. God, what was wrong with me?

"Thanks for doing that. I'll have to notify the landlord about the damage."

Nodding, he brushed his fingers down my cheek, sending chills all over my body. "Yes, Tomas should know about it, but I'll also call him. I know Tomas, and he's going to want to pay me back for the rushed repairs."

I wasn't sure what to feel anymore. Despite that, the fear about the stupid rock and that nasty note stayed in the background compared to this powerful attraction to Royce. His presence dominated the space and overwhelmed me.

While his thumb caressed my cheek, I studied him. Mutable green eyes that could be deadly or tranquil depending on the situation. A strong nose, high cheekbones, and a perfect square jaw with enough stubble that made me want to feel it against my skin. He had thin, masculine lips that could transform his face with a smile or a scowl. This versatile aspect of him made me want to understand everything about him.

Amusement flickered in his eyes, probably wondering why I was staring at him.

"Tomas doesn't have access to an immediate maintenance crew like I do," he said. "So he's going to be extremely appreciative."

Footsteps sounded outside the door, and Royce opened it to the police officers. Three men dressed in black uniforms carrying batons surveyed my apartment. It still surprised me that the police officers in Iceland didn't carry guns. I did a quick search after the purse snatching incident and discovered Iceland had a squadron trained to use firearms when necessary, but they were rare.

Royce and the men spoke in Icelandic as they peered out the window. The dark-haired officer asked if I was all right. When I assured him I was fine, he shook my hand, nodded at Royce, and exited with his team.

"Are these crimes normal in this area?" I asked when it was just Royce and me again.

"No. This is unusual on this side of town. The police will look into it. It could have been stupid kids thinking it was funny. This incident won't be a priority for the police department because you weren't hurt. They took the rock and the note for the case file. They'll get back to me as soon as they hear anything. I'll keep you posted."

"Thank you. It's nice to have an interpreter handy." I understood the police officers when they spoke English, but having Royce take the lead made me feel better. The stress eased exponentially.

I knew the minor vandalism case wouldn't be a priority. It was like that in the States too. Violent crimes took precedence, which was fine with me. As long as they had this incident on record, I was okay with that.

"That note seemed personal. Do you know anyone in Iceland besides me?" Royce glanced at his phone, staring at an image of the note. I didn't even see him snap a picture.

Fiona's face came into my mind. But why would she do something stupid that could ruin her career? But then again, she could be unpredictable.

I kept the suspicion to myself because I didn't want to point fingers when I didn't have proof. I hated assumptions. Fiona had started rumors about me, and that took forever to resolve. If I wanted vengeance, I could start a rumor about her, but I didn't want to.

I'm acting like a good girl right now.

I didn't need the drama. "Not really."

"Maybe someone's jealous of you." He walked up to me. "I can see why."

What did that mean? *Elaborate, please!*

He didn't.

"I have a coworker I don't get along with, but it's just business stuff. I don't think she would walk over here in her designer shoes and expensive outfit to whip a rock at my window. I don't think she's very athletic."

She could've hired somebody, but also I kept that thought to myself.

"From now on, be extra careful wherever you go. This is the second time you've been attacked."

I'd only been here for about two weeks and had experienced my share of unfortunate accidents. Were these signs that I should head home?

"You should stay with me at my place until the window is fixed. It'll get cold tonight. Weather here is not much different from Rhode Island."

"Oh, thanks, but I don't want to intrude. My bedroom is over there, and I can close the door, turn on the heat, and use extra blankets."

The greens of his eyes turned glacial, and his expression too serious to ignore. I understood his mood by simply looking at his eyes.

"I want you safe."

Those words entered me slowly, penetrating my chest and heart in the most profound way. If I could illustrate what I felt, it would be like watching some otherworldly force piercing through my skin, and traveling through muscles and tissues to settle into my heart.

My heart quivered, and I knew I was a changed woman.

CHAPTER THIRTEEN

ROYCE

"IT'S NOT safe for you to sleep in your apartment tonight. Let my men fix the window, and you can return after that. I'll sleep here if you don't want to go to my place."

"I have one bedroom and a couch." Her brows knitted together.

"I can sleep on the couch."

Michelle glanced at the broken window and back at me. "But you're going to freeze."

An odd warmth spread through my chest at her concern. Then an image of her and me in her bed popped into my mind, sending heat to my cock.

The baggy sweatshirt hid the immediate hard-on. I didn't know what brought on the sudden attraction to Michelle. She was a beautiful woman, and any man would be attracted to her. However, the attraction I felt seemed different, deeper somehow. I wasn't sure if I was making any sense, but I'd never felt this way before.

I was good at research, so I'd analyze this feeling later. Perhaps I could "research" my feelings by having her close by. What better way to study a specimen than by having it displayed in front of me?

I never said I was a decent man. Sometimes I crossed the line to get to the truth.

Michelle kept staring at me with those warm brown eyes that increased my body temperature exponentially. I glanced away for a second to gather myself—another reaction I had to investigate. Turning away meant I feared something, and I'd stopped fearing anything a long time ago. Fear made me feel weak, and I hated that feeling.

I'd never turned away from a woman's stare until Michelle. It was as though she could see through me, right into my soul—a place closed off to the world, even to myself sometimes. No one had come close to that part of me, but Michelle was stepping towards it without even knowing.

Why was this conversation in my head turning into something deeper than it should be? It was clear it frightened her. As a friend, it was my obligation to offer her security and comfort, right?

"If you care about me and don't want me to freeze, stay at my place. I have three bedrooms, each with its own bathroom."

She widened her eyes. "Why do you need three bedrooms if you live by yourself?"

"There's nothing wrong with having space. I own the entire building, so it makes sense that I have the largest unit for myself. The extra rooms are for when friends and family come to visit."

Was that relief on her face? Did she think someone lived there with me?

"So what do you say? Let me freeze to death or come stay

at my place? It's not an inconvenience for me. We're friends, aren't we? Don't you trust me?"

I had to reevaluate that last statement. Trusting me as a friend was different from trusting me as a man. I wasn't going to do anything inappropriate, but I couldn't promise there wouldn't be any inappropriate thoughts swirling around in my head knowing she was sleeping in my apartment.

Michelle sighed. "If it's not a bother, I would love to stay at your place."

"I wouldn't have asked if it was a bother."

"Thanks, I appreciate it. Let me pack some clothes and toiletries, and I'll head out with you."

CHAPTER FOURTEEN

MICHELLE

ROYCE'S APARTMENT WAS SPACIOUS, modern, and warm—something I didn't expect from him, but loved. I didn't know why I had expected dark colors, sharp edges, and some disorganization from him. Maybe it was because of the rugged look he'd preferred when we hung out as a group. The ripped jeans, worn T-shirt, and sneakers illustrated him as a simple guy. But Royce was no simple man. There was so much more to him.

The apartment possessed an earthy palette of taupe, gray, ivory, light green, and hints of purple scattered in various decor. He had a wide couch and several standing lamps in abstract shapes and sizes, all warm red or orange.

There was a lot of wood furniture in his apartment. Even some of the art on the wall was made from petrified wood. His dining room table was a slab of rock with thick wooden legs. Simple, strong, yet a focal point in the room.

"You have a beautiful home," I said, glancing around.

"Thank you. Your bedroom is this way." He gestured for me to follow him.

Royce carried my bag down a hallway with beautiful wooden floors. Fearing I'd scratch it or leave dirt on the surface, I removed my shoes and placed them against the wall.

"You don't have to do that. I have a cleaning service that comes once a week."

"Your floor is so beautiful. I don't want to track any dirt onto it. Besides, I'm used to it. When I'm at home, I leave my shoes at the door. Keeping the house clean has been drilled into me since I was a kid. Do all the apartments look like yours?"

"No. I had Grayson help me renovate the interiors a while back. He added a fireplace in the living room for me, and the windows in my apartment are the only tall ones."

"Grayson is exceptionally talented." I glanced around, admiring the architecture. "Maybe one day I can hire him to design my future home."

Feeling his stare, I turned to meet his gaze. I couldn't read his expression, but there was contemplation behind those green eyes that had somehow warmed to a shade I hadn't seen before.

"He'd do it for you. What are friends for?"

I didn't know why, but my body picked up on a minor irritation from his tone. Or was I imagining it? Why would he be irritated?

Royce opened the door to a bedroom with eggshell-colored walls and windows draped with beautiful, luxurious curtains. A queen-sized bed with lots and lots of pillows greeted me.

"Oh, the way to my heart." I picked up a pillow, testing its softness. "I love sinking into a sea of pillows. My favorite."

He smiled, and his entire face changed from minutes

ago. Standing close to me, I could see into the greens of his eyes, which possessed other gorgeous colors I didn't notice before. Spears of blues and purples burst from his pupils, mesmerizing me. I'd never seen eyes like his. From afar, they looked green, but up close, my god, they were indescribable. People said the eyes were portals into the soul. Right now, I believed that. His eyes reminded me of a storm contained within an extraordinary vessel that held stories I wanted to hear.

What are you holding inside, Royce?

"You have a thing for pillows?" he asked.

"You don't? What's wrong with you?" I grabbed a large pillow and whacked him with it. "Don't you love sinking into their softness? Pillow fights are the best!"

He laughed, and the sound echoed through the room. "Pillow fights?"

"Yeah, haven't you had one before?"

"Nope. I can't imagine having a pillow fight with the guys. We prefer playing video games."

"Well then, you're missing out, Viking."

Royce looked like a Nordic god with his height, build, and gorgeous face, but I wasn't going to tell him that. A man like him already had a sizeable ego and didn't need me to increase it.

He grabbed a strand of my curly hair and tugged at it before letting it bounce back to its natural state. "Why don't you show me sometime, angel?"

He offered a challenging smirk.

An idea popped into my head. This could be an opportunity for me to exercise my SSG 003 mission. Audri, Kiera, and I dressed up as spies for Halloween one year in college. We all loved the spy who preferred his martini shaken, not stirred, and came up with our own group of female spies.

What would my friends think if they found out I enticed Royce to a pillow fight? What kind of rules would I have? Did I need rules? What if I could make him open up to me? He seemed like a man who loved a challenge, and I was a woman who loved a challenging man. At least this man in front of me, anyway.

"If you dare." I grinned, narrowing my eyes. "A pillow fight between a Viking and an angel could be catastrophic to your pillows." I whacked him with the pillow again.

He reached for a pillow, whacking me back. "Indeed. I can always buy more." Whack! Whack! Whack!

"Stop!" I held up my hand. "We're not having a pillow fight now. You need to wait."

"Why?"

Because I need a plan to ensure I'll win, but I can't think right now.

"Because it would exert too much energy, and I need to work. I *dare* you to wait. Or are you too afraid of what an angel can do to you?"

The corner of his lips tilted up as amusement sparked in his eyes. "I accept your dare. Maybe after my banquet on Friday?"

Friday was in two days. Dammit.

I hadn't expected him to want it so soon. How could I have a pillow fight without knowing what we'd be fighting for? I mean, the spontaneous pillow fights I'd experienced weren't complicated. They all started with one of us whacking the other. But I couldn't just do that with Royce, could I? I needed to use the situation for something more, but what?

Why did this sound more complex than it needed to be? Maybe it wasn't a good idea . . .

"Wait a minute. You have a banquet Friday too?"

"I'm a speaker at the Volcanic Museum."

"No way. I'm attending with my coworkers. I'm working for NewYou Beauty. They just opened a resort not too far from here."

"NewYou Beauty has sponsored our Volcanic Sustainability Research Program. They're using some technologies we've uncovered for their products."

I remembered Audri mentioning Royce was a volcanologist. "Where do you find the time for it all?"

"What do you mean?" He quirked an eyebrow.

"Just curious how you manage Paradigm Excursions Group while being a volcanologist."

Amusement glinted in his eyes. "I'm a part-time volcanologist and full-time businessman."

"I admire a person with many passions."

"Passion gives life to things. You have them too. I see them."

He did? I wanted to ask what exactly he saw, but I was afraid of his answer or where this conversation might go. We all had things we didn't want to talk about, and if I asked the wrong question, I might be forced to discuss something I wasn't ready to.

"I guess we all have something that inspires us."

Something flickered in his eyes, but was gone in an instant. "We can go to the banquet together."

"That would be convenient. I was going to call your car service for a ride, but now I don't have to."

"Call me if you ever need to go anywhere. I'm just across the street. It's no bother at all."

His eyes pinned me, and silence thrummed between us. It was the silence that spoke more than any words could ever say. He wasn't joking about wanting me to call *him* and not the car service. But why? Did I dare ask?

"Why? I'm sure you're busy. I don't want to trouble you, Royce. I've already invaded your space."

"It's not an intrusion when you've been invited. And I don't invite people into my place often. Besides, I'd like to get to know what kind of angel you are, Michelle."

A thrill fluttered deep in the pit of my stomach.

He shifted to stand in front of me and tipped up my chin. He was so big, so tall. Energy sizzled between us, and my skin tingled from his touch.

"I'm no angel, Royce. But I'd like to know what kind of Viking you are. Are you the Nordic warrior like the movies portray, or are you someone new?"

"I guess you'll have to find out."

His lips were so close to mine. All I had to do was go on my tippy toes and our lips would touch. His musky cologne tugged at my senses, tempting me to kiss him.

The phone rang and popped the magical bubble we were in.

Cursing, he fished out his phone from his back pocket and stared at the flashing screen.

"I need to take this. Why don't you get settled? I'm going to call your landlord as well."

He walked out of the bedroom, leaving me weak, wobbly, and wondering what had just happened between us.

CHAPTER FIFTEEN

ROYCE

I STRODE into my office to take Oskar's call. He confirmed his men would arrive Friday morning to repair Michelle's window.

"The men can't come tomorrow," Oskar said. "They're still repairing the storage room."

A package in storage had exploded and caused a fire a couple of weeks ago. Luckily, no one got hurt. The package came in with other deliveries, and before anyone had time to sort them out, it burst.

"That's fine. Thanks." I smirked, loving the idea that Michelle wouldn't be going back to her apartment tomorrow.

"Someone can stop by tomorrow and cover the window with a tarp until repairs can happen." Oskar's words brought my attention back to the task at hand.

"Thanks. Let me know the time, and I'll be there to let him in."

In the past few months, one accident after another had created a substantial financial loss. Who in the hell was trying to sabotage my company? These disturbances wasted my time, money, and energy, none of which I wanted to divulge unnecessarily. A part of me feared these disturbances were just the beginning.

After the call ended, I dropped into my office chair and gathered my thoughts. In the last week alone, I sensed a change in myself. I had blamed it on the long hours at work, trying to sort everything out, including postponing projects, but now I wondered if there was something else.

I'd always been careful about my feelings. Keeping myself numb to emotions made things easier to deal with. Which was why I hadn't had any serious relationships. I never got close enough to a woman to *feel* this odd tug in my heart.

But having Michelle around evoked something in me. She was the whisper in the night, luring me out for an adventure without making me fearful of what might lie ahead. I should be terrified because she was daring me to open myself to her—something I'd never done for anyone. And yet, I found myself enticed because I wanted to know what she had to show me.

Was this another phase in my life where I just had to wait it out? This was the best opportunity for me to find out.

Michelle was affecting me on a level I wasn't used to. When she complimented Grayson's talent, an unexpected surge of jealousy erupted in me. What the hell was that all about? Grayson was my boy, and I'd never been jealous of him about anything. The idea that Michelle could like him bothered me more than I realized. I didn't want her to be with anyone, but I had no right to claim that.

While standing in the guest bedroom with her and looking at the abundance of pillows, I wanted to push her down onto the bed and kiss her. My sense of control wavered around her. I was a trained scientist, a man who followed logic to get results. Somehow, I'd gotten into a gray area where I didn't know where to go. I couldn't even trust my own thoughts.

I didn't like losing control.

Inviting her to stay in my apartment was probably a bad idea, but I was a man who loved a challenge. The more she enticed my sense of control, the more I wanted to know how far she could lure me before I snapped.

Did I dare travel down this route knowing I could get burned and never be the same?

Somehow, I knew Michelle was the end of one thing and the beginning of something else. I prayed the answer would come sooner than later.

CHAPTER SIXTEEN

ROYCE

MICHELLE and I walked to a nearby café for breakfast the next morning. I wasn't a breakfast person, so I had nothing to feed her at my apartment.

Walking beside me, her floral fragrance filled my space. I turned, studying her profile, and my chest tightened at how beautiful she was. How had I not realized this before? I loved the way her long curly hair cascaded over her shoulder. My fingers curled, itching to touch it.

A breeze blew by, and she pulled the lilac sweater jacket closer. I didn't mind the chilly weather and only wore a long-sleeve knit top. A stronger gust of wind sent dirt and leaves flying in our direction. Michelle squinted and turned, trying to block the debris with her hands. I wrapped my arms around her, cocooning her from the chill and the debris. It felt so good to hold her, and I stroked a hand down her hair.

When the wind stopped, she smiled up at me. "You give very nice hugs, you know that?"

I smiled back at her. "I do now. We can stay like this for a while if you want."

Her stomach growled, and we both laughed.

Breaking free, we continued our walk. I should have been in the office today, but I took a day off to attend to my guest. There wasn't anything I couldn't do at home. Just a few conferences with the directors on the status of our projects and anything urgent that needed my approval. Sometimes I liked going into the office for a change in scenery. But today, Michelle was more intriguing than work.

"What would you like to eat for breakfast?" she asked, bumping her shoulder into my arm. "It's my treat."

"I don't eat breakfast."

She stopped in her steps and gaped at me. "Why not? It's the most important meal of the day."

I shrugged. "It was never my thing."

Her lips twisted into an adorable pout. "What about coffee? Do you drink that? If not, I need to drag you to the hospital for an MRI. Something must be wrong with your brain. Coffee is life's blood."

I grinned at her serious expression. "I drink coffee."

"Thank God." She blew out a breath.

We arrived at the quaint café and got in line. She grabbed a muffin and a croissant while I ordered two cups of coffee and paid for everything.

"I was supposed to treat you."

"Now you owe me." I winked at her.

That hadn't been the plan at all. I just wanted to buy food for her. It was no big deal. But now she owed me something. Being linked to me meant she couldn't escape easily.

Why would she need to escape? Why was I having these odd thoughts?

Because you want her. You want to know why she's affecting you.

"Okay, I'll get you next time." As we headed back to my apartment, she glanced around. "This is a cute residential area. It's so close to everything." She blew on her coffee and took a sip. "The last time I was here, I didn't have time to see all the things I wanted to. I was only here for a few days."

"Did you come with someone?"

"Nope. Just me. It was a personal adventure—a spontaneous trip."

"Do you want me to show you around Iceland?"

Her eyes brightened. "When you have time, I'd like that."

"Wanna go today?"

"I would love to, but I have a scheduled visit to the NewYou Beauty Resort to experience their geothermal water lagoon. If you're not busy, you can come—"

"I'll go."

What the fuck did I just agree to? She was going to a spa where she'd put goo on her face. Why did I want to go with her?

Curiosity, remember? My inner voice annoyed me.

Like breakfast, going to the spa wasn't my thing.

Two hours later, we arrived at NewYou Beauty Resort—a manmade lagoon using the hot springs from a nearby area. It had luxurious amenities and spa packages that catered to both the regular crowd and celebrities.

After checking in, I followed Michelle as she wandered around the lagoon taking pictures with her phone and recording her observation. I watched her work with clarity and efficiency and felt the passion in her voice as she spoke into her phone. She was in awe of the lagoon and what it offered. We stopped near an artificial geyser—an opening in the Earth's crust pulsing with boiling water. When the pressure from the heat needed to be released, a spout of hot water shot out into the air. Michelle's eyes brightened as she recorded the event. I could understand why her blog was so successful. She transferred her sense of wonder into her work, which I had felt when I browsed her blog.

"Would you be interested in promoting my excursion locations on your blog? You can choose a site, visit it like you're doing now, and write about it. All expenses paid, including housing."

She didn't need to know that I'd also be present at her chosen site. It would be rude of me not to show her around.

Rude, presumptuous, arrogant, and other unfriendly adjectives had been used to describe me, and none of them were wrong. I was an adaptable man, acclimating to his environment. Right now, the terrain was a gorgeous woman who thought I offered the most exceptional hugs. It would be inconsiderate of me to prove her wrong, wouldn't it?

Michelle gave me a sardonic look. "With all the money you have, aren't you working with a marketing firm? I hear Starke Vision is exceptional at that."

Remington became Audri's boss when he bought the company. She now worked full time on her jewelry collection, Epiphanii, which was in stores all over the world.

"I'd already signed with a marketing firm prior to Remi's new business venture. Even with a PR company, there are other ways to get exposure. I've never thought about having a blogger promote my company. That could be untapped territory that could garner new business for me."

She searched my face. "Why me? Other blogs have a larger following than mine."

"Why not you? I've checked out your website and read your posts. You're thorough and informative without being pushy and 'salesy.' Your style attracts people, and I think that's a great way to introduce my exploring sites. A few more locations will be added to Paradigm Excursions Group, and I think you'd be perfect for promoting them."

She considered me. "What part of my blog lured you?"

"All of it. I learned a lot about *you* from the blog."

"Do you think that our meeting here in Iceland means something?" Her eyes fixated on me. "We've been friends for a while, but we never knew each other like we do now."

She sensed the inexplicable attraction too . . .

"Maybe it wasn't our time. Certain things have their time to flourish or time to succeed. There's a dude up there manipulating things." I pointed up. "I'm sure he gets to play an interesting game by putting people where they need to be."

Her brows rose in surprise. "I didn't know you believed in that kind of stuff."

"Sometimes you explore to make sense of things. For example, I need something to explain this odd connection between you and me. I can't explain it. Can you?"

Her face turned serious. "No. I can't."

Someone emerged from the corner of my eye and disrupted the moment. I turned and was surprised to see Fiona, a woman I'd dated for one week so many years ago. She met my eyes, and her face brightened. Two other women stood beside her.

I didn't need any complications right now, and Fiona had a way of creating chaos for me.

I wrapped my arm around Michelle's waist and whispered into her ear. "Can you do me a favor?"

She turned, and the hints of gold in her eyes hypnotized

me. At that moment, I didn't care who else stood beside us or around us. I was in my own world with her.

"You know Fiona, don't you?" she asked, flicking a glance at Fiona and her friends.

I loved that she could read me so well.

"I'll tell you about that later." My lips hovered around her ear, and the scent of her fragrance seduced me. "Pretend to be my girlfriend, okay?"

Michelle didn't have a chance to reply.

"Royce! What are you doing here?" Fiona barged in, disrupting the moment.

CHAPTER SEVENTEEN

I COULDN'T BELIEVE what I was seeing and hearing.

Royce just asked me to be his fake girlfriend. These things happened in books and movies, not in real life. And not to me. But the way Fiona scanned his entire body made my fingers itch to hurt her. I didn't like the person I became when she was around.

A weird possessiveness surged in me. I'd never felt this sensation before and had no clue how to deal with it.

Royce tightened his arm around my waist, pulling me closer.

Fiona came up to us and stood in front of him, ignoring me. She ran a hand down his arm as though I weren't there.

Don't touch him.

He wasn't mine to claim, and yet my brain believed he was.

"Fiona. How are you?" Royce asked casually.

"I'm wonderful." She beamed, biting her red lips invitingly. "But I'm better now that I've seen you, handsome."

Lust filled her eyes. "What hotel are you staying at? Are you busy tonight? We should catch up. It's been so long."

Fiona didn't know he had an apartment here. My heart twirled that I knew something she didn't.

Royce shifted his body, turning towards me, which forced Fiona's arm to drop from his.

He opened his mouth to say something, but I spoke first. "He's busy tonight. We've got plans. Right, honey?" I turned to him and smiled.

Fiona stepped back, blinked, looked at him, and then at me.

"You're kidding. You're dating *her*?" She laughed.

I narrowed my eyes, wishing I had magical powers. She should know that when she said mean things to people, there were repercussions. A zap to her body would turn her into an ugly witch with warts on her face. A zap to her brain would turn her into a nice person.

"Of course," Royce said, sliding his hand down from my waist to interlace his fingers with mine. "She's beautiful, smart, and sexy. Just perfect for me." He lowered his face to mine and kissed me.

My body jerked from the jolt of power upon his touch. Standing on my tiptoes, I kissed him back. Energy zapped me, and I felt electricity zipping through my body. At first, I kissed him to irritate Fiona, but then he cupped my face and coaxed my lips apart with his tongue. I couldn't resist and parted for him. Heat wafted over me, and I lost myself in the kiss. I loved how his skillful tongue explored my mouth. I wanted more, so much more, that it shocked me.

A delicious heat bloomed in my chest, spreading down to my core. Was this kiss an act for Fiona? Or was he kissing me because he wanted to?

What was his relationship with Fiona? Was she his crazy ex-girlfriend? What a small world.

Placing a gentle hand on his chest, I broke the kiss and licked my lips. I yearned for his mouth again, but knew better. His curious eyes pierced mine with a seriousness I hadn't seen before.

"I have the best girlfriend." He ran a thumb over my lips.

"Well, I guess your taste level has declined over the years." Fiona flicked her blonde hair.

Horns wanted to sprout out of my head and ram into her. "Based on your character, I'd say he leveled up." I pasted a fake smile on my face and fluttered my lashes, which I'd always thought was childish. At that moment, the gesture suited Fiona.

She glared at me, and I glared back. The energy between us sizzled. I didn't even know how we became this way. Was she still holding a grudge about how she was forced to apologize to her followers for posting untruthful things about me?

My God, move on.

I jerked when Royce slung an arm around my shoulder and kissed the top of my head. I should get used to his touch.

"People change, Fiona. I've changed just like you have."

She waved a dismissive hand. "Anyway, we should catch up."

Some girl called out to Fiona. "We're going to change and hop into the pool. You coming?"

"Be right there." Fiona smiled warmly at Royce and tossed me an indifferent glance, instead of the sneer I had anticipated. She strutted away, swaying her hips as though he were watching her.

I looked at him, expecting him to be staring at Fiona's swaying hips, but his eyes were on me.

"She didn't like me before, but now she *hates* me."

"We're in the same boat."

"No. She doesn't hate you. She *wants* you. Can't you see her *drooling* over you?"

He let out a half-laugh. "No. I only have eyes for my girlfriend."

"Your *fake* girlfriend." I snorted as an idea percolated in my mind. This could be my opportunity to make Fiona suffer and discover if Royce liked me as more than a friend. I should call this spy mission From Iceland with Love.

My Super Spy Girls 003 would appreciate the title. I couldn't wait to share it with them.

He whispered into my ear, "Is that a yes?"

A shiver slithered down my spine, and I lost my train of thought.

"Yes to what?" My voice came out soft and needy.

He smirked, and his green eyes darkened. "That we're fake dating. I don't know how long Fiona will be here, so we should date for the rest of our time in Iceland. Okay?"

"So I'm doing you a favor?" I arched an eyebrow. "What do I get out of it?"

I should just zip my mouth. Why did I have to complicate things? It was already complicated enough.

"What do you want?" His fingers traced my lips again.

For you to kiss me again and again.

"I don't know yet. When I figure it out, I'll let you know. Raincheck?" I held out my hand to shake on the business deal.

"You got yourself a deal, angel." He shook my hand as amusement gleamed in his eyes. "You want me to sign any papers?"

"No. I know where you live, Viking. On both continents."

"You don't have to worry about the relationship getting complicated. It won't. I don't believe in love. It's overrated."

The casual way he said it completely threw me. I didn't know how to reply.

What had happened to him to make him dismiss love like that? Despite my breakup with Julian, I still believed in love. I was just more careful now. Love offered me hope when life seemed too dark. We all needed something to guide us along the way. Maybe Royce found something else.

What happened to you, Royce?

"I'll meet you out in the waiting area." It was all I could say.

We both headed to our locker rooms to change.

CHAPTER EIGHTEEN

ROYCE

THAT "LOVE" comment was meant more for me than for her. It was my reminder, but it came out fast and careless. I couldn't take it back. She didn't seem bothered by it. Otherwise, she would have said something.

After changing into my swim trunks, I shoved my clothes into my locker. My thoughts wandered back to the kiss. I'd dreamed about kissing her, but never expected that potent force to slay me the way it did. The energy felt like a bolt of lightning slicing through me, zapping my nerves. I could still feel the robust charge between us.

The simple attraction to Michelle had risen to a new level that confused me. I liked my path clear and concise, with no interruptions, like a hypothesis with a definite conclusion. This thing with Michelle had too many variables to determine a positive result. As a scientist, I knew this, and yet I continued.

You're not thinking like a volcanologist. You're thinking like a man in heat.

When she looked up at me with those yearning eyes, I

couldn't resist. Who could resist a face like that? A part of me wanted to show Fiona that I was already with someone and prayed she'd leave me alone. But when my lips touched Michelle's, Fiona disappeared.

Everything disappeared from the vicinity. No one and nothing mattered except our joined lips. Her soft lips became my new favorite thing.

I loved how her body had melted into mine as though she'd lost control too. Was she shocked that I kissed her?

How she had sighed into my mouth made me wish we were at my apartment. She tasted like a forgotten treasure I'd misplaced and had just found again. That baffled me. Her floral scent intoxicated my body, blurring my logic. The scientist in me knew when a man lost his logic, he lost his mind. Yet I didn't care and needed the kiss like I needed oxygen.

That was the truth, and I hadn't dared to admit it until now. It made no sense, but some of the most extraordinary things in life didn't have an explanation, which was why they needed scientists and explorers to investigate.

I walked out of the men's locker room and waited for Michelle in a luxurious area with plush seating.

"Ready?" Michelle's voice cascaded down my body like a soothing waterfall.

I turned, and my breath caught in my throat. Praying that my cock behaved so it didn't embarrass the both of us, I reined in my desire to gather her into my arms and have my way with her.

She wore a pale yellow bikini, revealing a gorgeous chest that made my hands want to touch her breasts desperately. The bikini bottom triangle littered my mind with inappropriate images. Her ass was a thing of beauty, and I'd probably need a floatie to survive the lagoon so I wouldn't drown. My body and mind weren't themselves right now.

She waved a hand across my vision. "You okay?"

"You . . ."

I couldn't form words about how beautiful she was or how powerless I felt at this moment. Her curly hair was piled into a messy bun on top of her head. I wanted to untangle it and run my fingers through her brown locks.

Forcing myself to regain control of my body and brain, I said, "I'm ready."

Michelle grabbed my hand and led me through the glass doors to a tranquil oasis. The lagoon had a serene atmosphere that differed from the Blue Lagoon, which I'd visited a few times with Aunt Klara. I'd researched about NewYou Beauty because I was interested in what brought Michelle to Iceland.

NewYou Beauty Resort possessed a more mystical scenery with its plants, succulents, and moss-covered lava rocks. The mossy green and the aqua waters painted a gorgeous fairytale setting. Though this was an artificial lagoon using natural hot spring waters, the atmosphere looked natural, which would be a great seller to new clients, and fantastic competition for the Blue Lagoon. A section of the geothermal pool had an overhang with twinkling lights, most of which was an outdoor spa.

"Brace yourself for the heat," she said, releasing my hand.

My fingers curled, missing her touch.

Following behind her, I studied her gorgeous ass before it disappeared into the blue water covered with a layer of mist. People waded around the pool, but my attention was on Michelle. She turned and watched me enter the water that came up to my hips. The instant heat from the pool eased the bulge I'd developed while staring at her perfect behind.

Hissing, I waited for my body to acclimate to the thermal water.

"Most guys would react like you, especially guys who don't normally get cold in the winter. I love taking hot showers, so this temperature is perfect for me." She moved her hands around in the water. "You'll get used to it."

Now I was imagining her in the shower with me.

"My aunt laughed at me the first time I joined her in the Blue Lagoon. Let's just say there was a lot of cursing from me." The chilly air created more mist to blanket the lagoon, making the area more magical.

"Did you come here with your mom and aunt?" Michelle asked, making her way to an area where lava rocks created a ledge for her to lean against.

Though we'd been friends, she didn't know about my family. Only my boys and Audri knew I lived with my aunt. My past never came up, and I was fine with that. I didn't talk about my private life to many people, mostly because I didn't want to relive it. But I didn't mind sharing it with Michelle.

"No, just my aunt. My mom passed when I was eight years old."

Her eyes warmed. "I'm sorry to hear that. What about your dad?"

"He abandoned my mom and me before she passed."

Michelle pressed her lips into a thin line and nodded. "I never knew my dad either. He never stuck around when he found out my mom was pregnant. What's with these men with no responsibility?" She slapped at the water playfully and flicked a gaze at me. "Don't be like them."

"I don't plan on it." That was the truth. Keeping relationships simple prevented broken hearts—broken families.

A burst of laughter erupted and drew our attention to a group of women wading on the opposite end of the pool. Leaning against a boulder were Fiona and her two friends. In her red bikini, which revealed too much, she stared at me.

Don't come over.

Michelle dragged me to the mud bar, where the hostess scooped some white paste into Michelle's hands.

"This algae-infused mud will shrink the pores on your face and body. Wanna try?"

I had let Aunt Klara put some on my face once, but this mud paste had a different consistency. These beauty remedies were mostly for women, in my opinion. I'd never looked at the pores on my face and hardly ever used facial lotion except for SPF. Even that wasn't consistent. I was only in this pool—in this spa—to be with *her*.

"It'll make your skin *super* soft . . . like butter." She lifted the mud paste close to my face.

"You like soft skin?" I asked.

"Oh, I looove it." She leaned in, her breast touching my arm, and whispered, "Your admirer is watching. We should pretend we're a couple so she'll look away."

I placed my hand on her lower back, pulling her closer to me, where her breasts kissed my chest. My cock twitched under the water, threatening to pollute the entire pool.

Soft skin.

Oh, I looove it.

Those were the only words floating around my ears.

"Okay. Lather me."

I'm so fucked. Since when had I cared about having soft

skin? Since Michelle purred and made it sound like she wanted to kiss it.

Veering back, she created distance between us.

If my friends ever heard about me being lathered in mud paste for soft skin, I'd never hear the end of it. Each of them would create some dumb character in our video game to remind me of how pathetic I was being.

Fortunately, no one was here to witness this once-in-a-lifetime incident except Michelle. She could put whatever she wanted on me as long as her hands touched my body.

CHAPTER NINETEEN

THE HEALING thermal seawater was exactly what my body needed. Unlike the Blue Lagoon, an established resort of seawater, NewYou Beauty Resort offered both a seawater pool and a freshwater pool.

I scooped up some mud and lathered it on Royce's pectoral muscle, which flexed upon my touch. My internal organs reacted by doing something strange inside of me.

Trying to think of anything but his hot body, I asked, "Did you know that this mineral-rich water was harvested in a research and development center near the lagoon?"

"Oh yeah?" he answered in a husky voice.

"I read up on the company and its mission before I agreed to the job."

"Oh yeah?" He swallowed, and his gaze followed my fingers as I moved the mud down his abdomen.

Knowing I had this effect on him empowered me; I hid the smile that wanted to surface.

"The waters from both pools are enriched with silica, algae, and minerals."

"Oh yeah?"

I couldn't help but laugh. "You're in need of new vocabulary. I guess this mud has some magical powers. I should try it soon."

"You should definitely try it," he said breathlessly as my fingers traced the firm muscles of his abs.

Royce had a fabulous body corded with taut muscles. Every time a muscle flexed, something in me flexed too, as though our muscles were having a private conversation.

He had a body and a face that made women swoon, and I got to touch him all over. I felt his gaze on me, and my cheeks warmed as I took my time discovering the firm landscape of his body.

Was that a groan that escaped him? I couldn't be sure as I tried my best to prevent myself from moaning.

"You enjoy working out, Viking?" I asked in a low voice.

"I do."

Glancing up, I met his curious eyes, which had darkened to a dangerous green. I cupped the thermal water and splattered his body, washing off the mud.

He gripped my hands, holding them still. "My turn to lather you. Stay here. I'll be right back."

Royce went over to the mud bar, and I studied his muscled back and the lightning bolt tattoo. I'd been so focused on his face and abdomen that I hadn't noticed the beautiful artwork on his body. The lightning bolt sat along his spine, symbolizing an emblem of power.

He turned, came up to me, and his eyes flashed with heat, making me forget about his tattoo.

"Front or back." he asked with a handful of mud paste.

My inner thighs tightened, wanting his hands on my chest, but propriety won. "Back, please."

I shifted to give him access to my back while I took in the lagoon's atmosphere. I'd been too distracted by him to appreciate the surrounding wonder.

The cool paste felt like a lovely kiss on my warm body. Royce's large hand moved around my shoulder blades, massaging them.

"You've got skillful hands." My body relaxed when I tilted my head to the side.

"I know," he whispered close to my ear, sending a shiver through me.

I concentrated on my surroundings. The magical atmosphere felt like a universe of sacred wellbeing with a bridge that connected the separate pools. I couldn't wait to experience the freshwater lagoon. Perhaps another time because I was too comfortable in this spot and didn't want to move.

"What do you know about this NewYou Resort?" he asked, moving to stand in front of me while adding some paste to my arm.

"There's a Research and Development Center near here. That's where they harvest water with algae using LED light to mimic sunlight. When the algae is ready, they freeze-dry it into a powder, which they then add to their beauty products. It's pretty innovative."

"It is. I love how you know all of this." He added paste to my other arm. "Few people want to know the science behind the glamor."

"It's interesting to me." I shrugged. "Nature is beautiful, but *how* it functions is even more beautiful. I want to understand its little secrets because that's what I try to capture in my writing." His handsome face made me sigh. "What I love most about NewYou Beauty is they recycle carbon dioxide from their power plant to feed the algae. Isn't that cool?"

His green eyes sparkled, transforming his face from handsome to stunning. I wasn't sure how else to describe him.

Heat wafted over me, and I had to look away from his eyes before I melted into the pool.

"So you like innovative methods."

It wasn't a question.

"I do. I think it's a fantastic way to help the Earth. When I travel, I want to breathe fresh air, you know? So a company that shares that kind of philosophy shows they're helping the environment."

Royce continued to stare at me.

"Even their use of the natural hot springs fascinates me. I find lava interesting too."

He smirked. "Lava intrigues you?"

"When people think of lava, they feel fear—and they have good reason to. History has shown how destructive a volcanic eruption can be. But from the depths of the earth comes this heat, this sacred thermal passion that warms the earth, the water. I don't know. I just find it interesting. Isn't that why you're a volcanologist?"

"Partly," he said. "Lava has a darkness to it, but it also possesses beauty. Even after lava is no longer the liquid fire, it becomes these rocks with healing properties."

"Like life, you can't have the good without experiencing the bad. The good things come with a prerequisite."

I'd never understand why God made certain things the way he did, but if I looked deep enough, there were treasures to be found. Perhaps that was why I enjoyed exploring and seeking treasures for my blog.

My contemplative appearance must've fascinated him because he said, "What are you thinking about?" A sly smile crept onto his face. "Don't tell me you're thinking about me. Although that's what I would expect from my girlfriend."

"Fake girlfriend," I corrected.

"Same difference."

"No, it's not." I laughed.

He pressed the rest of the mud paste onto my neck, moving down and down, stopping just above the edge of my bikini top.

I gasped and stopped breathing.

"What should I do, Michelle? Should I continue . . ." His fingers hovered along the bikini edge, caressing my skin and sending heat to my core.

I desperately wanted him to continue, but I felt Fiona's stare cutting into my skin. I could see her looking at us from the corner of my eye. Her irritation slithered all over my body. If she wanted to look, I'd give her a show.

Right now, Royce was *my* boyfriend, and I had a claim to him. I had to show the world that he was mine.

"What do you want to do?" I asked, moving to a little nook in the corner away from the main area and lowering my body beneath the water, so people couldn't see what we were doing if they passed us.

A soft growl escaped him. "You're driving me crazy, angel." He palmed my breast beneath the water and watched my reaction with a smile.

My breath hitched at the sudden jolt of pleasure.

This "show" was to annoy Fiona, wasn't it? It seemed it didn't matter if she was around or not. We were both in our own world. I wanted to touch him regardless of her presence.

He could elicit powerful sensations from my body that I hadn't felt in years.

He slipped his hand under my top and played with my nipple. I gasped, and he smirked as heat flashed in his eyes. His mouth crashed into mine and muffled my gasps. His lips molded and coaxed mine, making me forget everything. Squeezing my breast and tugging at my nipple, he deepened the kiss. My pulse tripped, got up, tripped again, and quickened as desire soared, creating a sultry heat inside my body. My hands trembled as they roamed his chest, exploring the slickness of his skin and the beating of his heart.

I was pretty sure people were watching us, but I didn't care. There was nothing wrong with two lovers showing affection. My hands slipped around him, and my fingers tugged at his hair.

He removed his hand from my breast and cupped the sides of my face, angling the kiss. I moaned as his tongue twirled with mine in a seductive dance that made me yearn to know what else he could do with his mouth and tongue. He tasted of coffee and something so masculine and secretive that I didn't have a word for it. The slight hint of his cologne mixed with the seawater and earthly moss created this magical scent that captured him perfectly. I felt like I was kissing an earthly wonder that withheld so much pressure and power. He was the volcano I wanted to entice. The muscles in my inner thighs tightened. I had to stop this before things got out of hand.

I broke the kiss and licked my lips, still craving the taste of him. "This fake dating is getting dangerous, Royce."

"Don't tell me you're scared now." Rising to his feet, water dripped down his body as he tugged me to a standing position and washed off the rest of the mud paste from my arms.

"I'm scared we'll be kicked out of this lagoon and banned for life. I'd probably lose my job for indecency."

Smirking, he lowered his hands to cup my ass. My breath caught again, and he tossed me a wicked grin that promised a wild adventure in bed. It should be illegal for someone to be that gorgeous. The man had more sex appeal than anyone I'd ever known. Everything about him was just . . . *more*. Royce was monumental, overwhelmingly stunning, and possessed the power to make me weak with a simple gaze.

"If you lose your job, I can give you one. The offer still stands for you to promote my excursion business on your blog. I have several locations around the world. It's an enticing full-time gig."

Stop enticing me with that look.

His green eyes were like crystal balls, trying to lure me into seeing something that was probably not good for me.

Though the offer appealed to me, I didn't want to complicate matters even more between us. This fake dating didn't seem so fake. How could something fake make me *feel* so much? That kiss was everything. His touch brought my body to life. I could still sense the electrical charge running through my body.

Complications mean trouble. Trouble weakens my closet door, allowing the monster to come out.

Royce probably saw my concern and said, "What happens in Iceland stays in Iceland."

He saw through me, or his thoughts had just coincided with mine. I had thought the same thing not too long ago.

"So you don't have to worry. Have fun with me while

we're playing pretend." He cupped my ass, pushing my sex closer to his cock.

When I drew away, I saw Fiona from the corner of my eye. Or rather, I sensed darts flying at me.

"Is Fiona your ex-girlfriend?"

"Yes. For one week."

He dated her for only one week?

I couldn't help myself. "Why so short?"

He shrugged. "I was young and clueless. Hormones clogged my brain back then. When I came to my senses, I ended things. It was hard trying to keep her at a distance."

"She acts like she still owns you."

That idea bothered me more than I expected. My grip on his arm tightened, and my fingers dug into his muscles. I didn't even realize until he patted my hand, peeled off my fingers, and took my hand in his. That simple gesture soothed my irritation.

My new apprehension and anger towards her was just me being protective of my friend, right?

My dismay didn't have a chance against the power he had over my body. The heat between Royce and me could incinerate this hot spring.

"Let me give you a little background. I'd been studying for my master's and had just taken over a business. I was exhausted when I met her at the bar, and her invitation was what I needed. But she got clingy and wanted to date officially. I wasn't into that. I just wanted a hookup."

Would he dismiss me if I wanted more than this fake relationship?

Frustration flared in me. Fiona got to be with him first.

I shoved the ridiculous jealousy out of my mind. Why should I be jealous if my relationship with him was fake? I was doing him a favor. I shouldn't be jealous. Still, irritation nipped at me like porcupine quills.

"I'm going to explore the waters so I can write about it." I yanked my hand away from his and walked over to a new section of the pool with a wooden bridge surrounded by rocks and moss.

Royce followed behind me, saying nothing. Confusion overwhelmed me as I ran my fingers over the soft moss covering the huge rocks. Tears threatened and perplexed me even more. Why was I so emotional about this?

I was a mess for no reason. Ignoring him, I pretended to analyze the moss, rocks, and water. If I looked at him, I might cry. Then he'd ask why, and I didn't have an obvious answer, which would make me feel stupid.

Royce stood beside me, examining the rocks. My body was aware of his presence like a sunflower was aware of the sun. My body resonated with his body heat, his scent, his ability to make me weak and wobbly.

A burst of laughter from Fiona drew our attention to her corner. She was splashing water at two guys who had joined her group. Smiling, she waved at Royce.

He waved back and returned his focus to me.

"I want to do something again." He touched my chin lightly, his eyes darkening.

Something about his voice sent nerves rioting in my stomach. "Do what?"

"Something a boyfriend has a right to do with his girl-friend." He kissed me, his soft lips brushing ever so slightly over mine, teasing me. "Do you oppose this kissing practice?"

My heart quickened. "No."

I felt his smile on my lips as the kiss escalated from sampling to needy. Warm breath, soft lips, pounding hearts, and his body flush to mine were the only things in my awareness. He intensified the kiss, and I met his greedy demands.

My body trembled from the onslaught of sensation he drew from the kiss, and I wanted to know how my body would react if we went beyond this.

CHAPTER TWENTY

ROYCE

MICHELLE WANTED the kiss just as much as I did. She moaned, parted her lips, and my tongue slid in, met hers, and a wild battle ensued. A separate heat from the thermal water coursed through me, and my cock hardened.

She pressed her body to mine, and I deepened the kiss, wanting more of her. Her body sagged into me, and my arms banded around her slim waist. Was she kissing me as my "fake girlfriend," or was this kiss something she wanted?

Fake boyfriend or not, I kissed her because I couldn't resist her.

I was in dire danger—this fake dating situation would alter my life. I just knew it, but I couldn't stop myself.

The radical part of me wanted to know how this temporary relationship would affect me. The practical version of me crossed his arms, watching my downfall. Sometimes the best way to learn a lesson was to get through to the end.

What had I been thinking when I asked her to fake date me? My cock twitched as though it knew the answer had nothing to do with my brain. Our kiss was like a collision of stars, bursting with life and energy. I'd never felt anything like it, and I wanted to feel it again and again.

I dragged my mouth to her ear. "You're a fabulous kisser, angel. If we don't stop, we're going to give these people a show."

Sucking in a breath, she stiffened, remembering we were in a public area. Her cheeks blossomed to an adorable pink, making me want to continue kissing her. Something powerful simmered between us, and if I didn't step carefully, I could find myself in threatening territory.

Michelle was the danger zone, and I gave her access to me by being my fake girlfriend. What would she think if I backed away now? An intelligent girl like her would be curious. Curiosity provoked questions, and questions slowly eroded my privacy. That was too sacred to me.

She would probably assume I didn't like the kiss. Or that I wanted Fiona hovering around. From experiences with women, I understood that a woman's mind could produce frightening thoughts. Thoughts that could mutate into even scarier scenarios that had nothing to do with the original issue. I didn't need the extra complication or the drama.

So I kept my mouth shut, praying that Michelle and I would miraculously keep our hands off each other while we tried our best to succeed at this fake relationship. I had too much going on at work, and I didn't need Fiona hounding me.

Michelle looked at me with inquisitive eyes. "Should we have rules for this pretend dating thing? Like no kissing, no touching."

A sudden tightness cramped the muscles in my back. I didn't like her suggestion, even though it made sense to have boundaries.

"Like fake rules for the fake relationship?"

Her eyebrows furrowed. "Umm . . . I guess. It sounds weird, though."

This entire situation was weird, but something about it seemed right. At the moment, everything appeared foggy, like the layer of mist blanketing this lagoon.

I'd always been a man who knew his next step. It was like experimenting on volcanic lava. I could see the process and knew what to do to get results. But with Michelle, I was clueless. Carrying out a fake relationship shouldn't be this hard. With all those years I'd spent in college, I couldn't come up with a concise answer to a relationship question.

I needed a moment to think about my reply. Should I tell her there wouldn't be any intimacy? The idea constricted my chest.

"How about we have a safe word? You know, if things got out of control and you wanted to stop, then you say the word." I jerked a finger in Fiona's direction. "If she knows we're faking it, she's going to harass me even more. We have to make it believable, right?"

What the fuck was I talking about? I felt like I was two people in one body. One had some sense in him, knowing that more kissing would mean more trouble. The other guy wanted to do all kinds of inappropriate things regardless of the consequences.

I was a walking paradox in deep shit.

"I highly recommend a safe word." It sounded like *I* needed a safe word.

Whoever said spontaneity created the best ideas was a liar. This fake dating would be my end.

And yet you don't care.

Not when she was looking at me with such inquisitiveness.

"Okay. I've never had a safe word," she whispered, her cheeks pinker than before. "I've never *needed* it. People only use that kind of word when they're into the BDSM stuff, right?"

I laughed at where her mind went, but it was a natural thought process. There were many things I could tell her. Though the lighter version of BDSM could be fun, my angel needed a different tender loving care. BDSM wasn't her style. Those brown eyes sought a different excitement, something daring yet not as dark.

"Are you into that kind of erotic roleplaying?"

"Umm . . . no . . . not really . . ."

"Not really" just made my dick throb. I understood her more than she knew. Not BDSM, but something else.

She had no idea what she just did to me. Now I wanted to know. My *mission* was to find out what was behind "not really." I'd proven I had lost my mind, and I didn't give a damn.

Scooping up water into my hands, I whipped it at her face. She squealed, laughed, and sloshed water back at me. The echo of her laugh went on and on, enlivening the place.

She submerged under the water and came up. "What's your safe word?"

I'd never needed a safe word, but to give her peace of mind, I said, "Mine is a phrase: 'Dammit, I'm mad.'"

"What?" She looked at me as though I were an alien. "Are you serious?"

"Did you know that 'Dammit, I'm mad' is spelled the same way backward? It's a cool palindrome."

She twisted her lips as she thought. "You're right! I never knew that."

"You can have a safe phrase if it's easier for you."

"I was expecting something else from you."

"Like what?"

She shrugged. "I don't know. 'Emergency' or 'crisis,' or some other word that would *alleviate* the situation."

"My phrase will pause everything and *alleviate* the situation. Besides, I won't need it." I tapped her adorable nose. "People go into these kinds of relationship already knowing what to expect. They have safe words or phrases for when they can't handle something. A safe word is used to help bring on a contrast to the situation."

"And you know this because . . ."

"I've partaken in a few relationships that required such words."

But none of those relationships intrigued me the way you do.

"Oh." She pursed her lips, thinking.

I'd give anything to peek into her mind.

"Well then, my word is 'tomato.'"

"You feel safe with a tomato?" I tugged at her hair playfully.

She smirked. "Not so much 'safe' as it reminds me of something I've overcome. Don't give me that look. You're the one with the weird 'dammit, I'm mad' phrase. There's nothing wrong with my simple vegetable."

I held up a finger. "Technically, *scientifically*, a tomato is a fruit."

She rolled her eyes at me. "Doesn't matter. It's *my* safe word."

Now I had to know why. The more our conversation

continued, the longer my list of curious things grew. Not a good idea.

Michelle turned, saw Fiona and her crew heading toward us, and wrapped her arms around my neck.

Loving how she clung to me with that determined look, I slipped my arm around her waist, pressing her closer. Our fake relationship served two purposes. One, I could live out my fantasy of being with Michelle and satisfy my cravings so when things ended, we'd both move on with our lives with no strings attached. Our friendship could return to what it was. The second purpose was to keep Fiona away from me.

She was a mistake that kept reappearing, and each time she morphed into a bigger problem for me. Even after I'd broken things off, she kept showing up to my work, waiting for me. She kept calling and emailing. Her obsession was frightening. I'd considered a restraining order, but those things didn't work. A restraining order would only escalate the matter.

We make the perfect couple. You should give us a chance. Being with you was the best thing that's happened to me. Don't you feel our chemistry?

That had been her response every time after I ended the relationship. I remembered that day clearly. I had just gotten back from assisting some rafters who had gone overboard. People could have died at my resort on my first official day of taking over the business.

Years later, I'd bumped into Fiona a few times at galas, seen her with dates, and assumed things were fine, but then the emails started coming. Thank God she didn't have my new private phone number.

I wished I could delete her like an old email or sever ties like a bad business transaction, but it was more complicated than that. Her father, Andrew Clark, was the CEO of Global Bank, the biggest funder for the Volcanic Sustainability Research Program. To ensure the program received funding, I forced myself to look the other way as long as she stayed on her turf.

CHAPTER TWENTY-ONE

ROYCE

WHEN WE MADE it back to my apartment, I felt like a different person. Michelle went to shower in her private bathroom, and I strode into mine.

The event at NewYou Beauty Resort shifted Michelle and me to a different level. When we went there this morning, Michelle was my friend, but she came home as my fake girlfriend. The falsehood seemed more real than any relationship I'd ever had. She ignited a thrill I'd been searching for, but I kept that thought to myself. I didn't want to frighten her.

Something interesting was brewing between us. I sensed the charged energy thrumming whenever she was around me. There had been desire in her eyes, coupled with caution. I could understand her situation. We both had our reasons for this caution, which would make this relationship easy to end when the time came. Neither of us wanted more than to show the public we were together.

I owed her a favor, which she'd collect when she figured out what she wanted from me.

Why didn't she get along with Fiona? What had happened between them? Was it a personality conflict? I had a feeling Fiona didn't have a lot of friends unless those friends bent to her rules. Michelle wouldn't do that. Audri and Kiera were her best friends, as close as I was to my boys. I could trust them. Fiona wasn't the type to be trusted.

A thought occurred to me. Fiona also worked for NewYou Beauty, and Michelle had mentioned a difficult coworker. Could Fiona be the person who had tossed the rock into Michelle's window? Had Fiona written that note, which wasn't an outright threat but a catty comment?

If I were a detective, Fiona would fit the bill. When I had worked at the Whitewater Family Resort, she had left several notes on my car windshield asking me to call her or meet her for lunch. She stalked me for a while until I called the police on her. Her family had money and made everything go away. That was before I worked for the Volcanic Sustainability Research Program, which her father now funded.

Had Fiona developed a hatred toward Michelle because of me? Knowing Fiona, she probably researched Michelle and me and assumed we were together even though there hadn't been anything between us until now. I picked up my phone and called my PI.

"Can you look into Fiona Clark? I want to know if she had searched Michelle Yates or me and if she was anywhere near Michelle's apartment. I'll send you the address."

"Okay."

I had to thank Remington for referring me to his PI and for allowing him to take on this extra job, as he worked exclusively for Remi.

"By the way, Einar Hallsson's business is suffering, and

he's also going through a divorce. Other than that, he hasn't been up to anything out of the ordinary. But I'll keep looking just in case."

"Thanks. Make Fiona Clark your priority."

I had also been chatting with some associates, who confirmed Einar had cheated on his wife of ten years. People in stressful situations often committed unimaginable crimes. It was better to be thorough than to be sorry.

After a quick shower, I walked out to the kitchen and found Michelle on her hands and knees on my tiled floor, wiping something with a paper towel. She wore cotton pants and a T-shirt, nothing provocative. But damn, the way her body moved aroused the hell out of me.

Leaning on the wall, I folded my arms across my chest and enjoyed the spectacular view. If I were a decent man, I'd walk over to assist her. But at the moment, I preferred indecency because the seductive sight of her on my floor stirred up a slew of tempting images.

The way her ass shifted beckoned me, sending heat rushing through my body. I'd never been this turned on watching a woman clean my kitchen floor. She was the first woman to do so in my home, and I couldn't imagine anyone else.

What would she look like if she wore lingerie while making me coffee or dinner? Though I'm not the breakfast kind of guy, I'd have her every morning.

Michelle shifted into a downward dog position, stretching out her back. Her perfect ass was in the air, calling me as she stretched out one leg and then the other. *Fuuuck.* If she kept that up, I'd slap her butt for provoking me. Then I'd take her on my kitchen floor.

"Are you going to help, or are you going to stand there

and be creepy?" She straightened up, tossed the paper towel into the trash, washed her hands in the sink, and turned to meet my gaze.

Smiling, I pushed myself off the wall and walked up to her. Unable to resist, I cupped her face with both hands. "As your boyfriend, I have permission to be as 'creepy' as I want. Besides, there's nothing wrong with admiring my girlfriend cleaning my kitchen floor. That was the hottest thing ever." Then I kissed her lightly on the lips.

I figured since we were fake dating, I might as well take advantage of this and do all the things a boyfriend should do.

She made a face but didn't prevent me from kissing her once more before releasing her.

"You didn't need my help. You were doing a fine job by yourself." I jerked a chin to the spot where she had cleaned. "What happened here?"

She jabbed a finger at my chest. "I spilled some water."

"If you're looking to add to your resume, I'm always on the lookout for a dependable maid."

She narrowed her eyes. "Viking, I have enough to do, and I'm looking to hire an assistant."

"Oh yeah? What kinds of things do you need assistance with?" I wiggled my fingers. "As you can tell, I've got skillful hands and fingers."

"Is that how you charmed your other fake girlfriends?"

"You're my first fake girlfriend." Did she think I had a roster of them? It was probably best to let her believe that because it would make things easier when the relationship ended and we returned to Rhode Island as friends.

She tilted her head. "That makes me feel sooo special."

"So what kind of assistance do you need?"

"Someone to slay a monster and to be on his hands and knees for me." Her eyes sparkled as she teased.

"You have a monster?"

"Don't we all?" There was something serious in her voice, a hidden truth I wanted to discover.

"Just holler when you need me."

Smiling, she patted my cheek. "We should both go to bed. We have a full day tomorrow before the banquet."

With that, she walked past me and toward her bedroom, leaving me hot, bothered, and wondering how I could slay her monster.

CHAPTER TWENTY-TWO

ROYCE

A STRESSFUL DREAM woke me up at five in the morning, and I couldn't fall back to sleep. I went to the gym at the far end of my apartment and rowed for twenty minutes before doing sit-ups and then hopping over for some weights. I needed to sweat, hoping that would ease my lingering frustration.

In the dream, my mom asked me for my forgiveness. She looked distressed, and I wanted to tell her I wasn't mad at her. There was nothing she could do about her illness. I told her if I had to blame someone, it would be my father, who stopped loving us.

She responded by shaking her head at me. *"He's not to blame, Royce. Sometimes, life is too complicated for a young child to understand."*

I was no longer a child and still blamed him. It was probably wrong to hold on to such negativity, but I couldn't help it. My resentment was carved deep into my soul, preventing me from having a normal relationship. Yes, I blamed him for that too. My anger was unhealthy, but at least I acknowledged it. That was a positive step, wasn't it? I wasn't avoiding the issue. I *knew* the problem but didn't know how to fix it. Or if it could be fixed at all.

What would have happened to our family if he had stayed? Mom had needed him when my sister went missing and was never found. Hell, I needed him too.

After another thirty minutes in the gym, I showered, cleared my head, and got some work done before eight in the morning. I was on the third cup of coffee when Michelle entered the kitchen and found me on my laptop.

Seeing Michelle made me irritatingly happy. She was the reason I almost broke my vow. My mom's distress reminded me why I never wanted to see that pain in another person again. A broken heart had killed my mom. The guilt she must have felt when she left me with my aunt probably did her in. The ugly past crept up my spine, reminding me of what I should do.

"Morning." She smiled, sitting down across from me.

I looked at her pretty face and morning hair, all rumpled and wild. I shouldn't be aroused by the messy look, given my sour mood, but my cock hardened despite everything.

"Morning," I replied, returning my gaze to the computer screen, trying to focus on a new proposal from one of my directors, but all I could think about was her.

"There's coffee in the pot. Help yourself."

Though I kept my face to the computer, I could tell she stared at me for a while before getting up to retrieve her coffee and sitting back down.

After a few minutes of awkward silence, she asked, "Are you okay?"

"Yeah, fine. Just busy."

"Busy being annoyed?" She sipped from the white mug.

I glanced up. "Just busy."

She arched an elegant eyebrow. "Okay. I don't want to interrupt you. Let me go wash up and I'll get my things and work at my—"

"No," I said too quickly. The shock of her leaving snapped me out of whatever mood I was in. "You're not interrupting me." Not in the way she assumed. I couldn't explain what I was feeling without telling her about my past. There was nothing beautiful to share.

"You're obviously occupied and annoyed. I don't want to disturb—"

"You're not," I sighed. "I had a bad dream, and it annoyed me." For fuck's sake, I sounded like a toddler who needed comfort.

"Really? Is that the whole truth or part of the truth?" She peered at me over the rim of her coffee cup.

"What do you think?"

"Part of the truth. But I won't press you into telling me anything. It's not my business." She sipped her coffee again and purred, "This coffee is superb. We don't need to go to the café at all."

Seeing her satisfied face changed my attitude. I wanted to see her smile more.

"You can have all the coffee you want."

"We all have bad dreams. That's what they are, though— just *dreams*." She stared into the coffee, tracing her finger around the rim of the coffee cup. "Sometimes you get remnants of the past. Sometimes they're distorted versions of a traumatic event that still haunts you."

What was her trauma? But how could I ask her when I didn't want to talk about mine? So I left it alone.

It surprised me how she changed my mood so quickly.

When she said she wanted to go, my body and brain reacted, worked together, and told me to stop her. Her words yanked the annoyance out of me like a splinter that had been pulled out and was no longer irritating me.

This was also the first time I'd want a woman sitting at my kitchen table early in the morning having coffee with me. Michelle had given me many firsts today, and I had a feeling I'd be experiencing a lot more of them soon. Her presence filled my home with a softness I wanted to keep around. She was like a comfy Icelandic sweater that kept me warm in the winter.

Michelle belonged in my home, in the chair across from me, drinking my coffee and soothing me with her presence. Why had I let a bad dream ruin this precious moment?

"If you tell me about your monster, I'll tell you about mine."

The words flew out of my mouth without my permission. I wanted to grab them back, but failed. *Holy fuck!*

She looked at me for a long moment, and the silence in the room swirled into something else—something neither of us wanted to comment on. What had I been thinking?

Michelle made me comfortable enough to *want* to share this private part of me with her. Or maybe it was something else . . .

The need to protect her is stronger than the need to keep the secret.

Inhaling a slow breath, I pondered on the revelation. I wanted to know her monster so I could keep her safe. I'd never felt protective of a woman other than my mom and aunt. Even then, the need differed.

Something about Michelle transformed me.

Her eyes glinted with amusement. "Thanks. I've always wanted a Viking to slay my monster."

"I've always wanted an angel to show me the way."

She laughed, and the echoes of her voice resonated through my home and settled. "I'm not sure I know the way. I'm a lost angel. I might lead you straight to hell."

"I have a private stairwell and a special key for that place. No need to worry. I reserved my place there a long time ago. Me and the devil? We're like this." I crossed my fingers to demonstrate my closeness with the Lord of Hell.

"Then you tell him to stop the nightmares. Easy peasy."

I liked her lighthearted perspective. It made the darkness seem unimportant.

She glanced at the clock on the wall. "I'm going to get some work done." She rose from the chair, holding her cup of coffee. "I'll see you later. Don't forget, it's banquet day."

Fearing she'd go and take all the warmth from my home with her, I asked, "You're staying here to work, right?"

"The devilish Viking needs the lost angel to show him the way, correct?" She grinned. "This is the only place that makes no sense and at the same time feels right. I guess I'll have to stay."

I laughed at her accuracy.

"Maybe we can swing by my apartment before we head to the banquet. I want to see if your men have finished repairing the window."

It was selfish of me, but I didn't want them to finish the window repair.

"Sure, we could do that."

CHAPTER TWENTY-THREE

MICHELLE

I SAT AT MY DESK, turned on my laptop, opened the folder for NewYou Beauty, and stared at the images. Though I stared at the pretty pictures, I didn't see or think about anything regarding beauty products. My mind was swamped with Royce and the dream that had supposedly unsettled him.

When I first stepped into the kitchen, I sensed his frustration before I spotted him or even spoke to him. One thing was obvious: we both had something to hide. We skimmed the edge of truth by sprinkling the conversation with sarcasm and humor, none of which was bad or wrong. But it showed we weren't ready to share that intimate part of ourselves yet. I didn't know why, but I wanted him to trust me.

Then I need to trust him too.

Pushing that thought aside for now, I entertained something more lighthearted. I wanted to erase his nightmares and give him hope and laughter.

I didn't know why I felt the need to help him, but sometimes I had no choice but to go with the flow. Right now, the flow told me to give him the pillow fight of his life.

Laughing at the ridiculous idea, I planned a scenario that would either embarrass me or make him find me irresistible.

What if my plan backfired, and I became the victim who *couldn't* resist him?

I stopped my brain from thinking further because I sensed more what-ifs emerging, and self-doubt sabotaged my confidence.

Clearing my head, I focused on my next blog post.

CHAPTER TWENTY-FOUR

ROYCE

AFTER SLIPPING on my Eton shirt and adjusting my black bowtie, I put on my black Canali tuxedo. I had a selection of custom-made suits to accommodate my broad shoulders. Paying a little more for the enhanced fabric with stretch allowed for extra comfort. I wasn't one of those men who preferred wearing a suit all day.

With all my travels, I'd met many suppliers who produced innovative materials and introduced them to my tailor, whom I'd also referred to my friends. Enzo's tailoring business soared just from my referrals.

All dressed and ready to go, I glanced at my watch. We had plenty of time to swing by Michelle's apartment to check on the window repairs. Oskar had already notified me that everything was all set, and Tomas was also present, overseeing the repairs of his building.

I'd gotten an email from him thanking me and confirming his repayment to my company's account.

I walked out to the kitchen island and reviewed my

schedule for the upcoming weeks on my phone. An alert highlighted in red caught my attention.

Dinner date with Michelle.

Smiling, I checked my schedule for tomorrow. I had two conference meetings regarding renovations I needed to approve for two excursion sites. They'd been pushed back twice already. I moved the meetings to Monday, allowing me more time to review the updates.

I heard the clicking sound of Michelle's shoes, turned around, and lost my breath. The power of her presence—her beauty—stole my senses. Writers often described this moment in books, but I'd never fully understood it until now.

She wore a long black dress with a draped neckline that teased a lovely bosom. Thin straps hung over her elegant shoulders, making me want to drag my mouth along them. My gaze followed the flowy fabric down her hips to the floor, where pink toenails peeked out from black-heeled shoes. When she took a step toward me, the side slit revealed a lovely, toned leg with smooth skin that made my throat dry. I envisioned her long legs wrapped around me, and my cock pulsed.

"Sorry it took me longer than necessary. I had to send a file over to Becca."

I released a slow breath so I could inhale more oxygen to keep my brain functioning. "You're beautiful."

"You think so? It's such a simple dress. It's the only one I brought with me. I would've brought more dresses if I'd known I'd be attending a fancy gala."

Finally regaining my senses, I walked toward her. I took her hand, twirling her around. The low open back led my eyes down to her ass, making my heart speed up. I wasn't sure how I'd survive the evening talking about volcanoes and lava when the internal heat threatened to destroy me.

"Simple is perfect. Too much frill hides the true beauty." I twirled her again. "This allows me to see you."

Color deepened her cheeks. "Thanks." She adjusted my bowtie and met my eyes. "You look charming and dapper. A devilish Viking wrapped in elegance is irresistible and dangerous."

I yanked her body to mine, not caring if she felt my cock. "Irresistible and dangerous to whom?" I was the one in danger of her.

My fingers trailed down her flushed face and rosy lips. Her makeup wasn't overdone like some women I'd encountered. She wore crystal teardrop earrings that sparkled in the kitchen light.

"To every woman who will see you tonight," she whispered, looking up at me.

She wore her hair down, and I couldn't resist threading my fingers through the long curls.

"Does that bother you?" My fingers tightened in the brown forest of curls that seduced my skin.

The colors of her eyes shifted from light brown to a dark mocha with golden specks. I could almost see her struggling with a thought.

"Yes."

One simple word detonated a dormant emotion inside me. Was it joy? Satisfaction? Surprise? I couldn't be sure. All I knew was that I'd never experienced this eruption that shed layers of my heart. I was keenly aware of my body's reaction to her. It was like a silent lava leaking from the deepest part of my soul, scorching its way around me with slow seduction. In that moment, I knew Michelle was either a guardian angel offering me salvation or the fallen angel who would destroy me.

"Then make sure you're stuck beside me so they know who I'm with."

Something flickered in her eyes, and she broke free from my grasp. "I think we're doing a fabulous job at this pretend dating."

The comment rubbed me like sandpaper. Was everything an act?

It was your idea.

I asked her to be my fake girlfriend, so it was a role she was playing. Did I want it to be an act? What the fuck did I want?

Confusion stormed my brain, making me sound like a clueless man with no direction in life, which was wrong. I knew where my life was going. I oversaw a successful excursion empire that continued to flourish, allowing me the extra time to dedicate to my research project on volcanic innovation. That was the plan. Simple and concise.

"Indeed. Maybe you can try out for the community theater when this is all over," I said, still feeling tart about the relationship being an act.

"Did a bug crawl up your butt?" She arched an eyebrow.

"Nope."

She stared at me. "You sure? Your eyes just turned icy. That usually means something's bugging you."

"Nothing important." Was I that obvious?

"Okay. Let's go check out the window repair. I also packed up my things. Can we load them into the trunk? That way, you can drop me off at my apartment after the banquet."

My stomach quivered at the idea she'd be gone from my

apartment after tonight. I hated the concept, but how could I convince her to stay? What excuse could I have? Fake dating didn't require the couple to live together.

She didn't wait for my reply and returned to her bedroom to retrieve her two bags.

"I got them." I took the bags from her hands and stalked out to my car.

CHAPTER TWENTY-FIVE

MICHELLE

"OH, wow. Your men did a fabulous job. Thank you." I glanced up at the newly replaced window. "Tomas called me yesterday and apologized for the incident. He's grateful for your help."

"He's been in this neighborhood as long as I have. We look out for each other's properties. And you're welcome."

Silence hummed in the air as Royce drove toward the Volcanic Museum. We had started the day flirting with each other, but ended with irritation. Though we were fake dating, this game between us seemed more serious. This was no longer about Fiona, but a revelation for me.

I was very attracted to Royce.

He looked handsome in casual clothes, but in a suit? Oh. My. God. My heart had never palpitated the way it did when I saw him standing in the kitchen. The power of his presence constricted and relaxed my muscles on command. I'd never met anyone with charisma oozing out of him like Royce. No wonder Fiona and the other women couldn't keep their eyes off him. Even I had trouble.

Sitting beside him, I sensed the heat of his body caressing mine. I also knew he was thinking about our conversation regarding other women eagle-eyeing him. My honest answer to his question surprised me. The lie I initially wanted to say wouldn't make its way out. The truth was more powerful.

I didn't want any woman near him. *He's mine.*

But in reality, I had no claim to him. He wanted me as a fake girlfriend to chase away an old flame. That alone made me jealous of Fiona. She got to touch and experience him in a way I never did.

The man was also moody. One minute he flirted with me, and the next he gave me attitude for wanting to go back to my apartment. He liked having his space, but so did I. Not to mention, he only offered for me to stay at his place until the window was repaired. If he wanted me to stay longer, then he should ask. I'd consider, and we'd have a conversation about it. Instead, we kept our thoughts to ourselves.

I wasn't going to invite myself into a man's home. Self-respect was priceless, and no man could take that away from me. I'd learned a long time ago that self-worth was difficult for most people to maintain.

This had nothing to do with a woman asking a man out or anything like that. I believed in equal rights and all, but sometimes I would like a man to show me he wanted me enough to *make* that move. That wasn't so hard to ask.

Everything came down to having standards. I had mine, and his loss if he doesn't measure up to them.

The sexual tension in the car finally got the better of me, so I broke the silence.

"Are you mad?"

He met my eyes. "No. Why would I be?"

"You seem annoyed."

"Not annoyed. Just contemplative."

"Really? Your version of 'contemplative' is unique. The furrowed eyebrows, the pout, and the glacial look that could bring Earth back to the Ice Age."

He offered a half-smile. "I can be an intense man."

My heart leaped. "You're right."

He sighed, placing a hand over mine. "I'm sorry if my bitter mood is affecting you. That wasn't intentional. Forgive me. I'm just trying to figure out a difficult puzzle."

"For work?"

He met my gaze. "I think you've asked a lot of questions already. My turn. I saw you crying one time at Remi's house. You looked upset, and Audri consoled you. I asked Audri, but she only said you had a fight with your boyfriend. What happened?"

The question threw me off. That was a long time ago. At least in my book.

I debated on how much I wanted to share with him. If I wanted to know about his past, I had to let him in a little. Relationships were about compromise, and friendship was a different relationship that respected the same rule.

I inhaled a deep breath. "My two-year relationship ended that day. It should have ended sooner. I shouldn't have endured him for as long as I did."

His grip on my hand tightened as he pulled over to the side of the road, parked, and shifted to face me.

"What are you doing? We're going to be late."

"We have plenty of time. Besides, I'm the keynote speaker. They have no choice but to wait for me."

My brain spun as I recalled Becca mentioning a scientist being the keynote speaker. I'd assumed Royce was another attendee like me. Shifting to face me, his green eyes bore into mine, sharp and penetrating. I couldn't think or do anything but look at him.

"Did he hurt you?" he asked. The deadly look on his face surprised me.

Words jumbled in my brain, but nothing made sense. I couldn't break away from the intense eyes that held me in the spot. "What?"

"Your ex-boyfriend. You said you wished you didn't have to endure him. *Did. He. Hurt. You?*"

I felt the dangerous edge of his voice rubbing against my skin. The power of his gaze chilled my bones. This reaction painted him a different man from the friend I'd known for years. This was a man he kept hidden. Despite that, I wasn't afraid of Royce. The wrath he emitted wasn't toward me. I sensed an inexplicable security with him more than anyone I'd been with.

"No, not physically. I would've bruised his balls and used my hair clips to stab them if he'd dared."

Wincing, Royce loosened the grip on my hand. "Okay then." He shifted his seat as though trying to protect his family jewels.

I stifled a smile.

"I guess I should be more concerned about your ex." A smirk formed on his lips before it disappeared. "What did he do to make you cry?"

I couldn't believe Royce remembered that day. I must have made some horrific impression.

His genuine concern made me say something that surprised me. "He made me feel unworthy." That was a truth I was afraid to admit until now. How had Royce coaxed that truth from me so easily? So painlessly?

"You are *not* unworthy. What an ass."

"I didn't see that until it was too late. He only wanted me to be an accessory on his arm in public. I had to look a certain way. Eat certain things to stay trim . . ."

Shit. Fuck. What had I done? He wasn't supposed to know about my weakness—the monster in my closet.

Royce looked at me with deep concern.

I interlaced my fingers together and placed them on my lap, facing forward. "I think we should get going."

Royce didn't object and sped off. "Thanks for sharing your past with me."

"You owe me."

"Owe you what?"

"Something about your past. Since I shared mine with you, it's courteous for you to return the favor. That's what relationships are all about, right? Give and take. You don't have to tell me right now. I'll take a raincheck. Thank you."

He laughed, and the sound bounced in the car, making me smile too. "You're some negotiator, angel. If memory serves, I owe a lot. One is your compensation for being my fake girlfriend and now this. I feel like I'm losing in this relationship."

Grateful the conversation had turned to a different topic, I studied his profile. There was no annoyance on his face, just amusement. "There are no winners or losers, just two people trying to make this relationship successful. While we're at it, we're becoming closer friends, don't you think? I mean, I know more about you now than I ever did."

He nodded slowly. "A Viking and an angel make a wonderful pair."

I liked the ring of that, even though it seemed farfetched.

The closer friends we became, the higher the risk of destroying that friendship by adding passion to the mix.

Feeling too much had been my mistake when I dated Julian. I was attracted to his determination to succeed in his financial world, but that was the problem. He only had eyes for his career. I was an asset to make him look good. He ensured I stayed that way by controlling what I ate and wore and how I exercised. He made those basic needs I'd suffered —and was still healing from—into a chore. In doing so, he added to the monster already within me. He made it more frightening. I didn't want to give another man that power.

With Royce, my emotions were raw again. He touched something deep within me, and I couldn't describe it. It was primitive and thrilling. What if things didn't work out between us? I'd lose more than friendship—I'd lose my friend, my heart, and my soul.

CHAPTER TWENTY-SIX

ROYCE

I WANTED to kick her ex-boyfriend's ass for making her feel unworthy. Didn't she know how precious she was?

Why had she stopped mid-sentence? What was she hiding? The forbidden attracted me more than anything else. Even though every cell in my body wanted to, the horror on her face prevented me from asking further. I didn't want to frighten her.

Time. Michelle needed time to trust me. That became my mission. I needed to earn her trust.

Then you have to trust her too.

I parked in one of the reserved spots, got out, and opened the door for her.

"You didn't have to do that," she said, taking the arm I offered. "I can open the door myself."

"I believe in equal rights and all, but sometimes it's fun being a gentleman." I patted her hand.

"Is that your pickup line?" she asked with an arched eyebrow.

"No. It's the truth. If I were to give you a pickup line, it would be somewhere along the line of 'you must be a volcano because you're making all the geysers hot and bothered.'"

The corners of her lips quirked. "How are you still single?"

"Who says I'm single?" I clasped her hand in mine, a gesture that surprised me. Holding hands wasn't something I did with my previous girlfriends. It made things too intimate, but I'd been holding her hands more than I realized.

I tightened the grip on her hand as we passed a group of men staring at her.

She's with me.

"I have a beautiful girlfriend by my side." A whiff of her lovely fragrance snuck up my nose, and my body heated. "Have you forgotten?"

"You know what I mean."

I paused in my steps and looked at her. The light from the lamppost cast a soft glow on her face, making her appear like a goddess. "I'm searching for the right one. And you? Why are you still single?"

"Who says I am?" She grinned, tugging me toward the main entrance where more people had gathered.

A man chatting on his phone cut his eyes toward her, and I wanted to poke them out.

"Hey, no fair. I answered your question."

"Aren't we all searching for the right one?"

"What is your definition of the right one?"

She looked up at me with curious eyes.

"I'm not sure. I think it's different for everybody. What about you?"

"Someone who can move me from within. Someone who can inspire me to do something I'd never do."

"You want someone to *dare* you?" It wasn't a question,

but an accurate statement that sent a chill rippling down my body.

She pounded the nail on the head, showing how perceptive she was. She considered me for a long moment, and I wanted to jump into her brain to see her thoughts.

Finally, she said, "It's good to know you have standards." Then she swung our joined hands back and forth as we entered the museum.

What she didn't know was that I had already accepted the challenge when she became my fake girlfriend.

CHAPTER TWENTY-SEVEN

MICHELLE

AS SOON AS we entered the ballroom, people greeted Royce from several corners. I spotted Becca sitting at a table. She rose and waved at me, and I returned the gesture.

"I moved your seating arrangement. You'll be sitting with me," he said. "I've got to go over a few things with the organizers. I see your coworkers are dying to speak to you. Come back to me."

I wanted to ask him when he'd moved my seat, but the gleam in his green eyes made me ask something else. "Is that a *dare*? What if I decide to sit with my coworkers since you didn't ask or inform me about the new seating arrangement?"

"Then the devilish Viking must take matters into his own hands by tossing you over his shoulders and taking you out to his car to *punish* you." He leaned in and kissed the top of my head. "You don't want your peers seeing all that?"

I narrowed my eyes to sharp slits.

"I didn't mention the seating arrangement because I assumed you'd want to sit with your boyfriend. That's how relationships work, angel."

"I would've appreciated the information earlier so I could prepare myself for questions from my coworkers."

He tapped my temple. "You have a quick mind. I can already see the wheels turning. Make up something." He grinned and squeezed my hand. "See you soon."

When his hand severed from mine, an uncomfortable emptiness filled the space. I wanted his touch again.

Becca walked past Royce and said, "Hi, Dr. Viktorsson. I love what you're doing for the Volcanic Sustainability Research Program."

"Thank you," he said and went up to greet two men in suits.

Becca approached me. "You look gorgeous! Why didn't you say anything about you dating Dr. Viktorsson?"

Doctor? How had I not known this? I'd think about that later.

Right now, my mind raced for an answer to give Becca.

"First off, you look stunning. I love the French twist." I gestured to her hair. "And this red dress is exquisite. As for dating Dr. Viktorsson, I don't like to discuss my private life with people I've just met. Privacy is important to me."

"Oh, I understand, especially with Fiona around. Everyone knows she has the hots for him. She won't stop talking about him. Even the CEO is getting annoyed. Now I know why she wanted this job at NewYou Beauty—it gives her access to him."

The more I learned about Fiona, the more she seemed like a dangerous stalker. Was it her who'd broken my window? Was this how she eliminated her competition?

"Brace yourself. Here she comes." Becca gestured to Fiona in a glittering silver gown that enhanced her figure. She strutted across the ballroom, heading toward Royce. The low V-neckline showed off her full breasts that jiggled as she walked. She wore her long blonde hair in a fancy updo and sparkling earrings that matched her necklace. I wished I'd done something different with my hair instead of leaving it naturally down. My jewelry was elegant, a gift from Audri from her Epiphanii collection.

Stop comparing yourself to her. You're classier than her.

Still, I couldn't help but compare. It was a natural reaction when my enemy was trying to steal my man.

He's not your man yet, only your fake boyfriend.

I tuned out my inner voice because it wasn't helping me.

"NewYou Beauty made a nice donation to the Volcanic Sustainability Research Program. Their research is top-notch."

I only half-heard Becca's words because my attention was fixated on Fiona and Royce. She barged into his conversation with his associates, placing a hand on his arm.

Don't touch him. He's mine.

Royce turned, met my gaze, and waved. My heart jumped at how handsome he was. He had mesmerized me in his apartment when I first saw him all dressed up, but I didn't get to truly observe him because I'd been trying to calm down my body's reaction to him. But right now, I studied him like an undiscovered adventure that promised an exhilarating experience.

Royce stood out from all the surrounding men, towering over them. The dark tuxedo, the blond hair that looked silver under the massive chandelier, and the confidence oozing from his posture cut him as an elegant man wrapped in secrets. His broad shoulders reminded me of the leveled planes of the Grand Canyon—profound, heart-stirring, and irresistible. When I visited the Grand Canyon, I was in awe of the million-year-old rock strata that made up these wondrous layers. Like the canyon, Royce contained more than what people saw at a glance. I wanted to discover the Royce beneath the surface.

When his associates waved at me and broke my trance, I returned the gesture. Fiona surveyed me, probably comparing my dress, hair, and jewelry, just as I had done to her. I didn't need to wear all the high-end brands to feel worthy. Besides, I was wearing my bestie's jewelry, which was better than anything on Fiona.

"If I'm prying too much, tell me to shut up." Becca dragged me over to an empty table. "How long have you been dating Dr. Viktorsson? He gives a speech every year at the Volcano Museum. I didn't get to go last year because the company was just starting. Only the CEO attended."

"We've been friends for years, but recently started dating."

Somewhere in my brain, I should have known that Royce had a doctorate. He was a volcanologist, basically a scientist, and most scientists have their PhD. But he never boasted about it, even when we hung out at Remi's place. It never came up.

What else didn't I know? As his girlfriend, I demanded to know everything. With every extra surprise he swung my way, my heart beat a little faster and swelled a little more. The barriers I had built to protect myself were slowly weakening. That scared me.

"Oh, I heard friends to lovers make the best relationships. As friends, you already know each other and want something more. At least that's what the romance novels say."

"Don't believe everything you read, Becca. But yes, being

friends beforehand takes away the nerves of getting to know one another."

Romance novels weren't true to life. They were fantasies to give women like me and Becca hope. I'd never dated a guy friend before, so Royce was my first. So far, it had been eye-opening.

As more people showed up and filled the ballroom, I lost sight of Royce. A waiter strode up with champagne flutes and offered one to Becca and me.

"I loved the way you handled Fiona in *that* email. I couldn't believe she had the balls to ask you to change your job for *her*." Becca sipped her champagne. "Do you know how many emails I get from her asking questions or demanding I provide her info about the resort and products? Too many."

"There's a shared folder with all the information she needs."

"Exactly. She thinks I work *for* her. I don't. You, on the other hand, have caused me no trouble at all, and that makes me worried. Everything good?"

I patted her shoulder. "All good. Didn't you see my first write-up?"

"I did, and it's perfect. I haven't seen anything from Fiona yet. If she asks to see your write-up, I won't show it to her. It's none of her business." She sighed. "I can't believe you've already been here for two weeks. I hope the next few weeks will go fast because Fiona is driving me nuts. But then that means you'll return to the States too. And I don't want you to go."

The emcee with red hair and a beard alerted everyone to take our seats because the presentation would start soon. Finishing my champagne and handing the glass to a passing hostess, I joined Becca at my original table to greet the CEO and representatives from other companies I didn't know. After telling Becca we'd catch up later, I made my way to Royce's table.

On my way there, I spotted the little girl I'd seen at the grocery store. All dressed up in a pale pink dress, she looked bored and played with her napkin. Her mom sat next to Fiona, whispering. Fiona spotted me, stopped her conversation with the little girl's mom, and walked up to me.

"Royce said he'd meet me for lunch in a few days. You can join us if you'd like, but he wants to catch up just as much as I do. We had something special. I'm so glad he remembers. Nice dress, by the way. Very simple. It suits you."

A knot twisted in my stomach. Why would Royce meet her? The point of this fake dating thing was to keep her away, wasn't it? Was she lying?

"Thank you. How kind of you? Your dress is . . . very *loud* and busy. In my humble opinion, simplicity is better than being overdone. People who wear a busy ensemble usually do it to hide something. But it suits *you*. Enjoy your evening."

I sensed the little girl's mom eyeing me as I walked off. She was probably close friends with Fiona and had already formed an ill opinion of me. I didn't care.

CHAPTER TWENTY-EIGHT

ROYCE

AFTER SPEAKING with two representatives from an alternative medicine company interested in supporting the program, I made my way to my table and Einar Hallsson lifted a hand, gesturing for my time.

My competitor appeared thinner and older than when I last saw him at a camping gear convention about a month ago. In order to protect myself and my businesses, I had to investigate my opponent. It was the only way to survive. Survival meant scanning the horizon for potential threats and preparing. I'd done the same to the bullies who tormented me in high school. Those bullies helped shape me to become the man I was today.

No one fucked with me.

The only people I trusted were my aunt and my boys. Everyone else fell into a category where they'd pay if they crossed me. My boys and I came together because we all needed to survive a darkness that hounded us. Our lives could've gone the other way, but our passion to make something of ourselves drove us to succeed.

"How are you, Einar?" I shook his hand.

"Fine. You?"

"Could be better. I've been dealing with a lot of inconveniences at my excursion sites." I studied his face, which showed exhaustion.

Einar pressed his lips into a tight line. "Sorry to hear that. I didn't realize how involved you were with the Volcanic Sustainability Research Program. It's helping Iceland and other countries immensely."

"Thank you. We need programs like this to help us live longer and healthier lives."

I should have asked about the status of his business, but I already knew. It would be useless chatter, and I wasn't in the mood for that.

"Listen, are you interested in expanding your business here?"

I quirked an eyebrow. "In what way?"

"I'm thinking of selling Hallsson's Excursions. Interested?"

Buying his company hadn't been on my radar at all. It was smaller than mine, but he'd been in business a lot longer, and his location was prime real estate.

"Let me look into it." I needed to determine how it could benefit Excursions for You. "Why are you selling it?"

"With my divorce, I don't have time or the energy to put into it. No passion left," he said with a shrug. I could hear the truth in his words. This wasn't a man out to sabotage me. He was just a man trying to deal with a divorce and a failing business.

"I'm sorry to hear that. Does anyone else know your business is up for sale?"

Einar shook his head. "I knew you'd be here today, so I

got a ticket. Though I don't want the business anymore, I would like someone competent to take over. It's a great company and location. You can take it further than me."

Several ideas percolated in my head.

"You know what's strange? I spoke to a vendor who claims he knows you from the States. He said he's not fond of Excursions for You. Had an unpleasant experience or something like that. He jokingly said that if I wanted to 'eliminate' my competition, he knew of a few guys. I didn't like where the conversation was headed and told him I'd call him back."

Now my interest was piqued. "What's his name? What company was he from?"

Could this person be an unsatisfied customer who wanted to sabotage my business? If so, then Iceland should be his target, not all my excursion sites.

"Do you mind me giving the number he gave you?" It was probably a burner phone, but I'd have the PI look into it.

"Sure. I'll see if I still have it."

Turning my head, I saw Michelle with a scowl on her face. "I'll get back to you on the business proposal."

I made my way toward Michelle. What had happened? Did Fiona create more trouble?

CHAPTER TWENTY-NINE

MICHELLE

A GENTLE HAND cupped my elbow, stopping me in my steps.

"You okay?" Royce searched my face.

"I'm fine. Just a minor annoyance."

He tipped up my chin. "Who?"

"The girl who supposedly has a lunch date with you," I sneered.

He smirked, but kept his fingers on my chin. "Are you jealous?"

"As your girlfriend, I *am* jealous."

"As your boyfriend, I love your reaction. But it's not what you think. Me attending a business conference that she's also attending doesn't make it a date."

"Oh." I knew she was lying, but the idea of him being with her while I wasn't around bothered me more than it should.

He leaned in, kissed the side of my head, and whispered, "Have you forgotten why we're together?"

"No, I haven't."

"I'm giving my speech in a few minutes. Let me introduce you to my peers."

Royce introduced me to three scientists and their significant others and ensured I was in my seat before walking behind the stage.

"I didn't know Royce was seeing anyone until tonight. He's a lucky man," Lisa said with a warm smile. She was the wife of Dr. Anderson, a geologist who worked on the research program with Royce.

"Thank you. We like our privacy."

"He hasn't brought a date to these events before, at least not the ones I've attended," Lisa said.

That comment changed my mood, and I realized I shouldn't let other people's opinions affect me. I'd been irritated by Fiona's jab, and that irritation disappeared when someone offered a brighter perspective—one I should have seen and known.

I should focus on my relationship with Royce—the one brewing under the fake façade. I knew what I wanted, but was terrified of where it could lead me. For tonight, I didn't want to think about anything negative. I wanted to enjoy my time with him at this event where he had never brought another woman.

The host, dressed in a black tuxedo with a full head of silver hair, stepped to the podium and spoke while images of volcanoes splashed on two large screens on either side of him. I was mesmerized by how many volcanoes there were on Earth. The last time I was in Iceland, I wanted to tour a volcano, but didn't have time.

"Ladies and gentlemen, please welcome our keynote speaker, Dr. Royce Viktorsson."

Royce walked onto the stage, and I heard gasps and sighs

from the surrounding tables. I understood his magnificence because my body also gasped.

"If he hadn't shown up with you, sweetheart, I might have divorced my husband for him. The man grabs attention like he's a black hole in space." Carol, a former aerospace engineer, patted her husband's cheek.

Henry, who had a few wisps of white hair on his head, shook his head. "I don't think you're his type, love. He prefers girls his age, so you're stuck with me."

I smiled at the pair, who hadn't seemed to have lost their sense of humor despite their age. "You make a lovely couple."

The ladies whispered about wanting to introduce him to women they knew if he hadn't brought me tonight.

I turned my attention to Royce.

"Thank you, everyone, for being here this evening to support the Volcanic Sustainability Research Program. As you know, it's innovative research showing the world how using available resources can help keep our planet healthy and benefit us in unimaginable ways. We've only tapped the surface of how lava can assist us in creating 'energy' that can help charge our phones, tablets, and other small gadgets on the go. There are also health benefits proven in research labs regarding lava heat being used to infuse vitamins." He pivoted and pointed to the screen showing the lab workers using lava to "cook" something.

I wasn't a scientist, but I could tell from the easy-to-understand images that this research program was changing the world.

"Most people fear volcanoes, and they have good reason to. But like any natural wonders, there are benefits if you care to look. Lava creates new lands like the Hawaiian Islands."

He looked around the room where most people weren't volcanologists but individuals or investors with money who cared about the program or believed in this beneficial research. NewYou Beauty was one of those believers, and I was grateful for this job that connected me to Royce. If I hadn't taken the position, would I have gotten to know him the way I have?

This job delivered something priceless to me: a jumpstart to my heart. I started to believe in love again. It never went away; it just fell asleep. It scared me, but at least I knew I was ready to give it a chance.

As I looked up at the man who gave me hope without even knowing it, I sensed that I'd met him somewhere before. Was it a soulmate connection? Was this what people talked about when they said they felt a familiarity? I'd always assumed people were romanticizing it, but I felt it like a quiet liquid heat moving around my body in slow motion, waking up my nerves and everything else within me.

Confidence and knowledge oozed from Royce as he discussed the benefits of volcanoes. No wonder people wanted him to deliver the keynote speech. He made you listen to his words. He exuded charisma, which made him more spectacular in that elegant suit.

"Volcanoes also increase the water production we have on earth. How? Water comes out of the steam, out of the lava when it touches a water source." He looked around the room and his gaze met mine and stayed. "Earth is made of beautiful things. Some of them take our breath away, making us feel more alive than before. If we pause to appreciate and *explore* that beauty, we could come to an understanding beyond our imagination."

Royce held my gaze, and my stomach quivered. My heart

raced at his words as though he spoke directly to me. A rush of energy zipped up and down my body.

A realization dawned on me: I wanted him to *want* me not because I was his fake girlfriend, but because I was Michelle—his friend. There was an attraction between us, but did he feel the same way about me? My body lost control whenever he looked at me. Even now, as he spoke, my body reacted to his every word. A chill here, a tingle there, a tightening in my core, a subtle gasp from an unexpected shiver—these sensations occurred because of him.

In that suit, the potent sexuality he emanated increased tenfold, demanding all eyes on him. I could practically feel the energy in the room holding onto his every word. He inspired everyone, including me.

I wanted to know how lava could become a source of energy for the world. In my travels around the world looking for inspirational things, I found someone. Royce was an intelligent and interesting man disguised in the casual clothing and carefree attitude he exhibited in the company of close friends. But in this professional arena, he was king. I loved seeing the many aspects of him and wondered what else was underneath the stunning exterior.

I feared getting to know him was like walking toward an erupting volcano that could either incinerate me or offer answers to what I'd been searching for.

"I don't know everything, and neither do you," Royce continued, and everyone laughed. "But I know this: if we allow ourselves new perspectives, we'll learn new ways to improve our lives, the lives of our children and their children. You can browse our website and see for yourself what our research has done and what we're planning to do." He gestured to the new images on the screen. "Another important advantage of volcanoes is the fertile land created from the volcanic materials mixed with soil. We're currently harnessing a new species of moss never seen before. It's still in the infant stages, but we're watching it closely in our development center. We're changing the world, and with your contribution, we can continue to do so. My team and I sincerely thank you for everything you've done for this program."

Everyone rose and offered Royce a standing ovation as he stepped away from the microphone, walked off the stage, and sat down beside me. Another scientist replaced Royce and spoke at the podium.

Royce took my hand in his and held it throughout the speech until dinner was served. By the time we left the museum, it was already ten at night, but I wasn't tired. The late cup of coffee gave me the boost I needed to unpack my bags and settle back into my apartment.

"Don't forget to drop me off at my apartment, Dr. Viktorsson." I poked him playfully as he drove out of the parking lot. "How did I not know you're a doctor?"

He lifted a shoulder. "My PhD isn't the kind that can prescribe medications or offer surgeries."

"Still, you never talked about it whenever we hung out."

"Why should I? None of us talk about our jobs when we're chilling and playing video games. My job is another part of life. Besides, a title means nothing to me. I mean, it's nice, and I worked my ass off for it, but it doesn't change who I am. However, it gives me access to things others don't have, which is beneficial."

"You like things that are beneficial?"

"Depends on your definition of beneficial."

I laughed. "Here we go again with the definition. I think

by the end of my stay in Iceland, I'm going to have a brand-new dictionary with all new meanings to things I thought I had already defined."

"There's always room to learn new definitions."

"Seriously though, your speech was inspiring. It opened my eyes to the possibilities out there. When I was younger, I wanted to visit the Seven Wonders of the World, but as I got older, I made my own list. Iceland was one of them."

"I'm happy my homeland is on your list. Maybe you can share your list with me sometime."

"Only if you take me to visit—"

Jeez, I was thinking as if he were my real boyfriend. *Steer the brain back to the slow lane, Michelle. You're detouring . . .*

"I'd love to. My excursions sites are all over the globe."

I hadn't expected him to agree. But maybe he was being nice as friends should be to one another.

My attention returned to his volcanic research—safer territory to be discussed. "I had no idea you were working on such important research. Do you have to fly back and forth to do it?"

He smiled at me. "I'm a part-time researcher, so I don't have to be present in Iceland. I only visit the labs here whenever I return to Excursions for You, which is one of many companies under Paradigm Excursions Group. The private labs in Boston are where I do research. I spent most of my time expanding my excursion business and keeping it updated and fun."

"No wonder you're the most eligible bachelor. The women at the table had plans to introduce you to eligible bachelorettes if you hadn't brought me." A thought sparked in my head, and I narrowed my eyes at him. "Is that another reason for this fake dating?"

He smirked. "I can see why you'd think that. But no, it hadn't occurred to me until now. I guess this fake dating is very *beneficial*."

It bothered me that he saw our relationship that way. It made me feel like a business transaction, and my heart hurt at that thought. The tightness in my chest became uncomfortable, and I stroked it as though I had heartburn. But it was a different burning in my heart.

Feeling irritated, I stayed quiet for the rest of the ride. He was obviously contemplating something, probably how else he could "benefit" from this relationship.

When he stopped the car in front of my apartment, I finally looked at him and regretted it. My heart lurched at the intensity of his eyes. Those green eyes held something—a quiet conversation he wanted to tell me, but couldn't. How did I know this? Because it felt as though I was having a quiet conversation with him too.

We both had things to say, but something held us back.

A silhouette from my window caught my eye, and I gripped his hand in terror.

"Someone's in my apartment."

CHAPTER THIRTY

ROYCE

I LOOKED up at the window and saw a quick silhouette before the soft light died, and everything went dark. Who the fuck was in there? I called the police, reported the incident, and contacted Ludvik, a detective friend who lived in the vicinity.

This was the third time Michelle had been in harm's way since she landed in Iceland. After three times, coincidences went out the window. Something peculiar was happening here. Who was after her?

A lot of epiphanies emerged at the museum today, and I'd been trying to sort them out during the silence in the car. But now, Michelle's safety came first.

"Stay here," I told Michelle, who looked frightened.

"Where are you going?" She gripped my hand.

"Up there to check it out. I'm just browsing."

"No. That's dangerous."

Reaching for the glove compartment, I retrieved the gun and shoved it into my jacket pocket.

"Oh my God, Royce. No!" Her eyes widened at the

pocket where the gun was hidden. "How about we wait for the police to arrive? You're a scientist—*think* logically here."

I smiled at my angel. "Don't worry. It's licensed, and I'm a good shot. I'm not going into your apartment. Someone wants to hurt you, and I need to know who he is." I brushed a hand over her cheekbone. "No one touches what's mine."

She gasped at my admission. The words came out without me knowing. I supposed the truth had a way of sneaking out to the light.

I pressed a soft kiss to her lips. "Stay here. I need eyes on the street in case he has an accomplice. Don't leave the car. Don't go after them. Just observe, take a picture if you can, and call me. I need you to be the detective on the ground. Can you help me with that?"

Understanding dawned on her, and she heaved a sigh. "Be careful."

"Always."

I exited the car, locked it, and surveyed the area, looking for anything out of the ordinary. Nothing stood out to me. Across the street, a couple walked toward the retail and restaurant area.

I made my way into her apartment as though I lived there, looking like a man returning from an event. Taking the stairs instead of the elevator, I kept my ears open for any noises as I approached the door to her floor. Footsteps sounded, and I yanked the door open, hoping to find the asshole. I heard the door at the other end of the hallway slam shut. He probably ran down toward the back of the building. I rushed after him and out into a dark alley.

A car screeched away, and a loud boom erupted in the air.

Fire burst from the fourth-floor apartment. Terror

gripped me. *Michelle!* I rushed toward the front of the building. Relief settled when I found Michelle assisting a lady with her dog across the street to join the other residents.

Michelle spotted me and met me halfway down the street. Her arms swung around me. "Are you hurt?" She looked distressed, with tears in her eyes.

"I'm okay. Are you?"

"Yeah." She tightened her arms around me. "When the explosion happened, I thought you were still in there. I . . . I was so scared, Royce."

She cried because of me, and my heart shook. "I'm fine. I was chasing after the intruder."

"Did you see them?" She peered up at me.

"No." I kept my arms around her until the police arrived.

After giving my statements to Ludvik, I drove my car to my garage. Despite the extreme situation, it only garnered a few dents and scratches—minor things that could be fixed. I glanced at Michelle, who couldn't be replaced if something happened to her. The fear that she could have been hurt from the explosion knifed me deeply.

"Did a bomb go off in my apartment?" Michelle asked.

"Maybe. The police will investigate and let us know."

"Do you have any enemies?"

"No." Tension formed between her eyebrows. "The only person I know who hates me is Fiona."

Terror swam in her eyes, and I hated seeing that.

"Let's talk inside."

Michelle kicked off her shoes at the doormat. I followed suit and removed my jacket, draping it over the kitchen chair. She made her way to the living room, folded herself onto the couch, and released a shaky breath. She looked frazzled, and I wanted to strangle the person in her apartment. This was no accident. Someone tried to kill her. What would have happened if she'd been in her apartment all alone? The more I thought about it, the more infuriated I became, but Michelle didn't need my anger.

I slung an arm around her. "I'll sort this out."

She rested her head on my shoulder. "I don't understand. Who have I upset to make them want to hurt me like this? Fiona wouldn't want to *kill* me for you, would she?"

Fiona was capable of many things, but I didn't think she'd do something like this. "I don't know. She doesn't have a chance with me. Why would she risk something deadly like this? It's too extreme for her. But then again, I don't know her well."

Thoughts swirled in my head. A thief threatened her with a knife, wanting to mark her face and steal her purse, then a rock was thrown into her apartment. The explosion was severe compared to the other two incidents. Were the three events related? Would Fiona do this? Sharing my suspicion with Michelle would only make things worse, and I wanted her to sleep well tonight.

"How many girlfriends have you had? What's your favorite food? What's your favorite color?"

I welcomed the change in topic. "Three girlfriends. Each of them lasted less than a year. Women I've dated for less than two weeks aren't considered girlfriends."

"That's all?" She tossed a perplexed look at me as though I were lying.

"Why?"

She shrugged. "I assumed you dated more."

"Dating requires a lot of time, and I don't have much of that. However, I've been with women who aren't considered girlfriends, but that was during my younger years. How about you? How many boyfriends have you had?"

"Three as well. My longest relationship lasted two years. The others were one year. But the numbers need to be increased if you count the boys in kindergarten and first grade." She elbowed me playfully. "You didn't answer my other questions, and don't dodge them. I need to talk about something interesting to keep my mind off the explosion."

"I agree. I'm a *very* interesting man who's fascinated by an interesting woman. I don't have a favorite color, but I'm drawn to earth tones. If I had to pick one, it would be gray, which reminds me of lava rocks."

"I can see that."

"I know what color you like."

"Really?" She arched a perfect brow. "What is it?"

"Purple, more like a lilac or lavender."

Michelle straightened up. "How do you know?"

"Because I'm an 'interesting' man with a clever mind."

She shoved my shoulder. "Seriously, how do you know? A wild guess?"

"An educated guess. I've noticed you wear a lot of purple when you hang out with Audri and Kiera."

"You're very perceptive, Dr. Viktorsson." She ran a finger along my jaw, and my stomach quivered. "It must be the keen power of observation required for research, right?"

"That and interest. I only pay attention to what fascinates me."

A wild pink blossomed in her cheeks. "What about food? What's your favorite?"

"My aunt makes a nice fish stew with mashed potatoes and onions. Her Icelandic crepes are the best. They're filled with whipped cream and strawberry jam. Now that America is my home, I won't ever say no to ribs or a juicy burger."

"I've never had the fish stew or the crepes, though I've seen them on the menus here."

"We can try them when we have our dinner date."

Her eyes widened. "Yes, please."

My phone rang, and I answered the call. "Is anyone hurt?"

"Fortunately, no," said Ludvik, the detective I'd known since I opened Excursions for You. "The explosion was from a small bomb placed at the back of her apartment. Heavy damage to the infrastructure. Five residents, including your friend, will need temporary housing until repairs are done. My guys will look at the cameras from the nearby buildings and see what they can find out. I'll let you know."

"Thank you. I appreciate it." I ended the call and relayed the message to her. "Stay with me for the rest of your time in Iceland. I'll alert Tomas. It's one less resident he has to worry about. It's not a bother, and I enjoy having you around."

She bit her bottom lip, considering my request. "I feel bad intruding, though."

"Don't," I said firmly. This wasn't a negotiation, but I held back, not wanting to distress her even more. "You're my girlfriend, so it makes sense for you to stay with me." I rose from the couch. "Let me get your bags from the trunk."

Nodding, she got up. "Thank you. I'm going to take a quick shower and wash away the negative vibes from today."

The exhaustion on her face frustrated me. I wanted to wipe away what she'd experienced today. The person who placed the fucking bomb would pay. That was a promise. I'd rearrange my schedule for the next week to get to the bottom of this.

This overwhelming need to protect her surged in me, and I didn't know what to think of it other than she had somehow snuck into my heart, making me feel all kinds of things.

The current situation needed actionable steps to achieve results. Like a science experiment, there were variables I needed to observe. Only facts would help me resolve this problem for her.

At first, I had considered this fake relationship an experiment. But now it had turned into something more. That first kiss had shocked my system and changed the trajectory of the desired outcome. When I saw those men looking at her at the museum, I didn't like it. I wanted them to know she was mine. All those thoughts had slammed into me, confusing the hell out of me. But one thing I knew for certain: I wanted her.

"The shower would give you an energy boost. We can watch a movie later if you'd like."

"Thanks for everything." She offered a weary smile, then her eyes flickered with mischief. "I suppose there are benefits to having a boyfriend."

"I can show you my list of 'benefits' when you're ready."

That got a smile out of her, and the anxiety weighing in her eyes completely vanished.

"I'm sure you do." Her eyes sparkled. "You haven't seen my list yet, honey bunny."

I laughed at her endearing address. No one had ever called me that, but I loved hearing it from her.

Tilting my head, I considered her. "You surprise me."

"We're both full of surprises." She strode toward her bedroom, stopped, and looked over her shoulder at me. "For what it's worth, I love all the surprises I've discovered from you."

The smile stayed on my face as I went to the garage to retrieve her belongings. Everything I'd done so far wasn't because of the fake dating agreement. That had just been a tactic to deter the truth. My feelings for her had been real from the start, and I'd been meandering through the maze of emotions, trying to figure out what I should do.

At least for me, it had been real. I wanted her not because of some damn fake relationship.

On my way back from the garage, I called the PI, asking him to get me the videos from any buildings around Michelle's home for the entire week. He could hack into people's security systems and retrieve what I needed instead of me waiting on the local police force to do so. There were protocols law enforcement had to go through, and I didn't have the patience for that. My woman's safety was a priority, and I'd break any law to keep her safe.

Breaking rules wasn't new to me, and I'd do it over again for her. She might think I was a respectable doctor and a successful business executive who followed the rules. But no, I didn't succeed or survive in a new country by playing nice. I survived because I studied the rules, bent them, broke them, and remade them into my version. Which was why I loved running my own business—my world, my rules.

That was how I designed Level Two of WaterFyre Rising, which was behind schedule. Michelle had interrupted my life and thrown my routine off, but I didn't care.

The realization that I'd put the development of my video game on hold to focus on Michelle stopped me in my tracks. Where did Royce Viktorsson go?

I didn't recognize the person I'd become. He seemed

beyond me. I was now a man who had put a woman *before* an important project that had been my love since I was a teen. The WaterFyre Rising video game had saved me.

She's rebuilding you. She's remaking your heart.

I heard that quiet voice in my head. Though I didn't fully understand it, my body sensed a restructuring of my heart, which terrified me. I was feeling things I'd never felt. What if I got lost while I allowed myself to explore this unknown territory?

The best adventure is the one you know nothing about.

I'd scoured the world for the thrill, to find something that moved me. And now there was a woman who could do more than move me—she had the power to resurrect me.

CHAPTER THIRTY-ONE

MICHELLE

AFTER SHAMPOOING MY HAIR, I opened the rose body wash Kiera had given me for my trip. As a fashion photographer, she got a lot of free samples from high-end fashion and beauty brands. I did too for my blog, but her connections were better.

The floral scent mixed with something light and soothing was exactly what I needed to calm my body.

I was glad Royce offered to let me stay at his place because I couldn't imagine the anxiety that would've kept me up at night, wondering when that person would return to hurt me. Maybe the next time, I wouldn't be so lucky. Who was it?

Wash off the negativity. Rest your mind for the night.

My thoughts swung back to what Royce had said earlier. *I can show you my list of 'benefits' when you're ready.*

The muscles in my inner thighs tightened as I tried to imagine what kind of list he had. A soap bubble flew across my body and popped as an idea appeared in my head. What would it be like to have Royce touch me? How would my body react?

I wanted the intimacy with him. We were both adults, and we were "dating." Having sex fell into the dating category perfectly. I didn't need an excuse to want him.

For tonight, I didn't want to think about danger or someone after me. I wanted to feel something other than fear and stress.

I slipped into my cotton pajamas, wishing I'd brought my sexy silk nightgown on the trip. But it was fall, so it was more practical to bring warmer clothing. Seducing a guy hadn't been my plan until now.

After adding some leave-in-conditioner for my curly hair, I exited my bathroom to find my luggage near the bed. When I finished putting everything away, I went out to the living room to find some nature show on TV.

Sitting on the couch, Royce busied himself with his phone. He looked fresh and relaxed. His hair appeared toweled dry, which made it a shade darker. Wearing a white T-shirt and gray sweatpants, he stretched his long legs across the coffee table, crossed at the ankles. I swallowed the dryness from my throat at the captivating man blessed with such good looks.

Even in casual clothing, he looked just as delicious as he did in a suit. If Royce in a suit was escargot, then Royce in a T-shirt and sweatpants was a juicy burger that satisfied me. Smiling, I wondered what he'd think if I shared my comparison of him to food.

Food.

I sucked in a breath as the revelation dawned on me. I'd always been careful about what I ate and never saw food as something "fun." It had consumed my psyche—pun intended—as a child, a teen, and a young woman. Even now, I had reservations about my eating disorder, which derived from so much more than food. But food was the tangible thing I could describe. And yet here I was, comparing Royce to it with no reservations.

My chest constricted, not from stress or anything negative but from a liberation that shook me awake. Royce had somehow released a chain that had trapped me. I blinked back the hot pressure building behind my eyes. God, I didn't need to add another layer of confusion today. I accepted the liberating gift, which I would contemplate more on later. Right now, I had a desire that needed to be released.

I walked over. "Thank you for bringing the bags in."

He stopped typing on his phone and turned to me. "You're welcome. How are you feeling?"

"Better." I sat down beside him, trying to plan my seduction. I'd never done anything like this. It both thrilled and scared me.

"Good, because I don't like to see these worry lines on this beautiful face." He rubbed the space between my eyebrows.

"You have them too." I pressed my finger to his forehead.

He gripped my hand and held it. "That's because I'm worried about you."

All my playfulness disappeared, replaced by something so serious my heart hammered loudly. Could he hear it?

I looked into those green eyes. "Why?"

The green turned glacial, and the pupils darkened within seconds. "Because I care about you."

Why was my throat dry again? "As a friend or as your girlfriend?" I didn't dare say fake girlfriend because that word diminished my importance, and I didn't like it.

A smile formed on his lips. "Both. If you hadn't agreed to stay here with me, I would have made you."

My eyebrows shot up. "You can't make me do anything I don't want to." Grabbing a throw pillow beside me, I whipped it at his chest, but he blocked it swiftly.

"Wanna bet?" He grabbed the pillow behind him and taunted me.

What exactly did he believe he could make me do? This recent development shifted my plan to seduce him. My new scheme took root.

"I'm game. What are we wagering?"

"The loser has to answer a question truthfully or do one thing he or she *fears* but wants to do." That arrogant smirked enticed me more than it should.

I had questions for him, and I was certain he had questions for me. What I feared but wanted to do was exactly this: *seduce* him. I had other worries, but this particular one —this person—had overwhelmed me, and I had to resolve it by facing the issue. Perhaps then I could move on and concentrate on the job I was hired to do here. Not that I wasn't performing well or getting my work done. I just couldn't get him out of my mind.

"I'm game," I said. "Since you thought of the rules, *I'll* pick the game, and it comes with one more little rule: the first one to get three whacks in the head from the pillow loses."

"Fine." His mouth moved in a smile.

I jumped up from the couch, rushed to the armchair, and grabbed the biggest pillow. "Do you dare have a pillow fight with me? Or are you afraid?"

"One must overcome one's fear in order to be victorious." He whipped the pillow at me, but I blocked it with my massive pillow.

A silly pillow fight ensued, with me running around the living room screaming and laughing. He snatched several throw pillows and pitched them at me, one by one. He was quick, and I ducked and dodged while trying to block the flying pillows from hitting my head. I didn't get a chance to whack him at all.

"How do you like that, hmm?" he said.

"For someone who hasn't had a pillow fight before, you're a quick learner!" I picked up a throw pillow that fell and flung it at him. He caught it. *Damn.*

"I'm just good at fighting." His eyes sparked with amusement as he pitched a pillow at me, and it hit the side of my head. "One point for me!"

I had been too focused on his eyes and didn't pay attention. My bad. My brain went into overdrive, and a scheme finally popped into my head, ensuring my victory.

I tripped, hit the coffee table with my leg, limped, and dropped onto the couch with the pillow on my side. "Ow." I held my knee to my chest, wincing.

Tossing the pillows from his arms, Royce rushed over and placed a gentle hand on my knee. "Are you okay?" Concern swam in his eyes, and guilt gnawed at me, but I had a game to win here.

I yanked at the pillow and whacked him three times on his head. "I win!"

In a blink, he pounced on me, pushing me back onto the couch with his body covering mine. He gripped my wrists and lifted them above my head. Heat spread all over my body as I sensed the bulge pressing into me.

"You cheated, and that calls for a punishment." His eyes pinned me, while a mischievous smirk slid onto his face.

"I didn't cheat," I breathed as my nipples pebbled under

my thin bra. "There weren't any rules about fake injuries. I just *maneuvered* around you."

"You *manipulated* my concern for you. We're going to set hard rules for next time." He shifted his body, pushing one of my thighs up with one hand while still gripping my wrists with the other. I was at his mercy, and there was something sexy about that.

"Not my intention—"

His hand ran over my thigh and squeezed my buttock. "Oh, it was your intention, just like this is my intention." His free hand slipped under my ass, pushing my core into his hard cock.

I let out a moan as his cock throbbed against me, trying to punish me with need. God, I wanted him so badly. Grinding my hips against him, I studied his face.

He growled with satisfaction. Did he realize we were starting a new game?

"I should've known you're a she-devil. All this wild hair and the wicked glint in your eyes should have given me a clue." He pressed his face into my hair and inhaled. "I love the way you smell."

The need to touch and feel him surged in me. With my legs, I squeezed his ass, making my claim. "A she-devil is the perfect match for a daredevil, don't you think?"

"You're driving me crazy, Michelle. What game are we playing now? How to seduce Royce?"

How had he known? A wild guess? It didn't matter.

His eyes had darkened to a gorgeous mossy color. "Seduce away, angel. You know how to turn me on."

Royce swallowed, and the movement of his Adam's apple increased the need in me. I'd always considered a man's shoulders to be the feature I couldn't resist, but right now, his Adam's apple became the switch that lit me up.

I pressed my lips to the masculine bump on his throat and kissed it.

He crooned. "I'll accept this defeat."

"Willingly? You had no choice. You lost." My voice vibrated against his throat.

He veered back, creating a slight distance between my lips. "I love that you wanted to win so badly."

I *needed* to win because I wanted to know what he feared. That desire trumped everything else. "I like to win."

"So do I." His eyes flashed with heat. "Since l lost, I have to either answer a tough question or do something that frightens me." His body shifted, opening my thighs wider, not acting like someone who had been defeated.

Pinning me under him, he posed as the clear winner. Fully aware of his hot cock pulsing against my center, I surrendered to him, wanting all the sensations he could make me feel.

"What will it be? Answer my question or be fearless, Viking?"

As he stared at me, a golden strand of hair fell across his forehead, making him appear disheveled. I wanted to brush it away, but he still clasped my wrists in his hand.

"What frightens me is how you make me feel. I want to know how else you can make me lose control."

He crushed his lips to mine, kissing me with an urgency that jolted my body alive. The kiss sent an explosion of sensations through me. Any reservations about holding back snapped free. The fearless version of me wanted to feel everything he would give. I'd been depriving myself after my breakup with Julian. I had let a man hurt me, making me forget who I was. No more.

Royce had lured me back to myself in subtle ways—his concern for my safety, his protectiveness. He gave without asking me for anything in return.

Though restrained, I felt freer than I ever had. But the desire to break free had nothing to do with me feeling trapped. It was sexual energy wanting release.

I squirmed under him, creating more friction between us. "I want to touch you."

He released my wrists immediately. "Please do," he whispered, and I felt his smile on my lips.

My fingers dug into his hair as his tongue traced my lips, making me moan. His tongue slid in and seduced mine. Tongues twirled as gasps escaped from our hungry mouths. If that kiss in the lagoon had ignited me, this one was a volcanic eruption.

My body trembled from the glide of his tongue and the merging of breath. I'd remember this moment when all my senses heightened to unfamiliar levels. The masculine scent, his unique taste, the curious touch, the sounds humming around me, the feel of his hard body against mine—everything became *more* with this man.

His mouth moved along my chin to settle at my neck, nibbling on my skin. A shiver zipped through me. I breathed in everything about him—the scent of his shampoo, the softness of his hair, and the roughness from his five o'clock shadow tantalizing my shoulder.

Moaning, I licked my lips, wanting that unique taste of him again.

As though sensing my needs, his mouth came back to

mine. He held nothing back, and neither did I. We were like two desperate people starving for each other.

"I want . . ." I couldn't speak clearly from the onslaught of heat and need.

"What do you want, angel?" He nibbled my earlobe and sent a fiery trail down my neck with his mouth and tongue. He slid a hand under my shirt, under my bra, and palmed my breast. "Tell me." His darkened eyes demanded an honest answer I couldn't hide.

"I want more. I want your clothes off right now." I tugged at his shirt.

"And I want yours off too." He stood and removed his shirt, pants, and boxers, whipping them aside.

I rose to a sitting position and stared at the massive cock begging to be touched. He sucked in a breath as I ran my fingers along his length. I twirled my finger, signaling for him to turn around for me.

Smirking, he said, "As you wish."

"Wow." He had a strong and splendid back packed with muscles.

"Like what you see?" He glanced over his broad shoulders, meeting my eyes.

I loved watching his muscles bunch and lengthen with sleek fluidity as he shifted slightly. My eyes went to the lightning bolt tattoo at the center of his back. "I love this art on your back. What does it signify?"

Royce turned. "Clarity, truth, courage, strength, and renewal. When you're in a thunderstorm, lightning illuminates, showing you what's hidden, showing you the truth—sometimes ugly, sometimes not. It takes courage and strength to weather a storm. A storm clears out old energy, bringing in a new day."

My heart trembled at his touching words. I knew that for him to grasp this wisdom meant he'd been through hell. I wanted to know everything about him. I wanted to be his lightning bolt, to show him how exquisite, strong, brave, and worthy he was to me.

"I'll never look at a lightning bolt the same way."

Smiling, he jerked a chin to my clothed body and reached for my shirt. "Off."

I let him remove my clothes, dropping them on the floor. He stared at my body. "You're absolutely beautiful."

His smoky voice was like silk brushing against my skin, creating delicious shivers down my body. He hovered over me, bracing a hand on either side of the couch, trapping me between his powerful arms. He looked like a beast surveying his prey. I wanted to be his prey, wanted everything he'd offer me tonight.

I was desperate for him in a way I couldn't understand. Maybe there was no need for any understanding, just feeling was enough for me.

Royce captured my mouth in a powerful kiss that forced me to lean back further into the couch. His knee urged my legs apart, making me feel vulnerable. I was bare to him, but he didn't know that yet.

I was showing him aspects of me no other man had seen —the wild Michelle who wanted to explore in bed. With Julian, he only wanted to fuck missionary-style because it made him feel powerful and in charge. I never dared suggest anything else.

But with Royce, I felt I could be me—do whatever my heart desired.

I gasped when his hands cupped my breasts and teased my nipples. Liquid heat pooled in my core.

"Royce . . ." I begged.

"I know what you want, baby." He lowered his mouth to my breast and circled his tongue around my nipple, driving me insane.

While his lips and tongue worked one breast, his hand teased the other. Pleasure spiked in me as I arched into his mouth. My fingers dug into his hair, holding him in place as I watched him feast on me.

Chills skated down my spine, intensifying the need that ached in my core.

"More," I breathed.

"I'm going to fuck you so hard." He growled and suckled my breasts harder, faster.

I'd never watched a man devour me like this. He met my gaze, and I saw the frantic need in his eyes. I wanted him just as much as he wanted me.

He gripped my thighs and urged them apart. I gasped at how exposed I was to his gaze. My stomach quivered, and I bit my bottom lip as a thrill twisted my stomach.

"You're a gorgeous woman." He dropped his knees to the floor and flicked a devilish grin at me. "And I'm making you mine." Grunting rich and low, he leaned in and dropped gentle kisses to my inner thighs.

I gripped the cushion of the couch as the anticipation rose in me. Desire swarmed to my center and leaked out.

"Fuuuck," he crooned, then used his finger to wipe my cum and licked it from his finger.

That act aroused me further, and I shivered as more juices leaked from me. God, I couldn't stop my body's reaction to him. Embarrassed, I tried to close my thighs.

"No." He held them in place. "I love seeing what I do to you. Every sigh or moan from you, every quiver of your muscles, every beat of your heart, and every orgasm I coax out of you—they all belong to me now." He pressed his lips to my core, kissed me, then flattened his tongue, licking me.

Pleasure whipped my head back as I let out a satisfying moan. He spent his time feasting, sending me into a blur where I couldn't think or do anything but focus on the sensation of his lips and tongue. The long exploration of my body woke up nerves I didn't know existed.

"I could explore you all day, all night." His eyes met mine. "You taste so good. Do you like me fucking you with my mouth? My tongue? My finger?" He demonstrated with a flutter of his tongue on my bud and the thrusting of his long finger into my channel.

I squealed as a powerful wave of bliss surged in me. "Yes. I love everything you do to me. Fuck me like it's your greatest adventure."

He groaned against my sex, and the sound vibrated against me, pushing me even further toward the edge. As he feasted, he called me dirty names, asking if I wanted more.

The way he spoke to me differed from the professional demeanor of the respected doctor who had given an innovative speech or the businessman who ran a successful empire. This man devouring me had heightened sexual needs that matched my own.

He lifted my ass and flung my legs over his shoulders, making my body shift down on the couch. "This is mine. Remember that." He buried his face between my legs and plunged his tongue deep into me.

Pleasure spiked, and my body quivered. My fingers tugged at his hair as the orgasm ricocheted through my body, sending me off the edge. "Royce!"

My body bucked and trembled as he continued feasting.

The sensation was too much. I gripped the cushion to help stabilize the spinning sensation. It shot me up into the sky. As I slowly floated downward, he flipped me onto all fours.

"God, I can't get enough of you." He pushed my head to the cushion. I stretched my hands out in front of me like I was performing a yoga move with my ass in the air. "This is your punishment for manipulating me." He slapped my ass, kneading each buttock, spreading them wider as he dragged his mouth over my ass before giving me another slap. It didn't hurt, and I wanted more of it. "And this is for making me want you more than I can understand." He pressed his face into my ass and ravaged me.

"Oh my God!" I squealed into the cushion, feeling wonderful, alive, and completely undone. This man knew what I wanted and needed.

"I need to get a condom."

"Don't. I'm on the pill. I want to feel you inside me."

He dropped kisses along my spine, creating a trail of fire. His breath caressed my ear as he whispered, "You want to be my sex slave, don't you?" He inserted a finger into me, leaning over me. I turned my head to the side so his mouth covered my lips—lips that had explored my most secret place just moments ago.

I wanted to reply, but no words would form in my mind. He consumed me with the kiss that tasted of the two of us.

I purred against his mouth, and he moaned. "I want to fuck you in every position imaginable, and I know you want it too."

He *knew* me. A wash of blush overcame my face, even though what he'd been doing to me should have erased any shame or embarrassment. But knowing he could see into my desires shifted something in me.

"Yes. Fuck me like I'm your sex toy." I couldn't believe the words that came out of me. It was the truth, and Royce had yanked them free.

I'd never experienced this wild sex where I surrendered to a man I trusted. He could do whatever he wanted with me because I planned on doing what I wanted with him too.

A wide grin spread across that handsome face beaded with sweat. "Your dirty mind is going to destroy me, angel."

"You're a sex fiend, and I'm only conforming, *sir*," I purred, teasing and taunting him to show me how much he wanted me.

Growling, he positioned his cock at my entrance. "If I'm a sex fiend, then you're my sex hellion." He slid into me, one inch at a time. "You're so tight."

I gasped as my muscles stretched to accommodate him. Gyrating my hips, I tortured him with pleasure and knew this wasn't the end of my desire for him.

This one night was not enough for me. I wanted more with him.

CHAPTER THIRTY-TWO

ROYCE

WHEN SHE GYRATED HER HIPS, fucking taunting me, I thought I was going to explode. She was tighter than sin, squeezing at my self-control, but I held onto the tiny sliver of sanity, trying to milk every second of pleasure while I was inside her.

My desire to claim her increased every time I touched her, kissed her, and licked her. She lured this animalistic side of me out, and I obeyed without hesitation. Michelle held power over me even though it appeared she had surrendered to my needs.

Perhaps we were surrendering to each other because the passion on her face and the feverish urgency in her eyes slayed me. When she was at the mercy of my mouth and tongue, letting me do whatever I pleased to her, I embraced the trust she offered me like a precious present. She tasted of something that sparked a memory in me—a memory of when I was a child holding onto a dream that anything was possible.

And as I feasted on her, I remembered more about

myself. This revelation was new to me. I'd never fucked a woman and found myself in the process.

Michelle was the catalyst that made me re-evaluate my life.

I plunged into her, fast and furious, creating wet noisy sounds of sweat-slicked bodies slapping against each other. Her moans and my grunts filled my apartment with a melody I wanted to hear over and over again.

She arched her back. "More."

I loved her sex drive and sense of exploration in bed. Gripping her hips, I pounded into her, but I was missing something. I needed to see her face. At least for this first time, I wanted her to look me in the eye when I took her.

Lowering my body over her, I muttered, "Flip on your side."

Face to face, I lay beside her on my wide couch. Her thigh came up to my hips as I hammered into her fast and furious.

She wiped away the sweat on my forehead, but kept her gaze on me. The warmth in her eyes melted something cold and hard within me. I didn't understand what that was yet, but I knew I'd destroy the world for her.

I'd do anything to see that lovely smile stay on her lips. She bit her bottom lip, a sexy gesture that made me kiss her. Her muscles squeezed my cock, and her eyes gleamed with amusement.

"Hellion." I growled as I drove into her, feeling the rise of an orgasm.

Her hand cupped the side of my face. "I'm yours."

She had no idea what that devotion did to me. My body stiffened, bracing for the massive orgasm that shot through me like a bullet as it took me over the crescendo.

"Michelle!" I roared as the orgasm continued to ripple through me, making me tremble all the way to my soul.

My heart pounded so loudly that it was all I could hear. Still throbbing inside her, I collapsed to the couch, and she cradled me. With my head to her chest, I heard and felt her heartbeat. It thumped alongside mine, and I imagined them speaking to each other.

The odd thought put a smile on my face as I wallowed in her presence. "Who knew you were so wild and crazy?" My fingers skipped along her arm.

"You knew."

I laughed. "I had a feeling, and you confirmed it tonight and then some." I propped onto my elbow. "This isn't over. My appetite for you has just begun."

Her stomach growled, and pink bloomed on her cheeks. Of all the things I did to her, hunger made her blush, which made her even more adorable.

"Let me go wash up, and I can warm up some leftovers for you."

We got dressed, ate a quick dinner of flatbread pizza I'd ordered yesterday, and cuddled on the couch, watching a nature show. I never knew why I'd wanted this wide couch, but it served its purpose tonight when Michelle fell asleep with my arms wrapped around her.

Her hand was strategically placed on my cock. I was certain it was an accident, but I liked the look of it, so I didn't move. Instead, I dragged the throw blanket over her and slept beside her.

CHAPTER THIRTY-THREE

MICHELLE

I YAWNED and glanced over at Royce, who lay beside me, snoring. His hair was a sexy mess, making me want to run my fingers through it. One leg draped over the edge of the couch while the other was pinned under my leg.

That was when I realized something warm was in my hand—something hard and throbbing. I lifted my head and gasped. Horrified at what I saw, I yanked my hand away from his cock.

Oh my God. How long had I been holding his cock? I couldn't have held it all night, could I? It wasn't a stuffed animal—which I outgrew when I turned ten—that comforted someone to sleep.

"Why must you torture me?" he growled, opening his eyes and cracking a smile. "Your hand was *exactly* where it was meant to be." He dropped a kiss on my cheek. "Morning, gorgeous."

I didn't feel gorgeous. My hair was probably a mess, and my drool was probably crusty around my mouth. Self-conscious, I sat up and scrubbed a hand over my face.

"Why didn't you wake me so I could go to bed?"

"You looked so peaceful. I didn't want to disturb you."

"Why didn't you sleep in your bedroom? You could've just left me here. Your couch is comfortable enough for me."

"What kind of man would I be if I left you out here all by yourself? You might be scared." Amusement flashed in his eyes.

I tilted my head. "That's not the reason. Don't lie."

"Okay, fine. I didn't want to wake you because you had your hand strategically placed on my cock—the best place for it, by the way—and if I got up to leave, it would have woken up my beautiful girlfriend. I'm a very thoughtful guy—"

"Shut up," I muttered, feeling heat scorching my cheeks. Had I really held his cock all night? I did have a dream where I kept squeezing a stress ball.

"I can't believe I did that. That's a first."

"And only." He corrected and took my hand in his, kissing my fingertips. "I don't ever want you touching another man's cock."

I didn't know what to think of his seriousness. Or was he being sarcastic?

Only one way to find out. "What if I do?"

His eyes flashed with a darkness I hadn't seen in him. Deadly. Unstoppable.

"I know of places that could incinerate a man where no one would ever find his body. I'm a volcanologist, remember? I have access to places on Earth most people don't. I prefer to keep them untainted, but when and if necessary, I won't hesitate."

There were so many facets to him, and this was a darker side I hadn't known. I was about to inquire, but his phone buzzed on the coffee table. He glanced at it, answered, then stood up and walked into his office, shutting the door behind him.

I went to wash up and replayed last night's events in my head. No man had ever made my body feel the way Royce did. My body was still sore and wanting him.

Was he being a possessive fake boyfriend? Would all of this end when it was time for me to leave Iceland?

Did he think I'd touch another man because we were only fake dating? The sex wasn't fake. My orgasm was real. My core tightened remembering his skilled mouth, his talented tongue, and dominating cock.

A sadness overcame me, but I pushed it away.

What happened in Iceland stayed in Iceland, right? I would get my adventure with this fascinating man, even if it were temporary.

CHAPTER THIRTY-FOUR

MICHELLE

"READY FOR AN ADVENTURE?" Royce held my hand as he led me down a rocky path.

The mid-October chilly air mimicked New England weather. I wore a sweater jacket and soft corduroy pants with long comfy boots. He wore a long sleeved shirt with a puffy vest and dark denim jeans with hiking boots, looking rugged and gorgeous as always. He carried a backpack with our water bottles, snacks, binoculars, and other hiking essentials.

"Always," I said, stepping over a pretty patch of bright green moss. "How many girls have you brought here?"

"None." He gazed down into my eyes. "You're the first person."

My chest warmed at the knowledge.

"Do you come here often?"

"Whenever I return to Iceland for business, it grounds me, reminds me of where I've been and where I'm going."

The sex had changed us, whether or not he admitted it. It had shifted everything. This fake relationship wasn't working for me anymore, and I wanted the real thing. But I wasn't sure how to bring it up to him. He clarified that he only needed a fake girlfriend to keep Fiona away. It was obvious he wasn't looking for an actual relationship, or he would've been with someone already. Just look at him.

Before I confronted him with my proposal, I had to ensure that my thoughts were clear and concise. I had to be sure it was what I wanted and not because of how much I enjoyed the physical intimacy. To be with someone just because they made you feel safe wasn't a good excuse. I once thought Julian made me feel safe. He had in the beginning, but things changed quickly. I had a feeling Royce was different, but could I be sure? Wasn't any relationship a gamble?

My heart couldn't afford another gamble, so I had to think carefully. But for today, I could enjoy being with him.

As he took me to his secret place, it was like walking into his soul. Each step on the moss was a clue to discovering Royce. That was precious to me.

I understood why he liked earthy colors; they surrounded him, a part of him. From this moment onward, I would think of him whenever I enjoyed nature's wonders. He was my volcanologist, my geologist, and my video game nerd. He was also a man who fired up so much desire in me.

We continued trekking along a dirt path filled with mossy rocks, heading to a waterfall. "So the waterfall is off-limits to the public?"

"To everyone. No one comes here. I own this land, and if they're caught, they'd be trespassing."

My body sighed as I breathed in the fresh air. Pebbles crunched under my boots, and a bird squawked nearby. I heard the sound of water and glanced up at him. "We're close."

Minutes later, we arrived at a beautiful waterfall. It wasn't a massive waterfall, but a quaint wonder hidden between hills, rocks, and trees.

Royce stood beside me, taking in the captivating view.

"Nature never ceases to amaze me," I said, inhaling a deep breath.

"That's why I love studying geology and what lies beneath the earth. Symbolically, I believe humans are like that too. There's so much to discover."

"How did you find this place?"

"When I bought Excursions for You, I browsed the nearby area and stumbled on it. Then I offered the previous owner a price he couldn't refuse."

I turned to my right and gasped. "Oh my God, is that what I think it is?"

"You can see the volcano better from up there." He pointed to a rock and led the way.

From higher up, I could see the gorgeous volcano in the distance. It stood tall, proud, and watchful. I imagined it was like a guardian watching over its land. A deity that sometimes got angry when people didn't treat the planet with care and respect, therefore erupting with anger.

We were all alone on the massive rock that jutted out from the side of a mountain. Intensely green moss carpeted the surface. The witnesses to the beauty around Royce and me were the sun, the sky, and the earth.

I didn't know why tears started rolling down my cheeks. "It's breathtaking. This is the closest I've ever been to a volcano. It's my first time seeing one in real life. The images you see on TV don't do it justice. I can feel its power standing here."

"That's why I come here, to immerse myself in its power. But ever since I met you, I don't need it."

My heart constricted, and I met his gaze, filled with so much emotion.

Yanking me close, he kissed me, making me moan. I tugged at his hair, his jacket, needing him closer, wanting to touch him everywhere.

A wild thought sparked in me. "I want you right now. Right *here*. In the open. Do you dare?"

His eyes flashed with lust as a wicked smile pulled at his mouth.

Nerves stirred in me. I couldn't believe I said that, but it felt liberating to share what I wanted to do with him. Being with Royce allowed me to think and do as I pleased. There was nothing holding me back. With him, there were no restrictions.

"You read my mind, sex hellion." He shrugged off the backpack and dropped it on the ground.

I laughed, shoved him against the standing rock wall, and gripped at his waistband. Desperation coursed through me, sending a thrill that fired up my blood. Royce smiled as he watched me unbuckle his belt, dropping his pants to bunch at his boots.

His bulge greeted me through his boxers, wanting to burst free. I swallowed my dry throat. My hand skimmed his muscled thigh. The October air should have made his skin cool to the touch, but it was welcoming and warm.

I palmed him, and he throbbed in my hand, scorching like a furnace. "Ready for your adventure, sex fiend?"

"With you? Always."

In seconds, his boxers pooled at his boots. He was trapped, and that turned me on.

I gripped his cock and examined its power, my gaze riveted on the glorious force of nature, studying it keenly. He groaned as my fingers traveled along the length. With a quickening breath, his expression strained with need.

Still fully clothed, I dropped to my knees and licked his tip, circling it, before loving his entire length. He crooned, and the sound echoed into the vastness, becoming part of the landscape.

"Oh, fuck. I love your mouth on me." His raspy voice dripped with sin as he held my head in place. I felt like I was loving a delicious rod that held insatiable power.

Somewhere, a crow cried out as though it read my thoughts and cheered me on.

With his cock in my mouth, I gazed up at him. His lips parted with a gasp, his chest heaved with ragged breaths, and his skin grew hotter. My heart hammered at what I saw in his piercing green eyes—the apparent vulnerability that moved through them like fog rolling over the land.

"You make me feel so much, baby." He leaned his head back against the rock and released a wild growl that had my mouth and tongue working even faster and harder.

I wanted him to feel all the wonderful sensations so he'd always remember this moment when he brought me to his sacred hideaway.

CHAPTER THIRTY-FIVE

THE WAY her mouth devoured my cock was the most beautiful thing I'd ever witnessed. The rush of heat coursing through me was more powerful than the thrill I felt during skydiving or any of my daring adventures. Nothing compared to this moment.

I'd never been more aroused by a flick of a tongue on my cock, the wicked curve of her lips as she kissed my length, or the sparkle of lust in her eyes. Every facial expression she conveyed while loving me was etched in my mind like lava hardening to rock—solid, real, forever.

She took her claim, and I was a lost man wandering toward a territory I had long promised I didn't believe in.

Still clothed, she looked irresistible while she sucked me, showing me her undeniable skill. I relaxed my body against the stone slab, which should have been cold to the touch, but wasn't, not when there was so much heat blazing through me. My vision blurred as I took in the remarkable scenery, imprinting this moment in my head.

A breeze blew by, and her fragrance heightened my

senses further. Somehow, I'd slipped to a place between the conscious and unconscious, if that made any sense. The air became sweeter because of her. The wind hummed her a poem, the waterfall drummed her a song, and the fall colors brightened with vividness. I was no fucking poet. I was a man getting head from a virtuoso.

My perspective of everything changed because of her.

Passion pounded me as need tugged at my restraints.

"Angel." I cupped her face, pulled her up, and kissed her senseless.

Then I shifted her body so her hands braced against the stone wall and her back faced me. She arched, offering her gorgeous ass to me.

I slapped it. "All mine." Unbuckling her pants, I shoved them down, along with her underwear. My hand cupped her wetness, and I crooned. "You're dripping for me."

"Royce, please . . ."

I'd never heard a more beautiful plea and gave her what she wanted. I drove into her like a madman.

She moaned, and the sinful sound stimulated me even more.

"Yes, take me here in the wild," she breathed. "Show me how much you want me. Show the wilderness who's *wild*."

Fuck. This woman knew how to add fuel to the fire.

I gripped her hips, thrusting with everything I had. She cried out with pleasure, and I drove in deeper, faster, as sweat trickled down my body.

"Feel that?" My tongue traced the shell of her ear. "That's me taking possession of you." I pummeled harder into her. "Do you need to use the safe word, baby?"

"No," she moaned, taking my every thrust. "I love what you do to me. I trust you."

Her words only increased my stamina. With a mighty thrust, I slammed into her, and her muscles tightened.

"Oh, God, Royce!" She trembled as the ecstasy squeezed my cock.

I growled like an untamed beast as the orgasm ripped through me, shredding my mind into slivers of nothingness. Everything left my brain but one word: Michelle. I held her as the ringing in my ears became a distant drum. I inhaled the sweetened air, letting it fill me with her scent.

When our labored breathing calmed, I removed myself from her and cleaned her with the napkins from my backpack.

We got dressed, and she turned to me. "Wow. I like your sense of adventure, Viking."

"There's more where that came from." I gripped her chin, holding her still to admire her beauty. "We should mark every property I own this way."

She laughed, and her voice echoed into the distance. I imagined the landscape smiling the way my heart did.

CHAPTER THIRTY-SIX

MICHELLE

SADNESS OVERWHELMED me as we walked back to the car. I didn't want this fake relationship anymore. I wanted the real thing.

My steps slowed as my boots crunched on pebbles. I bent down and picked up an orange leaf. Like this leaf that had fallen from its tree, I'd fallen for Royce. I had pretended my feelings were all fake, but they'd trickled deep inside of me, creating a sacred lagoon that grew every time we kissed, every time we touched.

My chest tightened, and the hot pressure behind my eyes increased. Struggling to fight it back, tears slipped through the rim of my eyes and slid down my cheeks.

"What's wrong?" He placed a hand on my shoulder and looked at me.

"Nothing."

"It's not nothing. Tell me." He bore those gorgeous green eyes into me.

"Nothing" was the safe and silly response that most women replied. Why did we always say that? It was obvious that something was bothering me, but the fear of telling him and his reaction made me unsure if I should share my thoughts.

Royce said he didn't want a serious relationship, and our fake relationship was to keep his ex-girlfriend away. But if I didn't tell him now, then when?

"Just thinking about this relationship," I said, staring at my boots, kicking a pebble into the distance. If I had to look him in the eye, I'd cry like a fool in front of him.

He tipped up my chin, forcing my gaze to meet his eyes. "Our relationship has gone beyond what I initially thought. I want you to trust me. What's wrong?"

I frowned at the confusing thoughts in my head. If I didn't tell him my feelings, I would be running away from my issues. I stopped that when my relationship with Julian had ended.

With Julian, I had an inkling that something was wrong, and yet I ignored my discomfort because I feared the truth. And where did that leave me? Delayed heartbreak? Julian and I weren't meant to be together. If I had faced my concerns when intuition nudged me, it would've saved me time and heartache. Why drag out something that wasn't going to last?

I didn't know if this would last, but my feelings for Royce were so strong, I had to give it a chance. I didn't want to continue analyzing this because it drove me crazy. Honesty was always the best approach.

Inhaling a breath, I said, "I know I agreed to this fake dating, but I can't do it anymore." Needing to do something with my hands, I shoved them into my jacket pockets. "I want this relationship to be—"

"It was never fake to me, Michelle." He wrapped his

arms around my waist, and the warmth of his body comforted me. "It was a label to disguise what I wanted to sample—a disguise to protect myself." He brushed his lips lightly over mine. "You're the first woman to make me want this much. That scared and intrigued me, so I suggested the fake dating as an excuse to see where this relationship could go."

"So Fiona wasn't an issue?"

"She was an opportunity that became an excuse. I needed her to make it sound believable. Yes, it helped keep her away, but she wasn't the main reason."

Something satiny fluttered in my stomach. "So . . ."

"Starting right now, we're the real deal."

CHAPTER THIRTY-SEVEN

ROYCE

BEAMING, she threw her arms around my neck, rose onto her toes, and gave me a big, sloppy kiss. "If you had said no, I would've tackled you, tied you up, and had my way with you."

I couldn't get enough of her. "Go ahead. I'm not stopping you."

She laughed and clasped my hand. "We can save that for later at home."

I didn't realize how much I loved holding hands with her. Though it was a simple gesture, it meant so much more to me. She had inspired me to love it.

"Since you own so many excursion sites, have you visited the Seven Wonders of the World?" she asked as we headed back to the car.

"Not all of them. Do you have places you want to go?"

"I have my list of wonders to visit. I have eight left. Maybe we can go together one day." She swung my arm back and forth.

"Where do you want to go?"

"I'd love to see the Northern Lights, visit the pyramids of Giza in Egypt, Machu Picchu, Switzerland, Thailand, Vietnam, and New Zealand. There's also Mt. Shasta in California. It's not a 'wonder' per se, but it interests me. Supposedly, strange and magical things happen there."

I arched a brow. "You believe in that stuff?"

She shrugged. "I believe there are happenings that can't be explained. There's magic to them. I don't know. For me, it's like traveling and discovering something new. The unknown is scary, but it's also very interesting."

"I have a lot of *strange* and *magical* things to show you in bed."

She elbowed me with a giggle. "You're a science guy. Of course, you don't believe in this stuff because it can't be proven. Nor can you *see* it. Some things are *felt* and not seen or proven."

I understood what she meant because the way she made me feel was indeed magical.

"I sat next to a psychic at a conference once. She was at Mt. Shasta and saw fairy orbs and angelic lights. The history channel said people have spotted UFOs there too." Michelle shrugged. "I think the experience will make a great blog post. People like to read about weird things."

"Mt. Shasta is a potentially active volcano, but I'd go wherever you want."

"Smart man. You know the right thing to say to your girlfriend, and that makes you a keeper." She jabbed a finger at my chest.

"I *am* a smart man because I know what I have—the most beautiful and intelligent woman on this planet."

"Smart ass."

"Who wants to do all kinds of things to your ass."

That brought color to her cheeks.

We made it back to my car, parked in an open space with woods nearby. A man wearing a cap and dressed in black approached us from afar. His quick and focused movement told me something was wrong.

"Get in and duck." I opened the car door for Michelle and reached for the gun from the glove compartment.

The first shot smashed the driver's side windshield as soon as I shut the door. I was grateful it didn't hit the passenger side where Michelle and I were. Another shot rang out and broke the driver's side-view mirror.

I fired back at the man and hit him in the leg. He ran off into the woods. Either he was an awful marksman or the shots were warnings. I didn't want to run after him if someone else was hiding in the area. I stayed to protect Michelle. Seconds later, the police arrived, which surprised me because I hadn't even called them.

Recognizing Ludvik and some of his men, I showed them the direction in which the man fled.

"I shot him in the leg, so he shouldn't have gone very far."

Bang. Bang. Bang.

The three gunshots echoed in the distance.

"Go home," Ludvik said. "We'll take care of this. I'll call you later."

"How did you know to come this way?"

"We got a call saying an armed man was in the area."

Who had called them? Who was the man with the gun? Was he trying to kill Michelle or me? Could this be the same man who left the bomb at her apartment?

Michelle rushed to me and examined my body. "Are you hurt?"

"I'm fine." The concern in her eyes and the way she turned me around to check for injuries did something strange to my heart.

"Are you sure?" She looked terrified.

"Yes." I hadn't realized how scared I was. My life just got a jumpstart with this relationship, and now this fucker wanted to ruin it. She could've been hurt. Her safety was more important than mine.

I blinked at the shocking thought. No woman had ever been that important to me other than my mom and aunt. Michelle was transforming me, and I was just seeing it now.

She showed me I could feel an entire spectrum of emotions I didn't think I was capable of. She was a wonder, and she was mine.

I gripped her shoulders, looking into her eyes. "Are *you* okay?"

"Yeah, I'm all right."

"We can talk about this at home."

CHAPTER THIRTY-EIGHT

MICHELLE

BACK AT HIS APARTMENT, Royce made us tea with honey in two brown mugs.

Sitting on the couch, I sipped the tea, allowing its warmth to soothe my nerves. I placed the mug on a glass coaster on the coffee table and replayed the event in my head. Everything happened so fast. When the sounds of gunfire went off, I'd crouched on the floor of the car. Fear had stabbed me while I was worried about Royce. That intense fear reminded me of when I had to face my eating disorder. The overwhelming feeling consumed me.

I didn't realize I'd been trembling until Royce joined me on the couch, wrapping a powerful arm around me and rubbing his hand up and down my arm.

"Do you think it's the same man after me? Or is this someone else after you? Do you have enemies?"

"I didn't get to where I am today without making enemies. I've pissed people off, and people have pissed me off, but this assault seems different. My gut tells me this isn't the guy who left the bomb at your apartment. I don't want you to worry about it. The police will alert me if they find anything."

Now that we were officially dating, I had questions for him.

Turning to face him, I said, "Was it hard for you to adjust when you moved to the States from Iceland? How did you adjust to the language? Were you scared?"

His eyes gleamed. "You have a lot of questions."

"They've been adding up, but I didn't feel like I had a right to ask you until now."

"I love that you want to know. What can I say? I'm irresistible," he teased, another trait I adored about him.

Julian hardly ever teased me, and I was afraid to tease him. His replies always poked at my body, my diet, and how I should exercise more. His comments only got worse when I told him I suffered from an eating disorder. He didn't stop his criticism, as though my admission made me seem weak and unworthy of him.

He never inquired if I'd gotten treatment or how it started. Nothing. My flaw embarrassed him. He didn't want people to know, which was why he kept pushing me to maintain my strict workout regimen.

With Royce, I could say whatever I wanted. It was a pleasant change that I welcomed.

"You're irresistible and overconfident." My eyes narrowed with amusement.

"Most women find confidence attractive."

"As long as it doesn't inflate your ego to a dangerous level."

"My ego is adjustable." A smile played on his lips. "To answer your question, adjusting to a new environment wasn't easy, but I managed. There were moments of loneliness because I missed my mom and sister."

My heart broke at his words. His experiences seemed more serious than I had imagined.

"Kids can pick up new languages fast. But I'd been learning English in Iceland, so I adapted fine. Things got worse in high school, though. I got into too many fights."

"Did you clobber them? I hope you did."

Bullies were the worst. I didn't like hearing he'd been mistreated growing up. But I supposed they were typical growing pains because I also had my share.

"I got into a really big fight my senior year and made my enemy miss a few weeks of school. He was the one who started it, and I had to defend myself. I broke his arm and his nose and injured his friend."

"Two against one? Bastards!" I seethed. "You should have gone for the legs too."

Royce smiled.

"I can be a dark angel when necessary," I confessed.

"I see that. Now it's just Aunt Klara and me."

"I'm an only child, so it's been my mom and me too." The wheel in my brain spun. "What about business enemies? Anyone stand out to you?"

"I'm looking into it," he said. "Was that the first time you've been that close to a gunshot?"

I nodded, and the reality of the event sank in deeper. I could have been shot.

"Have you received any threats?"

"Are you practicing for a detective exam?" he asked, a glint of humor in his eyes that disappeared quickly. "No, I haven't received any threats. Let the police do their job."

Something in his eyes hinted that he wasn't telling me the whole truth. Maybe he didn't want to worry me.

Royce reached for his laptop on the side table and turned it on. "Let's not talk about today's event anymore. We've had enough fears and negativity for one day. Let's look up the wonders of the world. How's that?"

"I have a better idea. How about you show me some of the excursion sites you own so I know where I want to visit? Now that we're dating, you can give me a tour of your business sites without it being awkward."

"I could've given you a tour if you were my friend *or* my girlfriend."

"Yeah, but it's not the same."

"Come to think of it, I've brought none of my dates to my excursion sites. I always kept work and personal relationships separate."

I didn't want him to break any rules for me. "If you're uncomfortable with it, that's okay with me. It was just a suggestion."

"No, that's not what I mean. I've never wanted to share my business details with anyone . . . until you."

If my heart were a gymnast, it would've twirled, twisted, and done several somersaults.

"Let's start with my very first adventure site I owned while going for my master's."

"How old were you?"

"Twenty."

"That's young for a master's student, no?"

"I took extra courses during the summer and winter, so I graduated earlier than most."

"You and your friends are a bunch of nerds."

He smiled. "We're just men with a passion and a vision. Those are powerful weapons."

"I never thought I'd fall for a nerd. You're no typical nerd, though."

"And what does that mean?" He quirked an eyebrow and resumed typing into his web browser.

"You're more of a gladiator, a nerd, and a GQ model all rolled up into one fine specimen, Dr. Viktorsson." I ran my hand up his thigh, trying to distract him.

He paused and considered me. "And you're the clever angel who has tricks up her sleeve."

He clicked on the website, and the Whitewater Family Resort images splashed onto the screen. My heart raced as memories flipped through my mind.

"Wait a second," I breathed, gripping his arm. "Is that location in Corvallis, Oregon?"

"Yes. I went to Oregon State University and worked at that place until the owner got ill and wanted to sell it. I put all my savings into that business venture. Remi loaned me extra money, and I paid him back double."

My hands shook. "I've been there before."

"When?"

"When I was eighteen, I went with my mom." My stomach churned with nerves. How much should I share about what I'd experienced there? No one else knew about my suicide attempt that day.

"What happened there?" Royce searched my face.

Needing comfort, I took his hand into my lap. "I . . . I almost died that day. Let me rephrase that. I *wanted* to die that day."

Royce flinched, and a sharp V deepened between his eyebrows. Something flashed in his eyes, like a recollection.

"On my first day as owner, I was one of the guides on duty. A girl with red hair fell into the water, and I rescued her. It happened so fast. Once she regained consciousness and the EMT took her to the hospital, I went to check on my employees. That girl was you, right?"

My heart hammered as understanding settled in me. No wonder he felt familiar somehow.

Tears filled my eyes. "I dyed my hair red that summer because I needed a new look. The new look didn't make me feel better."

Royce drew me into his arms and held me. "We met all those years ago . . ."

"You saved my life."

His eyes sparkled with a tease. "I got my first kiss back then."

He tried to bring humor to the situation, and I appreciated his attempt.

"I was in and out of consciousness. When I came to, I remembered a silhouette helping me. I never got the chance to thank that person." I lifted my face to his. "Thank you."

He brushed his lips against mine and dabbed the tears from my eyes with a tissue from the box on the table.

"You're welcome. I'd always wondered about the girl I saved." He stroked a hand down my hair, and his gaze sharpened. "Don't ever do anything like that again, okay? I can't lose you."

I couldn't lose him either. This revelation—this fated connection—linked us.

He kissed my forehead. "Will you tell me what happened that day? I need to know what monster pushed my girlfriend to end her life."

I inhaled a deep breath. "I suffered from an eating disorder, terrible body image, and other issues that emerged from trying to please everyone. I'd been participating in beauty pageants since I was six. That kind of spotlight put a lot of pressure on me. I didn't enjoy it."

"Do your parents know?"

"My dad passed away from a stroke when I was a baby. My mom never understood how I felt. She knew I had an eating disorder but didn't know how bad it was. It made her happy to see me win, and I didn't want to crush her dream. But that day, everything came crashing down on me all at once. I'd just won my last competition and dealt with mean girls who hated me for winning."

Nerves continued to wreak havoc in my stomach. Even though that event had occurred a long time ago, my body still remembered it.

"The depression and the bulimia formed a monster that ripped me apart from the inside. I had no joy, and the pain was unbearable. That day, I wanted the pain to end."

He listened intently without interruption. I told him about my eating disorder, how I'd eat more than necessary, then regurgitate in private. When I got older and received treatment, I stopped the vomiting and focused my attention on working out. One pound over my "standard" weight used to ruin my entire day.

As I shared my story with Royce, I could see how I'd come a long way.

"I continued my treatment with medication and therapy. My skewed body image improved, and the obsessive work-outs decreased. By the time I was in college, my disorder was more of a mental thing. The therapy stopped working because I needed something different to tap into my psyche. The mind is a strange and scary place."

"It is, but with the right weapon, you can take control of what belongs to you. Your mind is yours." His eyes warmed with so much affection.

I couldn't help but fall for him even more. This man had given me a second chance at life. What were the odds of me dating my savior after all these years?

That aspect made life more beautiful, and I'd hold on to that beauty for as long as I lived.

"How are you dealing with that 'monster' now?" he asked.

"It's locked up in my closet." I reached for my cell phone, turned it on, and showed him the reminder app. "I have reminders to help keep me on track. Like eating healthy, planning my workout days, and so on."

Royce took my phone and glanced at it. "As long as it helps you, keep using it. You have a lot of apps."

Since meeting him, I hadn't needed the reminders as much.

Returning my phone, he looked at me with concern. "I don't like knowing the monster is still there. The best way to heal is to flush it out of your closet. I can help you." Lines creased on his forehead. "I *want* to help you. I didn't save you back then to have you suffer now."

"I'm not suffering now."

"No, but as long as that 'monster' is still in your psyche, it could return. We need to rid you of it."

I couldn't help the smile that formed on my face. "You're not responsible for my life, Royce."

"As your boyfriend—as your *savior*—I have a responsibility to ensure you live a happy and healthy life. Monsters of any kind will stop that. Let me help you. Please."

The seriousness on his face swelled my heart. No one

had been that concerned about me. No one had wanted to know about my monster, much less slay it for me.

Tears welled up again. Why was I so sensitive today? For the first time in my life, someone understood me and didn't make me feel like less of a person for having a disorder. Royce knew that although I claimed to have healed, I still needed work. A lingering symptom could always come back.

He was right because I sensed the monster's claws every time anxiety hit me hard.

"Why do you care so much?" I croaked, the tears making a mess of my makeup.

He offered me another tissue. "Because you're my girl-friend, and I want to be there for you."

It was such a simple statement that rang with a truth people often overlooked. You're supposed to care for one another when you are in a relationship. I had never felt that until now.

"Thank you." I swallowed the lump in my throat. "I accept your help."

He cupped my face in his hands and kissed me. "Let's order dinner and have it delivered. Then we can watch some TV if you're up to it."

"I need to finish a blog post and send it to Becca, then I'm all yours."

While watching a crime show with Royce, I started to drift off to sleep. I sensed his arms carrying me somewhere. With my eyes closed, I asked, "Where are you taking me?"

"Shhh. Just sleep, baby. I've got you."

His soothing words tucked me in for the night.

CHAPTER THIRTY-NINE

ROYCE

I SAT on the edge of my bed, watching Michelle sleep peacefully. I wanted her in my bed so I could feel her warmth tonight and know she was safe.

Tonight's revelation shifted my perspective. It explained the attraction I had to her. This connection we shared was beyond anything I'd experienced.

She made a soft sound, and her eyebrows furrowed as though she was having a nightmare. I clasped her hand, trying to let her know I was there. We had shared a kiss when she was eighteen and I was twenty, eleven years ago. Though that lip contact had been me saving her life and not a passionate kiss between lovers, it was still an unforgettable moment. That had been our first meeting, and now fate was ready for us to meet again as adults who had gone through several trials and torments.

Rising from the bed, I glanced at her once more. Her brown hair was a wild mass of curls over my pillow. She was so beautiful, and it hurt to know how dark her life had been.

I wished I had been there to help her. But back then, I had my own shit to deal with.

Would we have connected the same way if I had known her? My priorities back then were to get my master's, enroll for my doctorate at Stanford, and grow my excursion business. A serious relationship hadn't been on my radar. So even if we had dated, I wouldn't have been able to give her the attention she needed.

But now I could, and I treasured the opportunity. My powerful feelings for Michelle had been sown a long time ago. It had rooted over time, unseen, and yet just as powerfully. When I saw her that day during the thunderstorm, I felt the spark coming from somewhere deep. Now I understood where.

I brushed a hand over her cheekbone. "Sweet dreams." Shutting the door quietly, I walked to my office.

It angered me that Michelle's mother hadn't been as supportive as she should have been. A mother should always be there for her child, listening to their concerns. When my mom was alive, she did her best for me. Though she worked a lot, she put me in a good school and listened to what I had to say. We only had each other. Even when she was dying, she made sure I was taken care of. But I also had a father who abandoned his family. I supposed there were all kinds of parents out there.

As I sat at my desk, my phone rang with an anonymous caller. The PI used various numbers when contacting me. At first, I only wanted to hire him for a temporary job, but now he was an asset.

My thoughts returned to all the chaos surrounding us, and I picked up the call. "What do you have for me?"

"Fiona Clark's phone shows text messages about wanting

to scare Michelle with her friend. I'll send you some images. Nothing about planning any actual events, though. I'll keep tabs on her and let you know if something comes up. I got a recording from a neighboring building on the day of the explosion. Everything is in the encrypted email."

"Thanks."

Fiona had been a thorn in my side, but now she had crossed the line. Stalking and annoying me was one thing, but hurting the woman I cared about was another.

After a few more minutes of updates on other jobs he'd been working on, I ended the call and opened the email. Browsing through the images of chats between Fiona and her friend Brittany, I concluded Fiona hated Michelle. But nothing showed concrete proof that she'd hired anyone. I had a plan to deal with her.

The recording from the PI showed the face of the guy who had run from Michelle's building: he was the thief who had snatched her purse. I made a copy and sent it to Ludvik, saying that a neighbor had offered the recording to help the investigation. Hopefully, with his new information, his men could apprehend the asshole before I got to him. At least with the police, he'd be going to prison. With me, he'd be in the ground. I'd never forget that day when Michelle could've been in her apartment during the explosion.

From my recollection of the thief, he was taller than the stocky man who had shot at me. Were these two incidents separate or connected?

My phone rang again, and I glanced at the number. "Ludvik, did you get my email about the recording?"

"No. I haven't gotten to my desk yet. I'm calling regarding the shooter."

"Who is he?"

"He's your employee, Oskar. One of our men recognized him when he shot at them. They fired back, and he fell into a ravine. His body hasn't been located."

I blinked at the shock of Oskar's name. He had been a stellar employee. What had he gotten himself into? If he had wanted me dead, he would've aimed the shot at me and not elsewhere.

"Thank you for the update. Please keep me posted on any other news."

The police department would do what they could, but I needed to know who had killed Oskar.

I spent the rest of the evening looking into Oskar's employment. Did his wife know anything?

The next day, I informed Michelle about Oskar's death while preparing to head out for a meeting.

"I can't believe it," she said, looking dismayed. "He seemed so nice."

"Circumstances change people. He probably got tangled up with some dangerous people."

Concern weighed in her eyes. "Those people might want to hurt you too."

I didn't want to lie to her, but I also didn't want to frighten her, especially now that she knew about the thief being responsible for the explosion. She had too much on her mind.

"In business, sometimes things go awry. The detectives already know about my business competitors, and they're looking into it. Don't worry. I want you to stay in and not go out, especially when I'm not with you. I don't want anything happening to you, okay?"

"I don't want anything to happen to you, either." Her brows pulled together in a frown.

"Nothing will." I kissed the top of her head. "I won't be long."

Ten minutes later, I leaned against my new Land Rover and watched Fiona drive up in her Mercedes, parking next to me. She got out, wearing a black wool coat with a Dolce & Gabbana logo belt.

Smiling, she stepped up to me, looking around. "Why are we meeting out here? We could sit down at the café in the mall and catch up." She ran her hand down my arm.

"This isn't a date, Fiona." I pushed myself away from the car and straightened. "Listen carefully to what I have to say. If you don't take this seriously, I will do everything in my power to destroy your family. Andrew Clark has a prestigious position at Global Bank. He's funding your elite lifestyle, but that could easily end tomorrow. Do you understand?"

"I'm not sure what you're talking about." Her eyes filled with fear.

The Volcanic Sustainability Research Program could survive without Global Bank's support.

"It's time you stop causing trouble for me and Michelle. I have a lot of money at Global Bank. All it takes is one phone call from me, and your lavish lifestyle will crumble."

She extracted her hand from my arm and took a step back. People like her hid under the umbrella of wealth, which gave them the illusion of power. Without wealth, they were weak.

Though Fiona didn't show any evidence of harming

Michelle in her text messages to her friend, I played the game as if she did.

"Who did you hire to hurt Michelle?"

She gasped. "Hurt her?"

I lifted a hand. "Cut the crap. I don't have time for your excuses. I have proof that you wanted to scare her. Who did you hire to place that bomb in her apartment?"

Fiona clamped a hand over her mouth. "A bomb? I have nothing to do with that!"

I studied her widened eyes. "I want the truth. For every lie you tell me, your family will lose a business, and I know you have plenty. Don't tempt me. Who did you hire and what exactly did you have him do?"

"I only wanted to scare her so she'd run back to the States. I wanted a chance with you. My friend Brittany has hated Michelle since they were kids. Brittany hired her ex-boyfriend, Larus, to smash the window. She paid him for me, and I paid her back."

"So you have nothing to do with the bomb or him stealing her purse?"

"No!" The terror on her face proved she wasn't lying. "I had nothing to do with that. Brittany told me he just broke her window."

"He also left a nasty note with the rock he used."

Fiona blinked. "I didn't tell him to do that!"

I understood why women envied Michelle. She was beautiful, smart, thoughtful, and authentic, but those qualities often became a curse because people would come after her for having what they lacked. The world was messed up in so many ways.

"What's Brittany's last name?" I asked.

"Brittany Parker. They were in pageants together when they were kids."

"Do you know where Larus is?"

"No. He lives here and in the States."

Scrubbing a hand over my face, I said, "Michelle could've died if she had been in her apartment when the bomb blew up. This isn't some silly game. We never had a chance and never will. You should focus on improving your life and not destroying others. Stay away from Michelle and me. If you don't, you know what will happen."

Tears ran down Fiona's face. "I only wanted to scare her. Not hurt her."

"It's the same thing. Scaring someone is hurting them psychologically. Either way, you meant harm to her, and I won't have that. Stay away from us."

I got into my car and drove to my office, where I researched Brittany Parker. She had a website where she posted pictures of her in previous beauty pageants. I cringed at some images of her as a child. Those outfits weren't appropriate for little girls. Now I understood why Michelle hated pageants. They exploited children, making them into tiny versions of adults. I didn't find that attractive, but I knew sick men would.

She had a daughter, Lily, who was also enrolled in pageants. A recent picture showed a European pageant hosted in Reykjavik last week, which explained why they were here in Iceland.

What did Brittany have against Michelle? I tabled the issue for now and checked my calendar and reminders. I searched for James McNabb, the former police officer who had died at my Whitewater Family Resort. His social media profile showed he'd worked for the Providence Police Department but had been fired a few years ago.

I logged into a thread posted on his social media page. After reading through several posts, I discovered James McNabb was suing Dominic Bryson, the police chief. Apparently, James claimed he'd been framed and the chief was corrupt.

This was no coincidence. I had assumed my high school nemesis had changed his ways since he became chief but I supposed some things didn't change.

Did Dominic kill James McNabb because he had evidence of the corruption? But why in Oregon—at my excursion site? Perhaps that was a coincidence. Maybe he just wanted James dead somewhere far from Rhode Island and didn't know I owned the site.

I needed to think clearly to see the entire picture. I made a chart of all the issues, the players, and their connections. Thinking like a scientist would help me stay organized.

I had to assume Dominic was after me. Why was he suddenly interested in my life after all these years?

I remembered the day the police released me to go home. Thankfully, I was supposed to hang out at Grayson's house that night, so Aunt Klara had no idea I'd been in jail.

Dominic stayed away from me after that day, so this news about him coming back with a vendetta intrigued me. Why now?

My head throbbed with all this new information. Missing Michelle, I drove home wanting to see her and touch her. As I parked in the garage, my phone rang.

I picked up the call. "Yo, what's up, Remi?"

"You should check out the news for Providence, Rhode Island."

"What's going on?" I exited the car and entered my apartment. My body relaxed when I saw Michelle's smiling face.

"They just announced the name of the person whose bones were in my garage. I think you might know him."

Fuck. I didn't know how much more bad news I could take in one day.

"I just got back home. Let me settle in, and I'll look."

"We should all have a video chat when you're ready."

I agreed and hung up the phone.

"Are you okay?" Michelle slipped her hands around my waist, kissing me on the lips.

"Just a minor headache."

She kissed my forehead. "All better?"

"A little. I'll need a lot more kisses." I tightened my arms around her, loving the comfort she provided. Her scent and warmth eased the nerves in my body.

Something big was happening, and there was nothing I could do to stop it. I didn't want her near whatever was looming.

"You look stressed." She placed a hand on my face. "What happened while you were out? Who did this to you? Tell me, and I'll make him pay."

Her adorable threat eased the pounding headache. "Want to catch up on some current affairs in Providence?" I led her to my office.

"You can watch the news from the States here?"

I sat down in my armchair and pulled her into my lap. Grabbing my tablet, I turned it on. "I have access to a satellite that allows me to watch whatever I want in any country."

She leaned against my chest, and we watched the Providence news discussing the identification of the bones discovered in Starke Vision's garage.

"That's Remi's marketing company!" Michelle exclaimed. "I remembered Audri talking about it."

I doubted Michelle knew the entire story because Audri probably didn't know it either. Slash, a member of the crime organization, had saved my friends and me when we inadvertently witnessed the crime at the abandoned church. He had warned us not to share what we'd seen with anyone, or the organization would kill our families and us. As young boys, we'd been scared shitless.

Though some of us got glimpses from our drones, Remi and Grayson got the better view from where they stood on the balcony. That day, we'd been excited to meet and discuss our WaterFyre Rising video game at the abandoned church, our official meeting place. But a group of criminals murdered a man there. That man's body had somehow been buried inside the garage of Remi's marketing firm. A construction worker had discovered the body during renovation.

The reporter with the short brown hair said, "It's a sad day for the City of Providence. We have identified City Councilman Edward Bryson as the person buried inside a garage here in the city. Edward was reported missing by his family years ago and was never found. His services will be held next week. He leaves behind a wife and a son. His son Dominic Bryson serves as the police chief for our city. Our hearts go out to the Bryson family . . ."

I'd heard enough and tuned out the rest of the news. The pieces were falling into place, but there were still so many little gaps. Was Dominic after my friends and me? We had nothing to do with his father's death. What exactly did he know about the incident?

Reaching for my phone, I sent my boys a text.

You guys available for a chat tonight?

They all replied yes.

Michelle looked at me with concern. "Do you know the city council?"

"No. But his son was the bully I fought with in high school." What did Dominic want from me? He could hurt Michelle if he knew how important she was to me. "Let's have an early dinner, okay? I've got a conference with the boys tonight."

She considered me. I could tell she had more questions and was thankful she didn't press. "Say hello to the Water-Fyre men for me." Her eyes sparkled. "Or if you prefer to keep our relationship—"

"I want the world to know you're mine."

Her face brightened. "I need to tell my SSG 003 too."

"What's that? Sounds like a secret code."

"It is." She wiggled her eyebrows. "Super Spy Girls 003. The girls and I dressed up as spies one Halloween and it stuck. You know, I had a special mission for you." She poked me in the abdomen.

"Oh yeah?" My brows lifted with fascination. "What did you have in mind? Apprehend me for stealing your heart? Tie me up so you can have your way with me? All you have to do is ask, angel. I'll let you do whatever you desire."

This lighthearted conversation erased the darkness weighing on me from earlier.

"It's called From Iceland with Love. I wanted to know if you wanted me as more than a friend. Now I know. This country is special to me—it gave me *you*."

Her honesty penetrated my heart, filling it with so much love I didn't know how to react. My heart had never felt so soft, so vulnerable, and so completely bare to her. She didn't know she'd yanked off my armor with a simple statement that possessed more power than anything I'd encountered. This woman was the only woman who could truly hurt me.

I embraced her, and we stayed like that for a long moment.

"From Iceland with Love is my mission too. I'll give you everything you deserve."

"You already have."

I was going to wait and tell her about Fiona and Brittany, but it was probably best to inform her now. It could give Michelle time to evaluate the situation and prepare for the next step. Brittany Parker was on a mission to destroy my woman, and I'd make sure she knew my wrath.

Pulling back, I looked into her eyes. "Fiona had someone smash your window. She wanted to scare you off so you'd run back to the States and leave me here for her."

Michelle crinkled her forehead. "She's insane."

"She won't bother us anymore." I inhaled a breath. "But there's someone else who wants to harm you. She's responsible for the thief and the bomb. This person appears to be more unstable than Fiona."

"Who?"

"Brittany Parker. Do you remember her?"

A look of disbelief washed over her. "How could I forget her? She made my life hell. But gosh, that was so long ago. What happened back then was just something between rivals."

"She's in Iceland with her daughter Lily for a competition."

Michelle leaned against the wall as a revelation splashed on her face. "Oh. Shit." She placed a hand on her heart. "She was at the charity event. I didn't recognize her at all. She looked different. Why does she want to hurt me now? I don't understand."

That was something I wanted to know too. I told Michelle about Brittany's ex-boyfriend and how the police were searching for him. "Just be cautious about your surroundings."

"Thank you for letting me know." She blew out a breath. "I want to be informed about any updates, okay? I'd rather know, even if it's bad."

"You got it."

"Go meet with your buddies. I'm going to chat with my girls too."

CHAPTER FORTY

MICHELLE

AFTER ROYCE WENT into his office and closed the door, I took a moment to absorb the information about Brittany. Never in my wildest dreams did I think she'd come after me. Could she have held a grudge for that long?

I opened a new browser tab on my computer and searched for her name. Her website offered current photos of her. She didn't look like the Brittany I knew. Her cheekbones appeared higher, and the contours of her face looked smoother. The full lips were too pronounced. No wonder I didn't recognize her during my flight to Iceland, at the grocery store, or at the charity event.

I sighed when I saw photos of Lily in the inappropriate outfits. Brittany was grooming her daughter to be like her.

What had I done to Brittany to make her want to hurt me? Jealousy? We weren't kids in pageants anymore. If she wanted my tiaras and trophies, she could have them. They had no meaning other than as a reminder of my suffering back then.

Feeling exhausted and not wanting to look at stressful things, I turned off my computer and concentrated on the joyful news.

I sent a text to my group chat. *You busy? Wanna catch up?*

When they all replied yes, I started the three-way phone call.

"Give me the deets right now!" Kiera exclaimed.

"How do you know I have deets? Can't I just call my girls because I *miss* them?"

"You can, but we have radar for these kinds of things. Mine just erected. Spill it, Missy," Audri said with a laugh.

"Nice choice of words, Audri! I love the word 'erected!'" Kiera laughed over the phone. "Makes me *upright* and *alert*."

Gosh, I could always count on them to make me laugh.

"Royce and I are dating now," I said.

Audri gasped. "I knew it! How did it happen?"

"Did you do the deed yet?" Kiera asked. "How is he in bed?"

My smile widened at their enthusiasm, and I told them how the fake dating turned into something real.

"I'm so happy for you!" Audri said.

"He's a sex god in bed." I beamed, thinking about our time in the wilderness.

Kiera purred. "He looks like a Nordic warrior, so I can imagine the power he wields."

Oh, there was indeed some powerful hammering and then some, but I kept that to myself.

"I'm coming back in two weeks, so we should plan on a girls' night out."

"Definitely," said Audri. "I can't wait to hear about you two."

"Anything new with you guys?"

"Not really. I'm busy helping a friend throw a big fashion show for charity. I'm photographing a lot of stunning men. Did you know that Forrest models?"

"He does?" Audri asked. "He never mentioned it. But you know how the boys are when we're all hanging out. They only talk about their video games, food, and sports."

"Yeah, he was in a photoshoot with a bunch of guys. I was surprised when I saw him. The camera loves him, though."

"Like how I didn't know Royce was a doctor. He got his PhD in volcanology and mentioned nothing about that."

Kiera snorted. "We're surrounded by a bunch of nerds. Very handsome nerds, though."

"A brilliant mind is sexy. I love my hot nerd," Audri said. "Anything else exciting over there?"

"More like dangerous." I didn't want to change the energy of the conversation, but I needed to share about Fiona and Brittany with them. Audri and Kiera were like sisters to me.

"What?" Kiera exclaimed, cursing up a storm. I could imagine her eyes narrowed to slits whenever she got protective. "The bitches are just jealous."

"Be extra careful, though," Audri said. "A jealous woman can be unpredictable."

"I am. Royce is making sure I don't go anywhere without him."

"I love him more for that," Audri said.

We continued our conversation for a few more minutes until they had to go. I felt better every time I talked to my girls. Genuine friends were treasures I cherished.

I cleared my head as best as I could and went back to

work, trying to finish everything before I returned to Providence. Fiona and Brittany didn't have my permission to infiltrate my life more than they already had. I'd wasted enough energy on them.

CHAPTER FORTY-ONE

"THERE'S something you should know about what I've encountered recently. It ties back to that unfortunate event we witnessed years ago." I stared at my boys on the computer screen.

Remington, Grayson, Forrest, and Arrow looked at me inquisitively.

"What happened?" Remi asked, raking a hand through his brown hair.

"Dominic Bryson is the police chief for Providence. He was also my high school bully. I believe he's been sabotaging my excursion sites, even killing someone at the Oregon location."

"The fuck?!" Grayson exclaimed, looking angry. His black hair seemed shorter than the last time I'd seen him.

Ever since Grayson discovered his uncle had killed his father and betrayed the family, my carefree friend changed. Now, every time I saw Grayson, anger and sadness surrounded him. He used to throw parties at his house, but they stopped when his uncle was imprisoned for kidnapping Audri.

"Do you need our help with anything?" Forrest scratched his beard. "You can't do much when you're stuck in Iceland. We can handle things easier on our end."

"I'm still trying to figure things out. I'll let you know. We should all be cautious. We don't know what Dominic is up to. Is he after me because I broke his arm when we fought in high school, or does it have anything to do with his father's death?"

"We didn't have anything to do with that." Arrow adjusted the cap that hid his light brown hair.

"But he doesn't know that," Remi added. "The city probably informed him about the bone identification before it was announced publicly."

"Maybe he found out about our drones?" Grayson wondered.

"It could be anything," Forrest said. "Though we had nothing to do with Edward Bryson's death, anyone with a vendetta could frame us. It'll be an inconvenience for all of us and our families."

That was what I feared. They could come after me, but concern for my aunt and Michelle trumped everything.

Remi's jaw twitched, and I knew he was thinking about Audri. "We've extracted the recordings from our drones and saved them in a secured drive. We haven't needed to pull them out. It's our proof that we didn't kill anyone." He paused a moment before continuing, "But the killers could come after us because of the proof. Let's see what Dominic has planned and we can react accordingly. This is all speculation right now. We'll have to tread carefully."

We all agreed, and our conversation diverted to our video game, which was a better topic.

"I have a few more updates for Level Two before I can show you guys. I'll upload it as soon as I can."

"I can't wait, man!" Arrow leaned back in his chair, rubbing his hands together.

"We got a few more investors who want in on our venture. With their support, this video game will take the world by storm."

A cheerful roar erupted from my friends. We had bonded over this game, which symbolized so much for us. For me, water and fire were important elements of nature. Some would say they were opposites, but in truth, when different energies combined at a chemical level, magic occurred. It was like the process of lava meeting water. It sizzled and created steam. Steam became the magic as lava formed into rocks. So yes, opposites could create beauty.

In WaterFyre Rising, the "waterfyre" was the other-worldly force that kept the players alive. For each level of the game, the player gained new versions of waterfyre. I didn't realize the significance and depth of the game until I started building it. Each level represented the creator. Level Two was me, and I could make that world into anything I wanted. The game was my dream to make a better life for myself—my evolution.

To see each level created was to see the development of my friends.

Our conversation ended as it was getting late. I had to sort out everything in my head before I contacted the police department tomorrow. They needed to apprehend Brittany as well as her ex-boyfriend. She was probably back in the States or another country.

I had to shift my schedule and delegate tasks to my management team. I needed more time to look into Oskar, Brittany, and Dominic.

CHAPTER FORTY-TWO

MICHELLE

A SADNESS OVERCAME me as I embraced Royce at the airport. My stay in Iceland had ended, and I'd turned in all my blog posts to NewYou Beauty earlier than the agreed deadline. They had a few days to review what I'd written and request any changes. No new requests were made, and they loved how I portrayed their company and mission.

The first blog post went live on my site four days ago. It had garnered five hundred thousand dollars in revenue for NewYou Beauty. Fiona's blog gained one hundred thousand dollars in profits. I'd asked NewYou Beauty to create a discount code for me to offer to my readers. With that code, NewYou could track which sales came from my blog. With the tremendous success, NewYou hired me to create a monthly blog to promote their products. I accepted the offer with glee because I believed in their company and mission.

NewYou Beauty gave me a huge supply to take home, which was in the suitcase that Royce had checked.

I tightened my arms around him, inhaling his musky scent, never wanting to forget it. How could I leave him when someone was trying to hurt him? They hadn't located Brittany, and the police had discovered Larus's body in an alley with multiple gunshot wounds.

"It's safer for you to be in the States," Royce said. "You have more people you know around you."

I had other jobs waiting for me at home, and though they were mostly remote work, I had an apartment and other responsibilities that needed my attention.

"What about you?" I spoke into his shoulder. "When are you coming back?"

"I have some things to take care of before I can head home to Providence. But soon." Royce rubbed circles on my back.

"Don't go out alone," I muttered. "Hire a security guard."

He drew back and smiled. "I'll be okay. I have someone looking into all my employees to ensure they haven't been bought by someone else." He stroked my cheek. "I want you to be careful wherever you go. Text me as soon as you land, okay?"

Understanding his concern, I nodded. "I want you to inform me when you're out and about too."

He smirked. "I'm not used to answering to anyone, but I can bend the rules for you."

My feelings for this man had grown exponentially. Nothing could keep us apart, not even an ocean. The heart could sense things no matter the distance. I'd found the person who had saved me so long ago by crossing an ocean into a different country. What else did fate have in store for us? Only time could tell.

"I'm going to miss you so much, Royce."

"You don't know how much I'll miss you. I wish I could shrink you, put you in my pocket, and take you everywhere."

"Like a stress ball?" I laughed.

The green eyes sparkled, making it my favorite shade of green. "It made you smile, didn't it?"

He looked more exhausted than I'd ever seen him. "You need more sleep. That's an order."

"I've got some deadlines to meet, but I'll sleep early tonight."

The announcement for my flight boomed through the airport, and I kissed him, breaking free from his embrace. "Don't cause trouble without me. Save it for me."

I loved the handsome smile on his face. "I only want to cause trouble with you. Have a safe flight."

Waving goodbye, I headed to my terminal and discovered Royce had upgraded my seat to first class.

After tucking my carry-on into the overhead compartment, I settled into my roomy seat and closed my eyes. Two months had flown by, yet there were moments that seemed to have remained still. So many precious memories left their mark on my heart.

People were right when they said life could change in a split second. Mine did in Iceland. I fell in love. Royce didn't know it, and even I couldn't believe it. The feeling was new and exciting, and I needed time for it to settle. Perhaps the distance between us would allow the heart to acclimate to this newness. Right now, I was vulnerable because my heart was open to Royce for the taking.

"Crap!" a woman shouted near me.

I opened my eyes and turned. A stunning woman crouched on the floor, picking up scattered contents from her purse. She had dirty blonde hair piled up into a bun and wore an aqua top with dark knit pants.

I got out of my seat and picked up some travel-sized

bottles of lotions and creams from the Blue Lagoon for her. "Here you go."

"Oh, thank you very much," she said with a slight European accent. "I'm Natalie. Nice to meet you."

"I'm Michelle. I see you're a fan of the Blue Lagoon."

"Yes. I've been there a few times. But this visit was for a bachelorette party," she whispered. "I didn't want to go, but it's a family friend. You know how that is."

"I understand. Well, next time you should visit NewYou Beauty Resort. They have a freshwater lagoon, a seawater spa, and excellent beauty products. I *love* them."

I should get a commission for promoting NewYou Beauty like this.

"I'll try them out next time."

Natalie had big blue eyes that reminded me of a clear blue sky and flawless skin that would make women envy her. Even with no makeup, she looked gorgeous.

I returned to my seat and continued the conversation with my new neighbor, who sat across the aisle from me.

"Do you live in Providence or a nearby city?" Natalie asked.

"In Providence. You?"

"Same. I work for the city, so it makes it easier."

"I don't mean to pry, but you have a lovely accent. Where are you from?"

"France, but I've been learning English since I was a child."

The flight flew by, and Natalie and I became fast friends. She also liked to travel and promised to visit my blog when she got home. We exchanged numbers, and I invited her to our girls' night out. I knew Audri and Kiera would love her.

Royce had arranged for a car to pick me up. I checked my phone to find a message from him.

His name is Bob, and he's a trusted driver. You can go with him.

Royce even attached a full photo of Bob for me to see. He had short white hair, a friendly face, and a round belly.

Michelle: *Landed safely. Thanks for the car service.*

Royce: *You're welcome. Miss you.*

Michelle: *Miss you more. (heart emoji) Gotta go. Chat later.*

Royce: *(heart emoji)(kiss emoji)*

His thoughtfulness surprised me. As CEO of his excursion empire, he must have been used to preparing for things in advance. With so much going on lately, I didn't think he'd have time to schedule a car service for me.

It felt nice to be someone's priority.

Smiling, I let Bob take my luggage and escort me to the black SUV. "Thanks for the ride." He wore a puffy blue coat and dark pants.

"You're welcome." He recited my address, and I confirmed that was where I wanted to go.

Sitting in the back seat, I couldn't help but remember who had picked me up from the Keflavik Airport. Oskar had seemed like a nice man. What had made him turn against his employer? Was Bob like Oskar?

I flicked my gaze to Bob, who was focused on merging onto the highway. Royce had probably done extensive research on his employees after the incident with Oskar.

I texted my friends, informing them I was back in the city and for us to meet Friday night at the Krazee Tavern for drinks. That gave me some time to settle in and deal with chores.

CHAPTER FORTY-THREE

ROYCE

AFTER RESEARCHING DOMINIC BRYSON, I discovered he had a long list of crimes to his name. He should have never become Chief of Police.

I walked up to Oskar's house just as his wife, Sara, exited the front door. She had short curly hair, and dark circles formed under her sad eyes. Grief sagged on her face as she approached me.

"I'm sorry—"

"No. You lost your husband, and your children lost their father. *I'm* sorry for your loss."

From what I heard, Sara had a small funeral for Oskar, even though his body hadn't been found. Maybe the animals in the woods got to him, or the water from the ravine took his body elsewhere. The closure allowed Sara and her kids to move on.

"Thank you. Come this way." She gestured for me to follow her to a swing set on the side of the house. "The babysitter is watching the kids while I run out to the grocery store. The refrigerator needs to be stocked. Life has to go on."

She looked at me. "I'm sorry about what Oskar did to you and the company. I should have seen it."

"What do you know?"

"He left a voicemail for me, saying he was sorry he couldn't be there for the kids and me. He got into trouble with someone and was afraid they were watching him." She tucked her hands into her jacket pockets. "Even though he hadn't been working, he'd been acting strange, always talking on the phone, looking stressed. I remember overhearing him say he didn't want to do something."

"Do you know who he's been talking to?"

"No." She shook her head. "In his voicemail, he told me to apologize to you and that he never meant to hurt you." Sara touched my arm. "There's something you don't know. Oskar had lung cancer. There was nothing the doctors could do. He only had six months to a year to live." She paused and wiped away the tears. "I don't know what he got himself into, but I know it was for money to take care of the mortgage and raise our kids. My teaching job doesn't pay well enough."

This news filled in the gaps. Had Dominic offered Oskar money to hurt me? If not Dominic, then who?

A man who knew his life had an early end date would do anything to protect his family.

Oskar, you should have come to me.

Though he had betrayed me, I understood why. I didn't blame him. He was a dying man with limited options. He could have killed me, but he didn't. That made all the difference.

Sometimes, circumstances forced us to make tough choices. I was grateful to be alive so I could drag the fucker responsible for Oskar's death to hell. I had no doubt Oskar died because he failed his mission.

I looked at Sara. "Do you need my help with anything?"

She pressed her lips into a tight line. "No, thank you."

I sensed the lie and the pride, but didn't press. "Okay. Someone from my company will contact you to go over the life insurance policies paid out to employees."

"I thought he only had one policy there."

"No, he had three. We offered a special add-on just last year. He probably forgot to tell you."

Now it was my turn to lie. Sara's guilt and pride wouldn't allow her to accept my help, so I improvised. As I fabricated the lie, I realized that sometimes bending the truth was necessary for a positive outcome. Not everything was what it seemed.

At that moment, I truly understood what Oskar did. He lied to his family and me so he could protect us.

CHAPTER FORTY-FOUR

MICHELLE

AS I DEALT with the pile of mail, it reminded me that Thanksgiving was in two weeks, which meant my mom, Charles, and I would have a small dinner together like we did every year.

I tossed the miscellaneous mail into the recycling bin and looked out the window at the gray sky. A sense of longing blanketed me. I missed Royce tremendously. I'd only been back for less than a week, but it felt like a year. I hadn't worked out in a few days and felt sluggish. I also needed to do some grocery shopping.

My phone pinged with my daily reminder:

Food: *Food is your friend. Eat healthy. Don't overdo it.*

Daily Exercise: *1 hour of cardio. 30 minutes of weights. 30 minutes of yoga.*

Motivation: *You're doing fantastic! Wear that pretty dress you love!*

Don't forget this: *What are you grateful for today?*

Another message came through as I was about to plan

what I needed to eat. My heart skipped at Royce's name, and I swiped away the reminder to reply to him.

Royce: *How's my woman doing?*

Michelle: *Good. How's my man doing?*

Royce: *Busy wrapping things up. Will be back for Thanksgiving.*

Michelle: *I'm having Thanksgiving lunch with my mom. Wanna come?*

Royce: *Always want to come inside you. All over you. (laugh emoji)*

Michelle: *You're so bad. (eye roll emoji)*

Royce: *Your fault. Yes, I'd love to go. Wanna join me for Thanksgiving dinner with my aunt?*

Michelle: *Okay. I want to hear your voice.*

He called immediately, and I spent the next three hours on the phone with him until he had to attend an online conference. I couldn't remember the last time I chatted on the phone for that long. We talked about everything. Even the silent moments didn't feel awkward. It was as though the phone offered us the "invisible" touch we craved where words weren't necessary. The longing I'd sensed earlier lessened after our chat.

I sat on my couch smiling like some high school girl who'd just gotten a date with her secret admirer when a pretty image popped into my phone with the title Eat Your Monsters. I didn't recall downloading this app, but I often bought interesting apps or was given free ones from vendors I'd promoted.

I should probably delete all these apps I'm not using.

As I clicked on the beautiful landscape, my finger accidentally touched a flower icon, and the screen opened to an option for a male or female version of an adorable little creature. Before I knew it, I was a bunny battling beasts while trying to save a village of cute animals from being destroyed. My reward was a golden apple and a few reminders that looked familiar:

Food: *Whatever your heart wants.*

Daily Exercise: *Running around with compassion.*

Motivation: *You saved the Lavender Cuties from the Scaly Wolf. You earned five golden points for the accessory shop.*

Don't forget this: *You're awesome!*

Smiling to myself that I did indeed save a bunch of cute cranes, I rose and made a mental note to check out the app again later on. It looked like an updated version of my current reminder app. Regardless, I'd spent thirty minutes on the darn thing and didn't feel guilty one bit. Who said electronics were bad for you? That person had never played Eat Your Monsters.

I had an hour before I had to meet my friends at the Krazee Tavern at seven. The day had disappeared in a blink, and I only remembered doing two things: chatting with Royce and playing on the app. I wasn't sure if that was a good or bad sign.

CHAPTER FORTY-FIVE

MICHELLE

WEARING jeans and an ivory sweater under a light wool jacket, I entered the crowded Krazee Tavern, which Remi owned.

"There she is!" Audri waved from the table in the far corner and rose to her feet. As always, she looked chic and beautiful with her long black hair, classy makeup, and elegant jewelry. She threw her arms open.

I walked into her arms and squeezed. "God, I miss you guys!"

"Ditto!" Kiera jumped from her seat, offering me a hug too.

I glanced around. "Natalie should arrive soon. I want you to meet her. She's like us."

"As in gorgeous and crazy?" Kiera asked.

"And sarcastically amusing," added Audri.

Sitting down, I offered them each a gift bag full of NewYou Beauty products.

"Oh, these look fantastic." Audri peeked into her bag. "Thank you."

"Thanks, babe. You know how much I love lathering myself with beauty products."

"If anyone can set up a little shop from all the freebies she gets, it's you." I grinned at Kiera.

Kiera shrugged. "I can't help it if the vendors love me."

"Sorry, I'm late." Natalie approached and shrugged off her black jacket, revealing a light pink sweater with an asymmetrical neckline that made her appear elegant and stylish, but not overdone.

"You're fine," I said. "Girls, meet Natalie Chapelle."

"I love that sweater." Kiera eyed Natalie's outfit. "I don't mean to sound snobby, but I'm a fashion photographer and used to seeing various designs. I'm curious. Who are you wearing?"

Natalie grinned. "Oh, it's LaRue, a French label."

"Ohhh . . . I've heard of them. They're on top with Chanel and Dior."

"Yes, they are, but the House of LaRue is on a smaller scale."

"I'm Audri. Very nice to meet you."

"I'm so happy to meet all of you." Natalie draped the jacket over the chair and slid into her seat. "Thanks for inviting me. I don't know many people here in town."

"I hear you're working for the city." Audri grabbed a french fry and bit into it. "What brings you across the pond to work in a city like Providence when you could hang out in Paris? Providence isn't as historical or fashionable as Paris."

I hadn't had fries in a while and grabbed one too. The waitress returned to the table, and Natalie ordered a Mai Tai.

"Just family stuff." Natalie lifted her shoulder. "Sometimes you just want a change of scenery, you know?"

"Yeah, I hear you. That need for change took me to Iceland. It was well worth it."

"I told Remi that you and Royce are dating. He was surprised." Audri sipped her Blue Hawaiian cocktail.

Maybe Royce forgot to mention it to his friends about us. A sliver of disappointment pricked my skin. Why didn't he tell his friends? Why was I even thinking about that? With the danger surrounding Royce and his business, our relationship should be the least of his concerns.

I scolded myself for the pettiness.

"It's not something a guy talks about with a bunch of friends." Kiera set her margarita down. "They don't go into a gathering and say, 'Hey, guess what? I'm dating!'"

Her waving hands and silly face amused me, tossing out the fear that Royce didn't value our relationship the way I did. When she put it like that, I understood why the topic didn't come up.

"Men view relationships differently than women. They're all business or shooting the breeze about irrelevant things."

The three guys at the table close to us roared obscenities when a sports team didn't score. They argued with another group sitting across from them.

"Like sports, video games, or stocks." Audri arched an eyebrow at the loud men.

"Women, on the other hand, are smarter." Kiera winked. "Because we talk about said men. And their idiosyncrasies."

We all burst out laughing.

"By the way, I told my friend I'd help him raise money for the Youth Center and Food Pantry. It's almost Thanksgiving, so there are people in need. Want to paint some T-shirts for a silent auction?"

"Sure, I'd love to. When? Where?" Audri asked.

"Tomorrow at The Church of Compassion. They start at ten, but you can come at noon. I can paint about five T-shirts, but if we all paint five, that'll be twenty for the charity."

I didn't have any plans for Saturday and wanted to contribute. "I'm down."

Natalie also joined.

"Thanks, guys!" Kiera exclaimed.

A pretty Asian girl walked by our table as one guy cursed at another. She met my gaze and rolled her eyes. I smiled, understanding her annoyance. I'd never witnessed this kind of raucous behavior at the restaurant before.

The guy with spiky hair reached out and groped the Asian girl. She whirled around and slapped him. He jumped up from his chair and shoved her with so much force she slammed into Audri and they both crashed to the floor.

My heart raced at terror surfaced, reminding me of the explosion in Iceland.

"What's wrong with you, asshole?" Kiera shouted as she got up from her seat.

I joined her and helped Audri and the Asian girl. "You okay?"

The jerk cursed and hurled a fist at me, but the Asian girl leaped forward and blocked this arm. She threw an uppercut into his jaw, and he fell backward.

That action enraged Spiky Hair even more.

"You think you're big and tough, pushing everyone around?" she demanded with eyes sharp as blades.

"Bitch!" He charged at her, but men from a different table got to him first.

A fight erupted, and the bouncer tried to break it up but

failed. There were five rough guys and one bouncer. The poor guy was going to get hurt.

Two men from a different table approached, trying to break up the fight.

"Cut it out," said the man with short brown hair. Where had I seen him?

Remi, Grayson, Forrest, and Arrow appeared from the back like a pissed-off pack of alpha males, yanking the men apart.

With tundra aqua eyes, Remi whipped a glance at Audri, rubbing her arm. "You okay? What happened?"

"That asshole shoved a customer who fell onto Audri, pushing her to the floor." Kiera crossed her arms, narrowing her eyes at Spiky Hair, whose eyes looked glazed. He had to be on something other than alcohol.

"I'm okay," Audri said.

"The fuck?" Remi twisted Spiky Hair's arm back.

"Give him to me," said the familiar man. "My men will be here soon."

"Chief Bryson, what brings you here tonight?" Remi asked in surprise.

"Just having a drink after office hours. Then I saw these assholes causing trouble and tried to intervene."

My heart pounded faster at the recognition of Royce's former bully. I wanted to kick him, but that wouldn't help the situation. Was he looking to start trouble with Royce thinking he'd be here? Or was it a coincidence that I got to see Dominic Bryson in person? Regardless, my body shivered standing near him.

"Thank you for your assistance. I'd like them all arrested and banned from my restaurant." Remi dragged Spiky Hair to the front door.

Grayson wore an irritated expression as he gestured the other troublemakers to follow suit. Walking by, he flicked a glance at Natalie, who appeared surprised to see him. They knew each other?

Kiera eyed Forrest as he spoke to the witnesses nearby. He had olive skin and an athletic build. Turning, he met her gaze, nodded, and left.

Arrow walked up to me. "You okay?"

"I'm fine." I turned to my savior. "Thanks for blocking the hit. What's your name? I'm Michelle Yates."

"Vivian Vo, and you're welcome. Men who hit women deserve to be punished."

"They sure do." I shivered at how I'd frozen in place at that moment. The violence unsettled me. Maybe I should take some self-defense classes.

Arrow looked at Vivian. "Black belt?"

Vivian sized him up and nodded. "I know some kung fu."

Grayson hollered at Arrow, and he excused himself.

I whipped a look at Vivian. "Do you offer classes?"

She laughed. "No time. But I know of a place you can go for classes. Martial Arts Studio is a great place. I go there sometimes to work out."

I'd seen that studio before. It was at a plaza not too far from my apartment.

"I should sign up too," Natalie said. "Living in the city alone is dangerous."

"Kiera, Audri, want to sign up for self-defense classes with me? Maybe they have a group discount."

"Remi can teach me at home," Audri replied.

"But it'll be more fun with *us*, and you can use what you've learned to spar with him," I said, laughing.

"Excellent idea," Audri agreed as she helped the waiter move the chairs back to our table.

"Sign me up." Kiera sat back down, and we resumed our conversation and drinks, all of which were on the house.

CHAPTER FORTY-SIX

ROYCE

MY HEAD SPUN with all the issues I had to deal with. Each one required careful consideration because one misstep could make everything worse. Dominic Bryson could yank my friends and me into the limelight involving his father's death even though we had nothing to do with it. The spotlight would make us a target for more dangerous people who thrived in the dark. These were the people who killed his father—people with whom Grayson's uncle, Derek, had been involved. They belonged to a secret society that no one knew about.

I preferred to stay away from problems as best I could. I took a leave of absence from my project for the Volcanic Sustainability Research Program to deal with these looming issues.

After reviewing all the evidence I'd gathered and the information the PI had retrieved, I formed a plan to meet Dominic face-to-face.

Releasing a sigh, I leaned back in my chair, and Michelle's face popped into my vision. My apartment had felt cold and empty without her. Before Michelle, my apartment was a home furnished with everything a successful man could have and want. But after she made her mark here, it hadn't been the same. I missed the echoes of her laughter, the scent of her perfume, the warmth in her eyes when she looked at me, and the smoothness of her skin against my palms.

I never imagined I could miss someone this much, but here I was, wishing she were with me. Chatting over the phone for hours had never been my thing. I'd never had this much patience with other women. Twenty minutes over the phone was the longest conversation I could have before boredom set in. But with Michelle, I wanted to continue talking to her even after we'd been chatting for three hours.

What the fuck was wrong with me? What could we possibly be talking about for that long? Everything. I wanted to know everything about her. Her dreams, her fears. Listening to her voice was a song my heart needed to hear.

I was a goner, and I knew it. Now, I needed to tread carefully so that I didn't end up hurting her. What if I couldn't be the man she wanted me to be? Though I felt strongly for her, was that enough? Michelle seemed like she needed more. Could I offer her what she needed? Was I capable of that? As of right now, my answer was no.

My emotions had a limit. To go beyond that was entering unknown territory—dangerous grounds I didn't want to think about. How could I love when I didn't believe in it? Nothing in my life had proven that love was worth it. All I'd ever witnessed were heartache and suffering. Michelle didn't deserve that.

I didn't want to lie to her or make false promises, so I'd

keep my thoughts to myself and enjoy the present moments with her. What came next would be dealt with later.

Despite the anxiety stabbing me, just thinking about Michelle made me smile. All responsibilities mattered less when it came to her.

Helping her conquer her fears had been important to me. I knew how fear could hold a person back. It had held me back when I was younger. Back then, I discovered a way to maneuver around it to defeat it. With that experience, I'd help Michelle realize *she* had the power. Nothing outside of herself could take that away.

This acknowledgement allowed me to charge forth, claiming my success. The thought brought me back to WaterFyre Rising. I opened a new browser and logged into the demo for Level Two. Remi had created his Level One demo, where the player fought off several city kings. Remi created special portals from the fire basins that mimicked the ones the city lit during the actual WaterFire event in Providence. One of those portals took the player to my world only after they beat the last villain. Remi had injected parts of his life, hopes, and dreams into his world, making it unique.

I did the same with my world. Initially, it was a wilderness inhabited by fantastical creatures. Now I had other ideas to incorporate, all thanks to Michelle. Working on the game with my boys had taught me many things. I'd learned how to create sketches—extremely rough illustrations—of my ideas and thrown them into a program for image manipulation and coding. I'd acquired new skills necessary to make my dream come true. Would I have worked so hard to learn these skills if I didn't have this dream? No. When and where there was passion, magic happened.

Once the demos for each game level were approved by

all of us, we'd send them out to a service for finalization and testing, and so on. There were so many steps to making a video game, and each one was an intricate process. We took our time because this video game wasn't just to make money—though it was a side benefit. WaterFyre Rising was our evolution—the building blocks of our hearts and souls. At least for me it was.

So far, everything for the game flowed smoothly.

After working on Level Two for a few hours, a sense of satisfaction washed over me. I saved my work and logged off. With a clearer mind, I reviewed the proposal to purchase Hallsson's Excursions and sent it off to my lawyer to review. He could oversee the acquisition for me. Einar Hallsson would like the numbers I'd offered him. When that deal was finalized, I could think about renovating it to suit my needs.

I should have called it a night, but I thought about Michelle and stayed up working on a project close to my heart.

CHAPTER FORTY-SEVEN

MICHELLE

WHEN I ARRIVED at the craft room in the Youth Center and Food Pantry, Kiera, Audri, and Natalie were already there. Five long tables were scattered around the spacious room. My friends occupied the table near the window. Each table had about three to four volunteers.

The clock on the wall showed I still had ten minutes before ten o'clock.

Approaching my friends, I shrugged off my jacket and draped it over a chair. "I didn't expect all of you to be here so early."

"I was already up, so I figured I could help. Remi is with his boys." Audri held a paintbrush and stared at a blank white T-shirt spread out on the table in front of her.

Tubes of paint, a container of stencils, and other craft items lay in several containers.

Kiera walked over to a rack, grabbed a stack of T-shirts, and dropped them on our table. "Go wild and crazy. I want to see how much money our group will raise!"

"I'll make something for Remi and make him bid for it." Audri smiled.

"Exactly my thinking. All the T-shirts will be displayed on the website, so he can bid online." Kiera turned to me.

Understanding the intention, I reached for a T-shirt from the pile. "I'll have Royce place a bid too." That idea had already been in my head.

Smiling, Natalie shook her head. "Seems like you know how to network and run a successful charity."

Kiera slung an arm around Audri and me. "They're the only ones with billionaire boyfriends. Might as well put the rich guys to use."

"I feel so used," I teased. "Wait until it's your turn. Who are you dating now? I didn't have time to ask you yesterday."

"Right now, no one." Kiera squirted some paint onto a small plastic dish. "I'm taking a hiatus, which is why I have time to volunteer."

Kiera never had trouble getting dates. As a fashion photographer, she met gorgeous men all the time, and she was as hot as the female models she photographed. But I'd never know her to stay with a guy longer than a few months.

I bumped shoulders with Natalie, spreading out the T-shirt on the table. "What about you? Are you seeing anyone?"

"Not right now. Too busy getting the lay of the land at work. I'm trying to get an inspector into a building before the renovations can be approved, but the owner isn't cooperating." She took a floral stencil and placed it on the white shirt. "He was there at the Krazee Tavern. Grayson Wu."

"Grayson's my brother," Audri said. "I'm sorry if he's acting like a jerk. He has a lot on his plate these days, trying to merge companies and resolving some personal issues."

"Oh, okay." Natalie offered a warm smile.

The last few times I had seen Grayson, he seemed preoccupied. Everyone had issues to deal with in private. I could attest to that.

It occurred to me I hadn't been paying attention to the food and motivation reminder I'd set up on my phone. When it came up during my chats with Royce, I'd swiped it away. In the past, I'd always looked at it, even if I didn't follow the directions. It was simply a reminder.

Perhaps I didn't need it anymore. Besides, I'd spent more time playing the silly game on my phone. I wasn't sure if it was a good thing that I'd abandoned my reminders to play games.

Kiera handed out pieces of thin cardboard to slip between the shirt layers so it wouldn't bleed to the back. "You can also use fabric markers." She dropped a container filled with an assortment of markers on the table.

We all got busy decorating our shirts.

An idea sparked in my head as I reached for a paintbrush. Giggling to myself, I painted over the letter stencils. Twenty minutes later, I stepped back and studied my creation with SMART A.S.S. splashed across the front of the shirt. If I weren't creating for Royce, the words would have been entirely different—something safe for other people to auction. But since I was making this for him, I had no limits.

I am free with him.

Natalie stepped beside me. "What does A. S. S. stand for?"

"Achieve. Strive. Success." I beamed.

"Oh, I love it," Audri said. Her shirt had a simple straight line and a statement written on top of it. "Line Segment: Bringing Two Points Together—Me and You."

"Yours is so cool," I said.

Kiera lifted hers. "Mine has floral designs."

"Mine has abstract figures." Natalie showed hers off.

"Wow! We should start a T-shirt collection!" Audri exclaimed. "These are all so fabulous."

When I finished my five shirts, I wanted to wear them.

"That's a nice play on words." Natalie gestured to my shirt with "Nerd Lava" on it.

"Royce is a volcanologist. He'd appreciate it."

"You *are* a nerd lover and so adorkable." Kiera grinned.

"Adorkable should be on your shirt." I laughed.

"You mean smart and sexy." She fluttered her eyes at me.

When we were finished, the coordinator took photos of our shirts, giving each of them a number for the auction. We all took snapshots of our shirts before going our separate ways and planning to meet again soon. The craft session with my friends was exactly what I needed to feel at ease again.

Outside, I took a moment to inhale the fresh air. I'd always loved the chilly air of fall. I missed going to see the foliage this year. The warm colors always mesmerized me. Nature was a true wonder. It was its own painting, offering peace to those who knew how to appreciate it.

As I drove home, I noticed a black sedan with tinted windows had been behind me for several lights. Maybe I'd watched too many crime dramas and was becoming paranoid. When it finally turned the corner, I released a sigh.

Suddenly craving some chicken pot pie, I parked my car in the garage and walked over to Esther's Kitchen, a small restaurant run by two older ladies. They only had two eating tables. Most people ordered takeout. After getting my order, I exited the restaurant and from the corner of my eye, I saw the black car again. I couldn't see the driver because the windshield also had a tint.

Nerves stirred in me. After the fiasco with Fiona and Brittany, I couldn't be too careful. Was Brittany in Rhode Island? Though Royce said Fiona wouldn't bother me anymore, I was still hesitant. How could I trust Fiona? What were the chances that my former enemy was friends with my current enemy? The world worked in weird ways.

I had to be extra careful.

I pretended I didn't see the black car and crossed the street. When a car honked, my heart jumped. I whirled around, turning toward the sound, and bumped into a man, causing him to drop his bag of groceries. A woman rushed out from a building and slid into the passenger side of the honking car, and it drove off.

Blowing out a sigh of relief, I crouched to help him pick up his groceries. "I'm so sorry."

He wore a beanie with gray hair peeking out and had sharp blue eyes and a friendly smile.

"It's okay," he said, tucking all the contents back in. "I'm Viktor. I just moved into the adjacent building." He jerked a chin to the apartment building next to mine.

"Nice to meet you. I'm Michelle." I didn't realize my voice was shaky.

He looked at me. "Are you okay?"

"Yeah. I just thought someone was following me."

"Where?" He looked around, his eyes scanning the area.

I didn't see the car anymore. "It's gone. I think I'm just scaring myself." Changing the topic, I pointed to his groceries. "What are you making for dinner?"

"Ah, I'm not making anything. I'm bringing my friend some groceries. She's always cooking for me."

"A friend who cooks for you is a keeper," I said, assuming it was his girlfriend. "You have a good evening."

"You too." He offered a warm smile.

Feeling better, I rushed into my building with my chicken pot pie, showered, and couldn't wait to tell Royce about the charity auction.

CHAPTER FORTY-EIGHT

ROYCE

AFTER SURVEYING the area around Michelle's apartment, I walked into the lobby and turned to the mailbox, where a camera on the wall aimed right at me. I liked that she had security inside and outside the building. With the incidents in Iceland and Brittany still unaccounted for, I had to ensure Michelle was safe. I wondered if Dominic would turn to Michelle to get to me.

Wanting to surprise her with my early arrival, I spotted Michelle's name on the wall, pressed the buzzer, looked up at the camera, and gave her my biggest grin.

"Royce!" Her cheerful voice boomed from the speaker, followed by a buzz at the door, allowing me to enter.

As I got off the elevator to her door, she ran down the hallway and leaped into my arms. I buried my face in her hair, inhaling her scent as though it were all the oxygen my body needed.

"Why didn't you tell me you'd be home early? I could have picked you up from the airport."

I looked down at her eyes. "Because I wanted to surprise you."

She kissed me for a long moment and then led me into her quaint one-bedroom apartment with a good-sized kitchen and many windows adorned with solid-colored curtains. Photographs of tranquil, scenic views splashed on lilac-colored walls. The living room had a comfortable couch, an armchair that she could sink into, and a round coffee table filled with magazines and books. A soft rug sat over the hardwood floors.

"Are you hungry? I have leftover chicken pot pie."

"I'd love some."

"Any updates on Brittany?"

So much had happened since she left Iceland, but I didn't want my first night home to be discussing other people. I didn't want any pleasantries filling her apartment tonight. Tonight was about her. I missed her so damn much, my chest hurt.

I leaned against her kitchen wall and watched her prepare my meal. "We can talk about that tomorrow. I want happy and sexy thoughts of you tonight."

She tossed a seductive glance over her shoulder as she removed the plate from the microwave. "I made something for you, but you need to place a bid if you want them."

The gleam in her eyes made me smile. "Them?"

"Yes." She smirked, and my cock hardened.

"If you made them for me, then they belong to me." I walked over, placing a hand on either side of her, caged her in, and brushed my lips over hers. "Why should I bid on something that already belongs to me?"

She shivered from my touch. "Because it's for a good cause."

I whispered in her ear, moving my lips down her throat, "I've got a noble cause right now."

Her elbows pushed something on the counter, making a noise. "W-what cause?"

I smiled as her body sagged against mine. "It's called the principle of causality—cause and effect. I can show you exactly what I mean." I settled my lips on the crook of her neck, loving her soft skin. "This is the cause." I sucked on it, and she moaned, fisting her hands in my shirt. "Your reaction is the effect. But we're only scraping the surface."

She moaned again, tilting her head to the side. "Is this your prescription for relaxation after a long flight, doctor?"

"Indeed. Now be a good girl and do as I say." I lifted her, and she wrapped her legs around my waist with her arms slung around my neck. Cupping her ass, I made my way into her bedroom. "I'm having you in *your* bed tonight."

Amusement glittered in her mischievous eyes. "I've got some aches and pains I need help with."

My mouth jerked into a grin. "I'll lick all your aches and pains away."

She bit her bottom lip. "Sounds like a lovely remedy, Dr. Viktorsson."

Desire spiked in me as I kicked her bedroom door open, rushed to her bed, and fell onto her. "My hypothesis? To remedy Michelle's aches and pains requires a lot of licking, sucking, and orgasmic eruption."

Her eyes sparked with heat. "That is the most provocative educated guess I've ever heard. Let's test it out." She yanked at my clothes.

In seconds, we were naked in bed, licking, sucking, and performing all kinds of sexual acts that offered us mighty orgasms. Afterwards we sprawled out on the bed, letting the sexual energy drift around the room.

Michelle lay on top of me with her head on my heart, and I didn't think there could ever be anything more perfect than that moment.

I ran my fingers down her spine. "How was your day today?"

She shifted her head and looked at me. "Wanna see what I made for you?"

"Absolutely."

Michelle slipped into her robe, and I threw on my boxers, walking out to the kitchen.

"I need to get my luggage from my car for a change of clothes," I said, taking a seat at the table.

"You can do that later." She brought over her tablet. "You can look at all the T-shirts available to be auctioned off in a couple of weeks. I'll reheat your dinner."

I didn't know what to expect, but when I saw the unique T-shirts, pride and love filled me. She knew me well. "I love Smart A.S.S, Nerd Lava, Book Lava, Michelle's Viking, and Experience the Adventure." No one had ever made a shirt for me, never mind five. "Thank you."

She brought over the warm chicken pot pie. "You don't have to wear—"

"Of course I do. People need to know I've got a sassy girl-friend." I yanked her onto my lap. "You should make all my T-shirts."

"It was a fun activity with the girls." She scooped up some chicken pot pie with the spoon, blew on it, and fed me.

I opened my mouth, chewed, and swallowed, loving the intimate gesture more than I thought. I'd never been fed by any woman I'd dated. They never got this close to me.

She gave me the spoon, hopped off my lap, and brought a glass of water for her and me, sitting next to me. "So what are some updates? I'm dying to know."

I finished the delicious pot pie and looked at her big brown eyes. "You can't wait until tomorrow?"

"No."

I told her about Dominic Bryson and his corrupt police department, but I didn't share any other details about his father's death. I didn't want her to be involved in my past. Though Slash was no longer alive, his warning still rang in my ears.

Michelle told me she'd encountered Dominic at the Krazee Tavern, and I didn't like knowing he'd been that close to her. It wasn't unusual for Dominic to dine at a popular restaurant in the city.

If I wanted to keep my loved ones safe, my friends and I needed to keep our mouths shut regarding the incident we'd witnessed all those years ago when I was fifteen.

It seemed the discovery of Edward Bryson's body was the beginning of something. Though my friends and I had nothing to do with his murder, what we saw tied us to those involved in the crime. We were kids who'd been in the wrong place at the wrong time, and now the past was catching up to us.

Regardless, I wouldn't let anything or anyone get near Michelle—the woman who held my heart.

CHAPTER FORTY-NINE

MICHELLE

"IT'S OKAY, Mom. I'd rather you get well. We can meet you another time," I said over the phone.

We were supposed to meet Mom and Charles for Thanksgiving lunch at her place in Newport, but she'd gotten the flu the past week and hadn't gotten better.

"I'm so sorry, honey. I wanted to meet your boyfriend. This flu has been kicking my butt. Shows my age."

"Do you have enough food and medicine?"

"Yes. Charles has been taking great care of me." She coughed.

"Okay. I'll let you go. Say hi to Charles for me. Get well soon."

I turned to Royce, who sat on his couch looking perfect. He was reading something on his phone. His blond hair had grown long, with a few strands falling past his eyes. It seemed like every time I looked at him, I discovered something new. The past few days, I'd been staying over at his luxurious apartment that gave me a first-class view of the WaterFire event from the forty-fourth floor. The WaterPark was right below us. The living room windows were mostly glass, allowing for an abundance of light and a view of the city life.

To me, Royce was very much a nature guy, but he adapted well to the city's sophistication. There were so many surprising sides to him that made him irresistible, but I fear the more I discovered, the more in love I'd be. And that would make it harder when I had to leave, right?

Could this exquisite and intelligent man be all mine? But for how long?

Royce had made it clear that he didn't believe in love. What would happen if I told him I loved him? He'd probably freak out and break things off, telling me he'd warned me. A warning couldn't stop me from feeling what my heart wanted. Royce made me feel safe, loved, and free. I didn't regret falling for him, nor would I regret wanting to dive deeper.

I chose this path, and I'd live with the consequences no matter what.

Stop thinking negative thoughts. It's Thanksgiving. Be thankful.

I was grateful to him more than I could ever say.

"My mom still has the flu, so we can head over to your aunt's place early. Does she need help cooking or something?"

"Sure, Aunt Klara would like that. Do you need to drop anything off at your mom's?"

I patted his cheek, appreciating his thoughtfulness. "She's all set. Her boyfriend Charles is there with her."

Thirty minutes later, we were in the South Providence neighborhood. It had several multi-level homes, and many of the buildings were being renovated. Royce pulled his Land

Rover into a small driveway behind a Toyota Corolla of an adorable house with a fence all around the yard. It sat on a main road where city buses went by.

"How did you meet Remi and your other friends?" I asked, wondering how boys from affluent neighborhoods connected with boys in more impoverished areas.

"Through an RPG game called The Seven Realms. I took two city buses to meet up with them downtown. Forrest and Arrow lived only a few streets apart from me. We didn't grow up in rich neighborhoods like Remi and Grayson, but we became close friends despite our different backgrounds."

Royce grabbed a fruit basket and a bottle of wine from the backseat and used his key to open the door. "Aunt Klara, we're here."

She wore a bright red apron that read "Love is the Best Ingredient."

Royce placed the fruit basket and the bottle of wine on the kitchen table and offered his aunt a big hug.

Aunt Klara turned to me. "It's so lovely to meet you, Michelle. I'm Klara Smith, his favorite aunt."

"My only aunt," he said.

Aunt Klara had the same green eyes as Royce. She pulled back her shoulder-length blonde hair with a simple fabric headband. A strong-boned face and good looks ran in the family.

"Likewise. Thank you for having me over for dinner. Royce told me you're a superb cook."

"Did he now? I guess he was raised well." She winked at me.

Royce flexed a bicep. "Look at what all your food did to me."

I sensed the love between them.

"Do you need any help?" I glanced at the kitchen island with containers filled with stuff.

"If you wouldn't mind, the potatoes need peeling." She turned to her nephew. "Royce, there are some boxes in the hallway. Could you please bring them out to my trunk? I'm donating some of your old clothes to the local shelter."

"You should have told me you were cleaning. I would have come to help."

"You're busy, and I had time on my hands."

"I'll do some cleaning while I'm at it." He strode down the hallway.

While I peeled the potatoes, Aunt Klara asked, "So, how long have you known Royce?"

"We've been friends for years, but started dating recently. I didn't know how wonderful he was until now."

Her green eyes gleamed, and I couldn't help but wonder if Royce's mom had similar eyes. "Love takes time to develop. It's like cooking. There's preparation, the simmer, the display, the taste, and how the food made you feel. It's a special process, but well worth it. Don't you think?"

I got the sense she was asking me an indirect question. Turning to her, I saw love and caution on her face. "Yes. Sometimes fate takes us on detours to prepare us for the most profound experience of our lives. We can only be open to love once we accept that we're worthy of it. Like you said, it's a process. I'm still learning, and so is he. We're both learning together." I placed the peeled potatoes into a bowl and smiled. "Between the two of us, I think he's making excellent progress."

She looked at me for a long moment as tears welled in her eyes. Offering me an embrace, she whispered, "You're exactly what he needs. I've never seen him this cheerful and relaxed. Thank you."

"He's helping me too."

"Royce is very intelligent and determined, but he's got a stubborn streak too." She stirred a pot that smelled delicious. "I wanted to meet his girlfriends, but he's never brought any of them home. He has reservations about love, but I think you're changing that."

Soft and silky butterflies fluttered in my stomach. I was surprised he hadn't brought home a date before me. Knowing I had shifted something in him made me believe in the power of love.

"He's the scientific type, so he likes facts and things he can see as proof. But there's a part of him that believes in something more."

Aunt Klara's lips curved into a sweet smile. "You sure know him. Whatever it is you're doing to him, keep doing it."

"He told me you took him in when he was young. That's very kind of you."

"He's family, and I love him." I finished peeling the rest of the potatoes and asked if she needed help with anything else.

"Thanks, I'm good. I prepared everything the night before, so there's not much left to do now. Go check on him."

"Just let me know if you need help." I washed my hands, dried them, and headed to Royce.

I stood at the open doorway, watching Royce sit in a wooden chair, flipping through a comic book. Two other Thor comic books sat on top of his desk. I imagined a young Royce, lanky and ambitious, reading in his room and dreaming about big plans. Was he lonely back then? A twinge of sadness tugged at me.

I remembered growing up with just me and Mom, and the loneliness became unbearable, especially when no one understood the darkness in me. I'd desperately wanted someone to show me the way, but no one came. This was probably why many people lost faith in the higher power that was supposed to appear when asked. I'd like to believe that he or she was helping someone worse off than me. There was only one God and so many needy people. If I were him, I'd need a timeout too.

You're strong, and you survived on your own. God knew you could create your own path.

My inner voice seemed to have gained some wisdom today. Perhaps it was the man standing before me, helping me understand myself better.

I stepped inside, and he flicked a gaze at me, grinned, and closed his comic book. He reached for my hand and dragged me onto his lap. I straddled him, winding my arms around his neck. "What are you reading?"

He jerked a chin at the Thor comic book. "A book about how to wield power to gain sexual favors from my woman."

"There's a price for sexual favors."

"How about we exchange a massage for a massage?" He squeezed my ass and gestured to the bed. "We can defile my childhood bed right now."

I laughed just as a cough sounded in the doorway. I flew off his lap, heat burning my cheeks as I stared at Aunt Klara.

She waved a hand, grinning. "Coffee is ready if you're both interested, but I think you're busy. Carry on. Coffee can wait." She closed the door tightly.

I covered my face with my hands. "Oh my God. I'm so embarrassed."

Smiling, Royce brushed his thumbs across my inflamed

cheeks. "Next time, we'll close the door. All done peeling the potatoes?"

"Yup. I'm here to help you clean your room." Trying to forget my embarrassment, I jabbed a playful finger at his chest and glanced around the small room. He had a bed against the wall and two bookcases filled with books on Earth, volcanoes, and superheroes.

He pointed to two boxes on the floor. "There's not much to clean. I'm giving away all my books, even the comic books." Why did he sound sad about the latter?

I reviewed the knickknacks on his shelf and spotted a wish bottle that looked oddly familiar. It was about ten inches long, filled with shells, sand, twigs, and a rolled-up piece of paper. The glass was clearer than the one I had at home. My heart skipped when I saw a lightning bolt etched at the bottom of the bottle as though someone had used a sharp tool to carve into it.

"Where did you find this?" I asked.

"I didn't find it. Aunt Klara gave it to me. When we returned to Iceland for a special memorial for my mom, we each made a wish bottle for fun. I tossed mine out to the ocean, but Aunt Klara kept hers and gave it to me." He took the bottle from my hand and ran a finger over the lightning bolt. "I think mine is at the bottom of the ocean right now."

Inhaling a breath, I placed a trembling hand on his arm. "No, it's not. I think I have it."

CHAPTER FIFTY

ROYCE

AFTER DINNER, we thanked Aunt Klara and left with two containers of leftovers. I promised her we'd visit again and told her to leave the donation boxes for me to take care of the next time I came over. The boxes were too heavy for her to lift.

The visit to Aunt Klara had been more wonderful than I expected. I loved seeing the two most important women in my life get along so well. Before I left, Aunt Klara thanked me for letting her meet my girlfriend. That was when I realized tonight hadn't been a simple Thanksgiving dinner. Michelle was the first woman I'd ever told Aunt Klara about and the first to see my childhood home.

It was a tremendous step for me, and I'd done it as though it were natural. There hadn't been any hesitation on my part. What did that say about me?

I had it bad for Michelle.

Inside her apartment, Michelle led me over to her bookcase, where she retrieved a box from the top shelf and brought it over to the coffee table. Her hands shook as she removed the top lid and took out a worn and scratched-up wish bottle.

My heart hammered when I flipped to the bottom and saw my lightning bolt. "Where did you find this?"

"When I was at the beach about five years ago. I was walking along the shore and came to an area with rocks and found it covered in seaweed. At that time, I was blogging about treasures you find at the beach."

I couldn't believe it. "I made this bottle about ten years ago, the year after I bought Whitewater Family Resort—a year after I rescued you." I placed the bottle on the table and cupped her teary-eyed face in my hands. "You found me. In a special way, you rescued me. What I have in that bottle are bits and pieces of my soul. It carries a wish I never thought anyone would see. It could've sunk to the bottom of the sea, but you found it, took it home, and cherished it. Thank you." I kissed her for a long moment. The kiss was soft and slow, like gentle waves of the ocean rippling through us, letting us know we were destined long before we knew each other.

How could I not believe in the universe's magic? I believed in nature and the power of observation during my research because they yielded a tangible truth I could touch and see. This weaving of serendipitous moments resulted from something beyond Michelle and me.

I opened the cap and took out the rolled-up piece of paper. "I'm surprised how intact it is."

When I unrolled the paper, a small seashell clattered to the table, and Michelle picked it up, examining the iridescent shell. "The ocean took care of it."

"I guess nature was hinting at my future girlfriend's name to me back then. 'Shell' in Michelle." My grin widened as her eyes sparkled with the connection.

"I guess so," she said as she stared at the message scrawled on the paper in my hand.

Risk lies in the space between love and no love. What do you dare to choose?

"You've read this message before?" I asked.

"I was hesitant at first because I felt like I was intruding, but curiosity got the best of me. Somehow, I believed the message was meant for me." She stroked the paper as though remembering that day she found the bottle.

"When I tossed the wish bottle into the ocean, I never expected anyone to find it. I'd just visited my mom's grave, wishing she could have lived longer. Sadness overcame me along with anger, and I needed to get away from those suffocating feelings. Aunt Klara took me to a gift shop offering a class on creating your own wish bottle. I stuffed my emotions into that bottle and set it free."

Though I'd been the one to toss it into the waters, the recipient must have felt fortunate to have found something profound. I'd seen it in movies, but to actually find one was extremely magical. It seemed like every moment linking me to Michelle was extraordinary—magic in the making.

Was that love? *What do you dare to choose?* Could I answer my question from the bottle?

I believed I had already made my decision. My heart galloped from a combination of fear and excitement. Human emotions were so confusing, and now I understood how they muddled even the brightest minds.

Warmth and hope filled her eyes. "You can have it back if you'd like."

"No. You found it, so it's yours. It's more magical being with the person who found it."

She held it up to her chest. "Thank you. I love it. It's like I have a part of you with me."

She had more than she realized.

"The day I found the bottle, I felt defeated because I didn't get the job I'd wanted and had a fight with my mom regarding a gala I didn't want to attend. Feeling sad, I just wanted to be alone and walked the shore. When I spotted the bottle, hope sparked in me, and I wanted to know the message the universe had for me. The message resonated with me."

"How?" I wanted to know everything in her mind and heart.

What had she been feeling that day? Did the bottle make her heart skip the way she made mine erratic just looking at her?

"It asked me a simple question that opened a door to other issues. Had I been taking risks? Sort of, but not intentionally. I was living my life dodging certain issues rather than walking through them. Because when I walk around them, they might reappear again. But if I walk into them, *through* them, I conquer the issues by breaking them down, right?"

"Not only are you sexy and stunning, but you're also wise, angel."

She rolled her eyes even as a small smile curved onto her lips. "Must be the Viking with a wicked mouth always saying stuff to make me blush. Now stop distracting me so I can finish my thoughts."

I said what ran through my mind, which had been occurring more frequently. Ever since I met her, I'd transformed into a guy who saw things through a poetic scope. I wasn't sure if I liked that or not.

She turned the glass bottle around in her hand. "When I opened the bottle, something in me also opened up. I had been blogging mostly about traveling and tourist stuff, but I wanted to introduce other topics that interested me. Basically, I was getting a bit bored and wanted to branch out. I took a risk and changed my blog to suit *my* desire and not someone else's. That was when my follower count grew exponentially." She turned to me. "Yet again, you changed my life."

Michelle was the only woman who moved my body and soul like tectonic plates, but admitting that to her would solidify a truth I was still afraid to admit. When it came to fear, I'd overcome it many times, but I was still terrified by the idea of love. I didn't know if I could put myself back together if things didn't work out with Michelle and me.

She saw me as an accomplished businessman and a doctor, but she didn't know the version of me that could be so cold and emotionless. I had been like that for the first few years living in America. It had worried my aunt when I retreated into myself, questioning God, life, and even the superhero I had looked up to. Where was this higher power that was supposed to save people?

No one saved my mom when she was ill. No one saved my sister when she was kidnapped. When I sat in that dark corner, no one saved me.

What if that emotionless version of me returned one day? It would crush Michelle, and I'd rather not tell her anything than give her hope only to smash it later. I knew I sounded like a coward, but I didn't know what else to do.

"Seeing how happy and hopeful you are makes me believe in superpowers and magic again."

Something flickered in her eyes. "Don't ever stop."

If my feelings for her were magma, it was slowly traveling up from the earth's core, wanting to erupt to show the world how much I cared about her. There had never been anyone who touched me this deeply.

"With how wonderful I make you feel, I deserve brownie points. Don't you think?" I asked.

She threw her arms around me, dropping kisses all over my face and counting them as she went. I laughed like a fool, loving every damn kiss she offered me.

Her phone rang, and I cursed it to hell.

She paused and scowled. "My email notifications are going crazy."

CHAPTER FIFTY-ONE

MICHELLE

ANXIETY TWISTED knots in my stomach as Royce scrolled through my website.

"It's been hacked," he said calmly as he stared at the words on what was supposed to be Finding Life's Treasures' website.

I'm a cheating bitch. I fuck men to succeed.

An image of my face on a topless woman's body flashed on the screen. She sat on a chair with a man's head between her thighs, smiling provocatively.

Don't cry. Don't cry. Don't let them get to you.

Too late. The pain broke through, and tears streamed down my face even though I tried my best to stop it. Why were people so cruel?

"She'll pay for this." Royce flared his nostrils and swapped to another tab, trying to protect me.

Shock, anger, and despair coursed through me, numbing all other emotions.

"I want to see it. Please go back." He did as I asked.

The damaging image and the malicious words etched in

my brain like an invisible tattoo I'd never forget. The false words pounded like a hammer trying to smash my dignity, reputation, and career. Who the fuck did this? Fiona? Brittany?

The anger was easier to deal with because it carved an outlet for me to release my emotions. A surge of violence rose in me, and I hated feeling that way, but they left me no choice. These people pushed me into a corner and stepped on me, smearing my character. I'd worked damn hard to build my career—to become the Michelle Yates who was proud of her work. No one had permission to destroy it.

I let the anger move through me like a virus, infecting me with something malevolent. Something that wanted to hurt the person who did this to me. I allowed myself to feel the animosity, the violence, and the vengeance toward the person assassinating my character.

"That's not me," I choked, unable to speak properly.

"I know, angel. They'll pay, I swear." Royce cupped my face with both hands. "I'll sort this out." Reaching for a tissue from the nearby box, he dabbed my eyes tenderly.

His gentleness and promise decreased the anger in me. Looking into his green eyes, fury burned in them. I didn't want him to do something reckless that would get him into trouble.

"I need a moment to let the shit settle. I'll be okay." The lie tasted bitter on my tongue, but it was necessary to protect the man trying to protect me.

Setting the damp tissue aside, he pulled me into his arms. When my head rested on his strong shoulder, my internal barrier faltered. I thought I had my emotions under control, but I was wrong. Once I felt the comfort of his arms around me, the dam burst, and emotions poured out.

"It's okay, baby. Just cry. Let it go."

"My readers will see this and think it's me. The entire world will see this, Royce. What am I going to do? How will I recover from this?" I sobbed into his shirt.

"You will bounce back from this harassment, I promise." He stroked my hair.

I now understood the drawbacks of the internet. One slanderous act could ruin a person. Even if I got my website back up, the damage was already done. How many people had seen me as *that* woman?

A headache throbbed in my head from too much crying. My phone buzzed with messages from my friends and colleagues who probably saw the image or got email alerts about the down website. My body shivered thinking about it.

Breaking free from Royce's arms, I said, "The girls are worried about me. I'll need to reply and alert my clients about the website being compromised."

"Go ahead. I'll get this image removed immediately. Arrow knows some hackers."

Royce made a call to someone while I went to the kitchen table. Sitting down, I sent my friends a text message, informing them I was aware of the spam email and the image on my website and for them not to worry about it.

I spent two hours sending emails to clients alerting them of the situation, and saying I'd inform them once things returned to normal. I had a promotion for NewYou Beauty at the moment. Feeling awful, I offered them a free promotional post when my website was back up and running. I had to maintain a professional relationship with my vendors if I wanted to continue doing business with them. NewYou Beauty had been kind to me, and I would treat them in the same manner.

My head throbbed and my stomach began to ache, all signs pointing to extreme stress levels. I swallowed two painkillers and sat at the kitchen table, watching Royce's determined face as he spoke on the phone.

"I need this done immediately. Let me know what you find out." After he ended the call, his fingers flew across the keyboard.

The crying and anxiety exhausted me, and I couldn't think coherently anymore. I needed something to take my mind off of this horrific event. Who would have thought anyone would see me like that? Had my mom seen it? She would've called already.

In minutes, my career had crashed and my stress level shot through the roof. The situation was probably worse in my head, as most things were when you were in the thick of it.

The worst scenarios played in my head. My clients could sever ties with me after seeing that image on my website, which was inappropriate and unprofessional. Who would want to work with me after that? My sponsors would want to stay away from me. I'd lose the trust and respect of my followers as well.

Stop thinking about it. Rest your mind.

Sighing, I leaned back in the chair, swiped to the Eat Your Monsters app, and began playing. Just looking at my cute bunny made me feel better already. Nibbles, the name I'd chosen for him, had grown to be as big as the monster trying to take over my village. I'd also graduated to new levels, which offered new findings and motivations. I could eat whatever I wanted—an exceptional ability. With each food I discovered and devoured, I gained new powers and motivation stars and earned coins and gems in my bank to purchase adorable accessories. Even an avatar needed the right wardrobe to intimidate enemies.

In my mind, I imagined destroying my adversaries—Fiona, Brittany, and all of my fears trapped in my closet—with my berry bombs. My enemies died in a pile of mush, which grew into a beautiful tree studded with blooms.

I smiled as the victory screen flashed.

Motivation Star: *You are awesome. You are fearless.*

Coins and Gems*: One hundred new coins and three diamonds.*

My avatar grew another inch, and I bought her a crown as she gained a new backyard with a cool obstacle course that offered her opportunities to earn new coins. This bonus section didn't have any enemies to fight. The faster I cleared the obstacles, the more coins I received.

Thirty minutes later, I felt like I'd purged enough stress to make me feel lighter. Was that why Royce and his friends played video games all the time? It had the power to eliminate stress by tossing you into a world where you lost yourself. Not only that, but I also became someone new during that role-playing game.

I never realized that a video game could help me deal with my stress.

"How are you doing?" Royce pulled up a chair beside me. "I like the smile on your face. You look like you just defeated someone."

"I defeated a beast and earned a crown for my bunny."

"Sounds fun." His eyes sparked. "The image has been removed and replaced by 'Down for Maintenance. We apologize for any inconvenience.'"

I gasped with joy. "That was fast! How did you manage it?"

"I know some people." He smiled. "It's down, but my guys are working on getting to the source. You need to get away for a bit. I want to take you on a brief vacation with me."

"Where?"

"To a place that's on your Wonders of the World list. It'll be good to get away."

My heart veritably jumped onto his lap, and I wondered if he felt it. I knew he'd help me resolve this website issue, but he achieved it in a manner that was efficient and painless for me. I had so much appreciation for him.

Too emotional, I choked, "You are truly a gift."

"Then I suppose we're a gift to each other." He grinned.

Royce thought of everything. My brain was beaten to a pulp, and I couldn't think of a better idea than a surprise vacation. This entire scenario had unsettled me to the core. I didn't think anyone could hate me this much. Despite the alarming situation, Royce was by my side and made everything easier to deal with. He met my immediate needs with a smile, and a flame burst in my soul.

I had a gift for him, but it was still in the works. Hopefully, he'd love it.

"Sure. I can't wait to see what wonderful place I can cross off my list. Let me go pack some clothes, and we can head over to your place." My stomach growled, and I had a craving. "Can we order a deep-dish pizza and fries?"

"You can have whatever you want. I'll place the order."

See? Efficiency.

As I packed my clothes, a thought occurred to me. I had just requested a deep-dish pizza and fries without a sliver of guilt. It was as though my relationship with food had changed. Normally, I'd feel guilty even *thinking* about eating something so bad for me. But I didn't care today. Pizza and fries would give me the comfort I craved.

Was it because I was with him that I didn't feel the guilt?

My brain was too exhausted to care what the reason was. All that mattered was that guilt and fear stood at bay.

CHAPTER FIFTY-TWO

ROYCE

WHILE MICHELLE SLEPT, I conducted more research regarding Fiona, Brittany, and Dominic. The PI was working hard on uncovering who the fuck created that image of Michelle and hacked into her account. Arrow knew some hackers and sent me their contact details. I didn't care who got me answers first—I just wanted to know who I had to destroy.

Fury had spiraled in me when I saw the image. It escalated when she shattered against me. I felt her pain reverberate in my body, my cells. The despair was unbearable, and I understood why. She was portrayed in the most disgraceful way for the world to mock. I had contained myself so she didn't see how irate I was. She needed my composure and support to help her at that vulnerable moment, and I tried my best not to pop a vein.

Seeing her broken devastated me. I wanted to burn down the fucking world for making her cry. I wanted those responsible to scream in pain as I watched lava devour their bodies slowly, eating up their flesh and bones.

There was more to this predicament than simple slander. I had to proceed with caution if I wanted to uncover everything.

Michelle was important to me, and someone knew this.

CHAPTER FIFTY-THREE

MICHELLE

DRESSED in thick coats and boots, Royce and I trekked around the campsite. Domes that looked like glass igloos offered the residents the perfect view of the night sky. Royce had reserved a dome near a cliff for us.

Royce squeezed my gloved hand. "Are you warm enough?"

He didn't have his hood on, whereas I wore a knit hat and scarf. "Yes."

Snow crunched under my boots as I observed the illuminated domes surrounded by pine trees. The domes offered a lovely glow to the night sky. It was only eight in the evening, and we'd just had dinner at a local restaurant.

Before I left, my website had returned to normal, but I still got emails from random trolls who asked if that was me. Most of them were men, and I'd blocked them. I'd asked Royce if he knew who was behind it, but he didn't have an answer for it. I dropped the subject because I didn't want to waste any more energy on it.

Usually, when I took a vacation around Christmastime,

it was to go to a warmer climate, but this year, I exchanged one winter wonderland for another. Winter was the best season for a glimpse of the Northern Lights.

I glanced around and smiled as we made our way toward our dome. "They must look like glowing eggs from afar."

He grinned. "Very perceptive."

We arrived at our dome, which was more private and a lot bigger than the others.

"Do you want to look inside?"

We took two steps down, entered with a key, took off our snow-covered boots at the door, and browsed. One large bed sat at the center, and a tiny kitchen took up one section of the dome. An electric fireplace flickered on the opposite side. The sign on the wall gave directions for internet access. I could see the sky from all directions. Anyone walking by would need to be extremely tall or require a ladder to see into our space.

"When did you buy this resort?" I asked.

"A few years ago when the owners didn't want to take care of it anymore. It's a magical place. I didn't buy it for profit, though that has increased since I took over. I got it for what it offered. The view and the feeling you get when looking at the Northern Lights is priceless." He pulled me to him. "I wanted you to experience it with me. This dome is reserved for me only."

I rose to my toes and kissed him. "Let's go out and wait for it."

"You sure? You can see everything from here. It's also warmer for you."

"No, I want the real deal. I'm not cold if you're hugging me." I tightened my arms around him.

We sat on a metal bench, and he gathered me into his

arms, keeping me warm. I glanced at the beautiful landscape with snow-covered mountains in the distance and the vast sky and sighed. The foggy breath slithered into the air, and I waved a gloved hand through it.

All the concerns that had boggled my mind seemed minuscule compared to the magnificent scenery before me. Life was about the profound wonder and joy that made us speechless. These were the moments that counted—not issues I had no control over.

"Thank you for this trip. I appreciate it." I tilted my face to look at him.

This beautiful man had been there for me long before I knew about him. He saved me when I didn't have the will to live. When I lost hope, he gave it back to me through his wish bottle. And now he'd helped me rebuild my reputation, my career, my heart—my soul. He did all of this without asking for anything back—without a guarantee that I would reciprocate anything. There was no guarantee in love. A person in love gave because they loved unconditionally.

Did he love me? Did he even know what love was? Would it frighten him if I pointed it out?

No, let him acknowledge it for himself.

I'd let him find his answer just as I discovered mine. Emotions swelled within my chest, and love glowed in me like the dome radiating through the night.

I love him so much.

As tears blurred in my eyes, a stream of light flowed across the sky and took my breath away.

I straightened and clasped his hand. "It's more beautiful in real life, Royce."

My body relaxed from the peaceful glow of the Icelandic

starry night sky with curtains of light moving slowly in front of me. I was completely immersed in the beauty and wonder. Nothing compared to seeing the real Northern Lights. The colors mesmerized me as they changed shades when they fluctuated. In the distance, a ribbon of pinkish-purple emerged as though God had splashed a new neon paint onto the dark sky.

"What gives off the colors?" I asked, making a mental note to cross off seeing the Northern Lights from my bucket list.

"It's the solar wind from the sun entering the Earth's atmosphere. When the protons, electrons, and neutrons from the solar winds react to Earth's particles, they release energy and create this magical palette."

I smiled at my gorgeous nerd and remembered something from high school science class. "Be a proton, always positive!"

He laughed, and his voice echoed through the vastness as though it moved over the flatlands to the mountains and beyond, spreading joy. The sound went on and on, making me grin at my silly attempt at incorporating what little science I knew.

"Yeah, I know it's cheesy, but it suits this moment."

"Not cheesy at all. It's brilliant, and I love it. I'll remember that when I'm feeling 'negative.'" His eyes sparkled, and the ribbons of light illuminated them, making his eyes brighter.

A seriousness moved through me as nerves stirred in my stomach. "I guess there's magic in science."

"Of course. There's magic in whatever you love and believe in." His eyes bore into me, like that statement.

My heart quickened, preparing me to share a truth I held deep within my heart. "I love you, Royce."

A quiet gasp escaped him, and his face softened. Emotions stormed his eyes, and I wanted to know what he was feeling, but I was also scared. What if he didn't feel the same way? What if my confession forced him to define something he wasn't ready to?

The struggle in his eyes showed he was conflicted, but then he pulled me into his arms and kissed the top of my head.

Silence hummed between us as my declaration hung in the air. My admission was like the ribbon of light, glowing in the night. But unlike the Northern Lights that were for everyone to love and appreciate, my affection was meant for only one man. A man who didn't comment on my declaration. I knew he didn't believe in love. He'd said it before, and yet I couldn't help but hope my admission would inspire him to give it a chance. He had time to consider.

His phone rang and disrupted the moment. *Damn stupid phone.*

Royce didn't pick up, but it rang again. Pulling back, he stared at me with eyes that held so much emotion. "It's my urgent ringtone."

He fished his phone from his coat pocket. "Yeah?" While he listened to whatever the person told him, a V formed between his brows, and his jaw ticked. "Thanks. I'll be in touch soon." Turning off his phone, he tucked it back into his coat pocket. "Let's go inside for a drink, okay?"

Rising from the bench, I studied him. "Is everything okay?"

He smiled. "Yes. There's nothing for you to worry about."

I knew he was lying. Not wanting to ruin our evening, I shoved it aside for now.

Inside the dome, we hung our coats in the closet and changed into soft pajamas. He tossed his phone and wallet onto the bed, and something clanked from his wallet onto the tiled floor. Reaching down, I picked it up, and my heart stopped. My hand trembled with joy as I stared at the stud design that was half an inch long. I couldn't speak as I held the gold emblem in my palm.

Royce came up beside me. "You like my lightning bolt? It's cool, isn't it?"

"It's not a lightning bolt," I whispered, as my hand shook from elation and surprise. "It's an abstract letter M. See?" I turned the stud earring horizontally. "M for Michelle. It's my earring. I lost it during my first trip to Iceland. The backing must have fallen off. I only realized it was missing when I was already on the flight home."

Taking the gold earring from my palm, Royce examined it, turning it vertically, which made the design appear like a bolt of lightning. Then he turned it horizontally, which showed the M.

"It's a masterpiece," he said, still admiring it. "It's us. I'm the bolt of lightning, and you're the M."

"I'd sketched it for the designer, and he made it for me. The jewelry store that I was looking for closed. I wanted a new one to match the one I had at home."

"You weren't meant to have another," he said, giving it back to me. "You're now reunited with the person meant for you."

"I can't dismiss the idea of fate. It's the only explanation for this magical event. I thought I'd lost it forever, but it was only being kept safe by you."

"The day I found it, I'd been debating selling all of my Thor comic books. I used to believe in him, but after my mom died and I moved to live with Aunt Klara in a new country, I lost hope. I thought to myself, if there was a power beyond me, why didn't it save my mom? Why didn't it save my sister, keep my family together? As though God heard me, something glistened on the sidewalk. When I picked it up, I thought the lightning bolt was a sign. So I held off on selling the comic books. I'd had those books since I was a kid. Finding this earring—though I didn't know it was an earring back then—was a sign of hope for me."

"We literally found each other in the most profound way," I said, making another mental note to call his aunt to do me a favor about his belongings.

"Do you trust me?" Something in his eyes worried me.

There was no one I trusted more. "Yes."

"Don't forget that," he said. "I'm asking you not to worry about anything and enjoy this vacation with me. We leave tomorrow for a new destination."

"We are? To where?"

"To an adventure that will make your heart palpitate, take your breath away, and offer you one of the best views of your life. Most of all, it will help you overcome your fear once and for all."

You make my heart palpitate. You take my breath away.

Instead, what came out was, "I'm ready for this adventure."

"But first, there's an adventure inside this dome that must be experienced." A wicked smile slid onto his face, and the muscles in my inner thighs tightened.

"What is that, Viking?"

"Making love to my angel while she gazes at the Northern Lights and screams my name."

Our clothes flew off our bodies and landed all over the room.

My gaze was riveted on his body as his arousal called to me. But I wanted to do something first.

"Wait," I said and walked around him until I faced his back. I ran my fingers down the lightning bolt tattoo and kissed it. It was an emblem that told his story. He was the lightning bolt that illuminated the truth, the thunder that made fear scatter, the power that made me feel safe. "I'm sealing this with love. Now you have more power to achieve whatever you want." I kissed it again, and he shivered.

He whirled, gripped my waist, nudged me to the bed, and prowled over me like a man-beast. His eyes darkened with so much passion I'd do anything he wanted.

Lips collided, and tongues twirled and danced while hands touched and claimed. My body melted to his as he fulfilled his promise and more. This wasn't the raw fucking I was used to. This was a slow lovemaking that set my body ablaze. His hot mouth created rivers of fire along my chin, my neck, over and under my breasts before capturing my nipples in a wild sucking. I cried out his name while he took his lazy time adoring my breasts, then licking his way down my stomach, heading to my core.

My body trembled as his curious lips roamed around my hips and my inner thighs.

"Royce," I begged and bit my bottom lip to suppress the need scorching through me.

He lifted his head and offered a devilish smile. "Yes, angel?"

"I need—"

His mouth covered my center and explored my folds with his phenomenal tongue. My back arched, surrendering to his exquisite mouth as I cried out his name again and again.

Above me, the Northern Lights pulsed and became the witness to the love between Royce and me.

CHAPTER FIFTY-FOUR

THE WEATHER IN FORT MYERS, Florida, differed from the winter of Iceland and was a much-needed contrast. I wanted something warm, bright, and colorful for Michelle. Life had been dark recently, and she needed something uplifting.

While I assisted Michelle into her skydiving jumpsuit, I remembered our lovemaking two days ago inside the dome. Her eyes had danced with wildfire as though magma stirred in the depths of her soul, and she exposed all her secrets to me that night.

I love you.

Michelle's words rang in my ear like a song, one I replayed over and over since I heard it the first time. That night, she gave me the most precious gift.

I'd never brought a woman to the dome until her. It had been my sanctuary when I craved solitude. Being with Michelle had changed me. I wanted to show her places that were precious to me. Solitude was nice and necessary for a man contemplating his career and what he wanted in life.

But now there was something else I wanted more. She sat in the center of my heart, and I'd do anything to protect her.

I prayed she'd understand in the next few weeks.

I love you.

The power of those words cracked the brick wall around my heart. For the first time in my life, I felt the rawness of my emotions leak through like the unstoppable magma that rose to the surface of a volcano, becoming lava. Nothing could stop the flow.

My heart was bare, exposed in the most vulnerable way. There was no safety net to keep me from getting hurt. The emotional numbness I was used to disappeared, along with the doubts regarding love. How could I not believe in love when it stood before me? When it flooded my brain and took over my heart?

I'd be a fool to dismiss her declaration. What she didn't know was that I'd felt the same all along. Our love for each other had started a long time ago when we'd each found parts of ourselves along our life's journeys.

I believed in love. It was my oxygen, the air I breathed, the silence that hummed in her absence, the sweet fragrance that tantalized me whenever I missed her, and the lovely mist that blanketed the morning landscape before it was ready to wake. She was all these beautiful things and more to me.

Michelle was the most precious treasure I had in my life. Because of that, I had to protect her at all costs.

Aunt Klara was right about love being inexplicable and profound. I couldn't wait to inform her I'd been wrong to dismiss it. Finding my definition of love had made it mine.

I'd wanted to tell her I loved her that night, but shock and emotions stymied me, delaying the message. When I received that pertinent phone call, I had to delay telling her.

She'd find out later when everything was resolved. Right now, I didn't want to risk her life.

All dressed, Michelle faced me, looking worried. "I'm scared to death. I don't know why I agreed to do this."

"You like embarking on an adventure. Do you trust me?"

She placed a hand on my cheek and pinched lightly. "With my life."

Smiling, I placed a hand on either side of her shoulders. "We'll be doing tandem skydiving. You'll be attached to me. There's a harness and a parachute built for two."

"Oh." She glanced at the equipment next to us and faced me again. "That makes it better."

I pulled out a black feather from my pocket and waved it in front of her. "I want you to hold this in your hand and let it go when you're in the air. Think of this feather as the 'monster' in your closet—the ugly thing you've been afraid of." I brushed the feather against her nose. "I know you said you're healing because the monster is behind closed doors. But it's still there in your psyche. You need to eradicate it, remove it permanently. It's time to empty the closet, Michelle."

Her eyes glistened, and I could tell she held back tears.

"I never considered the monster to be soft and pretty like this feather," she said with a laugh.

"Everything is perspective, love. You saw it through fear —your imagination from the side angle, from upside down, from a skewed view, never fully seeing it for what it is. It's an opportunity to learn about yourself and regain your power." I placed the feather in her palm. "You can imagine the ugliness however you want. Some people believe crows are birds of the underworld. So return it—and everything associated with it—to where it belongs."

She tilted her head, emotions swirling in her eyes. "How long have you been thinking about this?"

"For a while now." I shrugged. "Symbolically, you're releasing pain and darkness. Let the wind take care of it. Let it go."

Tears made sparkling rivers down her cheeks. "What are you, a philosopher now?"

"No, just an observer." I wiped her tears with my gloved hand. "Being with you has grounded me, allowing me to see things clearly."

"And you took me here to experience danger. Skydiving is risky."

"Love is riskier. Love can destroy your soul, whereas skydiving can destroy your physical body. I can deal with physical pain, but not an injured soul. You're my soul."

She threw her arms around me. "Thank you for everything."

CHAPTER FIFTY-FIVE

MICHELLE

ERRATIC NERVES WRANGLED inside me as I stood strapped to Royce at the opened door of the plane. The sun was bright, and there were a few clouds in the distance. My heart raced at the excitement and fear.

You're my soul.

But after thinking about these words, the fear subsided. Was that his way of saying he loved me? It felt like it, and I folded the sacred message and tucked it into my heart.

I wanted to tell him I wasn't scared anymore, but thrilled to be experiencing this with him. The wind roared like a beast. The movies lied when they showed people having conversations while they leaped from the plane. I couldn't hear anything but the rushing wind, much less chitchat.

I gripped the black feather tightly and let out a slow sigh, bracing for the jump.

It's time for you to go, monster. Thank you for the lessons.

I didn't know why I was being nice to it. It had terrified me, but also taught me strength, perseverance, and courage. So I was grateful for those lessons.

Be a proton, always positive.

I smiled at my silliness in trying to see the positive side of things.

Royce wrapped his other hand around my waist, and we jumped. The wind slapped my face as we dropped with Royce strapped above me, allowing me to face the stunning landscape below. Nothing could compare to this freefalling sensation. My stomach churned and twisted with excitement ten times more prominent than a rollercoaster ride.

My heart rate skyrocketed, making me feel so alive—so invincible. I held up the feather for Royce to see and released it. The wind yanked it away. In a blink, it became a black dot in the distance—no longer near me, no longer affecting me.

The monster was gone because *I* let it go. Feeling as light as a feather and as free as a bird, tears blurred my eyes at the realization of how far I'd come. I'd been crying way too much since I met Royce, but these weren't sad tears. They were a form of release.

The adrenaline soared in me, clearing my mind of all the clutter I'd collected. Royce deployed the parachute as we descended, and love and gratitude for him overwhelmed my heart and soul.

CHAPTER FIFTY-SIX

MICHELLE

TWO WEEKS after we went skydiving, Royce jumped back into work, and so did I. We saw each other less because of his schedule, where he had to fly to different states and countries to resolve business issues.

We texted and chatted over the phone whenever we could, but I sensed something was wrong. I couldn't help the insecurity that nipped at me. I trusted him, but then a voice whispered in the back of my head, *You also trusted Julian.*

Shut up.

I focused on writing more blog posts for NewYou Beauty and other companies who had reached out to me after reading about the Icelandic beauty products. After that, I spent time on my secret project as well. When I missed Royce, I touched the stud earring in my ear. Now I wore it every day.

Still, I couldn't shake off an uncomfortable feeling. What was about to happen?

Three weeks later, I got back from the gym and noticed a black sedan without a license plate parked across the street from my building. How could it get away without a license plate? Where were the cops when you needed them? The car had followed me to the gym and back. Fear twisted my stomach.

Who was it?

When I got into my apartment and locked my door, I walked toward the window but stayed against the wall, peeking through the curtains. The black sedan was gone.

Feeling relieved, I dropped to my chair and texted Royce.

Michelle: *Hi. Are you busy?*

Royce: *Meeting starts in 5 mins. What's up?*

I didn't want to worry him since he had a meeting to attend. Apparently, there had been new accidents at some of his resorts. He didn't need the extra stress right now. Besides, as long as I stayed alert whenever I went out, I should be okay.

I missed him so much, and I feared something unsettling was brewing between us.

Michelle: *Are we okay?*

Royce: *Of course? Why?*

Michelle: *Why is there a wall between us?*

Royce: *There is no wall. Do you trust me?*

Michelle: *Yes.*

Royce: *Been busy. Things will return to normal soon. Trust me.*

He kept asking me to trust him. I did, but somehow, I still felt like I wasn't in the loop on things. What was he hiding from me?

Michelle: *When will you be home?*

Royce: *In a few weeks. Gotta go. Miss you.*
Michelle: *Miss you too.*
Things appeared fine outside, but why did I feel so sad?

Valentine's Day came, and I received a gorgeous bouquet. I had expected Royce to be home by then, but he'd called me a few days ago, saying something came up and he'd be coming home a few days later.

I felt like a dark cloud had appeared above my head, sending drizzles of sadness over me.

I placed the stunning bouquet of roses and peonies on my kitchen table and opened the card with a message. *Trust me. Miss you.*

Annoyed, I tossed the card aside. What the hell did that mean? The more he kept repeating those words about trust, the more my brain spiraled out of control. Why did he want me to trust him? Did he do something wrong that needed my forgiveness?

Feeling irritated, I needed air and wanted something sweet to eat. A big piece of chocolate cake or a gooey brownie would satisfy me right now.

The temperature was warmer than usual today, and I wore a light coat with a hat on. Driving to the nearby bakery, I picked up some apple tarts, a slice of chocolate cake, a decadent brownie, and a latte. I drove to a park overlooking the ocean, sat in my car, and sipped the caffeinated life force. The warmth traveled down my throat and into my stomach.

Perhaps I'd overreacted with Royce. He was working on recovering his business and also trying to get proof of who had sabotaged my website. He told me the IP address was linked to a property owned by Brittany Parker. The police still hadn't been able to locate her.

A silver BMW pulled into a spot a few down from me and parked. The door opened, and Fiona got out of her car and strode to a bench facing the shore. I blinked at her sudden emergence. I didn't know why, but anger surged when she intruded into my vision, distracting my pretty view. She and Brittany had given me too much grief. I had tried to be a responsible adult, dealing with the matter patiently. But these past few weeks, my patience had run thin.

Fiona needed a taste of her own medicine. I'd always refrained from telling her how I felt because I had to maintain a professional appearance since we worked at NewYou Beauty together. But right now, I didn't give a shit. The world already had the worst ideas about me after that image had been posted on my website. If I had learned anything from the past several months with Royce, it was taking charge of my life.

I had no monsters in my closet. *I'm now the fucking monster.*

Exiting my car, I slammed the door and strode to stand in front of her. I pasted a fake smile on my face, glaring at her.

She blinked, smiled, pressed something on her phone, and lowered it to her lap, smiling at me with her red lips. "Fancy meeting you here. What can I do for you, Michelle?"

"Stay away from me."

"You're the one who came up to me."

"I know what you and your friend Brittany did. You hired a thief to steal from me, placed a bomb in my apartment, and now tried to smear me through my business. What the fuck?"

Fiona's face turned serious, a look I hadn't seen before. "Look, I'm sorry those things happened to you. I had nothing to do with them. Brittany had a tiff with you, and my jealousy got the best of me. The smashed window was a mistake, but I wasn't involved with any of the other crimes." Guilt stirred in her eyes. "I just gave Brittany information on you, that's all."

How could I believe a fox when she'd never shown me an ounce of kindness?

"I'm trying to make things right."

The statement shocked me. Why was she being so nice? Suspicion sparked in me.

"How?"

"By apologizing?" She lifted a shoulder.

I rolled my eyes. That made me think there was something else going on.

What was she trying to do? This was not the Fiona I knew. What tricks did she have up her sleeve? Did she still want Royce back?

I crossed my arms. "You're not getting Royce back." I sounded like a jealous girlfriend, protecting what belonged to me.

She let out a laugh, and amusement glittered in her eyes. "What if I want him?"

"Then you'll have to deal with my wrath. Just because I've held back doesn't mean I don't know how to play dirty."

Fiona's lips twisted into a sly smile. "What exactly can you do?"

"To start, I can also mock up fake images of you and blast them out to the internet. Since you want to be famous, I can make sure your face is on every continent. I have loyal followers who'd be happy to help me spread the news when they find out you're responsible for smearing my name."

"But I had nothing to do with that!"

"I don't care." My eyes widened. "Besides, you said you gave Brittany information about me. You're guilty by association. Why should I give a shit about your feelings when you don't care about me or anyone?" My chest heaved as I let out my frustration. "You're a selfish bitch who thinks the world revolves around you. You have no respect for anyone and flaunt your family's wealth like a DDD chest. People look at you, and all they see is your money. Where's your self-respect?" I inhaled a deep breath. "Stay away from me."

Fiona gaped at me and made no comment, which surprised me.

I guess I wasn't done yet. "If you don't, I'll have to resort to calling Lucille from Lucille's Salon. I understand she's paying you a lot of money for a promotion on your website. I can easily alert her that you've spent time with her husband in Paris."

She gasped. "H-how did you know?"

Lucille's husband had also asked me to accompany him to Paris a year ago when I met him at a banquet, but I'd declined.

"People talk, Fiona. You're not the only one he's been with. And no, I haven't been with him, nor do I have any interest in men who could be my grandfather. I'm sure his wife would *love* to know her precious client had fucked her husband."

Fiona twisted her lips, looking worried. "I told you—I'm making things right."

"Also, stay away from Royce. He's *my* boyfriend, and as a

mature adult, you should respect that. Don't make me show the world who Fiona Clark truly is." I turned and walked away.

"Do you love him?" she asked.

I whirled and faced her calm and curious expression. "I do."

"Does *he* love you?"

Why so many questions, Fiona? The truth was, I didn't know.

"It doesn't matter," I said. "When you love someone, you don't need it to be returned. You love because the person makes you feel cherished more than anyone ever did, and that's enough for me. I hope you find someone to make you feel treasured too." I meant that and left her sitting on the bench to return to her phone call.

Walking back to my car, I opened the door and sagged into my seat, blowing out a hefty breath. I should have shown her my true feelings a long time ago. Perhaps things wouldn't have gotten this bad. Fiona was one person; Brittany was another. I couldn't anticipate the mindset of crazy people.

Feeling drained, I headed home to finish my cake and brownie.

CHAPTER FIFTY-SEVEN

ROYCE

I WORKED LATE into the night to get everything done before my flight back to Providence. I missed Michelle more than I could express, but I had to keep my distance until the entire shit show was over. She had to understand her safety was my top priority.

From my investigation, I discovered that when Edward Bryson was alive, he had used his office to launder drugs and city funds to solicit underage girls for sex. He deserved his horrible death. Anyone who abused children was the lowest scum in society.

The crime organization responsible for his death was expansive and secretive, making it extremely hard to determine who ran it and where they were stationed. In order to protect myself and my loved ones, I had to know who my enemies were. Though these crime lords weren't my "direct enemies," their crimes were close to my friends and me.

We were linked to them on that fateful day so long ago. When innocent young boys with big dreams only wanted to meet up to discuss their video games. That day changed all of us, and I couldn't help but wonder what the universe wanted me to know.

Edward Bryson's body wouldn't have been found if Remi hadn't renovated the garage of his office building. I supposed nothing could hold back the truth, not even concrete. The truth had a way of revealing itself in its own time.

From what I gathered, Dominic Bryson was heading down the same path as his father. A smile curved onto my lips as I flipped through the mental file in my head, containing his crimes.

Did he know how his dad had died? Did he care he could end up with the same fate?

I'd find out in two days when I surprised him at the private event to which I hadn't been invited. Once I showed him what I could do to him, he'd stop trying to ruin my life.

CHAPTER FIFTY-EIGHT

MICHELLE

I'D GOTTEN a lot of writing done and could take a few days off to rest my brain. Royce should be back in a couple of days.

My phone buzzed with an unfamiliar sound. When I checked my lock screen, it showed Eat Your Monsters had new updates.

I logged in. "Sorry, Nibbles. It's been hectic, and I haven't fed you."

A few minutes into the game, I survived a dangerous new terrain, and my bunny devoured multiple beasts, saving more villagers. Feeling happy, I waited to see how many motivation stars and coins I'd earned so I could purchase a new outfit.

Motivation Star: *Be a proton, always positive!*

Coins and Gems: *Two hundred new coins. Three diamonds. Two rubies.*

I gasped, not at the coins and gems, but at the motivational message.

It had to be Royce! No one knew about that line but him

and me. Had he hacked into my phone?

I exited the game and researched the maker.

"No way." It showed the creator as Paradigm Excursions Group. It *was* him.

Why hadn't he mentioned it to me? He probably downloaded the app onto my phone when I wasn't looking. I played it thinking it had been an update to something I already had. It didn't even occur to me to look into it.

Why did he create this app? I had to know. I couldn't wait for him to come back, but I didn't want to call him in case he was in a conference.

Michelle: *Viking, are you busy?*

Royce: *Angel, I always have time for you.*

Michelle: *Did you create the Eat Your Monsters app?*

Royce: *You figured it out. (smile emoji)*

Michelle: *Why didn't you say something to me? Why did you make it?*

Royce: *Do you enjoy playing it?*

Michelle: *Yes. Answer my question.*

Royce: *It's training your mind. Eat Your Monsters is literally killing the monster in you.*

My heart raced at his proclamation. He'd created an app to help me overcome my eating disorder—to steer my brain away from fear by letting me play and making me forget my issues. I hadn't needed my reminders to eat healthy or work out. I knew what to do and hadn't felt guilty if I craved fatty foods or missed a workout.

Love burned in me for this man, and I wanted to hear him say those words to me.

Michelle: *Why?*

Royce: *Why not?*

Dammit. Why couldn't he say it? I knew he loved me,

but I guess it was harder for him. The app and the skydiving were his way of showing his love. I should be satisfied with that.

Michelle: *Thank you.*
Royce: *You're welcome.*
Michelle: *See you soon.*
Royce: *(smile and heart emoji)*

I should be overjoyed, but I couldn't shake this awful feeling still nagging at me.

Perhaps I was overanalyzing things again.

My phone rang, and I picked up the call. "Hi, Mom."

"Sweetheart, there's a banquet we should attend. Celebrities and talent agents will be there. You could land a fabulous job. It's next week at—"

"No. I have a job I love, and I'm not going anywhere." I sighed, no longer having the patience for my mom's inability to listen to my needs. "Are you home?"

"Yes. Why?"

"We can finish this conversation at your place. I'm heading over."

Forty-five minutes later, I arrived at my mom's luxurious townhouse and folded myself on her couch. Charles was traveling for work, leaving Mom home alone to spend time at the spas and salons.

"It's so good to see you, honey." She placed a glass filled with a green drink on the coffee table. "My fitness trainer told me this celery drink is beneficial to your health."

I'd tried it once before and didn't like it. I was done doing things people assumed were good for me. Celery drinks had benefits, but not to me. There were other things I could do to ensure good health.

Ignoring the drink, I faced my mom, who sat beside me.

She'd dyed her hair blonde, wore less makeup, looking more beautiful now than I remembered. She'd always taken good care of herself. I had her brown eyes and high cheekbones.

"Mom, I have something to say. You might not like it, but I need you to hear me."

"Okay, but after that, we can discuss this banquet—"

"No!" I shouted, my arms flying akimbo in the air. "You never listen to my needs. I. Am. Not. Attending. Any. Banquets." I breathed between each word so she understood this wasn't some simple statement.

My mom stared at me as though I'd turned into some fantastical creature from another world. I could see the shock and hurt in her eyes.

"I know you love me, and you've done your best to raise me. But there are things I've been trying to tell you, and you've shoved them aside."

Her lips trembled, and she probably didn't even know what she'd done wrong.

"I just want the best for you."

"I know, Mom." I held her hand and squeezed. "I know you love the pageant world, and you wanted me to shine the way *you* wanted to shine."

She winced at the statement. "I—"

"It's okay. You wanted me to have everything you never got to have. I understand that. You did everything you could to give me the best life." I swallowed as tears filled my vision. "But that life you envisioned suffocated me. The need to be perfect and slim made me ill. I developed an eating disorder, which was a lot worse than you thought. I fell into a severe depression."

Mom placed a hand over her heart and cried. I reached

for the box of tissues and offered her one, then took one for myself.

"I wanted to die that day we went whitewater rafting. When I fell in, I didn't attempt to get out. The pain was too much, and I wanted it to end."

She clamped a hand over her mouth, sobbing uncontrollably. I wrapped my arms around her, knowing this truth hurt like hell. But it was necessary for both of us. This was the only way for us to maintain a loving relationship going forward. I didn't want a wedge between us. She was my mom, my only family.

We cried together for a long moment. Mom pulled back, her mascara all messed up, but she looked more beautiful to me.

"I'm so sorry, honey. I failed you," she said with trembling lips. "I didn't know you were in so much pain." My mom kept pounding on her chest as though punishing herself.

It wrecked me to see her like that.

"Stop it." I gripped her wrist, pulling her hand to my heart. "It's in the past. I'm telling you everything now, so you understand why I don't want to attend those kinds of banquets again. I don't want you to feel guilty. You didn't hurt me on purpose."

"My baby." She touched my face. "What have I done?"

"You raised a strong woman who knows she's worth more than any tiara or title could ever make her feel."

More tears flowed from her eyes as she kissed my forehead.

"This industry can put a glamourous veil over what's real and what's not. I survived."

Her eyes lit up when I told her Royce had saved me from the waters that day and how he found my lost earring.

"You were meant to be together. Now I *have* to meet the man who saved my daughter and thank him personally."

"You'll meet him soon."

I stayed a while longer chatting with my mom. The energy between us changed as though all the muddiness had been replaced by joy. It uplifted me.

Feeling hopeful, I decided to surprise Royce by making him a lovely dinner.

CHAPTER FIFTY-NINE

MICHELLE

I STOPPED by a grocery store near Royce's high-rise to pick up ingredients for BBQ ribs and meatloaf. As I headed out of the parking lot, I drove by a car that looked like Royce's Land Rover. Did he get home early? Was he trying to surprise me too?

I parked the car just as Fiona exited the passenger side. She blew the driver a kiss and wandered over to her silver BMW, parked three spaces away.

Confusion hit me first, then anger and betrayal after. I heard the pieces of my heart shattering and falling to the ground. Each shard stabbed me as it fell. I didn't know why I didn't feel the pain the way I should have. Perhaps my body went into shock.

The man I loved had been cheating on me with a woman he claimed to dislike. Had it all been a lie? How long had this been going on? Was he even traveling for work, or had he been spending time with her?

Was Fiona the reason he hadn't stopped by to see me?

Excuses, excuses.

Why was I surrounded by cheating men? Was it my dark aura? Did I do something bad in my past life to deserve this?

I couldn't think clearly. My mind whirled with scenarios that made me want to hurt Royce and Fiona. Was the fake dating in Iceland an agenda for something else? Did they think I was a fool? Shame and anger boiled in me.

I'm no fool.

Hot tears burned my eyes even as I convinced myself of that. My chest collapsed in on itself, and my breath caught in my throat. I didn't know it was possible to feel this. A strange numbness overtook my body.

Was Fiona the reason he never said those words to me? He didn't love me because he already had another woman. I had been the most vulnerable I could be to him, letting him see all my flaws and fears.

Wanting to be home, I sped up out of the lot, almost hitting a lady with a cart.

Calm down, Michelle. You're better than this. Don't let a man determine your worth.

I heard someone call my name, and I didn't give a damn that it was Royce.

CHAPTER SIXTY

ROYCE

FUCKING HELL.

I didn't expect to see Michelle in my rearview mirror. What were the chances she'd be shopping at the grocery store near my home?

I called her phone, but she didn't pick up and left a message asking her to return my call. When I got home, I gave her thirty minutes before calling again. No answer.

I texted her instead.

Royce: *I need you to trust me.*

Michelle: *Trust what? That you and Fiona made a fool out of me?*

Royce: *It's not what it seems.*

Michelle: *It seems to be a lot more. She blew you a kiss. Did she blow you somewhere else? Don't wanna know.*

I could sense the anger in her messages.

Royce: *Calm down. You'll understand everything in a few days.*

Michelle: *Go to hell. I'm done with cheating men. Leave me alone.*

Her words cleaved my heart in two. My body jerked from the shock and pain. I felt my body fall apart like overcooked meat sliding off, leaving the bone bare. I collapsed onto my couch, clutching my chest. I hadn't felt this much anguish in so long.

She meant it. She was done with me.

I sat for a long moment, trying to piece myself together. Shit had to get done, and I'd explain everything to her later. I loved her too much to risk her safety.

I thought back to a few days ago when I overheard her conversation where she'd threatened Fiona to get her to leave me alone.

My angel was trying to protect me. Love and pride had surged through me when I heard her voice over the phone. I'd been having a conversation with Fiona, finalizing the plan for tomorrow, when Michelle unexpectedly disrupted the call. I had been on the line, listening to everything.

Working with Fiona was the last thing I wanted, but she had tickets for tomorrow's private gathering that I had to attend. Helping me was her pass out of the mess she'd caused with Brittany, who had been off her meds for some time. She'd also dated Dominic.

I had no doubt Dominic showed Brittany how to stay under the radar. The Icelandic police were working with the US officials to search for her. Brittany had several residences in New England and California. She could be anywhere.

There were so many possible scenarios where I could confront Dominic. My initial method would have been to surprise him after work, show up at his gym, or wait for him after his doctor's visit. These scenes ended with me beating the shit out of him. But after careful consideration, I decided patience yielded better results. Every scientist knew time and dedication were crucial.

I'd been watching Dominic, reviewing his past and present. The PI had delivered helpful information which offered me new insight into his vendetta against me. Phone records from Dominic's private number showed he'd been the phony vendor conversing with Einar, trying to sabotage Excursions for You. Still, an established police officer with a beautiful wife and two sons like him should forget the scuffles from the past.

Despite the pros and cons weighing in my head, Dominic was the chief of police now, and he could create more issues for me. I didn't need any more fires to put out.

With enough information on hand, I could blindside him and rattle his mental state.

Fiona didn't have anything to do with harming Michelle. Fiona's words and personality made her the perfect substitute—the scapegoat for all the wrongdoings. She didn't know I had already cleared her, but I needed leverage. If she helped me, I'd keep her name out of the files I'd soon offer to the authorities.

With me researching Dominic, it made sense that he had men following me too. For that reason, I didn't want to risk them finding out about Michelle. My aunt and Michelle were the most important women in my life. If I kept my distance from them, Dominic would assume I lived only for myself.

He could target me and leave everyone else alone.

Michelle had misunderstood me. I loved her. And I had to refrain from saying those words because if I gave her hope, it would have hurt her more during the past month with me staying away.

There was no other woman for me. She was my soul.
I'd explain everything to her after tomorrow.

CHAPTER SIXTY-ONE

ROYCE

DRESSED in my slacks and my Robert Graham shirt, I accompanied Fiona—who wore a blue dress—to an elite country club reserved for Dominic's birthday.

The hostess with red hair checked our tickets, glanced at Fiona, and smiled at her. "It's great to see you again. How are your parents?"

"They're wonderful, Annabelle. Thanks for asking."

Annabelle looked at me and grinned. "Have a good time."

Two more couples came up behind us, and we broke off from the check-in desk. I observed the fancy decorations that made me think of a wedding reception. Someone stationed birthday balloons around the large dining area. A band had set up on the side of a stage. People stood around tables drinking cocktails or nibbling on finger foods.

Did adults still have birthday celebrations like this? I'd been to a fiftieth or eightieth celebration because they were pivotal milestones in one's life, but nothing in between, especially this extravagant. Outrageous birthday parties were for kids or men who still needed attention. Just my opinion.

A group of women waved at Fiona, and she offered me a nod, signifying I was on my own and that her deal with me had been fulfilled.

I walked up to the bar, browsing for Dominic. Spotting him chatting with two men in crisp white shirts and dark slacks, I studied how he talked with suggestive hands. He'd always wanted to be the center of attention. A respected high school athlete. A popular kid who had most boys wanting to be him. All except me. I didn't have friends in high school, except my video game boys. I kept pretty much to myself, although the football coach had approached me several times, trying to recruit me. Maybe that was another reason Dominic hated me.

As though he sensed a foreign energy on his turf, he turned, met my gaze, and said something to the other men.

Walking toward me, his blue eyes glared. He'd gained some weight and muscles. He still wore his brown hair short, but he was balding. I went to a public high school and had always wondered why Dominic wasn't in private school. Apparently, his family had owned several properties in Providence and wanted to save money by keeping Dominic in a public school, not that there was anything wrong with public schools. Some of the most successful people I'd encountered attended public schools.

Education was important, but the drive to succeed determined a person's success.

Dominic's jaw tightened as he came up to me. "Follow me. *Now*."

"Are you talking to me?' I looked around. "I don't answer to you, Dominic."

Dominic flared his nostrils and changed his demeanor as more men approached the bar, wishing him a happy birthday.

After he chatted with his friends, he turned to me and forced a smile. "Let's have a discussion in the back office. Shall we?"

"We shall." I slapped his back playfully. "Happy birthday, man! It's been a long time. You're the same asshole I knew from high school." I grinned at the bartender. "We go way back."

"It's nice to have good friends," said the bartender as he made a drink for someone. "My friends and I used to pound on each other for fun."

"Oh, 'friends' isn't the right word to describe us."

Indignation flashed in Dominic's eyes as he gestured to the hallway. I stepped into the spacious office, and Dominic closed the door. A desk sat in one corner with several file cabinets. Dominic stalked over to a round mahogany coffee table surrounded by dark brown leather couches and armchairs.

"What are you doing here? Who the fuck let you in?"

"Manners dictate you ask me to sit down, Dominic." I stared at him, no amusement in my voice. "We're no longer high school boys, but grown men with social status. I'd like to think we can resolve our issues maturely, *Chief Bryson*."

His jaw tightened as he jabbed a finger at the armchair. He took a seat, and I folded into the one across from him, needing to see his face.

"Just like you, I also have friends who can buy me a ticket. Besides, I'm here to wish you a happy birthday. To ensure you have plenty more to celebrate, I think it's wise to leave me and mine alone."

"I'm not sure what you're talking about," he said, looking smug.

I glanced at my watch. "Well, check your email right now."

The PI should have already sent Dominic a file with embarrassing images of him with several women in Las Vegas. He'd been drunk with his friends—some of which were in his department. All were married.

He gaped at his phone, and his fingers tensed an angry white. "Where did you get these? These are fake! You want me to arrest you, fucker?"

"You know they're not fake. I also have a video if you'd like. There's also clips of it on social media with your face blocked out. That's what you get for cheating on your wife with some girl who was obviously pissed. I like her sass, though."

"What do you want?" he barked.

"Why are you trying to destroy my business?" I eyed him. "I know you hired Oskar to sabotage my excursion site, but he failed and died for it. You also hired an ex-con to kill James McNabb at my resort in Oregon." He opened his mouth to deny it, but I held up a hand. "I tracked the ex-con down and offered him triple the amount of money for the truth. He's living comfortably in another country right now."

"You have no proof."

"I have enough to destroy your career. Your family."

He sneered with contempt. "You ruined my life."

"How?"

Dominic lifted his arm, pulled it back, and winced before he pitched an invisible ball. "You broke my arm, injured my shoulder, and destroyed my dream of playing baseball. I had a full-ride athletic scholarship, but I couldn't go."

"Don't blame me for something *you* started," I reminded him. "You and your friend jumped me. It's called self-defense, Chief. Wasn't that part of your law enforcement exam? I sat in a jail cell because of *you.*"

He balled his hands into fists.

"You had all these years to come after me. Why now?" When he didn't answer, I added, "Does it have something to do with your father's death? I heard about it on the news. He got himself into some shit."

Dominic shot me a look that told me he knew something I didn't. "My father was an abusive asshole. I don't care how he died," he said callously. "Did it ever occur to you why the police let you go so easily?" He studied me. "How you didn't even have a record of any wrongdoing?"

I'd never even considered that, but now that he brought it up. What did Dominic know that I didn't? I doubted he'd tell me.

"It's because I'm an exceptional citizen."

"I wanted to press charges, but the detective told me it would be difficult since we were all fighting. Normally, it would've been easy to pin something on people like you. My family has connections to the city, but the detective told me to let it slide." A smirk slid onto his lips. "Someone made sure you had a clean record to attend college. Your life isn't on the straight and narrow either."

The news shocked me. Who had been helping me? Why?

"Maybe that someone believed I could be of service to society." I gave him no indication that I was clueless. "I can't help it if other people want to help me. Whereas you *inten-*

tionally want to destroy me because you can't let go of a grudge. In a courtroom, 'intention' is very important. I'm sure Brittany Parker—whom you also fucked—will have a lot to say on the witness stand."

"Get out!" He shot up from his chair and flung an arm at the door.

"Happy to." I got up from my seat. "That email is just one piece of evidence. There's more where that came from. If you know what's good for you, leave me and mine alone. I can easily send you a bill for all the damages you've done to my global business. That alone will bankrupt you."

"You destroyed my dream, my life," he seethed.

"You cheated your way through high school. You ruined your life on your own. Besides, you made my life hell back then. Do you see me coming after you? You framed the former chief and forced him out of office. I have evidence of that too."

Fuming, he stared at me for a long moment. "This isn't over. I'm Chief of Police, and I'm going to make your life hell."

It's already over with your statement, fucker.

"Do you know how your dad died?" I asked. "Why was his body buried inside the wall of a garage? Are you connected to the same people who killed him?"

He glared at me. "I'm an asset to them. And you're in my way."

"So you know who killed your father? And you're working for the same people?"

I considered the silence to be admission. How could he work for a dangerous organization when he knew what they'd done to his father?

"Just so you know, I can destroy a man just as easily as

you can. Money can buy many things that don't leave traces of DNA. Remember that when you touch what's mine."

His face twitched, probably already plotting while weighing the pros and cons.

Arriving home, I downloaded the recording of our conversation to my computer to be sent out to the news station upon my request. I deleted the sections with my threats. That wouldn't benefit my career or research program.

The meeting was to coax Dominic into incriminating himself. He wasn't the smartest guy back then, and I made an educated guess nothing had changed. My sudden appearance ensured he wouldn't be prepared to have cameras at the birthday party. But I was prepared.

Dominic didn't even flinch at my threats, which meant he had someone powerful backing him. Or he already had a backup plan.

Either way, I sensed a storm brewing. But he brought up a good question I needed answers to: who had helped me back then?

CHAPTER SIXTY-TWO

MICHELLE

I HADN'T SLEPT at all last night. The image of Fiona leaving Royce's car kept replaying in my head, mocking me. Now the sun had risen, and I was wide awake.

It was stupid of me to keep thinking about it, but I couldn't help it.

Had everything been an act from the beginning? Had he been with her while he was with me? I hated myself for not being able to stop the insecurity stabbing me in all directions.

What was missing here? Why didn't it make sense? I caught them with my own eyes. The pain was too much for me to think clearly. I had to let it go so I could function properly.

Right now, I felt like my body was in one place while my mind was in another, and my soul was still in bed under the covers. I was all over the place.

Logically, it didn't make sense, but the scattered pieces of me *understood* it. Still in bed, I stared at the ceiling, feeling sorry for myself, which I knew was a bad idea. I was human, and I could feel crappy and have bad days. But that didn't mean life ended.

Life went on after a breakup. Everyone had gone through some type of suffering, and my life wasn't defined by a man.

I had a splendid life, a fabulous career, and dreams of traveling the world. Just because my heart was in pieces didn't mean I couldn't achieve everything else. I could glue my heart back together piece by piece. In doing so, I'd make it into a better heart, a stronger one.

Bolting up from my bed, I switched my mindset from gloomy to grateful. Ready to seize the day, I walked into the bathroom and organized a plan: a good workout to start my day, order some delicious food, and then binge some TV shows. I was in the mood for some crime shows where I could be the anti-hero who went after those who had hurt me. Yup, that sounded like a superb plan. Then the next day, I could hang out with my girls and vent.

Already feeling better, I put on my workout clothes and glanced at my phone. *Ugh.* I cursed myself for not remembering to charge it last night. I blamed *him* for upsetting me.

I drove down the street to the local gym instead of walking because I needed my car for shopping later.

Don't look. Don't look.

I glanced at my phone one last time. No message from Royce. No voicemail or email either. Why did I do this to myself?

Because you're in love.

He'd gotten under my skin—no, even deeper than that. It would take extensive surgery to extract him.

While checking my email, I noticed I'd missed an email from Kiera. She'd emailed all of us girls to thank us for helping with the charity. Between Royce and Remington, they donated a total of two million dollars to the charity. It was the charity's largest donation to date.

Royce donated one million for the five shirts I'd made for him. Would he wear them now? Royce and Remington had loads of money, so one million for each of them was nothing.

Still, it was a generous donation that deserved my gratitude. I should thank Royce. Maybe after my workout and shopping spree when my heart didn't ache so much.

I found off-street parking right in front of the gym, got out, and prepared to enter the building when shouts erupted across the street.

"Get the fuck off!" My friend Viktor was struggling with three men. One of them punched him while another covered his face with a cloth. The third man opened the side door to a van and shoved Viktor in.

It happened so fast and petrified me. I got in my car, dialed 911, turned on the speaker, and placed my phone on the passenger seat while I tried to catch up to the van. A part of me couldn't believe this was happening. Fear knotted my stomach as concern for Viktor spiked.

The operator picked up. "911. What's your emergency?"

I told the operator the situation, and that I was following the van, but keeping my distance.

"Do you have the license plate? Can you describe the car? What street are you on?"

"I can't get close enough to see the plates. The van has a red star painted on the side. They're turning down Francis Street, passing the Providence Place Mall."

"Okay, miss. Thank you. We have police heading that way. You should—"

"Hello? Hello?" I looked over at my black screen.

Shit! My phone died. I'd forgotten to charge it last night. I probably had a charger in my trunk, but there was no time for me to stop the car and search for it. Those critical seconds could cause me to lose sight of the van.

I prayed the police could locate the van before something awful happened. Adrenaline pumped through me as I concentrated on the white van that was two cars in front of me.

Was Viktor okay? Who were these men? Why did they kidnap him? I didn't know Viktor well, but I'd met him, spoken to him, and he was nice to me. Now he was in danger. Any normal human being would try to help.

If I were kidnapped, I hoped someone who witnessed it would try to help me.

As I kept my gaze on the van, fear had me grasping for hope and safety. Royce's face popped into my mind. Would I get the chance to hear Royce's voice, hear him explain? Tears filled my eyes.

No time to cry, Michelle.

The tears came anyway. I'd tried to stop loving him by counting all the bad things he'd done. Only one incident hurt me. Before that event, he'd been the perfect man for me.

Love was a force of nature; it couldn't be stopped when it was real and raw. How could I stop the sun from shining? Love was that bright light that gave life to everything. It warmed my heart, healed me, and gave me the courage to reclaim myself.

How could I not love the man who yanked the door open to stand beside me while *I* battled my monster? He knew the best way for me to truly move on was to do the killing myself.

Tears blurred my vision, and I wiped them with the back of my hand.

Realization overcame me. I could still love someone who didn't reciprocate. We'd talk when all this was over.

The van turned into a junkyard. I drove past it, parked on a small street, got out, and headed toward the entrance on foot. I had no clue what I was doing and functioned mostly on intuition and adrenaline.

A few old buildings surrounded the junkyard, but I wasn't sure if they were in business. I crouched at the entrance, looking for any signs of men. When I didn't see anyone, I darted in, staying close to broken cars and stacks of tires.

I spotted the white van up ahead near a blue warehouse. As I prepared to leave, a cold surface pressed into my neck.

"Get up."

A bald man dressed in black with a mean face zip-tied my wrists, leading me to the warehouse. Terror spiked in me.

For some reason, I glanced back and saw a familiar black sedan drive past.

CHAPTER SIXTY-THREE

ROYCE

WHO HAD KEPT my records clean in high school?

I'd spent most of the evening trying to research, but came up with nothing. Another issue that hovered was how to approach Michelle and explain everything. I gave my brain a rest and showed Grayson the demo of my Level Two, and he showed me portions of his Level Three.

"It's looking good," said Grayson over the computer screen.

"Thanks, man. I'll upload it to the website for the others to see soon."

My phone rang, and I glanced at the number, my stomach knotting.

"I'll be right back," I told Grayson and walked away from the screen.

Standing by the window, I picked up the call. "What's up, Jett?"

Jett was a bodyguard I'd hired to watch over Michelle since she came back from Iceland. He was told to keep his distance unless she needed his assistance. He'd been following her around and giving me updates.

"Ms. Yates is in danger."

"What happened?"

"She's been captured in a junkyard. I'm heading in, but I wanted to alert you. I'm not sure how many men are in there. Her neighbor was kidnapped, and she followed the van."

"Give me the location. I'll meet you there. Keep me posted when you can." A sick feeling settled in my gut. "Did you alert the authorities?"

"I did." Jett was a retired police officer, so he knew the drill.

Ending the call, I returned to my desk and told Grayson, "Gotta go. Michelle's in trouble."

"Do you need my help?"

"You busy?"

"Not anymore."

Twenty minutes later, Grayson sat in the passenger seat while I alerted the PI to send my files to all the news stations about Dominic Bryson. The file would come from an anonymous source, showing the people of Providence that their chief of police was corrupt. The city and media could take what they would from that statement.

Not knowing who I could trust in the Providence police department, I'd asked the PI to alert his FBI friends. Being a former CIA agent, he had useful connections.

Was Dominic behind the kidnapping? Was he retaliating against me for threatening his ass? But it appeared Michelle hadn't been the initial target. Who was Michelle's male friend?

"She'll be fine," Grayson said, probably sensing my concern.

I nodded and pulled up behind Michelle's car, got out, and tapped the image the PI had sent me. It showed a bird's eye view of the junkyard.

Grayson patted his waist where he had his gun. We were both licensed and practiced often at the shooting range.

A shot rang out in the air, and my heart stopped as concern for Michelle sucked the air from my lungs. I rushed toward the blue warehouse, using the back path to stay out of view in case there were cameras. My heart pounded with fear.

Please be safe, baby.

If they hurt Michelle, I'd kill them all.

Grayson followed beside me, and my heart dropped when I stumbled on Jett, who lay bleeding on the ground with a hand to his stomach.

"You okay?" I asked, checking out the wound on his abdomen.

"Yeah." He smiled and winced. "She's in the warehouse. Be careful. The cop shot me."

Fucking Dominic, I should have broken both his arms on his birthday.

"You go to Michelle. I'll take him to safety," Grayson said, hauling a pale Jett to his feet.

Pulling out my gun, I cocked it and made my way toward the warehouse, staying close to the wall. I stopped by a small window with a crack.

"Let her go," said the male voice with an Icelandic accent. Terror twisted my stomach. I'd heard his voice before. On that fateful day, when I'd returned to the abandoned church to retrieve my cell phone, he'd been scouting the area.

I tried to see his face, but there were boxes in the way.
Was he working with Dominic?

CHAPTER SIXTY-FOUR

MICHELLE

"WHY WOULD I LET HER GO?" Dominic smirked.

To say I was shocked to discover the police chief was behind Viktor's abduction was an understatement. Added to that, Fiona and Brittany's unconscious bodies slouched against the wall close to me.

Dominic Bryson had entered to inform the guard "to bring the girls out" on his request. What did that mean?

Viktor glowered at Dominic, and for a moment, I could see Royce in him. It hit me that Viktor could be related to Royce. Was that the reason for the capture?

"What do you want, Chief?" Viktor asked.

"You betrayed the organization by killing a member. They're out to torture you. I've got some interesting information about you too. I'll let the organization review it first." He looked my way. "As for her, I'll be selling her along with these two"—gesturing to Fiona and Brittany—"to the highest bidder. Wealthy men would love them as sex slaves." He stared at me and smirked. "I can't wait to show Royce pictures of you with other men. I'll destroy whatever belongs to him. Did you enjoy the image on your website?"

Oh my God. My mouth dried up like the Sahara Desert. Nausea rose as my stomach twisted into painful knots.

"No one leaves until I say so," Dominic said to the guard standing at the door—our only way out—and left the room.

Fear numbed me, but the will to survive brought me back to my senses. *No time to be numb.*

Viktor bumped his shoulders with mine. "Don't be afraid. Help is coming."

I appreciated his attempt. He was worse off than me, with a bruised face. What organization was he involved in?

"You look like my friend Royce."

Viktor smiled. "Just as good-looking?"

"Better," I teased.

He leaned in and whispered, "He's my son, and he hates me."

I sucked in a breath at the shocking news. Royce told me that his father had abandoned him and his family a long time ago.

I didn't know what to say. I had a lot of questions, but this wasn't the time for that conversation. How would Royce react?

The name intrigued me. "Your name is Viktor, and Royce's last name is Viktorsson. Is there a correlation between the father's name to the surname?"

"Very perceptive. In our country, the children take the father's first name and add a suffix. Royce is literally Viktor's son. My daughter's last name is Viktorsdóttir—Viktor's daughter."

That was so basic and interesting. "It makes so much sense. Simple and to the point."

His blue eyes crinkled in the corners. "My son loves you."

My eyebrows furrowed. "How do you know?"

"I've watched him grow up from the sideline. I had dangerous things to do and didn't keep in touch the way a father should have. I wanted him safe. He's never been happier than when he was with you. I see it in his eyes, the way he walks. There's love and joy in him."

Fiona and Brittany woke from their sleep, looking drowsy. Wincing, Fiona glanced around and met my gaze. "You're here too? Where are we?"

"Warehouse. Looks like we're all in the same boat," I replied, not wanting to think about my qualm with her.

Brittany glared at me and looked at Fiona. "What the hell is going on? Dominic told me he'd take me somewhere exotic. I felt dizzy after he gave me a drink." She rubbed her head.

"He told me he got tickets to Armani's new fashion show and gave me a drink. The asshole drugged us."

It was ironic how I ended up in this situation with two of my enemies.

Looking frantic, Brittany cried out, "Dominic! You killed Larus, and now you want to kill me too? Where the fuck are you?"

She kicked her legs and continued shouting for him. Fiona tried to calm her down, telling her to be quiet. Brittany glared at me. "It's all your fault. When I told him you were with Royce, something in him changed."

I shot her an irritated look. "I don't know what your deal is, but we could die any minute. Let's conserve our energy so we can escape. Your hatred toward me isn't going to help you get out of here."

"I should have won all those tiaras! You stole them from me!"

Was this really happening? She sounded like an adolescent, throwing a tantrum about something that happened a long time ago.

"I donated them to the local shelter, but you're welcome to go there and get them."

Tears ran down her cheek. "I should have been the winner! I was the most beautiful! You stole the pageants!"

"It's not her fault," Fiona said, surprising me.

Brittany cried, placing her head on Fiona's shoulder.

"Shh . . . We should be quiet before Dominic comes back to kill us," Fiona said.

While the female drama occurred, Viktor kept his gaze on the guard, who appeared to be glued to his phone.

Fiona turned to me. "I'm sorry for being such a bitch. I was jealous of what you had with Royce. He was right. I should have moved on a long time ago. He's crazy about you. Sorry."

I never thought I'd hear those words from Fiona's mouth. Was she still affected by the drugs Dominic had given her? So many surprises occurred today, making me wonder if I was having some massive nightmare.

I was an adult and didn't want any drama in my life. "Apology accepted."

Dominic strode in, and all the attention went to him. "The truck is here. Take the women out. I'll deal with him."

The guard took Brittany and Fiona first. They kicked and screamed. "Leave us alone, asshole!"

"I have a daughter. Please don't hurt me," Brittany begged, sounding more like an adult. "Lily needs me. Please stop. You're hurting me!"

The guard appeared irritated by her cry. This fluctuation in personality showed how unstable she was.

Dominic slapped her. "Shut up! Where are your fucking meds? You're irritating the fuck out of me!"

Anger spiked in me. The jerk was inciting her, knowing she was unwell.

"You only got the balls to hit women?" I said.

He stalked over and gripped my shoulders, yanking me to my feet. He dragged me to the door after I kicked him in the shin. I wasn't going to be someone's sex slave. I'd rather die. My teeth sank into the hand on my shoulder.

He shoved me away, glanced at the red marks, then charged at me. Viktor used his body and slammed into Dominic, pushing him against a wooden table.

The sounds of a helicopter startled me. When the police sirens roared close, hope sparked in me.

Ignoring everyone, Dominic spoke into his phone, "What the fuck is going on?"

A loud explosion erupted outside and shook the entire warehouse.

The door flew open, and Royce charged in, shot the guard in the chest and blasted Dominic in his legs. He dropped, screaming in agony.

Royce grabbed a pair of shears on a shelf, rushed over, clipped my zip ties, and stared at Viktor for a moment before releasing Fiona and Brittany.

The unfriendly look he tossed at Viktor had me saying, "He saved me, Royce." I grabbed the shears from his hand and released Viktor.

"Let's get out of here. The front is burning." Royce gestured to Fiona and Brittany, who exited first.

"You fucker!" Dominic screamed and lifted his gun at Royce.

My heart raced as I rushed to push Royce out of the way, but Viktor got to him first. Viktor took the bullet aimed at Royce and collapsed to the ground. Blood poured from the back of his shoulder.

Royce cursed and fired three bullets into Dominic's chest, ending his life.

CHAPTER SIXTY-FIVE

ROYCE

THE DOCTOR EXAMINED Michelle and cleared her to go home. She hesitated and wanted to stop by to check on Viktor, but he was still in surgery. I had someone looking after him who would give me updates. That was the nice thing to do for someone who took a bullet for me. It didn't matter if that person was my father.

I'd need to face that issue soon, but I wasn't in the proper headspace to deal with that mess right now.

Entering Michelle's apartment, I said, "We need to talk."

"Let me shower off the filth first." Fatigue weighed on her face.

"Take your time."

If it had been a different day, I would ask to join her, but I knew she needed the time alone to refresh her mind and settle her heart.

Jett would recover soon. If he were interested, I'd hire him to be full-time security for a new building I'd purchased. I made sure his hospital bills were sent to me.

With a moment to breathe, I leaned back on the couch

and glanced at the ten voicemails from my aunt, probably wanting to know when I'd visit Viktor. I needed time, dammit.

People couldn't expect me to just wipe away all those years he hadn't been present. Where was my father when I needed him to teach me how to ride a bike? Where was my father when I needed help with a science project or someone to cheer me on at my game?

Tears tried to push their way out of my eyes, but I pushed them down. I wasn't the eight-year-old boy all alone after the death of his mother. I wasn't the frightened kid who wondered where his dad had been when he needed him most.

I knew I couldn't avoid him, and I didn't want to. It was delayed action—a pause in my life's hypothesis. Sometimes the pause revealed more than the action itself. Questions needed answers. Why did he leave his family? What was more important than *his family?*

My fingers curled into fists. The more I thought about it, the angrier I got. This emotional drain exhausted me. I needed energy to repair my relationship with Michelle. She didn't even know I loved her.

Love made me give my father a moment's pause. Before Michelle, I couldn't have cared less if he'd shown up. Why should I welcome him into my life when he never attempted to visit? But love transformed people. I believed it now because I wanted to hear his explanation. And Michelle said he'd saved her, so he got points there. He also saved my life, so I supposed he was racking up points.

I was about to put away my phone when I received an incoming call from Oskar's wife.

Unsure of why she was calling, I picked up.

"Sara, is everything okay?"

"It's been a while," Oskar said. "How are you?"

I blinked as chills skidded down my spine. "Oskar? It's really you?"

He mentioned the date when he'd been hired at Excursions for You.

"Where have you been?"

"In hiding. Now that the fucker is dead, I'm back. He would have come after Sara and the kids if he knew I was alive. A good guy saved me and offered me a place to stay until I was well again. Now I'm back, but with a new identity. I don't think Dominic's associates would track me. Oskar Karlsson is now dead, okay? My family and I are moving to Finland. My new name is Arto Eskola."

I agreed new identities were the safest route for him and his family. The elusive crime organization needed to be uncovered. At our last get-together, the boys and I discussed this. It would be another side project we'd work on besides the video game. We couldn't just sit around and pray that someone wouldn't link us to that day. Perhaps no one would find out, but it gave us peace of mind that we were doing something about it.

We had more than ourselves to protect now. For Remi, it was Audri. For me, it was Michelle.

"That's wonderful, Arto. Who helped you?"

"I'm not sure. I was out of it when I felt someone drag me away. When I woke, a guard offered me the phone to speak to the unknown man. All I know is that he doesn't like Dominic or his father. I didn't pry, though. I had issues of my own." He sighed. "Thank you for taking care of my family. The money helped Sara a lot. I know I didn't buy as many policies as you told her. I'm forever grateful. I should probably buy more now, though." He laughed.

"Thank you for not shooting me."

"I couldn't kill you. You gave me a job when others denied me one. I'd never forget that. I should have come to you when Dominic first threatened to kill my family. Did you check all the other employees? Maybe he got to them too."

"I did. A few have been arrested. Dominic would've eventually asked them to blow up my excursion sites. He didn't want to see me succeed."

"What did you do to him to garner this revenge?"

"During a fight in high school, I broke his arm, injured his shoulder, and that stopped him from being a baseball player."

"What an asshole."

"The more power a man gains, the bigger the ego. A massive ego blinds a man. He believed the organization could protect him, so that gave him free rein without consequences."

"I'm glad he's dead. My first cancer treatment starts next week. I got a scan the other day, and the tumor has shrunk. Must be God's will."

"Make the best of it."

We chatted for a few more minutes until he had to help his wife.

I was thrilled for Oskar—Arto—and his family. His kids could now grow up with their dad. An uncomfortable ache pulled at my chest.

"Why are you smiling?" Michelle strode over to the couch and stood in front of me, looking more refreshed.

"Oskar is *alive*," I said, gripping her wrists to check on the markings left by the zip ties.

"That's fantastic news!" Her eyes glittered. "How? What happened? I thought they said he died."

I updated her and said we could visit Arto and his family soon.

She let out a sigh. "At least that's one bit of good news to balance out the day."

I brought her wrists to my lips, kissing the markings and wishing I could erase them. Though Michelle hadn't been seriously injured, the fear she must have experienced wouldn't be forgotten.

"He should've died a more painful death." I pulled her down onto my lap and studied her. She was stunning, perfect, and mine. I could have lost her today. Every time I closed my eyes and thought back to when I heard the first gunshot, my heart lost its function.

The anger that should have been in her eyes wasn't there. Maybe she was too tired to feel anything. Or maybe she didn't love me anymore.

"Are we okay?" I asked.

"I don't know." She shrugged. "I'm ready for your explanation."

The distrust in her voice pricked my heart. "There's nothing between Fiona and me. Dominic was on a vendetta to destroy me, and I didn't want him to know about you. So I kept you at arm's length for your safety. Fiona had connections that were useful, so I asked for her help in exchange to keep her name out of the news."

Confused, she furrowed her eyebrows.

"Information was sent to the media about the corrupt police chief and those associated with him. Fiona didn't have anything to do with hurting you. That was all Brittany. I knew you'd react the way you did, which was why I kept reminding you to *trust* me."

"It's hard to trust when my eyes tell me otherwise. All trust and logic left my brain at that moment. When I saw you with her, I lost it. You would have reacted the same way."

"I would have killed the guy."

"I was devastated, but a part of me clung to hope. I knew I was missing something, but I couldn't find the piece." She brushed her fingers over my chin, feeling my stubble.

I shifted Michelle's body to straddle my thighs, facing me. Nerves churned in my stomach as heat rose in my body. I was a grown man who went skydiving like it was my pastime for entertainment. I loved the thrill, the edge where my breath hung with danger. The sensation liberated me. Yet here I was, frightened to confess my love to a woman who opened my heart. She was the only woman who made me feel vulnerable . . . and alive.

My heart palpitated as though I was preparing to jump off a bridge. It pounded, pumping blood through my veins, making me fully aware of the rhythm of my breathing. I should be used to this stimulation, but exposing my deepest feelings was uncharted terrain. I'd never done it before. Was I doing it correctly? Would there be quicksand waiting to swallow me up?

Courage was having an affair with that which frightens you. I gave courage my most intimate offering—my genuine and unprotected heart and all its facets.

I blew out a breath because my body needed to loosen the tension.

Just tell her.

Michelle looked at me with suspicion. "What are you still hiding from me?"

I looked her square in the eye and bared my soul. "Before you, I lived life like an adventure, moving from one to another with no real emotions—not the intimate kind. I'd locked those up deep inside me—sort of like a dormant volcano, never imagining it would come alive." Grabbing her hand, I placed it over my erratic heartbeat.

She pressed her lovely lips together, but didn't interrupt me.

"But you penetrated that depth, ignited that fire, and my soul erupted with all these raw and unfamiliar feelings. They spilled out of me, scorching, unstoppable, and unforgettable, like lava carving into my soul, making me *feel* all the emotions. Making me aware of my body, my heart, and even my surroundings. The air is sweeter, and the sun is brighter *because* of you. Everything is more vibrant because of you. Your love has permanently transformed me, and that scared me. I didn't think I deserved love."

"Everyone deserves love, Royce. It's what we all seek even if we might not know it."

I interlaced my fingers with hers. Before I could say those sacred words on the tip of my tongue, she had to understand how she'd changed me.

"You make me feel wanted—like I have more to offer this world. Your love makes me feel *alive*."

A jewel of a tear glistened as it slid down her cheek. "Ditto."

I wiped the tear away with my knuckle. "To feel is to never forget, and I'll never forget how loving you has changed me."

She sucked in a breath and bore those beautiful brown eyes into me.

"I love you." The words came out like a graceful current of air, carrying my deepest and sacred emotions to her.

She blinked.

She cried.

She smiled.

Cupping my face with her hands, she showered me with sloppy kisses. I remained still, allowing her to decorate my face and mouth with kisses.

Drawing back, she said with tearful eyes, "Say it again." A kiss landed on my cheek.

"I love you."

"Again." Another kiss landed on my forehead.

"I love you."

A third kiss landed on my lips, and she threw her arms around my neck, touching her forehead to mine. "I could listen to you saying those words over and over again."

"Then you'll hear them every day . . . *if* you move in with me." I wiggled my eyebrows.

She narrowed her eyes. "Is that an ultimatum?"

"It's whatever you want it to be. Consider living with me as an 'adventure.' An indoor 'excursion' for you."

Her face brightened. "What kind of excursion are you thinking about?"

"I'll leave that to you, angel. You've got a wild mind, so surprise me." I tapped her forehead. "Think about it. I've got a huge place, and you'll save on rent and other expenses."

"I can't live with you for free."

"Who says it's for free? I'll be taking advantage of you every chance I get. Like right now." I kissed her long and hard. "Now that we're 'lavas' again, let's take this relationship even further."

She burst out laughing. "You don't have to wear those T-shirts, you know. They were for charity."

"Hell, yeah, I'm gonna wear them. You made them for *me*. They're brilliant." I placed a hand on either side of her shoulder. "If you had money to do whatever you want, what would it be?"

She twisted her lips, thinking. "I'm doing what I love now, which is blogging about things I'm passionate about. But I've developed a new passion ever since I met you."

I smiled. "Like what?"

"I want to help you expand Eat Your Monsters. I've got some ideas. Are you currently selling it?"

"No. I made that just for you. It was an idea I wanted to incorporate into WaterFyre Rising video game and let you play a variation of it."

"It works, Royce. It's a brilliant game that can help people overcome their traumas. We can create different scenarios that mimic an illness, a phobia, a fear, and public speaking—whatever. I read you can incite the brain by targeting it creatively. You did that for me, and I think other people will love it."

Could I possibly love her any more than I already do?

"I already started on it. You can lead that project. Then we'll sell the app."

"I love you so much." She embraced me. "Why do you have to be so perfect?"

"I'm not perfect. It's because you love me and transformed my imperfections into something worthy. I'd do anything for you."

"Do you mean it?"

"Of course."

"Then visit Viktor with me. It's time to heal that part of you. Don't you want closure?"

"I do."

"Then why wait?" She eyed me curiously.

"I haven't seen him since I was five years old. It's been too long." I swallowed the lump in my throat. "I forgot what he looked like, Michelle. There's a big gap in my life without him. He abandoned us. Yes, he took a bullet for me, but I'm not sure how I should feel. Right now, I feel more resentment than gratitude. I can't help it. There are questions I need to ask, but the emotional storm in me is churning up debris, love."

"I'll help you sort out the debris." Her expression softened as she touched my face gently. "*If* you go visit him, I'll move in with you. We don't need to go today, though."

"Is that an ultimatum?" I grinned at the woman who knew how to work me.

"I learned from the best." A teasing smile quirked the corner of her mouth, and I wanted to nibble it.

My palms lowered to her ass and squeezed. "You've got me under a spell. I have no choice but to comply."

CHAPTER SIXTY-SIX

A FEW DAYS LATER, Royce and I headed to Aunt Klara's home. February had gone, and March had come, bringing a sense of hope in the air. Hope was ready to sprout. I resonated with the feeling because it mimicked what Royce and I had experienced. Or rather, were still experiencing.

We'd overcome some dark stuff, and now we deserved a season of renewal—a much-needed breath of fresh air.

For me, I'd achieved closure with my mom. We were now closer than ever before. I also released the monster—the eating disorder that crippled my psyche. It was gone. I didn't have any urges to turn to food when I was scared or anxious. I didn't force myself to work out for hours on end. Now I had a nice schedule with a three-day workout, and that was it. I didn't feel guilty about it.

I didn't realize how much I'd grown until I looked at the old Michelle.

Looking at Royce, love swelled in me. He'd helped me reclaim myself, and I felt stronger and more worthy because of him. This man had saved me more than once. I looked up at the sky and thanked the heavens for gifting me this amazing man. I couldn't have planned it better. And I believed in fate wholeheartedly. It had woven an intricate plan for Royce and me. We couldn't have avoided each other. Our lives had intersected so many times without our awareness. When we were aware, it became even more powerful.

I wanted him to find his closure too. He deserved it.

Studying his profile, I asked, "What are you thinking about?"

He turned and smiled. "You."

"I'm serious." I rolled my eyes.

A part of me understood Royce's hesitation. This was a massive surprise that would shake up anyone's life.

We gathered in Aunt Klara's living room. Royce sat beside me on the maroon couch, and Viktor folded himself on the opposite couch with Aunt Klara. She made us all coffee, and I grabbed my mug and sipped.

Viktor looked better today. He had more color on his face, unlike that terrifying day.

I broke the silence and asked, "How are you feeling?"

"I'll live. The bullet missed my vital organs, so that's a blessing." He looked over at Royce. "I know you're angry at me, but please listen to what I have to say."

"Wait." Aunt Klara placed a hand over his. "Let me explain."

Royce scowled as he glared at her hand gripping Viktor's.

What was going on? Was Aunt Klara having an affair with her brother-in-law?

CHAPTER SIXTY-SEVEN

ROYCE

I DIDN'T KNOW how much longer I could sit there and not explode with anger. The woman who took me into her home and raised me like her own was touching my father's hand affectionately. Was I wrong to feel this inferno burning inside me?

Drawing in a deep, harsh breath, I seethed. "Then explain."

Looking more nervous than I'd ever seen her, Aunt Klara said, "I knew what Viktor was doing all these years. That was why I moved to America. To ensure he succeeded with his mission." She looked at me with sorrow in her eyes.

The people closest to me seemed to have another life than the one I knew. I understood family issues always hurt more and dug deeper. As a scientist, I valued objectivity, not allowing my subjective view to blur the facts. Clinging to that objective view was my saving grace.

"Let me tell you a story of two people in love. They had two adorable children they loved—a boy and a girl. The girl was abducted, so the father went after the kidnappers, tracking them to America. She was taken by a man who works for a powerful crime organization that ran a sex trafficking ring. By the way, the kidnapper was recently killed. When the father couldn't locate his daughter, he joined the organization, hoping to find her alive. The son went to live with his aunt, who agreed to watch over him for as long as necessary." Tears rolled down Aunt Klara's face as she squeezed Viktor's hand, her knuckles turning white. "The boy's mom had her husband get their daughter back."

The muscles in my body constricted, stiffening me. "You . . . You're my *mother*?"

Michelle grabbed my hand, trying to calm me.

Aunt Klara nodded. "Alda, who raised you until her death, was your real aunt. We needed to keep your profile low in case your dad and I were caught. They'd no doubt come after you. We paid for your private school in Iceland and ensured you had a comfortable life."

Questions bombarded me, and I asked the one that came to mind first. "Did you wipe my record clean in high school?"

"We paid someone in the police department," Viktor said. "You got into a lot of fights back then. Dominic got what he deserved. He actually found evidence linking your mom and me to you. He was going to send a file to the organization, but my friend and I destroyed it."

Stay objective. Ask the questions. Don't let your emotions blur the facts.

"Did you find Emma?" It had been so long since I'd spoken her name.

Aunt Klara—or should I call her Mom?—sucked in a breath as more tears flowed from her eyes.

Viktor answered with a shaky breath. "I did. Emma lay

on a bed with three other dead girls around her age. She was taken when she was two years old. I found her when she was six, living in a secluded home with a lot of abducted girls and boys of all ages." He sobbed, and the tears rushed out of him like powerful rivers.

Something twisted in my heart, as though the betrayal I'd felt spiraled into something else.

How long had he bottled up these emotions? I couldn't imagine living life the way he did. He had to be someone else in order to survive being in that crime world. What crimes had he committed?

"I failed her." Victor's lips trembled. "I couldn't save my Emma. What they did to her and the other kids was unimaginable." His jaw tensed as anger filled his eyes. "I killed every fucking man and woman who abused those children. Emma would have been twenty-seven now, probably dating or falling in love."

Yes, she would have. I hated that I didn't have a clear image of her. I'd been a child myself when she left.

"Do you have any pictures of her? She's just a blur in my head."

Aunt Klara got up from her couch, pulled out a small album, and offered it to me. "I kept it safe. We didn't have many pictures. I'd planned on a family photoshoot, but . . ."

She didn't need to finish the statement.

"Emma is adorable. She looks like you!" Michelle pointed at a picture of my sister and me at the park. She had curly blonde hair. She would have grown up to be a beautiful woman.

"Why didn't you alert the authorities when you infiltrated the organization?" I asked Viktor.

"Because I couldn't trust anyone. Some people I've met were cops. Some worked for the Pentagon. Others were politicians. It's a massive network of ruthless people, and I didn't want to ruin all my hard work by making a mistake. It took me years to find Emma's location, and I was *in* the organization. A regular police officer wouldn't be able to help me. He'd end up killing us both." His body sagged into the couch.

"How did you get in there?" Michelle asked.

Her soothing voice was a blanket of calm around my unstable heart. Her presence softened the edges around the sensitive situation.

"I met a guy who got me a job, and I worked my way up. I did things that changed me, and I should have been dead already." He lifted his shirt, revealing a patchwork of scars. "But God still had work for me to do. When I discovered Royce was dating you, I made sure you were safe."

"You didn't live in the building next to me, did you?" Michelle eyed him with warmth.

"No."

"Thank you." She turned to me. "If I knew I had two bodyguards watching over me, I wouldn't have feared seeing the black sedan."

I had told her about Jett, and she'd spoken to him over the phone after he left the hospital.

Viktor bore his blue eyes into me. "I'm sorry for keeping you in the dark about everything. I didn't want to put you in danger, but once Dominic started trouble, and other members began investigating, I knew I had to get out."

A sudden wave of nausea overcame me. I wanted to comment on everything I'd heard. But it was too much for me to take in all at once. My heart and brain couldn't handle this emotional influx. My entire body hurt. Even breathing became difficult. I was a mess.

Aunt Klara and Viktor were hurting from reliving the abduction. I didn't know how to move forward. I needed to think, to breathe.

Scrubbing a hand down my face, I got up. "I need some air."

Michelle joined me and told Aunt Klara and Viktor, "We'll be back."

"I know it's a lot to take in. Take all the time you need," Aunt Klara said.

When we stepped outside, I wanted to release this frustration inside of me. The rock at the tip of my shoes became the target. I kicked it, and it flew into the street.

"Feel better?" Michelle cocked her head.

"A little."

The chilly air soothed me, and I inhaled, filling my lungs with much-needed refreshment. The sun shone bright against the blue sky with hardly any clouds, but my darkness in my soul right now couldn't appreciate it.

"I'll drive." Michelle reached for the driver's side door handle. Her earring—the lightning bolt or letter M I'd found and returned to her—glistened in the sun. That subtle spark of light speared the darkness from my soul.

I touched her earring, hoping to absorb the vibrancy of it. It had given me hope when I found it, and it offered me a new way of looking at my issue now.

The truth had many faces, and not all of them were pleasant. I should know the truth didn't always live up to my expectations. It was like my scientific research, which often yielded disappointing results. I either had to accept them and move on to another theory, or beat myself up about something I couldn't control. Trial and error. Live and learn.

What I'd heard from my remaining family members was eye-opening and heart-wrenching. I tried to place myself in their shoes, and my body trembled. I didn't know if I could have lived like that. It took courage, persistence, and a constant glance over your shoulder, hoping your enemy wouldn't strike unexpectedly.

Viktor worked in the lion's den, full of hungry beasts. It took a man with a strong will to survive that dangerous life. Aunt Klara must have worried herself to death every day, not knowing if her husband would return safely and also worrying about her son, who thought she was his aunt.

I thought I'd lived on the edge by taking part in daring adventures around the world and owning businesses that offered the same thrill to people, but compared to what they went through, my lifestyle couldn't measure up.

If my life were a movie, the director would have a tough time connecting all the pieces and trying to make sense of it. Perhaps that was the issue. I was having a hard time placing all the parts into an order where I could see everything. It was a big mess, like looking at an intricate cellular division under a microscope. Too many tiny pieces happening all at once, and it was hard to focus on one thing.

Despite my understanding of Viktor and Aunt Klara's motivations—I couldn't call them Mom or Dad yet—I couldn't help feeling betrayed.

I wanted to listen to their explanation, accept it, forgive them, and start over as a family, but I couldn't. Someday, yes, but not today.

"Where are you taking me?" I slid into the passenger seat, loving that she was chauffeuring me.

"I have the perfect place for you." Her eyes gleamed, and I surrendered to wherever she took me.

CHAPTER SIXTY-EIGHT

THE OCEAN GLISTENED from the sun like a blanket of diamonds.

I sat with Royce on the slab of rock, looking out at the water. The March weather was chilly, but it wasn't so bad with our jackets on.

Two seagulls landed in front of us and cawed as though asking us for food. A couple walked along the shore in the distance.

I looked over at Royce, who stared out at the waters with an impassionate expression. I could only imagine the storm brewing inside him.

Gripping his warm hands, I brought them over to my lap. "What's on your mind?"

He met my gaze. "Just thinking of life's trials. I'd rather weather the storm with you than enjoy the sunshine with anyone else."

I sucked in a breath. He always knew how to touch my heart.

When my heart calmed, I said, "This is where I found

your wish bottle, over there by all the pebbles and shells. It gave me hope that day. I was shocked that it had remained intact after all these years of being tossed around by the powerful waves, wind, and storms. Somehow, it miraculously made it to me." I squeezed his hand. "We don't have all the answers. Sometimes we just take what life offers and do something about it. For me, I took it home and treasured it."

Royce jumped off the rock and dragged me with him. "Show me the spot."

We stood amongst pebbles and shells, listening to the gentle waves.

"Do you hear that?" I asked.

"Hear what?"

"The ocean is telling you to purge. Let it go." I tapped his heart. "Empty your heart of pain and sorrow. The water will dissolve them, and you'll feel better."

"Is that your hypothesis?" He smiled, already looking better. The sadness in his eyes was now replaced by amusement. I'd take that.

"Yup."

"Okay, angel. How do I purge?"

I didn't know, but crafted a method on the spot referencing the idea he'd used to help me when I released the black feather. Bending down, I gathered up a handful of pebbles of various colors and offered him half.

Holding a pebble between my fingers, I said, "Think of this as a pain or sorrow you want to release. Then you toss it into the ocean. The ocean will wash it away and take it wherever it's meant to go. Maybe it'll go into some treasure chest waiting for treasure hunters to find. Maybe it'll be used to build a home for some sea creature. It doesn't matter. It's being recycled, becoming useful for something or someone else."

His smile stretched wide, and my heart leaped at the gorgeous face I was used to. "How did I get lucky enough to have such an intelligent and beautiful girlfriend?"

"Because I'm in love with every aspect of you." I rose onto my toes and placed a gentle kiss on his lips. "You don't have to state anything out loud. Just say it to yourself. The pebbles and the ocean will hear everything."

Just as I had heard his painful cry when he sat in front of his parents, trying to absorb the shock and forgive them but not knowing how to do it.

I loved him with all my heart. He was there for me at every crooked turn, and I'd make sure I was present whenever he needed me. That was love. He was the landscape that expanded my horizon, allowing me to see the beauty in everything.

"I'll start." I waved the pebble in the air. Instead of purging, I made a wish. This pebble-tossing method worked either way.

Please give Royce the strength he needs to heal his heart.

My pebble sailed through the air, broke the surface of the glistening waters, and disappeared.

Royce chose a pebble and whipped it into the waters with a sidewinder. The pebble skipped along the surface, creating this beautiful pattern before disappearing into the water.

"Show off," I teased.

He smiled and continued whipping pebbles and bigger rocks, making the ocean gleam even more.

CHAPTER SIXTY-NINE

ROYCE

A MONTH LATER, I organized my comic books into a new bookcase with a glass door. The books never made it to the charity. Michelle had asked my mom to save them and delivered them to me a while ago, and I hadn't had time to organize them until now. I'd taken extra time off from work to deal with family matters. My team could handle the load until I returned. Though I was on "vacation," I still checked emails and updates, making sure everything ran smoothly.

I picked up an old Thor comic book that was probably worth a lot if I were to sell it now. What had I been thinking, wanting to donate it?

"This is your past. You loved it, and Thor gave you strength and hope even when you didn't know it," Michelle had said. "Don't give them away. They're yours to keep. The magic and power are still there."

She knew me so well, and I loved her so much. I didn't think it was possible, but my heart grew bigger to accommodate what I felt for her.

The past month had been an important pivotal point in

my life. Everything changed, including my mindset. I'd always thought I'd been abandoned, and that conviction twisted certain beliefs. Love was one of the things I never believed in. But it saved me.

When I was done organizing the comic books, I was ready to move forward. Michelle and I headed to see Aunt Klara and Viktor.

Michelle sat beside me as I listened to their entire story. By the time they finished, I realized how much they'd sacrificed for my sister and me. My father didn't abandon the family the way I thought he did. He dedicated his life to bringing my sister back. I couldn't fault them for leaving me with my aunt, who wanted to help. I still considered her my mom too. She raised me, and I was grateful to her.

How could I blame Aunt Klara and Viktor when all they wanted was to complete the family? The realization lifted the heaviness that had hovered over me since I was a kid embarking on a new journey in a new country.

I discovered my sister's ashes were sent out to sea long ago. Perhaps she and my aunt were the ones who made sure my wish bottle found Michelle. I'd like to think that they did that. I'd make a copy of the photo album so I could remember her again.

It's not what it seems.

Those were the words I'd told Michelle when she thought I had cheated on her. Sometimes the truth was skewed either by circumstance or timing.

Love is the only thing that matters. Aunt Klara, my mom, had told me that all my life. She kept repeating the words even when she knew I didn't believe in love. It must've tortured her to know she was the reason for my belief.

I should have been the one comforting them.

Viktor met my eyes and gestured to the sunroom. Understanding him, I got up and joined him. We both stood staring at the backyard, where some tulips and daffodils had come up.

I was taller than him by a couple of inches.

"Thank you for coming back," Viktor said, his hands tucked into his pants. "It means a lot to your mom and me."

"I know."

"I wanted to speak with you alone regarding what I saw and heard while I was undercover. Your mom and Michelle don't need to know these details."

Nodding, I looked at Viktor, and the blurry image of him when I was young cleared to this respectable man before me. He was no longer a memory, but a real person.

"I heard you that day after Edward Bryson was killed at the church. I came back for my cell phone."

He furrowed his eyebrows. "That was you? I thought I saw a kid run off. On that day, I was on the phone with your mom. I knew you and your friends hung around that area, but I didn't know about the murder until the day after." He held up a finger as if remembering something important. "Dominic tried to have someone kill your friend's uncle in jail, but failed. Derek still had money and paid people outside the organization for protection, which explains why he's not dead yet."

"Thanks. I'm not sure if Grayson cares whether his uncle lives or dies, but I'll let him know."

Derek had killed Grayson's father and kidnapped Audri last year. That betrayal changed my friend.

"The crime organization calls themselves The Trogyn. It's not something spoken out loud. I only overheard someone reference it. You can use this information to do what you need to do. I know you and your friends have an interest in this organization. Just be very careful. I'll give you all the information about them, their safe houses, and so on."

These people killed my sister. I had to know who they were. It was a starting point for my friends and me to investigate later.

"How did you live like that?" I asked.

He shrugged. "One day at a time. Some days were tough. When you immerse yourself in the dark world, the ugly aspects of it get into your mind. You need to clear it out every night before bed to remember why you were there in the first place." He placed a hand on my shoulder. "My family gave me the strength to continue. I had a purpose, and I knew my presence could benefit someone someday. There are other children out there somewhere waiting to be helped."

"Thank you, Dad." Warmth burst in my chest as I patted his hand.

He pressed his lips into a tight line as tears sparkled in his eyes.

My dad had stayed in the organization after he found Emma because he wanted to expose them. The longer he stayed, the more he discovered how interconnected this dark web of crimes was, and just how far it spread. He met none of the "superiors" in the organization. He knew some were kings, princes, presidents, and wealthy people who didn't flinch at hurting women and children. Sex trafficking wasn't their sole business. It expanded to drugs, money laundering, and other corruption I didn't even know existed.

An hour later, we returned to the kitchen and enjoyed a lovely dinner. After dinner, we sat around the dining table, chatting.

"You're not safe from the organization," I said. "You

killed one of their respected members, and if they dug deeper, they'd know you destroyed that house which held the children and that you're not dead. You need to go into hiding."

Though the media reported my dad as one of the dead bodies caused by the explosion at the warehouse, if the organization investigated, they'd know that wasn't true. Dominic made it seem like he hadn't shared his suspicion that Dad had a familial connection to me. Another good reason Dominic wasn't alive to carry out his intention to ruin my dad.

"We've already discussed this. We're moving out of the country. Not sure where yet."

"Let me take care of that." I took out two folders and slid them across the dining table. "Mom and Dad, these are my gifts to you."

Joy rushed through my body as I addressed them the way they deserved. Mom and Michelle teared up. Dad smiled because he'd already experienced the power of my words earlier.

Mom opened the envelope, staring at her passport under a new name. She whipped a glance at my dad. "Check yours."

I'd bought a house for them in Costa Rica, near an excursion site I owned. "You're now Oliva Davis, married to Michael Davis, retiring to a warmer climate after working as librarians in the Northeast."

The library had been where Mom and Dad secretly met to talk while he was still in the organization. No wonder she never wanted to retire.

Mom embraced me. "Thank you, Royce."

Dad joined the group hug. "I dreamed of this day for a long time."

I peered over my dad's head, looking for Michelle, who dabbed her eyes. She smiled and declined when I waved her to join us.

The family hug felt weird and wonderful. It was new to me. I never expected to have a complete family, but here I was, embracing them.

"Jett is moving down there to work for my excursion site and to be your bodyguard."

"We don't need one," Dad said.

"It's better to be safe. Besides, I need extra help at my excursion business. So he's there for you and for me. It's already done. Don't argue with me."

Mom narrowed her eyes and slid a glance at Michelle. "Crack the whip tonight for me."

Michelle winked. "I'll use the new one I just got."

The entire room roared with laughter, and I didn't even care that they were laughing about whipping my ass.

Dad looked at the plane tickets. "We fly out in five days?"

"It's not that I don't want you around, but I want you safe. It's been a month since Dominic's death and the truck explosion. You don't know what these people are going to do. I don't want to risk your safety. It's easier for me to visit you. And I will."

"Yeah, that explosion occurred at the right time," Dad said. "I have to thank my friend before I leave for Costa Rica."

"Who's your friend?" I asked.

"He prefers to remain anonymous."

I looked at my mom. "I'll sell the house and transfer the money to you."

"No, you keep it," Mom said.

"I don't need it. Use it for your retirement."

Michelle leaned into Mom's ear and whispered something that had her laughing instantly.

I had to know what they discussed since they both flicked their gazes at me before erupting with glee.

CHAPTER SEVENTY

MICHELLE

ON OUR DRIVE HOME, I asked Royce, "What's going to happen to Brittany?"

With so much going on, I'd almost forgotten about her. I knew Fiona had gone off to some retreat. At least that was what she'd posted online. I was surprised when she suggested people visit my website for inspiration. The near-death experience seemed to have changed her for the better.

"She's being extradited to Iceland in a few days for the crimes she's committed there."

"What's going to happen to her daughter?"

Royce shrugged. "She'll probably be in foster care for now. I don't think Brittany knows where Lily's father is."

I listened as Royce explained what would happen to Brittany and Lily. It didn't sit well with me.

"Royce," I whispered. "Putting her in jail isn't going to help her or her daughter. Brittany is mentally unstable. She needs treatment, not a jail cell. If you throw someone with an untreated injury in a cell, that wound will fester. She's not going to understand what she did wrong. Her daughter will suffer too."

I could only imagine what Lily would experience seeing her mom in prison and not having the love and support she needed to grow up. I saw myself in Lily.

"Lily needs her mom. Her mom needs her. I want Brittany to receive treatment. She was a victim of this child pageant industry too. I could've ended up like her. I dealt with my monster. She didn't deal with hers too well. If we lock her up, her daughter will develop an inner monster—I can already see it."

Royce pulled over to the side of the road, parked the car, and shifted to look at me.

He cupped my face in his warm hands. "Most people would want their enemy locked up, punished. But you? You're an angel." He kissed me lightly on the lips and pulled me into his arms. "Are you sure that's what you want?"

"Yes, I've been thinking about it a lot. Imprisoning a sick person isn't going to make me feel better." I cut my eyes toward him. "Remember the favor you owe me for agreeing to be your fake girlfriend?"

"Yeah." Warmth and love filled his eyes.

"I'd like to redeem the raincheck. Can you help Brittany?"

"If that's what you want, I'll make it happen. We'll get her the treatment she needs here in America. You just saved her and her daughter."

I hope so.

"Thank you."

"You're welcome." His eyes sparkled with mischief. "What did you say to my mom earlier?"

He's been thinking about that?

A smirk tugged at my lips. "Oh, nothing unusual. Just that she should get a nice whip for your dad too."

Royce laughed as he drove back onto the street, heading home. "You're such a sex hellion."

"I learned that from my daredevil sex fiend."

He offered his panty-melting grin. "I dare you to go on an adventure tonight. But as far as I know, you don't have any whips."

I reached over to his thigh and walked my fingers to his crotch, loving how he flinched at my touch. His arousal grew, pushing at his fly. "Viking, I've got a list of adventures ready for us to try. And a bag of toys you haven't seen yet. You gave me free rein for this 'private excursion,' remember?"

"I'm yours tonight and every night. Do as you please." He sped home at a speed that could get us a ticket at any moment, but he didn't seem to care.

Neither did I.

Michelle

I finally unpacked the last box of my belongings and settled comfortably into Royce's massive apartment. He had two guest rooms, and I took the bigger one with the eggshell-colored walls for my office. After all my books, binders, and decor had filled the office, I placed the wish bottle on the middle bookshelf beside the picture frame of us. Standing back, I studied it.

Thank you for bringing me Royce.

I ran my fingers along the glass surface, appreciating everything it had given me and continued to give me. There was so much hope and love in this bottle.

Royce coming to save me from the thunderstorm had triggered something in my psyche. I didn't know it then, but I understood it now. Something in me released, a veil that blurred my reality, perhaps. He was the powerful storm that rolled in and cleared the surrounding energy, allowing me to see clearly.

He'd done so much for me. It was time he knew how I felt about him.

I went to look for Royce. He'd been talking to someone in his office earlier. The front door opened, and he walked in with a stack of mail in his hands, wearing the T-shirt with Nerd Lava splashed across it—a T-shirt that had cost him two hundred thousand dollars.

Smiling like a fool, I leaped into his arms, making sure my face rubbed against the super-expensive shirt that cost more than what I made all year.

He dropped the stack of mail to catch me, and the envelopes scattered all over the floor.

"I love this kind of greeting, but what's the catch? Pun intended." He squeezed my ass.

"Can't a woman miss her man?" I kissed his chin. "I thought you were working in your office."

"I changed into your shirt and figured we could go shopping today." He released me onto my feet and picked up the mail.

"Shopping? Where? I didn't know you liked to shop."

"I don't usually go to the mall, but there's a special event happening at Providence Place." He looked through the mail and offered me a pink envelope. "You've got mail."

Surprised, I read the sender's name and smiled. "It's from Lily Parker."

I opened it and read the invitation to a STEM Presentation by young children around the world. It was at the Children's Science Museum in Boston. She also sent a photo of her working with a group of kids, looking happy. The girl in the photo differed from the unhappy one I saw at the gala with all the makeup on.

"I got invited to Lily's STEM presentation. Will you come with me?"

"Of course. I signed her up for it. There's no way I'd miss it."

"You did?" I eyed him. "When?"

"When I met her and her mom to let them know how lucky they are. I told them what you did for them. Lily confessed she hated the beauty pageants and wanted to get into STEM." He tipped up my chin. "She's a smart girl, and she'll go far."

My heart burst with joy. "Thank you for doing that."

Royce kissed me lightly on the lips. "You're welcome. Brittany is also doing well with her treatments."

I didn't expect Royce to take on the extra responsibility. "You didn't have to follow up on all that."

"I know. But you gave them a second chance. I need to make sure they don't screw it up."

Smiling, I clasped his hand. "I've got something for you."

"Oh? Another 'private excursion?'" He smirked and playfully smacked my butt.

"Maybe later tonight if you behave the rest of the day." I led him to my office and placed him in my chair, facing my computer. "Sit and watch this."

I clicked the folder and opened the first blog post from my For Those Who Seek Love and Wonder series.

Standing beside him, I let him read the post and looked at the images I'd gotten from his team at Whitewater Family Resort in Oregon. It was where he'd saved me, where we first "met."

When he finished, he yanked me onto his lap, where I

loved to be. "That's an incredible promotion. I love it. Where did you get the videos and images?"

"David, your director, was very helpful. I told him I was making something special for his boss and needed his help with current images and videos. He also provided me with a list of all the other directors from your various locations. I've acquainted myself with your entire team."

"Where did you find the time to do all of this?"

"Oh, here and there. When you love someone, you make time for them, right?" I gestured to the computer. "There are three hundred and sixty-five blogs to promote all your excursion sites. One for each day of the year."

"That's a lot of work you did." The green eyes that always saw through my defenses sparkled, turning into a darker shade. "You love me that much?"

"I love you a whole lot more. This is just one way of showing it." I shifted to straddle him, studying his face. Emotion stirred in me as I absorbed everything about him.

"You okay?" he asked, looking concerned.

Nodding, I inhaled a deep breath to prepare myself for what I was about to share. "Being deeply loved by you gave me strength, while loving you gave me back myself. I love you the way the river runs toward the ocean; it doesn't know any other route. I love you the way the storm loves the wind; the force makes it stronger. I love you the way the volcano transforms under pressure; it creates the burning beauty beneath the surface. And I love you the way the night sky admires the Northern Lights; one complements the other." I swallowed as my lips trembled with the truth. "You are the essence of everything around me, and I didn't know how to appreciate them until you loved me."

Royce sucked in a breath as emotions transformed his eyes and face. He kissed me long and hard.

"That is the most spellbinding declaration I've ever received." His thumbs brushed across my cheek. "Does that mean you'll take my offer and work with me? Be the promoter for my excursions?"

I loved how he said work *with* him instead of *for* him. He respected me and acknowledged my self-worth and identity.

"I'd be happy to be your partner in crime, Viking, Daredevil, Sex Fiend—a man with many names."

He laughed. "Now we can go to the mall. Something is waiting for you there."

Royce

Holding hands, we browsed Providence Place, a busy mall I hadn't visited in a long time. I did my shopping mostly online, but seeing what shops were available was a pleasant change.

My heart still hammered at Michelle's declaration. I knew she loved me, but I didn't know the depth of her love. It matched what I felt for her.

With love overflowing inside me, I took her to a new popup shop by a group of young entrepreneurs I'd met at a convention with Remi last year. Game Genius was a temporary retail space used to promote new products and generate awareness.

"Are you buying a video game?" she asked as we entered the busy store.

It was a lot busier than I expected. One wall had a wide selection of video games, while the other offered a variety of apps.

I led Michelle to the app section, where a group of people sat in lounge chairs and on the floor, playing on their phones.

"Oh my God, Royce! Look!" She rushed up to the poster of Eat Your Monsters. Her bunny avatar, Nibbles, was in the image. "It's real!"

Her reaction was exactly how I'd pictured it.

She walked up to the group of people, ranging from teens to older women and men immersed in the free version on their phones and tablets.

"I like your cat avatar," the teen wearing a baseball cap said to his mom, who sat beside him. "We should get this game. It's on sale today."

Michelle gripped my hand and squeezed, joy beaming in her eyes.

"It's fun, isn't it?" she asked the kid.

"Yeah. My sister would love it too." He grinned.

More people entered the shop, asking about Eat Your Monsters.

"Do I have the updated version?" Michelle asked me while checking her phone. When she saw it was already there, she smiled. "I can't believe you released it already."

"It's the right time. You're getting half of the profits."

"I am? Why?" She blinked, looking adorable.

"Because you inspired it and helped me figure out how to enhance the game by playing. I saw all your moves."

"I was your guinea pig?" She narrowed her eyes.

"The most gorgeous guinea pig ever."

We left the shop, headed across the street to the Water-Park, and sat on the bench, looking at the canal.

Excitement still glistened in her eyes. "This will help people overcome their monsters. You're a genius."

I let out a half-laugh. "It's just observation and applying that creatively. You helped me see it from a different perspective. Life is all about perspective."

"I love you so much, Royce." Her lovely brown eyes bore into me.

True love was someone who could thrill me just by looking at me. Michelle was the only woman for me. I hadn't dared to open my heart to love, but Michelle was the catalyst that changed my life.

The space between love and no love was risk. Loving her was my biggest risk . . . but also my biggest reward.

"I love you too." I clasped her hand. "I used to believe that if I loved anything, my exposed heart would be wrung dry and eventually break. So I kept it under wraps by staying busy with my thrilling adventures, business expansions, and volcanic research." A gentle breeze blew by, causing a curly strand of hair to fall across her face. I tucked it behind her ear, admiring the lightning bolt earring that meant so much to us. "Despite all of that, my heart was still seeking something beyond itself. I didn't know what it was until you entered my life and yanked the veil away, making me want you—be vulnerable to you. You've remade me, love."

"We've remade each other." She kissed me, her lips and tongue slowly tantalizing me. If she kept it up, I'd have no choice but to drag her back to the garage and have her in my car.

But right now, I had to let her know what was in my heart. "Love flows through all of us like magma flowing through the earth. Sometimes it takes an eruption for you to understand its beauty, its power, its essence—the love that is steeped within nature. You're the magma that flows in me. Without you, there is no fire to light my path, no warmth to thaw the chill in my soul, no hope for me to grasp onto." I thumbed away the tears on her cheek. "I believe in love because of you. It's the most profound emotion, and I now understand why people do crazy things for love."

She kissed me for a long moment, showing me her heart. When she drew back, her eyes glittered with mischief.

"Are you in the mood for a dare?"

"What dare?"

"I've got some new products that arrived in the mail yesterday. They're edible lotion. I figure I could be your masseuse today." She wiggled her eyebrows. "Then after your massage, we can play Eat Your Monsters. First to win gets to do whatever they want to the other player. It's an all-day event. What say you?"

Initially, I had planned on a casual day with her, but my love had an irresistible adventure planned I couldn't object to.

Imagination sparked, and my lips bowed into a sly smile. "Is the massage part of the Eat Your Lover game?"

A hot pink washed over her cheeks. "Something like that. Any particular area that's aching for attention?" The tip of her tongue swiped across her lips.

My cock hardened, and I didn't care there were people around us in the park. "I've got a few." My voice grew hoarse. "I can't wait to defeat you in Eat Your Monsters." My eyes slid to the secret space between her legs.

"Seems like you already have plans of your own." She tapped my forehead.

"When it comes to loving you, I always have plans. Let's head home now because my body is screaming for my masseuse's touch. I'm tense all over, angel." I tugged her up from the bench, held her hand, and we raced back to my car.

Thank you so much for reading Michelle and Royce's story!

For Natalie and Grayson's romance, order **The Innovator** (Book 3) now!

https://nadiahan.com/books/

Read Michelle and Royce's **bonus scene here** or scan the code below. They're visiting Mt. Shasta!

If you enjoyed The Daredevil, I would appreciate a review on your chosen platform(s). With your support, I can continue to write more stories.

For exclusive content, new releases, and giveaways, sign up to my newsletter.

https://nadiahan.com/newsletter/

Stay in touch with me! You can scan the code for easy access to me.

Instagram: https://www.instagram.com/authornadiahan/
TikTok: https://www.tiktok.com/@authornadiahan
Pinterest: https://www.pinterest.com/authornadiahan
BookBub: https://www.bookbub.com/authors/nadia-han
FB author page: https://www.facebook.com/authornadiahan
Goodreads: https://www.goodreads.com/author/show/
22312698.Nadia_Han

ACKNOWLEDGMENTS

With each new book, I have more people to thank for helping me make my stories gleam. Thank you, Anna, for being the amazing editor and friend who knows my voice and for understanding me all these years.

To Lindsay, for your splendid copy edits and the way you work your magic.

To Violet and Melissa, my eagle-eye proofreaders, for catching all my typos.

To Ingunn, my wonderful Icelandic friend. Thank you for teaching me about your beautiful country. I can't wait to go back and take a dip in the Blue Lagoon.

To Sharon, my incredible beta reader, there's no one more supportive than you. I am truly grateful to have you by my side.

To my ARC Team, who I met on Instagram and TikTok. Words cannot express how much I appreciate each and every one of you.

I'm so grateful to my children for showing me love and the wonder that exists in their minds. That flicker of light inspires me every day. I wouldn't be able to publish this book without my husband, who is okay with me spending time with my book boyfriends and creating new ones as I see fit.

ABOUT THE AUTHOR

Nadia Han is a dreamer, a visionary, an artist, and a believer in karma and kindness. She lives in New England with her family and spends most of her time crafting stories. When she's not writing, she practices yoga, reads, creates art, explores nature, and eats all kinds of foods.

f facebook.com/authornadiahan

instagram.com/authornadiahan

BB bookbub.com/authors/nadia-han

a amazon.com/author/nadiahan